GW00391074

BOLEYN CURSE

DEBORAH COHEN

CITY OWL
PRESS

This book is a work of fiction. Names, characters, places, and incidents either are products of the author's imagination or are used fictitiously. Any resemblance to actual events or locales or persons, living or dead, is entirely coincidental and not intended by the author.

BOLEYN CURSE
The Boleyn Bloodline, Book 1

CITY OWL PRESS
www.cityowlpress.com

All Rights reserved. Except as permitted under the U.S. Copyright Act of 1976, no part of this publication may be reproduced, distributed, or transmitted in any form or by any means, or stored in a database or retrieval system, without the prior consent and permission of the publisher.

Copyright © 2019 Deborah Cohen.

Cover Design by Mibl Art. All stock photos licensed appropriately.

Edited by Yelena Casale.

For information on subsidiary rights, please contact the publisher at info@cityowlpress.com.

Print Edition ISBN: 978-1-949090-59-8

Digital Edition ISBN: 978-1-949090-60-4

Printed in the United States of America

For my father

AUTHOR'S NOTE

The legends surrounding Anne Boleyn were the inspiration for this book. **Though this novel is based on real characters in history, this book is a fantasy.** I wanted to weave together fact with fiction so it would difficult to tell where one stopped and the other began. After all, isn't that the essence of every good story?

The web of mystery surrounding Anne Boleyn is an alluring one. Depicted in history either as a heroine or a villain, the second wife of King Henry the VIII has captured the hearts and minds of people all over the world. But what is it about our beloved Anne that draws our collective interest?

For years, Anne Boleyn has fascinated me. Perhaps it is because, beyond some basic historical facts, we know little of her true story. We don't actually know, for example, the year of Anne Boleyn's birth, nor whether she or her sister Mary was the eldest Boleyn daughter. Much of Anne Boleyn's story in popular culture comes from legend, a medley of micro-fictions and truths that have given rise to the mythical creature we know today.

For the record, Anne Boleyn was not a witch. And she may, or may not have had six fingers on her right hand. In a piece of writing meant to demonize her, the Catholic propagandist Nicholas Sanders noted that Anne Boleyn had a 'projecting tooth under the upper lip', 'a large wen under her chin' and 'six fingers on her right hand'. Though this description was written some fifty years after her death, it is arguably one of the most influential in defining our memory of Anne Boleyn, and one that helps promote the witchy image that many have come to believe.

What do we know about Anne Boleyn for certain? We know that Anne was Queen of England for only three years from 1533-1536. After a seven-year courtship, Anne and Henry were married on January 25, 1533. On May 23,1533, Thomas Cranmer, the newly appointed Archbishop of Canterbury denounced Henry's first marriage to Catherine of Aragon and validated Henry's marriage to Anne. In less than one month, Henry Tudor was excommunicated by Pope Clement VII and so marked the beginning of the Church of England's break with Rome and the English Reformation.

Anne was crowned Queen of England on June 1,1533, already roughly six months pregnant with Henry's child. Throughout their short marriage, Anne gave Henry only one living daughter. Elizabeth Tudor was born on September 7, 1533. This little girl would go on to become the last of five monarchs of the House of Tudor. Following Elizabeth's birth, Anne had multiple miscarriages, cursed by some unknowable force that prevented her babies (one a boy) from living. By the time little Elizabeth Tudor was three years old, Henry had already cast aside his new wife, Anne, and was courting Jane Seymour.

Anne was arrested on May 2, 1536 and taken to the Tower of London. She was found guilty of high treason against the King, adultery, and incest. She was beheaded on May 15, 1536. Many people have suggested that Anne was also charged with witchcraft, although there is no formal acknowledgement of this indictment on the public record.

Perhaps even more fascinating than Anne's rise to power at English court is her life prior it. Anne's time in France is almost completely unknown. Most scholars believe that Anne Boleyn travelled to France to accompany Princess Mary Tudor as a bride's maid for her marriage to King Louis XII. Intended as an act that would seal a negotiated peace treaty between England and France, the wedding took place in Abbeville on October 9th, 1514 when Mary Tudor was eighteen years old and King Louis was fifty-two. Their marriage was a short one. King Louis died on January 1, 1515, rumored to have been 'worn out in the bedchamber' by his new wife.

It is widely believed that Anne remained in France for at least seven years in the service of Queen Claude. Queen Claude suffered from a severe form of scoliosis and had a noticeable hump on her back, though her deformity was not a source of hatred from her father. In this novel King Louis was portrayed as villainous and unkind, however this was a departure from the historical record, one I took intentionally in order to forward the plot line. In fact, King Louis XII was best remembered as 'the father of the people', a King who cared for his proletariat, eased tax laws and was generally well loved.

During her time in France, Anne met Marguerite de Navarre, a cousin to the King and a proto-feminist in her own right. Marguerite wrote the Heptameron, a book of seventy-two short stories, though the short story portrayed in this novel was not part of the original text. Although Marguerite did not tutor Anne in witchcraft, she was an important mentor to young Anne, helping her to become the thoughtful strong woman she grew up to be.

Leonardo Da Vinci arrived in France in 1516 at King Francis' request, two years after the wedding of Mary Tudor and King Louis XII. Leonardo lived out his remaining years at the Chateau Clos Lucé, and was reputed to be one of King Francis' closest friends.

Given that Anne spent seven years in France, it is likely that she met Leonardo Da Vinci, although there is no absolute evidence of their relationship. Leonardo's famous painting, *Lady with an Ermine*, was not actually inspired by Anne Boleyn. The Lady in this infamous portrait was most likely Cecilia Gallerani, the mistress of Ludovico Sforza, the Duke of Milan, whose nickname was 'The White Ermine'. Leonardo painted this portrait in 1489 when he was in the Duke's service.

This painting however is shrouded in a mystery of its own. In 2014, Dr. Pascal Cotte used a specialized scanning technique to reveal that Leonardo Da Vinci actually painted this portrait in three phases. The first version was a simple head shot with no animal whatsoever. In the second version, a small grey ermine was added. On his third and final attempt, Leonardo painted the large white ermine we see in the painting today. While Leonardo Da Vinci's motivation for doing this in unclear, it is one of the many intrigues surrounding this great man who was clearly the light of the Renaissance.

PREFACE

Of Anne Boleyn, fair legends told
Some tell false, fables old
But in the place twixt not and true
Her curse doth linger, conté anew

VOLUME 1

YULE

Darkness ends as day begins
Mother Goddess gives birth to the Sun
And the witches keep vigil

1514

VILLAGE OF HEVER, ENGLAND

Three hooded figures, hands clasped tightly, hurried through the winter night. A biting gale blew the snow in all directions, its swirling tempest a wall of white fury. The group leaned into the storm with the weight of their bodies, their heavy cloaks beating like bat wings in the wind.

The tallest pointed to a narrow close off the main street and they stumbled past tilted half-timbered houses towards it.

"Who's there?" a haggard voice called into the darkness. A dim lantern seemed to float mid-air.

The figures moved toward the light, their steps more certain in the murky glow of the flame.

"Who's there, I say?"

"'Tis Lady Boleyn," hissed the tallest. "Hurry, girls. We mustn't be discovered."

A door slammed shut in the alleyway ahead, but the group continued, edging towards the sound with determination now. At the entrance of the little cottage, a shadowy face emerged from behind a crack in the door.

"Aga... Let us in or we shall catch our deaths."

As the door crept slowly open, Elizabeth Boleyn and her daughters shuffled inside, the low light of the cottage wrapping itself around them like the fine strands of a spider's web.

An old woman stood by the hearth, a tattered shawl pulled around thin shoulders. Only two brown teeth remained in the dark hole of her mouth. A milky film clouded one eye. The other revealed a blue iris, a sharp pupil dancing with a life of its own.

"Elizabeth, it has been some time," she crooned.

"These are my daughters, Aga." Lady Elizabeth brushed the snow from her skirts. "Anne is sixteen. And Mary, not but a year behind that."

The old woman approached slowly. Scrutinizing the youth with her good eye, she dragged a thickened fingernail along each of their jawlines in sequence. Her eyes narrowed when her finger reached the eldest girl's chin. "This one I have seen."

Lady Elizabeth took the old woman by the arm. "Aga, I hate to rush an old reunion, but I come to you in desperate need."

The crone closed her eyes. "Yes. I wondered when you would come. But are you certain you wish to save him?"

"He is the father of my children." Elizabeth paused. "I love him."

"Do you really?" Aga sneered. "I have often wondered how a woman could love such a man. But you have risked great things in coming, so you must at least need him, if not love him." She shuffled to a chair by the fire. "Now then, what ails him? How many days has he been ill?"

The ancient Aga eased herself into the seat and gestured for her guests to join. Wide-eyed, the girls shuffled to the hearth. The cottage was but one room. Dried herbs hung from the exposed beams in the ceiling. A low fire crackled within a simple hearth and a black pot hovered over the cinders. Teetering shelves along the wall housed a dozen mismatched jars, each containing dark and unrecognizable things.

Lady Elizabeth wrung her hands as she paced the floorboards. "It began four days ago when Thomas came home from the hunt. He felled a deer but had not an appetite for it once it was served."

The girls sat perched, backs straight, along the bench by the table. They leaned forward to hear what their mother had to say.

"The next morning, Thomas said he was much refreshed but took little bread to break his fast. Later that day, he began to cough." Elizabeth turned to Aga. "He took to bed with fever and has gotten worse by the day. He does not eat. He barely drinks." She knelt down, grasping Aga's gnarled hands in her own. "I think he is dying."

The old woman stared into the flames for a time. "I have seen it. He will not last the week. But are you prepared for what is to come if you interfere?"

Elizabeth's face hardened, but she did not reply.

"You vowed fifteen years ago not to live this life anymore." Aga's lips twisted into a smile.

"I have no choice," Elizabeth finally whispered.

The old woman drew herself up with some effort, nodding as though she already knew the answer she would be given. She cleared away a surface on the careworn table and began pulling jars from the shelves.

"You will require assistance, Elizabeth. You are unpracticed of late and will lack the fortitude required to shift things."

Aga opened the first jar and pulled out two dried frogs, long since dead, hardened and black. "One frog that will never become a prince, one prince that will be ever more a frog." She tossed them into a wooden bowl, their dried bodies skittering across the basin's surface. Next she added four pinches of gray powder, filling the air with a pungent smell of fungus. "A pinch of wort for each day your husband has been ill."

Her fingers searched the top shelf, feeling for another vessel. She found a jar filled with thick red liquid and poured the contents over the other ingredients. A metallic scent layered atop the earthy one in the room, creating an odor consistent with that of a slaughterhouse.

"Blood of the pig, in place of the blood of your husband—although I'm not sure which one is more of a swine."

Lady Elizabeth interrupted. "Aga, I am committed to do this, but I will not involve the girls."

Aga sprinkled in some dried rosemary and rosewort, and gave the girls a knowing look. "Two innocent roses, two innocent daughters. Both will be required." She added a bit of fetid brown water from a jug in the corner, and then tossed in a pair of twisted bird's feet. "Crow's feet to help him claw his way back from death."

As she ran her fingers through the bloody brew, Aga pierced Lady Elizabeth with her dancing blue eye. "And finally, the spit of a witch…"

Elizabeth glanced at her girls and back to the clouded gaze of the woman. A pained expression pinched the fine skin along her nose.

"You must do it, Elizabeth. There is no other way." Aga's lips trembled in anticipation.

Elizabeth hesitated before moving to the table. Then, puckering her lips together, she bent over the bowl and spit fiercely. She stared down at the vile concoction for a moment before wiping the spittle from her mouth with the back of her hand.

"Mother!" exclaimed her eldest daughter, Anne.

But the two women took no notice, lost in their old ritual. Aga poured the contents of the brew into a jar as Elizabeth slid it into the embers. They held hands as they watched the small glass pot boil, mumbling a strange incantation as the elixir took form, a hot little wind swirling around them. Finally Aga pulled the glass from the flames with an iron poker and placed a stopper in the top.

"You know what to do from here. The moon has entered its healing phase. It will assist you."

Elizabeth nodded.

Aga wagged a finger in the air, still red with pig's blood. "You will require your coven. A powerful coven you have, a mother and two daughters. If you attempt this alone, he will die a painful, watery death. I have seen it."

"But I want my girls far from the Craft," said Elizabeth softly.

"Then why did you bring them? Why make them witness?" the crone shot back.

The two women stood face to face, one tall and elegant, one crooked and haggard. Their silhouettes cast an eerie shadow on the floor.

Finally, Elizabeth bowed her head. "I promise."

"There is one last thing." The old woman grabbed Lady Elizabeth's arm, turning her so her back was to her daughters. "I have seen your eldest in my visions. Anne... Anne... Anne Boleyn... You must send her away when this is done."

Aga's lips almost touched the lady's ear. "Your daughter bears the mark. I have seen it. In time, she will be a danger to herself and your family."

Elizabeth stumbled back, avoiding the dancing blue eye. She deposited the small glass jar into a hidden pocket in her cloak and gestured to her daughters. "Thank you for your help, Aga. But we must go."

Lady Elizabeth and her girls stepped into the night, back into the driving storm that brought them to this strange little cottage not but an hour ago.

PRESENT DAY
QUEEN'S UNIVERSITY, CANADA

The treadmill whirred beneath my feet, its driving pace keeping my restless mind at bay. The machine was set at level eight with a thirty percent incline. Suicide speed. My heart was beating so hard I could hear the blood coursing through my ears. Killing myself on the treadmill was usually the best way to relieve my anxiety, but today, no matter how hard I ran, the threat of failure taunted me like a schoolyard bully.

What if you're not smart enough, Ellie? What if you're too stupid, stupid, stupid?

The university's undergrad students had scurried off to their nine a.m. classes with professors ready to begin their first-of-the-year lectures. The early gym crowd, the pretty girls with screechy laughter and messy hair buns, had left without a whiff of perspiration. Only a straggle of graduate students, with their strange schedules and independent studies, remained at the gym this morning.

I hit the treadmill's acceleration button to fend off the negative thoughts jostling through my mind. My legs were on fire but the pain was pleasantly distracting. It allowed me to forget my fear for a few more minutes, and I dug into my unladylike perspiration with a vengeance.

My cell phone sat on the treadmill's water bottle stand. Its silence was maddening. I flicked at it and cursed under my breath.

"Come on, let's have it. Send the bloody exam question already," I muttered.

But the phone remained unresponsive. I considered hurling the device across the room but decided against it. The exam would arrive soon enough and I would finally have to face it. I would see if the months of preparation and study had been enough.

The Comprehensive examination was a PhD's worst nightmare, set to snag even the brightest students. And history students had the worst of it. "In preparation for your Comprehensives, you will be expected to study all major periods of human history since the Bronze Age. That shouldn't be too much to ask, should it?" Dr. Fishburn had announced with an arrogant chuckle at the History Department barbecue last summer. "No one ever said becoming a PhD was going to be easy, now did they?"

The Comprehensive exam was legendary for sending graduate students right off the edge, and we had all heard the rumors. Peggy Parsons had fled from her orals last year when she had been unable to provide a response to a question about ancient Mayan weaving traditions and the role of female fertility. Several years before that, Bernard McAllister had vomited on his examiner when he had been asked details about Lord Byron's pet bear. That story was the favorite. It usually incited a healthy dose of pride amongst the graduate student body.

But the Comprehensive examination was no laughing matter. Students who failed it were thrown out of the university. Simple as that. My insides churned at the thought of it.

Run, run, run, Ellie. Stupid. Stupid. Stupid.

BING...

The phone's cheerful trill signaled the moment I had been waiting months for. A shiver ran up the back of my neck. I should have hit the treadmill's emergency stop button, but somehow after all those months of worry, my legs wouldn't give up their dogged pace.

"Come on, chicken," I whispered as I eyed the blinking screen. The disappointed face of my father flitted through my mind. He always said I would be great, but now I wasn't sure I could live up to his expectations.

I pushed away the worry that had been growing inside me for months like bacteria in a petri dish. The screen displayed its foreboding message and I grabbed it up from the water bottle stand. Before my eyes could focus, my body wobbled on the conveyor belt and I seized the side rail. I slowed the machine to a safer speed, level four—somehow it seemed better than stopping altogether—and clicked the email open.

To: Ellie Bowlan

From: LFishburn@queensu.history.ca
Subject: Department of History—PhD Comprehensive Exam

This email marks the commencement of the Comprehensive Examination period for PhD students in the Queen's history program. Your exam question is contained in the attached file. You may not communicate with your thesis supervisor, faculty, or any other student in the history program during this process. You will have two weeks to develop a defensible paper. An oral examination will follow where you will be expected to demonstrate the depth and breadth of your knowledge of the subject matter. Per university regulations, only the students who pass the Comprehensive will continue in the PhD program. Those who fail will be asked to leave Queen's University immediately.

Best of luck,
Dr. Landon Fishburn, PhD
History Department Director, Queen's University

Sweat dripped into my eyes and I wiped at a stinging pupil. The cursor hovered over the attached file as I prepared to review the examination outline. I expected to see several long-winded paragraphs detailing the position the committee had taken in selecting the examination topic. I expected a full description of the contextual framework, word counts, and formal evaluation criteria. Instead, there was only one cryptic line:

Anne Boleyn. Woman or Witch?

The five simple words loomed black and large against the otherwise empty screen. I gave the phone a shake, hoping to make more words appear. But nothing happened. The words blinked at me, unsympathetic and daunting. I read them again.

Anne Boleyn. Woman or Witch?

I fought off a surge of nausea. Was this the exam? Comprehensive exam questions were never this short, this simple, this terrifying.

I swallowed hard, trying to control the anxiety that was starting to crawl up my arms and into my neck. The muscles were tightening under my collar, a slow-moving pressure closing in with gradual force. Suddenly an invisible set of hands seemed to wrap themselves around my neck and squeeze. I felt my throat close up, cinched tight like a boy scout's knot, as a full-blown panic attack set in.

In all my months of study, this wasn't something I had prepared for. Was it a trick question? Was it a joke? The exam question was too brief. It was too weird. Who the hell asked a question like that?

As my brain drained of oxygen, my legs turned to jelly. My head swooned and my stomach lurched. Soon, I ran out of air entirely. My body wobbled on the treadmill as my running shoe caught the edge of the conveyor belt and without a moment's notice, I was flying through the air with arms flapping like an ostrich wearing spandex. I hit the floor with an ungraceful thump.

Shit... It hurt.

For a few moments, I lay in a crumpled heap behind the treadmill, clutching my cell phone. *Nice job, Ellie—very smooth.* I glanced around the gym. Thankfully, not many people had witnessed my maneuver. Even my fellow graduate students had left by now, making their way to tiny closet offices around campus.

Anne Boleyn. Woman or Witch?

I reread the question from my splayed, belly-up position on the floor. The disappointed face of my father flashed before my eyes. Dad had been a professor of history here at Queen's. He was the one who instilled in me a love of research, a love of books. "Our capacity for greatness is born from those who came before us. And when you study, Ellie, you will stand on the shoulders of giants, and you will be great too," he used to tell me. And I believed him. That was, until he died.

"Ellie, what are you doing on the floor?" a voice scolded from above.

From my horizontal position on the spongy gym tiles, I spotted a large man dressed in a white lab coat. He was blurry at first, but I knew him in an instant.

"Hi, Dez." I tried to reply casually from my crumpled position on the ground.

My best friend Dez was a nerdy academic like me, but he did a much better job of hiding the nerd part. He'd been watching me all summer, worried I had become obsessed with this Comprehensive exam. He seemed to think I was close to a having a nervous breakdown. Maybe he was right.

Dez knelt down and looked me in the eye, no doubt checking for signs of concussion. His hands were stained purple, as always, from the gentian violet he used in the biology lab. "I thought you might be here beating the hell out of yourself while you were awaiting the almighty exam." He gave my arm a squeeze and left a violet smudge on my skin. "Are you hurt?"

"Nope. Just trying not to puke." I smirked. "The treadmill tripped me while I was reading the exam question."

Dez broke into a grin. "Honestly, do you have a death wish or what? You didn't think of getting *off* the treadmill before you read it?"

I smiled at him sheepishly and handed him the phone. I wanted his honest reaction. Maybe I was freaking out for no reason.

He winced when he saw the five short words on the screen. "Damn. That is nasty. I've never seen an exam like that before."

My eyes bulged. "What am I going do? What if I fail?"

As Dez reread the email, a look of determination passed over his freckled features. He shook his head. "Listen, El. You're not gonna fail. You can do this. Hell, maybe Anne Boleyn was a witch. Do your research —like you always do. You're the smartest person I know. Youngest student in the PhD program, and all that."

But his pep talk didn't register. The fear of failure was swallowing me like a snake, and I was in the belly of the beast up to my toes.

He tried again. "Ellie, come on. The exam isn't what you expected. I get it. But you've got to stop panicking. You always do this—panic first, think second. And it doesn't help. It *never* helps."

One of the reasons Dez was my best friend was because he understood my neurotic Type A personality. Usually he was placating me when I panicked about academics, forgiving me when I retreated to my study like a hermit crab. But today he was less permissive.

"Listen, I have an idea," he continued with mounting enthusiasm. "Jane's sister, Mindy, is holding a séance tomorrow night. She and her theater friends have got some lady who claims to be a spirit medium coming to their house."

I gave him a dirty look. "Please tell me you're kidding. I'm facing the biggest challenge of my academic career and you're asking me to go to a stupid séance? I only have two weeks to figure out how the hell I am going to answer this crazy exam question."

But Dez persisted. "Don't you see? It'll be an opportunity to wrap your head around this witchcraft stuff. Hell, we can call up the ghost of Anne Boleyn and talk to her ourselves, if you want to."

I remained silent, but Dez was gaining ground. "Mindy's friends will be there. Half of them are Wiccans, so if nothing else, you can pick a few brains about modern witchcraft religions. It will give you some insight. A good place at start."

I stared up at him.

"Come on, Ellie. Don't make me go to the séance by myself. I can't handle Jane and Mindy without you."

That was it. Dez had established his argument, linked it back to my most recent academic obsession, and finally played the pity card. How could I resist?

"Okay, but I want it on record. I think this is the stupidest idea in the world." My acquiescence sounded like more of a whine.

"Duly noted." He extended his hand. "Now get off the ground. They're going to call the paramedics if you don't get up, and that would be really embarrassing." He pulled me off the floor and gave my sweaty shoulders a squeeze. "You're gonna have this thing in the bag in no time. You were born to do this. So quit whining and go do it."

Dez always knew how to get me back on track. Sometimes it was with a reassuring hug, and sometimes it was with a swift kick in the pants. In this case, it was the latter. I was still stunned, but being upright did provide a renewed sense of empowerment.

I allowed myself to think, to breathe. My panic levels came down and a little of my own determination returned. I gave the schoolyard bully in my mind a firm shove and she stumbled back into the shadows. I could do this. I would do it for my father. I just needed to break it down like I always did, stick to my research plan, and make it happen.

"Thanks, Dez," I said.

He kissed me on the cheek and gave me a light push towards the changing room. "Now go have a shower, Ellie. You stink."

Anne lay in bed, examining her fingers. She scanned her manicured nails and the soft pink skin of the nail bed. The winter sun shone through a beveled windowpane, a beam of light setting upon her face. Her sister Mary lay asleep next to her, breathing slow and deep.

Anne rotated her palm and scrunched up her nose. The sleeves of her white cotton shift bunched at the elbow, revealing a long slender forearm, a delicate wrist, and six lovely feminine fingers. She scowled at the sixth one on her right hand. It sat beside her pinky, as though it were perfectly natural, as though everyone had one. Sucking on its rounded nail, Anne remembered what she had overheard the old woman say last night. *"She bears the mark, I have seen it…"*

Could this be the mark? Anne had always hated her right hand. It made her different, but she never thought it might be a mark of significance.

Her head swirled with the previous night's events. They had returned after midnight, speaking little on their long walk home, opting to go on foot to ensure their privacy. They had arrived home frozen and miserable. Anne and Mary had climbed into bed shivering, toes icy, cheeks red. Now, in the light of the morning, the evening's events seemed more like a dream.

"Mary, wake up," urged Anne, poking her sister under the heavy quilts.

"Mmmmmmm...not morning yet," Mary murmured.

Anne looked at the back of her sister's head. Her long blonde hair fell across the pillow, nightcap askew from a night of tossing and turning. Leaving her alone, Anne swung her legs out of bed, her feet reeling against the frigid floor. She grabbed for her housecoat, tied it snug at her waist and went barefoot. Cold as it may be, she could move through the castle more discreetly without footwear.

She slipped from the bedroom and padded down the hallway to the room that held her dying father. The heavy oak door groaned on its hinges as a foul odor accosted her senses. A hint of sweat mingled with the cloying scent of illness. Anne willed herself to approach the sleeping form in the bed. A large man with a graying beard lay on his side in a pool of perspiration, woolen blankets kicked aside. She listened to his breathing, something she had not noticed until her mother had pointed it out last night. A dangerous rumble emanated from within his chest.

Fear crept over Anne like a shadow. Her father, the Earl of Wiltshire, had been reduced to this. She recognized little of the former man. He was the very image of vulnerability. The old woman said he would die.

"Aye. I'll take it up to him, my lady," a kitchen maid called from downstairs. Her mother was obviously awake and dispatching the orders. Anne spun on her heel and slipped from the room. Racing down the hall, she launched herself back into bed, jostling Mary beside her.

"What?" Mary blinked her blue eyes against the morning sun.

"Shh... Pretend you are sleeping," Anne hissed, pushing Mary's head back into the pillow. "Mother is coming..."

The oak paneled door swung open to reveal their mother, posture poised and chin high. She was a vision of calm with her hair tucked under a coif, a rich velvet gown of deep russet framing her elegant figure. Only her eyes gave hint that something was amiss.

"Girls," she announced as she sailed through the room, surveying the dresses tossed in the corner. She eyed the gowns with mild irritation as she strode towards her daughters.

The girls sat up in bed, the image of innocence, hair unkempt and night shifts askew.

"Mother?" said Anne, feigning a voice thick with sleep.

Elizabeth perched upon the edge of the mattress, taking each girl's hand into her own. "Today, I shall require much from you. Today, you must ask no questions."

Mary rubbed her eyes. "Maman, what is happening?"

"Bathe," Elizabeth whispered. She seemed to summon her strength in the words as they came. "You must each bathe in lavender and lye."

Mary's face was alight with uncertainty.

"Maman?" pressed Anne. "We could catch our deaths. It is January."

But her mother's tone was firm. "I shall call for the servants to bring the copper basin and boiling water. You shall not catch cold. I will order a great fire in the hearth. Soak for a good long time, wash each other's hair, and let it dry by the fire. Come to dinner dressed in your night shifts. We will sup in your father's sick room."

"But why?" exclaimed Anne. "What will we tell the servants when they ask questions? What will we tell George?"

Elizabeth turned to her daughters, her back rigid with resolve. "Today, I require your absolute obedience. You shall tell the servants to mind their business. And you will never breathe a word of this to George. You brother is fetching a doctor so he will have no cause to ask questions. This must remain our little secret."

"Yes, Mother," said Mary immediately.

A pause hung in the air like a soap bubble waiting to burst.

"Promise me," pressed Lady Elizabeth, her eyes focused now on Anne.

"Yes, Mother," Anne finally agreed.

PRESENT DAY
QUEEN'S UNIVERSITY, CANADA

The dream was always the same. It had plagued me for years. I was a child, standing in the miserable rain. A dark river rushed behind me. A clock tower rose in the distance and rang out the time, the peel of the bells calling out to the now abandoned city—twelve o'clock midnight.

A flannel nightgown clung to my skinny legs and I clutched a stuffed animal under my arm. The little elephant was shaggy and well loved, with black shiny eyes and a tattered trunk. A French braid ran the length of my chestnut hair, frazzled after a night of sleeping. I pushed a loose strand behind my ear but it dripped with water and it wouldn't hold its place.

From the shadows, my mother and grandmother begged upon their knees. Soaked with rain, hands held in the air, they stared into the face of a loaded revolver.

"Please don't," my mother pleaded. "Don't do this."

Grandma put a hand up to shield her daughter. "Take me. Please take me."

I tried to run to them, to come to their aid, but it was no use. I was only an observer in this recurring nightmare, not part of the terrible tableau.

"Mom!" I cried. But she could never hear me.

Instead, she remained focused on the weapon pointed at her head, a look of resolve set upon her face. She closed her eyes and reached for her mother's hand, ready to accept her fate. Grandma closed her eyes too.

A third voice called from the darkness, but it was too late.

Three shots rang out in the night. Bang. Bang... Bang.

* * *

I gnawed on my favorite wooden HB pencil deep in thought. It was already bumpy with a day's worth of bite-marks and bits of yellow paint had chipped off onto my lower lip. I was enjoying a mid-morning cup of tea, and the taste of pencil wood mixed with the soapy essence of bergamot on my tongue.

I reflected on my Comp exam progress so far. Though my research was not as far along as I wanted, it was probably vastly further ahead than most of the other students in the program. I was always the one that raced ahead of the pack, desperate to get out in front, desperate to be the best. It was a need for perfection that went far beyond the reaches of normal. But the truth was, I was not normal. I had known that much all my life. To my chagrin, I had been born a nerd—an unfortunate character trait embedded within my DNA, a deep-seated need for perfection that could not be wished away.

My abnormal nerdy-ness manifested at a young age. While the other kids in kindergarten were learning their A-B-C's and putting glue in their hair, I gripped my childproof scissors with surgical precision. I had started a year earlier than most because I was already reading *Charlotte's Web* instead of *See Spot Run*. I didn't make many friends in my first year of school, but I did manage to produce a spatially accurate replica of the solar system made from Styrofoam balls and Popsicle sticks. The childish school project still hung above my bed today.

The theory I had developed over the course of my educational career was this: Nerds walked among the normal. They were desperate to be normal themselves but were hopelessly unable to achieve it.

For the last twenty-four hours, I had locked myself away in my study, breaking down my Comprehensive exam question the best way I knew how. With plain old fashion fact-finding. I had focused most of my study preparation on Ancient Greece, an area I was considering for my thesis dissertation. And I had to admit, sixteenth century Europe was not my speciality.

Based on my findings, Anne Boleyn had been a very interesting woman. As the second wife of Henry Tudor, King Henry the VIII of England, she was queen for only three years. Her marriage to the king was rather political because he was still married to his first wife, Queen Catherine of Aragon. In order for them to marry, King Henry needed to have his first marriage annulled. When it became apparent that Pope Clement of Rome would not grant the annulment, King Henry broke with the Roman Catholic Church and so marked the start of the English Reformation.

I highlighted the more interesting bits in the next passage. After several years, Anne and Henry married, but they could not have a son. They had only a single daughter, Elizabeth, and this little girl grew up to become Elizabeth I, Queen of England. Henry became unhappy in the marriage because of Anne's inability to bear him sons. Three years after their union, he had Anne investigated and thrown into the Tower of London. She was found guilty and was executed by beheading on May 19, 1536 on charges of high treason, adultery, and witchcraft.

Witchcraft. I circled the word a few times with my wooden HB pencil and rubbed my face with fatigue.

"Bloody ridiculous," I grumbled.

I scratched at a little scar on the side of my hand. It had always been there, a little white line at the side of my knuckles. I couldn't remember how I got it, but it always got itchy when I was frustrated. And this morning it itched like crazy.

The idea that Anne Boleyn was a witch was pure tomfoolery, plain and simple. You didn't need to a PhD in history to know that. An accusation of witchcraft was medieval power at its finest. In the 1500's, a powerful man only had to accuse a woman of witchcraft and she would be hauled away, tortured, and put to death. That is what happened to Anne Boleyn. She got screwed and everyone knew it. It was Medieval History 101. So why would the Comprehensive examination committee ask such a stupid question?

Downstairs, a door slammed shut and the unique sound of my great-grandmother's footsteps echoed up the stairs to my study: *schlumb-bum, bum...schlumb-bum, bum...schlumb-bum, bum.*

I recognized Grapes the minute I heard her, but I didn't get up. She'd always been fiercely independent and never liked the extra help. But ever since she had broken her hip two years ago and needed to use a walker, she had become a nightmare of determination.

She arrived at the doorjamb, looking hot and flustered, but wearing a certain amount of pride on her face. I knew it made her feel good she could still conquer those narrow steps at the ripe age of ninety-three.

She shuffled into the room—*schlumb-bum, bum...schlumb-bum, bum*—and planted a kiss on top of my head. "Did you get my note? I taped it to the Cheerios, so you'd be sure to find it." Grapes looked pleased with her cleverness.

"I had oatmeal this morning," I said.

"Shoot." She sat on the bed and caught her breath. Today Grapes wore a lime-green yoga pantsuit. Her sculpted hair was a curly white helmet, Ms. Clairol's firm-hold hair spray holding strong. "I would have been home earlier, but I took Bernice and Gerty to the senior's social last night for the dance marathon."

I couldn't help but smile. In spite of her walker, Grapes was as competitive as ever. A dance marathon would have been right up her alley.

She shook her head with a hint of frustration. "It was going well until Bernice had a dizzy spell. We were beat by Mr. and Mrs. Kontiki from the senior's residence. They were unstoppable."

"Well not everyone can be super-granny like you, can they?" I tried to sound a little stern. Grapes needed to be more realistic about people's physical limitations. The woman's friends were ancient. She would end up killing them if she wasn't careful.

"Did Gerty tell you about our poker tournament?" Grapes changed directions. "Do you think you'll be able to make it? If you don't come, we'll have to ask Vernon. And you know he has that terrible gas."

These three old women were the Titanium Trio. They had been aptly named by my great-grandmother after she had hip surgery and could claim all three of them had steel reinforcements holding their bodies together. Since her operation, she had begun thinking about their threesome as indestructible.

My shoulders sagged. "I'd love to go, Grapes, but I'm snowed under."

Grapes studied me. She'd always been able to see right through me. Grapes knew me better than anyone. She took me in at the age of eleven when my parents and grandmother died, and had been my greatest defender ever since.

"Well, what's the exam question? I can take it." She growled with mock ferocity.

"They want to know if Anne Boleyn was really a witch," I scoffed.

"Oh?" A shadow flitted across my great-grandmother's eyes.

I tucked the chewed pencil behind my ear for safekeeping and settled in to tell Grapes the whole story. She listened as I covered the major points of my experience yesterday: the queasy stomach, the evil treadmill, the brutal exam question, and the spongy gym floor tiles. She plied me with questions, intent on understanding the complexity of the research and its potential pitfalls.

All the while Grapes' eyebrows bobbed around like snowy white caterpillars. I'd seen it a thousand times before. She was thinking deep thoughts. Once the caterpillars finished their dance, the thought was ready. Ding!

"Now dear, perhaps this isn't as bad as it sounds. It may be a stroke of luck," said Grapes.

I scoffed. "Not bloody likely."

"Darling, listen. Don't you see? The sixteenth century? That's the era your dad was researching before he...well...before he...died."

A momentary silence fell between us, stopping the conversation short. My parents' death was the toughest thing for Grapes and me to discuss. It always had been. Ever since the day we got the awful news, I simply could not talk about it. Grapes had always understood not to push me too hard. Every few years, she would raise the parent-talk topic in conversation and then back off when I gave her the silent reaction.

I gave her the silent reaction now.

"Ellie, it's been years. I think it's time we talk about this. Maybe this exam is a sign you need to reach out to your family, even though they're not with us anymore. There are endless boxes of your dad's research in the basement. It would be a way for you to understand your father's work. To find that 'history' connection between you."

I stared at the floor. She was right. I wasn't a kid anymore, but a part of me resisted. The dream from last night pushed through my mind.

"The nightmares are back," I confessed.

Grapes put a wrinkled hand on my knee. "Oh dear." She winced. "I thought you were finished with those awful dreams."

I shrugged. "They started again yesterday."

After my parents died, I was plagued by terrifying dreams. They never made much sense. They were more like a string of terrifying flashes: A gun to my mother's head, drizzling rain and a clock tower, three gunshots in the night. I often woke up screaming. Grapes would hold me for hours until I fell back to sleep. The dreams stayed with me for a long time before they faded. It was such a relief when they finally went away.

Grapes' voice was softer now. "Maybe the exam triggered something in your mind. This might be your opportunity to deal with the ghosts of your past. I'm telling you, sacrifice a half hour tomorrow and go down to the basement. Open a few boxes. Your father's research has been waiting for you all these years."

"Maybe." My shoulders gave way to another involuntary shrug.

Grapes' white hair helmet glimmered. "Maybe is a good start."

She patted my hand. Grapes had this way of easing me into new ideas. Despite her age, she was the free spirit in this family.

"Oh darling." Grapes gripped her walker as she eased herself off the bed. "Would you stop by the liquor store and pick up a bottle of gin? A splash of gin in the tea always makes for a more interesting poker tournament."

I laughed. Now that Grapes had patched me up, she could return to her vibrant social life.

"Sure. But maybe I should buy nose plugs too—if Vernon is coming along."

The door at the end of the hall was ajar, the light from within casting long shadows. A fire surged in the hearth, copper flames devouring thick logs in the grate. Bread and cheese sat atop a simple table, three silver goblets and a flask of ale standing aloft. The washbasin sat at the room's center, now filled with hot fresh water that wafted steam.

The scent of illness had receded, but it continued to hover over the bed, forming a cocoon around their father's dying body. Anne shuddered at the sight of him. He was ashen gray, hair askew and hanging in damp clumps about his forehead. His chest rumbled with every breath, as though an ocean of water boiled within his lungs and he would soon drown upon the waves.

Mary ran to his bedside and sobbed. "Father."

It had been two days since the girls and George visited their father. And in that time he had deteriorated rapidly. Whereas before he had managed a weak conversation and drank a little tea, now it was as if it took all his effort to heave one great breath, rest, and then muster the strength to take another.

Anne saw her mother standing in the shadows of the sick room, dressed in her shift, her long red hair flowing down her back. She stood with her eyes set upon the night sky. A white sliver of moon hovered in the dark void outside.

"Mother?" whispered Anne.

Elizabeth reached upward and pulled at the iron latches holding the window in place, hinges squeaking as they gave way from their mounts. She lifted it down, leaning it along the wall in the corner. A cold wind wafted in but receded quickly, the scorching temperature in the room holding firm.

"It is unlucky to view the moon through a pane of glass," murmured Elizabeth. "Especially when you are meeting her for the first time."

Anne found her voice. "Maman, it is cold outside. You will let all heat out."

"Not tonight. The warmth shall stay within." Elizabeth glanced at her daughters. "Girls, you must trust me. I will try to explain, but much shall remain unclear. Do as I say and your father will come out of this all right."

This time Mary spoke. "Mother, I am afraid."

Elizabeth smiled sadly. "Don't be frightened. There are things in this world that can endow great power. But you must trust in it, swallow it, and accept its spirit—the dark and the light."

The girls looked at their mother, two sets of large unblinking eyes set upon her face.

"Just follow along with me. In time, you will come to understand." Elizabeth moved towards her girls now. "First, take off those night caps and unwrap your braids. A maiden must meet the moon looking the part."

Curiosity snatched up Anne with a vise-like grip as she pondered this strange request, but she knew better than to ask questions. Instead, she untied her nightcap and helped Mary with hers. When the girls had finished, their hair hung loose in rich waves of russet and gold.

"Better," Elizabeth announced. "Now turn to face the moon. I want you to hold it in your gaze, swallow in its energy, and curtsy three times."

Anne looked up at the sliver of white light against the black, and tried to breathe it in, feeling its power, as her mother had explained. She curtsied three times as she held her eyes constant on the pulsating arc in the night sky.

Elizabeth spoke barely above a whisper:

"Crescent moon, Goddess of Light, I give you two Boleyn daughters. A new coven is formed."

A surge of energy coursed through Anne's body, her cheeks flushed and her fingertips tingled.

Elizabeth moved through the room as if retracing the steps of a dance she had performed as a child. She crossed to the hearth and picked up a pot of ashes. Breathing steady now, she sprinkled the ash in a large circle on the floor, enclosing the three ladies, the washbasin, the bread table and the bed that held their dying father. When the circle was complete, she looked into the faces of her daughters, determination on her brow.

"Girls, stand at the edge of the circle."

The girls exchanged glances. Mary's eyes were full of bewilderment. Anne's eyes danced with adventure.

"Quickly," Elizabeth ordered.

The three women stood in a triangle flanking the edges of the circle of ash. A hot wind swirled around its outer rim, pulling at their hair, twisting and curling in all directions. Elizabeth took her position at the northernmost point of the circle and called for the wind to gain strength, her body a comely silhouette against the light of the fire. The wind eddied around the circle of ash, gaining vitality as Elizabeth spoke. She raised her voice above the gale and commanded the room and the objects within it.

"Virgin Moon, Maiden's head,
Bring your light, from once was dead.
Swell with life, wax and wane,
Share your light, squelch his pain.
Virgin moon, I give you thee,
My daughters chaste, our coven three.
For his life, a price is paid,
Blood doth charged, a virgin maid."

The wind picked up, a storm raging within the chamber. Elizabeth braced herself against it and grabbed the knife from the bread table. She moved to the steaming bath, hovering her hand just above the water. She ran the sharp blade across her palm, watching calmly as her blood dripped into the water, turning it a rich crimson red.

Elizabeth looked at her eldest. "Now you, Anne!" she called over the gale.

A prickling energy danced through Anne's heart at the sight of the blood. Her fingers tingled as she gripped the knife, her belly hot with the power. She lowered her hand to the bath and slid the blade across her palm. Blood dripped into the water, but this time it hissed as it hit the surface. Anne clenched her fist to stop the bleeding and handed the knife to her sister.

Mary was ashen gray, her face frozen in horror.

"Do it, Mary. It doesn't hurt!" Anne urged.

Mary had not moved from her position along the circle since her mother had begun the incantation. She wrung her hands but otherwise remained inert.

"Mary, you must!" insisted Anne.

Mary glanced at her sister and stumbled toward the bath. She took the knife from Anne's bloodied fist and held her hand over the hissing water.

"God forgive me," she sobbed. Mary closed her eyes and sliced the blade deep across the flesh of her palm. As Mary's blood dripped into the water, a swell of bubbles rose to the surface. The red liquid boiled hard, popping and spurting violently.

"Excellent," Elizabeth called over the lusty gale. "There is much power tonight. Help me carry your father. We must place him in the bath."

She heaved her husband by the armpits as the girls took hold of his legs. Still unconscious, his head tipped back with weakness. He was surprisingly heavy, despite his weight loss, and the women struggled to lift him from the bed. They breathed heavily as they lowered him into the bubbling red water, liquid spilling over the edge as his body displaced it.

"Anne, be sure his head stays above the water. Mary, fetch the elixir."

Mary retrieved the auburn liquid the old crone had conjured and emptied its contents into the bath. The oily brown ooze dripped from its container. Two hardened frogs floated on the surface. A bird's claw sat atop her father's chest.

The wind surged as Elizabeth flew to the basin and hovered above her husband's head. She placed her hands on his chest and pumped her palms on his ribcage. With every thrust up, his chest swelled. With every thrust down, blobs of green phlegm flew from his mouth. He coughed and sputtered as he expelled the vile illness, and with each new breath, he inhaled the steam, now putrid with the contents of the potion.

All the while, he remained deep in his slumber, unaware of their efforts. Anne held his head to ensure it did not slip below the water's surface, but she struggled to keep her father in place. Just when she wasn't sure she had the strength to hold him any longer, Elizabeth shouted over the tempest,

"We implore you, Goddess. Heal him!"

With one great heaving breath, Thomas Boleyn, the Earl of Wiltshire, bolted upright, eyes open but looking nowhere, body stiff with magic. A long, high-pitched cry escaped from his lips. The cry of a child. The cry of terrible suffering. The women looked around, gripped with uncertainty.

Everything stopped. The wind dropped instantly. Only the cry of Thomas Boleyn echoed through the night. His wail continued from somewhere deep within for much longer than any man could muster a single natural breath. All at once, Thomas Boleyn ceased. Unmoving, eyes glazed, his body stiff with magic. His mouth was a black gaping hole, his fingers gripping the side of the tub that held him. He drew no breath. He exhaled no more. He was a rigid frozen statue.

The three women stood immobilized, eyes wide with fear.

Finally, Thomas Boleyn drew one great heaving breath, his spine curved back like a viper. He emitted a painful wheezing as his body resisted the life-giving breath, but the magic gripped him hard. It filled him and filled him until he could take on no more. Then, as the force that breathed new life into him was satisfied, he fell back into the bath in a deep, exhausted sleep.

"It is done," Elizabeth announced. "Girls, help me get him back to bed."

PRESENT DAY
QUEEN'S UNIVERSITY, CANADA

I ran along the waterfront this morning rather than subjecting myself to the evil treadmill. For forty-five minutes, I cleared my head while looking out over the deep blue water of Lake Ontario. The waves were coming in like Poseidon's fury, rolling white caps smashing up against the rock barrier of the seawall. I got soaked a few times from a rogue spray that squirted from between the breakers, but overall, I found the whole thing to be therapeutic. After a lot of serious sweating, I was ready to face my day.

The limestone houses in our neighborhood boasted a well-preserved demeanor with stately facades and manicured lawns. Majestic iron lamp posts stood like soldiers along the tree-lined streets. Our English cottage seemed a bit out of place amidst the other homes on Gate Street. The Bowlan family residence was folksy rather than imposing, complete with a rounded front door, lead glass windows and a crooked chimney. Bluebells climbed the garden walls and wildflowers filled the garden beds. The ivy growing up the brick had turned a fiery red, hinting with color that autumn was around the corner. It was a little odd, it was a lot eclectic, but it was home.

A familiar face on the porch looked up with enthusiasm. Two big brown eyes, a stout black body and one large swishy tail rose up to greet up me. In the commotion of our reunion, the enthusiastic tail knocked over a planter full of Grapes' prize-winning begonias.

"Hey Zach. Are you here to hang out with me today?"

The black lab dropped a hockey puck at my feet. The Ottawa Senators hockey puck was full of slobber, its logo all but licked away. This well-chewed little puck was Zach's favorite thing in the whole world. Zach was the neighbor's dog. Grapes and I had known him since he was a puppy. His owners occasionally got too busy for him, so Zach came to visit us through his doggy door.

I threw the drool-soaked puck across the lawn. "Go get it, you psycho."

Zach bolted away to retrieve it. I waited for him to gallop into the house at full speed. *Slam.* The door closed too hard against its frame. It was one of those home repairs we hadn't gotten around to fixing. It had been that way for years.

Zach made his way into the kitchen and plopped himself down by the food dish. He gave me his best 'good-boy' face and I grinned. Like a well-trained human, I scooped a blob of peanut butter into his bowl and watched him eat it, his licks growing slower as the stickiness took hold of his tongue.

"I'm glad you showed up, buddy," I said. "Because today, you and I are going into the dreaded basement to dig around in Dad's old research."

Zach wagged his tail as he ate the last of the peanut butter.

The heavy oak door squeaked on its hinges as a smell of mildew wafted from the bowels of the house. I reached in and flipped on the light. A bald sixty-watt bulb dangling from the ceiling came to life, casting a dull glow over the basement. I took a deep breath and headed down the narrow steps. Zach followed behind me. The place didn't seem to creep out the dog at all, but my skin was crawling. The basement of our century home was not a pretty sight. It was more of a hole than a basement, barely a step above a root cellar.

Most of the subterranean space below our house contained antiques and heirlooms. Spinning wheels and butter churns, rocking chairs and armoires, and enough cobwebs to host an award-winning Halloween party. I grabbed a well-worn blue and green quilt from an old armoire—no doubt made by someone in my family from generations ago—and threw it across the floor for Zach. It was a comfortable bed and he stretched out with his hockey puck, ready for a rigorous day of sleeping.

My heart skipped a beat now that I had found the courage to come down here. The darkened north corner of the basement had been untouched for over a decade. Despite the thick layer of dust and a few creepy spiders, it was perfectly preserved. Almost fifty office boxes sat stacked along the wall. White labels with names and dates identified each box with crisp efficiency. I picked up my box cutter and wiped the dirt from the first few labels.

"Which one should I open first?" I asked the dog with forced optimism.

Zach thumped his tail.

I selected the box entitled 'Arthur's Published Papers.' It seemed like a good place to start. Running the cutter along the top, I tried to contain the nerves working their way through my intestines like greasy motor oil.

"Come on, Ellie. Don't wimp out now," I whispered.

I peeled back the cardboard lid and peered inside. Manuscripts filled the box in question, each with a pink top page stating the title of the paper, the academic journal, the dates, co-authors, etc. A cover page crowned the first package in the pile.

Matriarchal Naming Conventions in the 16th Century
Author: Arthur Wright, PhD

Traditional patriarchal European naming conventions are the foundation of modern genealogy. That a family name is passed from father to child throughout generations, allows the modern researcher to establish genealogical lineage across hundreds of years. However, there are rare circumstances in which a family name is passed from mother to child across generations because of some particular title or prized trait bestowed upon the mother. It is critical to the study of modern genealogy to grasp the circumstances of this unique naming convention to establish appropriate and accurate lineage, especially in the Middle Ages when other forms of documentation were limited.

"This stuff isn't related to my Comp at all," I scoffed.

Zach looked up from his hockey puck. His eyes said, "Suck it up and keep looking."

I tossed the first package of papers beside a now cold cup of Earl Grey tea and continued digging. After an hour, I felt completely deflated. I had found nothing but mind-numbing genealogical records and enough information about that bloody matriarchal naming convention to wilt a willow. I stood up and stretched my back, popping out the bits of compressed cartilage. Dad's disappointed face flitted through my mind.

"Zach," I said with an accusing tone. "There's nothing here."

The dog stretched his back too, a big bushy tail shooting up in the air. He seemed satisfied I had done my best. He dropped his hockey puck at my feet and looked up. I gave him a pat on the head and headed towards the stairs with promises of another game of fetch.

As we headed out, my eyes caught on the box I had been sitting on. This box, brown and benign, was marked 'Personal.'

"Hold on, bud," I whispered.

Zach lay back on the quilt, happy to wait a little longer.

This box held a jumble of paper clips, sticky notes, staples, and dozens of wooden HB pencils in a dizzying array of chaos. I ran my hand over a childish-looking clay horse with googly eyes sitting amongst the other items. I had made this trinket for my father when I was a little girl. A rush of happy memories flooded my mind. A birthday party, silly hats, Mom, Dad, Grandma, and Grapes. Dad was blowing out his candles, a new mountain of gifts piled high on the kitchen table.

Without warning, the warm laughter faded and the images blurred together. My throat constricted as the memories began to strangle me. I backed away from the box in question, giving my head a shake to fend off the memories. I simply couldn't deal with these happy images. They were the stuff of nightmares.

"Keep looking Ellie. Focus on your Comp exam," I said steadily.

A red and blue folder from Kingston Travel flashed from within the box. It didn't seem related to my Anne Boleyn research, but something about it made me take a closer look. I flipped it open, pleased at having skirted a full-blown attack of memories.

The folder contained travel receipts for three plane trips to London, England for my father, mother and grandmother—Arthur Wright, Eliza Bowlan, Beth Bowlan. The plane tickets were set to fly from Toronto, Canada to London, England on August 20 and to return August 28, 2007, the year my parents died.

"Look at this," I whispered. "This travel receipt says my parents and grandmother would have been in London, England on August 25."

Zach tilted his head.

"But that's impossible. My parents died on August 25 on a camping trip here in Canada."

More memories swirled through my mind in the dim light of the basement. The harder I fought, the greater the memories grew in clarity and strength.

I was a little girl again, waving goodbye to my family as they loaded the car. Mom and Grandma, dressed in matching sweatshirts and hiking boots, argued about what order the camping gear should go into the trunk. Dad wore his special vacation hat as he peered over a guide map, ready for their grand adventure. Grapes tickled me as we disappeared through the rounded red door with promises of cookies and milk.

A familiar set of invisible hands grabbed my neck and squeezed. I closed my eyes and tried to push back the hurt, the loss, the pain. In spite of my efforts to contain them, the memories kept coming in flashes.

The police officer with the white moustache stood on the porch. "I'm sorry ma'am," he said to Grapes, his eyes strange "They've gone missing... in the park...we suspect there was an accident..."

My throat threatened to close completely. Still the memories came, relentless and cruel.

"Based on the broken tree branches and the fallen rocks on the cliff face, we believe they fell to their deaths in the rapids below..." The officer's voice was stiff.

I shook my head to be rid of his words, but Grapes was wrapping herself around my eleven-year-old frame, tears streaming, her cries ringing through the chaos. "They're dead, Ellie. Your parents are gone... gone...gone..."

I brought my hands to my ears to stop the horrible memories from echoing through my mind as another full-blown panic attack swept in.

"Stop," I shouted into the silence of the basement as my legs gave way.

"Stop." I buried my face in the dog's furry body.

"Stop, please stop."

PRESENT DAY
QUEEN'S UNIVERSITY, CANADA

Dez and I were fifteen minutes late to the séance at Jane and Mindy's house. We looked like two waddling ducks as we raced down Water Street with elbows flapping.

"Hurry, El," Dez wheezed. "You know how Jane gets when we're late."

I considered making a snarky retort about the séance, but Dez seemed so enthusiastic, I thought it best not to start a fight before we even arrived.

Dez and I had a strange friendship. Most of the time we bickered about petty things. We argued about things even when we agreed on them, just for the sheer pleasure of the squabble. In spite of it all, Dez was my best friend in the whole world.

We met in first year university. We were younger than the first-year crowd, both of us having skipped a grade in high school. But we had more in common than our ages. Dez and I were both dealing with some rather profound family issues, so the connection between us felt rather natural. My issues were related to the death of my parents. Although they had been dead for years, I still felt betrayed by the world. Dez's issues were of different nature. He had come out of the closet that summer. The week before he left for university, he screwed up his courage to tell his mom and dad he was gay. Unfortunately, his parents didn't react the way he had hoped. In fact, it got pretty ugly. Dez left for Kingston three days early.

In spite of our troubles, we made a great duo. In the first few months of school, Dez showed me how being social could actually be fun. I had always preferred the quiet solitude of my study. But that semester, with the help of a couple of fake ID's, we partied like savages at the university's nightclubs, hung out with the cool crowd and rebelled against the world. In spite of his elephant-like proportions, Dez was a great dancer and every weekend we twisted, shimmied, and wiggled into the wee hours of the morning. The party scene was a phase that didn't last long for either of us. We both found it rather exhausting. Eventually, we reverted to the quiet lifestyle that suited us better. Through it all, Dez and I always stuck together.

"Are you gonna try to be open minded tonight?" asked Dez, a little out of breath.

I crossed my arms in protest, my legs straining to match his stride.

Dez pulled a journal article from his jacket pocket, a hint of his own nerd showing through.

"Listen Mrs. Skeptic, I dug this up for you. It might help put a little science into the supernatural. It's called "The DNA of Witchcraft." Some guy named Ivor Cullen studied the genetic sequence of witches. Maybe it's not hocus-pocus after all." He put the paper tube in my hand like has was passing me a baton in a relay race.

"Okay, biology nerd." I tucked the paper package into my back pocket. There was no way to read it now, so it would have to be safe keeping for later. "Figures you'd bring DNA into this somehow."

"Hey, it always come down to DNA in the end."

* * *

The party at Jane and Mindy's house was well underway and melancholy music moaned in the background. It had to be The Smiths. No other band could make a person want to sing along and commit suicide at the same time. A crowd of strangely attired theater people gathered in the living room, draping themselves over the furniture. Candelabras filled the room, with smaller pillar candles covering the remaining surfaces unoccupied by human bottoms. The flickering glow of three dozen wicks made for a dramatic effect.

Jane plunked an oversized glass of red wine in my hand and gave me a stiff hug. Jane was a clinical psychology major and everything about her reminded me of a female Sigmund Freud, right down to her little round glasses.

"Hi, Ellie. How are you doing? Are you coping? Are you well?" She psychoanalyzed in her usual low-pitched tone.

I hesitated, not sure how much information to divulge. Jane always had a way of making me feel like I had lost my mind, even on the best of days.

A small crash in the corner saved me from Jane's meddlesome probing. Mindy, Jane's little sister, flitted across the room, carrying a humungous bowl of cheese doodles and a tray of fancy drinks.

"Oh my God, Ellie," Mindy cooed. "I can't believe your Comp question. I was so excited when I heard. I mean, who gets to study witchcraft for a Comprehensive? I would kill to be in your shoes." The girl was practically vibrating.

Taking a long sip of wine, I gave Mindy a tight smile. Mindy was more my age than Jane, in spite of my PhD student status, but I always found her to be a little too 'high school.' Not only was she over the top, she was also really weird.

"Umm, well, witchcraft isn't really my thing."

"O-M-G... You have to let me help you. I have books and spells. I can show you everything," she said with dramatic flair, her eyebrow ring reflecting in the candlelight.

My eyes darted about the room, looking for an escape, but the place was too crowded. Black lipstick and face piercings were everywhere. I was cornered.

Mindy checked her phone. "Why don't we meet at the Sleeping Goat tomorrow morning? We'll grab a coffee and I'll give you the rundown on the ways of the Wiccan." There was something about her irritating enthusiasm I couldn't deny. Good intention and kindness just oozed from her.

"Okay," I said flatly.

Mindy squealed and gave me a quick hug. She passed the cheese doodles to Dez and dashed off into the crowd, trailing after a well-tattooed fellow who gave her butt a squeeze.

Jane, Dez, and I found ourselves a vacated spot on the couch. It didn't take long before Jane started into a one-way conversation about her latest clinical psychology research. She droned on about things like how to identify a mild depressive episode with a reflexive mirror gazing, how to cure insomnia with a hot towel, and the reason Freudian couches were no longer part of the modern psychotherapeutic experience. I faded in and out. Finally she returned to the topic of her crazy sister Mindy.

"I like to support Mindy in these supernatural interests of hers. I think it's a kind of subconscious over-compensation. I promised my mother I would take care of her."

"Take care of who?" asked a tall athletic guy coming from the kitchen.

"Oh hey, John." Dez looked up. "Glad you could make it."

Jane smiled up at John with those circular glasses and patted the seat to my left.

"John, have you met Ellie?" Dez asked, stuffing a cheese doodle in his mouth. "She's been hanging out with her laptop for the last few months, so you may not have met. Ellie, this is John Chelsea. He is our latest housemate recruit. Remember the vacancy we had this summer? This is the guy who moved in."

Jane leaned in to provide precise details about the psychological connection between John and me. "It turns out you are both writing your Comprehensive exams right now. We thought you two could commiserate. You know, provide each other with moral support?" She was stiff and clinical, but I worried she might be trying to set us up.

John smiled with curiosity and then with a hint of recognition. He leaned back for a second as if to see me at a different angle. "Yes, we have met." He sounded rather incredulous. "But I only know you as the girl in my kitchen."

My eyes slid over John's muscled torso as the memory came flashing back.

Two months ago, I had gone for a long run on a Saturday afternoon. It was a scorching summer day, but I had to get away from the books. As I was heading home from a grueling 20K, I passed by Dez's house and popped in to get a drink of water. No one ever locked the door at his place, so I let myself in like I always did. When I realized Dez wasn't home, I had a drink from the tap in the kitchen. I was standing at the sink, face as red as a tomato, slurping down water like a woman in the desert, when this half-naked beautiful guy in a towel walked in. He was muscular and tanned, still wet from the shower.

The half-naked guy said, "Oh."

Then I said, "Oh."

He said, "Do you live here?"

I said, "No... Do you?"

He said, "Yeah, I moved in yesterday."

There was a rather long pause. Then I said, "Well, thanks for the water." And I left. It was very embarrassing. I felt like Goldilocks caught red-handed.

My shoulders sagged with humiliation. I tried to hide my horror by taking a large sip of wine, but the glass was now empty. Instead, I gave John a weak smile.

A commotion by the door distracted us from our embarrassing exchange. A large woman, well over six feet tall and wearing a purple muumuu, sailed through the room. She gave orders about clearing away furniture and arranging the candles. Theater people rushed about, obeying her every command. This was the infamous Madame Lazarre.

"Dis won't do," she barked at the four of us on the couch. "I need you out of de way. We need to clear de floor...clear de karma...clear de energie."

A crowd of colorful hairdos, nose rings, and black leather jackets shuffled about. The room filled with excitement, conversations intensified, and every sentence seemed to be finished with the words 'Awesome Dude.'

"We will soon begeen," Madame Lazarre announced. She clapped her hands as though she was speaking to a group of five-year-olds. "Everyone gather round and find a nice spot on de floor. We will form a circle. T'must be nice and round." She made a round circle with her fingers in the air.

"Oh dear God, here we go," I sneered.

Dez poked me in the ribs.

After a great deal of shuffling and confusion, we made a satisfactory ring of bodies on the floor. It was like circle-time in kindergarten and this motley crew would begin show-and-tell. I was sitting cross-legged between Dez and Mindy's boyfriend, Tattoo-Carl. It was rather claustrophobic, but I tried to ignore it. Madame Lazarre turned out all the electrical lights and gave each of us a candle to hold. Mine was a creamy white color and smelled like gingerbread cookies.

"We come togedder in perfect love and perfect trust. I call de Guardians of the West to bring de airre. I call de Guardians of the East to bring de water. I call de Guardians of North to bring de Earthe. I call de Guardians of the Southe to breeng de fire."

Madame Lazarre looked around the room with a severe expression, making a silent pact. "Our protective circle is formed."

Everyone was quiet. Mindy looked as though she had fallen in love.

The Madame pursed her over-sized red lips together and instructed us to hold hands. I put my candle down and glanced at Tattoo-Carl. His palms were sweaty, but I held his hand anyway. Once the Madame was satisfied we could follow her instructions, she slid an empty wine glass into the middle of our ridiculous magic circle.

"Dis is our glass, de reflective surface, our grounding to dis world. Dis glass will form de creative center of our circle, to geeve power to our union, and allow de spirits beyond to enter."

The theater people seemed wildly impressed, as though the wine glass had become an object of worship. I snickered under my breath.

The Madame closed her eyes and began meditating, shutting herself off from the watchful stares around her. She sat cross-legged on the floor with her hands held to her lips in prayer, like an oversized purple Buddha.

"Spirit plane, we welcome our guests from de odder side to our circle, uniting de positive and de negative energie, de dark and de light, in harmonee, we call to you." She inhaled through large nostrils. "Who will be de first to call to de spirit world?"

The room filled with whispers. Mindy nudged her boyfriend with a light punch to the arm.

"I could go first?" Carl squirmed in his uncomfortable cross-legged position. "I have an uncle who died last year?"

The Madame nodded with approval. "Well den... Call to heem and see if he will join us in de circle of trust."

The whispers petered as the infamous Madame Lazarre began her creepy performance. She held the group transfixed with impressive theatrics and well-timed stage cues. Her eyes rolled back into her head, her face transformed into a macabre mask as she affected the voices of half a dozen spirits from the great beyond. The candles flickered and the tension mounted in a rather entertaining show of ghosts and ghouls, spine chilling and spooky. It was a fine performance. But I wasn't sure which was more amusing, Madame Lazarre's theatrics or the fact that the theater people had all fallen for it.

After one final spirit encounter, the Madame's head snapped back into position to indicate the spirits no longer inhabited her body. She called for silence as she cleared the karma from the room. The group waited in obedient quietude as Tattoo-Carl and Mindy mouthed O-M-G to each other.

From upstairs, a window slammed shut with a heavy crash. Madame Lazarre's eyes flew open and she looked around warily.

"Shh," she whispered. "Someone else is come. Someone unbidden."

The theater people shifted in their spots, eyes wide. I had to admit, it was creepy. We listened as set of slow footsteps made their way down the stairs, light-footed, like a woman in high-heeled shoes. Mindy gave me a no-one-else-is-here look, as the footsteps came closer—*clipunk, clipunk, clipunk*—across the hall to the entrance of the living room.

I looked towards the doorway, but no one was there, though I could have sworn someone was in the shadows. A strange new energy filled the room and brushed, light as a feather, against my skin. It made the hairs on the back of my neck stand on end.

After a long pause, the Madame found her voice. "Who is among us, spirit? Dis is a protected circle."

The partygoers gawked in the darkness but there was no response. The effect was unnerving.

Jane began to look strange. She didn't seem to know where she was. Her eyes swirled in the candlelight. She sat up straight as a pin and then collapsed into the lap of Mr. Face Piercings beside her.

"I seek Elizabeth. I seek Elizabeth Bowlan." Her voice was shrill and impatient.

Without warning, the wine glass the in middle of our human circle slid violently across the floor and hit my knee. It was thrust with an impossible velocity, as if moved by an invisible hand. The glass, now touching my leg, pressed firmly.

"Elizabeth, is that you?" the shrill voice demanded.

Pulsating with heat, the wine glass throbbed against my skin. It sent a jolt of electricity up my spine. The candles in the room glowed, the intensity of their light doubling as the wine glass continued to press against my flesh.

I looked helplessly around the room. The darkness was dotted with dozens of orange points of light. But the flames atop each candle were no longer dancing upward to the ceiling. Instead, each flame in the room bent over its wax frame, pointing like an accusatory finger directly at me.

"Yes?" I replied in a small voice.

Jane's eyes remained closed, but her lips moved around the strange voice. "My name is Beth Bowlan. I wish to deliver a message to Ellie Bowlan."

My heart beat wildly in my chest. I could feel the familiar invisible set of hands grip my throat, squeezing tighter, tighter.

The voice continued.

"Beware the dark mark on your name
We have felt it for many generations
Seek your father's research for answers

Among the boxes, unheralded work, hidden within."

Warm bile was rising in my gut, readying itself to burst forth as the voice continued.

"Only a Bowlan among the living can end the curse

To do it, the circle must be completed

Find the beginning to find the end

And save the life of the man who killed your parents."

There was an audible gasp from the room. Though I wanted no part of it, I had become the star of this bizarre freak-show. My heart pounded and my head ached. It was too much to bear. The room spun, circles of candlelight swirling through the darkness. I felt myself falling, falling, falling.

"Stop!" I shouted.

At my command, the room went black. Dozens of fiery flames extinguished with a pop as a hush fell over our gathering. Only the wine glass shattering into a thousand tiny pieces echoed through the room.

"Get the lights." A shaky voice croaked as the dark room erupted in a state of confusion. People bolted upright, struggling to secure their footing in the darkness. Furniture bumped, chairs scraped along the floorboards, and footsteps crunched over broken glass until the light switch was located.

I remained seated in my cross-legged position watching it all happen in slow motion. I was trying to process what I heard, trying to understand what just happened. Once the lights were back on, the world stopped spinning, but my legs were still jelly.

Dez knelt down and put a reassuring hand on my knee. "You alright, kid?"

I smiled weakly, my pallor as ashen as Jane's. "I think I want to go home." I tried to keep my voice light, but I was shaken.

Dez signaled to John, who was crossing through the mayhem to join us. John looked as relieved to be leaving as we were. The three of us pushed our way through the crowd to make our escape from this creepy theater party. Madame Lazarre was barking orders and stirring up new commotion.

Mindy intercepted us at the door. "You're not going, are you Dez? Jane's still acting weird," she pleaded. "Can't you stay for little while longer?"

A small crowd had formed around Jane as she lay in the lap of Mr. Face-Piercings. Her breathing was rapid and her eyelids fluttered, but she had found her usual low-pitched voice again. She was in the process of denying she had channeled a spirit.

Dez wore an exasperated expression.

"It's okay, Dez. Stay here with Jane," I answered for him. I tried to muster a certain bravado even though I did not feel brave. "John and I can walk home. We'll be fine."

* * *

I walked home beside beautiful, athletic John, lost in my own little world.

As a scientist in my most basic beliefs, I didn't know how to process what had happened. In my world, the supernatural simply did not exist. It never had. Yet, in spite of my hyper-skeptical nature and all the crazy stuff that happened, the thing that bothered me most was Beth Bowlan's message: "And save the life of the man who killed your parents."

Truth be told, everything else seemed inconsequential. The flames, the sliding wine glass, being visited by a dead relative—none of it mattered. But the suggestion my parents were murdered had undermined my sense of reality. The words played over in my mind like a scratched record on an antique Victrola. Wisps of nightmare trilled though my psyche, but I couldn't put any of it together.

"Sorry if I'm a little distant," I said when I remembered John was walking with me.

John's footsteps fell heavy on the pavement in the quiet of the night, wisps of the creepy feeling still lingering.

I shook my head, struggling to make sense of it all. "The voice introduced herself as Beth Bowlan. That was my grandmother's name. She died with my parents."

"That's pretty intense," said John.

We continued through the darkened streets. A homeless man dug through an overflowing trash can. A couple of pigeons cooed from the attic of an unkempt student house down a blackened alleyway.

My voice was hollow in the dark night. "My parents died when I was a kid. But they weren't murdered. When I was eleven, my parents and grandmother went missing in Algonquin Park. After an extensive search, they were assumed dead. I spent years waiting, hoping, they would return. But it was just a childish wish." My voice trailed. "They never came back..."

We continued walking but John didn't push with questions. Normally, I might have found the quiet between us uncomfortable. I'd always had this unexplainable need to make polite conversation with strangers. But tonight John and I walked along in companionable silence like old friends.

"You know, Ellie," John finally broke the quiet. "It's okay if this stuff is freaking you out. A small nervous breakdown right about now would be perfectly...normal."

I knew he was trying to be supportive, but his comment hit me like a punch to the gut. 'Perfectly normal,' I thought. Nope, I was anything but. I'd never been normal. And this embarrassing fiasco served as a solid reminder of that fact.

"Look, let's change the subject. Okay?" I suggested, ready to focus on something else—anything else. "Tell me about your Comp exam. What hellish question have they tasked you with?"

John shook his head and I thought he might be blushing. "That hardly seems relevant right now."

"Please tell me, John. Help me take my mind off tonight. We can 'commiserate' and 'support each other' like Jane said." I elbowed him in the ribs to lighten the mood.

John's discomfort was apparent, but I continued to press. With a little more nudging, he acquiesced.

"Okay...My exam question is about proto-feminism," he confessed, a hint of his own inner-nerd showing through. "I'm a sociology major. I've been asked to take a position on whether proto-feminism is a valid sociological construct and use a case study to defend my argument. Exciting, eh?" An uncomfortable smirk crossed his handsome features.

Now that the conversation was about him and not me, I started to relax. My mind engaged in the comfort of an academic conversation, and I responded with enthusiasm. "What is proto-feminism?"

"Ellie. You don't want to know about proto-feminism," he said, hesitating.

The craziness of the night's events made me forget my awkwardness and this new line of discussion had me feeling playful. I grabbed him by the arm and gave his large bicep a squeeze. "Come on. I want to know. What is proto-feminism?"

He looked as if I was torturing him. "Uhh... Okay... Proto-feminism is about the feminist movement before the feminist movement."

"Give me more info..." I closed my eyes, ready to sink my teeth into this problem like a piece of chocolate cake.

John continued. "The formal feminist movement happened in the nineteenth century. But there may have been important feminist ideas floating around before then. Technically speaking, proto-feminism is a term used to define the philosophical tradition of female empowerment that existed before the modern concept was born."

He sounded like an academic giving a lecture. It was quite sexy. There was definitely a nerd lurking beneath the surface.

"Some have argued it isn't possible for a feminist to exist in history before the nineteenth century. Others argue that feminist ideals existed as a precursor to the modern movement and that is proto-feminism." John glanced at me, worried I was finding this boring.

"Okay, Dr. John." I smirked. I was loving this conversation. And it was like a Daily-Double because it meant I didn't have to think about my dead parents. "What's the answer?"

A smile formed on John's perfect mouth. "I can argue that proto-feminism is a valid construct. The part I'm having trouble with is the case study. I mean, I'm no history major. Where do I start?"

Now I was in the zone. My mind whirred at the academic challenge he had presented. "If it were me, I would go way back to the sixteenth century. Any woman who moved women's rights along back then would be a proto-feminist. Right?"

"Okay, good idea," said John with surprise. "But who?"

I flipped through my mental rolodex of sixteenth century women. I had done a boatload of reading already for my Anne Boleyn research and there was a lot of useless knowledge rolling around in my head. I pulled an answer from the historical figures database in my frontal cortex. "Have you ever considered Marguerite de Navarre of France? Cool lady. Surprisingly feminist for a woman of the 1500's."

"Who the heck was Marguerite de Navarre?" John asked with a goofy smile.

"Trust me. You should look her up."

With a few more steps, we arrived at my house and stood on the welcome mat at the front door. We had run out of road and it seemed all too soon. The magic of our intellectual exchange vanished as nerves overwhelmed me once again. I was just a nerdy girl walking home with a handsome muscular jock. I hovered on the step, not sure what to do.

"We're here." My voice was soft.

John glanced up at our red brick English cottage with its crooked chimney and round front door. Amidst the other stately homes on the street, it looked like a family of hobbits might live here. It was quirky and awkward, just like me.

"Well it was nice to meet you," said John. He lingered on the doorstep, unwilling to turn and go. "I'm glad I finally know your name, Ellie-from-the-kitchen." He dug his hands into his pockets and gave me a long look.

I lingered too. I couldn't find any words, but I was equally unable to drag myself away. John held my gaze in a mind-numbingly sexy way. He looked intrigued. He looked shy.

"I better go in." I blushed. "Thanks for walking me home, John-the-guy-in-the-towel. And good luck with your Comp."

VOLUME 2

OSTARA

Winter dies and warmth returns
Mother Goddess grows young and fertile
And the witches come of age

The morning air was fresh and cool, carrying with it the sweet scent of spring. Tulips lined the garden, boasting shades of crimson and yellow in the crisp light of day. A magnificent fountain stood at the center of the grounds, a fat cherub cast in bronze spouting water from its tiny genitals. Dozens of mature apple trees in the north orchard, covered in puffs of pink, painted the landscape with delicate pastels. Thick blankets of new green ivy hung heavy along the gatehouse and walled bailey, the eldest parts of the castle. The grand house rose from behind the gate keep. Two towers flanked the three-story main entrance of the Boleyn homestead.

A deep rumble over the hills signaled the arrival of the royal hunting party. Anne and her sister found themselves at the center of a commotion as dozens of horses, riders and carriages arrived in entourage. Flags of green and gold danced in the light wind, announcing the Tudor king and queen. From within the carriage, a tiny face looked out. Anne could see, even from her position on the lawn, that the queen did not look well.

Anne had not expected however, the man who dismounted to greet her father. She imagined the King of England to be older, perhaps of stout form and balding pate. But this man was all exuberance and youth. He was tall and muscular, his broad shoulders giving way to a slim athletic waist and long, brawny legs. His face was young and handsome, with a fine jaw and a firm chin. Anne's breath caught at the sight him.

Sir Thomas bowed low. "Sire, it is my honour to introduce my daughters, Anne and Mary Boleyn."

"Thomas," replied the king, "I must pay you compliment, with a strong son like George and these two beautiful damsels."

Anne and Mary curtsied.

From the equestrian barn behind the main house, George led Anne's black mare, saddled with a hunter's mount, skittish with the energy of the hunt. Mary's horse followed too, reposing and safe, ready for a slow day of trundling along at the back of the party with the other women.

"A fine set of horses," Henry praised as he eyed the well-muscled mare. "But who rides the black Murgese?"

"The horse is my sister's, your majesty," said George with a modest bow. "Anne is a fine equestrian and an accomplished scout at that. She will make an excellent addition to the hunt, if you please, sire."

"She's welcome to it, if she can win her place," Henry replied as he mounted his own stallion. He gave Anne a nod and trotted off toward the hunt party.

Anne watched as the preparations for first hunt of the season drew the king's attention for a time. He oversaw the operation as horses were watered and weapons assembled. He called orders as his men tightened the bows and sheathed the arrows, sharpening swords and stowing the axes.

Amidst the commotion, the king circled his stallion away from the crowd and lifted his eyes to the lush forest beyond. All at once, he gave a swift kick to his horse's flank.

"Yah!" he shouted.

The game had begun.

Startled men mounted their horses and gave chase to the young king. Riders howled and raised their swords, kicking hard to move into a gallop. Henry rode ahead of the group and howled with pleasure as he raced to the wood at the east end of the property. His men knew this game well. The one who caught the king would ride at his side for the day. A marvelous prize indeed.

George gave Anne a nod of encouragement. "Show them what you are made of, sister."

Ready for the challenge, Anne leapt into the saddle with the athleticism of a boy. She surged with pleasure as her mare bolted forward under her command. George and Anne raced side by side across the castle grounds. As she gained speed, Anne's hood fell back and her long dark hair whipped about in the wind, bouncing and tumbling wildly.

The king's men did not know the Hever woods well, but Anne and George had grown up here. She had raced her brother through this thicket a hundred times or more. Brother and sister surged forward, losing track of the race with the others.

"You won't win, dear sister," George shouted. "I taught you everything you know!"

"The student has finally exceeded her teacher, I am afraid!" Anne shouted over her shoulder as she overtook him.

Anne spotted the king in the distance and kicked hard again, her body bent low as she matched her mare's rhythm. The riders behind her kicked up a cloud of dust, but none of them could catch Anne.

As she closed in on the king, she saw Henry's face alight with joy, the weight of the world lifted from his shoulders. With a straight back and a loose reign, he moved in perfect unison with his stallion. He was a glorious rider, but no match for Anne. She overtook him and as she did, she snatched the handkerchief from the breast pocket in his doublet. Once she had it firmly in her grasp, she waved the scarf in the air like a victory flag.

King Henry bellowed with surprise at the incredible feat. Anne Boleyn had caught the king. The game was up.

Anne and the king dismounted, pleasure dancing across their faces. Henry laughed as he tried to catch his breath, looking upon her in wonder. Anne's face had flushed a soft pink, her dark eyes dancing with mischief. She laughed too, unable to speak. Within minutes, they were both laughing deep belly laughs. It was magical, their shared moment in the woods, a new comradery born.

"You are delightful," Henry breathed as he eyed the stolen handkerchief she held in her hands. "Never in my life have I seen a woman ride thus."

"You, sire, were the true competition." Anne's long dark hair danced down her back.

They held each other's gaze and time seemed to slow. A dewy mist held the moment in check, unwilling to let it pass by. All formality and airs between them were gone. They were simply two young people brimming with the pleasure of the ride.

Cardinal Wolsey was the first to arrive to break their magic spell. His horse panted, white slobber dripping from its lips. He circled around Anne and the king as the others in the hunting party began to assemble.

"Sire, you will kill me with these chases." The cardinal mopped his brow. "And who is the young lady that has bested me?"

"You, sister, have risen your game. I was beaten by a girl," laughed George as he arrived with the rest of the group.

Wolsey's smile faded imperceptibly. His dark eyes darted between Anne's face and the king's. "My question is answered thus. Anne Boleyn, you have some skill as a horsewoman. I will give you that."

"Some skill?" Henry beamed. "She is the finest horsewoman in all of Kent, I would wager."

Anne blushed at the compliment.

The king tugged at the stolen piece of material still tucked in her palm and kissed the top of her hand. "Mistress Boleyn, you have earned your place as scout at the front of the hunt." He smiled, squared jaw flexing. "And you have won my handkerchief. Care for it well. It was my favorite."

Anne flushed as a warmth spread through her belly. "I shall."

* * *

The hunt party jostled through the forest with enthusiasm, primed and ready for an early kill. The cool morning welcomed them, beams of dappled sunlight dancing upon the forest floor. The woods echoed with birdsong and the first few hours passed with lively jests and laughter. Anne, ever alert in her role as scout, rode out in front, her eyes and ears straining to detect any small movement from within the brush. In spite of her effort however, the early morning woodland would not give up its bounty.

As the sun rose higher and the day grew warmer, Anne became frustrated. The forest seemed empty. The men had become sluggish in the heat, no longer cavorting and jesting. Instead, they adjusted their heavy weapons and fidgeted atop their mounts. As time dragged on and morning turned to noon, Anne grew anxious. She had not yet spotted a single brown body or puffy white tail.

Cardinal Wolsey took advantage of the silence. "Sire, I wonder if Lady Anne's skill as a scout may have been overstated."

The king did not reply.

Anne's skin prickled at the cardinal's reproachful comment, but she held her tongue. Perspiration had formed upon her brow and dampened her armpits. Her dark hair frizzed with humidity. She knew it would be most unfortunate to stop for their midday meal without a single kill, but Wolsey's insolence fed a fire in her belly. If she could only find a deer, she could put that pompous man in his place. Anne fixed her eyes in the shadows of the forest, more determined than ever.

The hunt party rode on, lumbering and hot. Several horses snorted with fatigue. Anne was desperate to find something, anything to show them she could do it. "I need to find a deer. I need to find a deer," she whispered.

Almost as quickly as the thought had been spun, Anne spied her prey. A great red hart with six marvelous points stood in the distance chewing trilliums on the forest floor. A hot energy surged through her core. She raised her hand and signaled the hunt party to halt. Only Henry moved forward with her with the stealth of a warrior.

The king advanced through the shadows until he found the perfect place to take the shot. Positioning his bow, he pulled back the string and made ready to unleash the arrow. In the distance, Wolsey's horse stepped on a branch and a loud crack echoed across the wood. The hart's ears pitched forward, its dark brown eyes alert. As Henry pulled his arrow back to release it from its keep, the great animal took off through the glade, long legs bounding through the thick underbrush.

Anne and Henry gave chase. In a moment, they would lose sight of this magnificent animal altogether.

Anne's desire to please the king grew strong. She allowed her instincts to drive her. As she raced through the thicket, something serene descended upon her, something otherworldly. As she watched the deer speeding away, running for its life, Anne began to feel the beast's energy within her core. She smelled its fear. She tasted the half-masticated grass in its mouth. Its heartbeat thumped in her ears.

"Freeze," she whispered.

Across the valley, the hart halted in its tracks. It turned to look at Anne in surprise, black eyes shining in the dappled sun.

Anne needed to drive the beast to the king before it took off through the wood. Yards away, a dappling of sunlight upon the forest floor shimmered with life. From the far reaches of her mind, Anne imagined a small spark within the fallen leaves, a flame just large enough to startle the deer back towards them. A warmth spread through her belly as the image of the fire grew clearer in her mind. She didn't question the sensation, she just allowed it to grow within her, imagining a tiny blaze into place amidst the rustling leaves.

At her will, a tiny flame ignited beneath the hooves of the beast. It flickered hot and red under its feet for long enough for the animal perceive its dangerous heat. The hart reared up and in a great panic, it bounded back towards Anne.

The king raised his bow. With one precise motion, he sent his arrow straight into the chest of the steed. The deer fell dead with an ample thump. It was a clean kill, swift in its delivery. The first deer of the hunt—a hart—had been felled.

Dismounting in awe, they both gazed at the animal.

"You are incredible, Anne Boleyn. Most incredible," Henry whispered, taking Anne in his arms. He smelled of musk and leather. The rough hairs of his beard ran coarse against her cheek.

Anne's heart flip-flopped as she relished King Henry's embrace. She glanced over his shoulder to the distant spot in the woods where she had imagined the fire. The flame had disappeared as swiftly as it had begun, and she wondered if she imagined it at all.

"No, dear king. It was your perfect shot, not mine," she whispered back, intoxicated by his closeness.

Henry pressed a kiss on her cheek and turned to face the hunt party who were now arriving.

"Thanks to Anne Boleyn, the first deer is felled," Henry announced, his voice booming in the clearing. "To the mistress of the hunt!"

"To the mistress of the hunt!" the king's men echoed. A raucous cheer erupted, swords flashing in the dappled sunlight.

The group jostled and bumped to get a better look at the six-pointed hart that marked the official start of the hunting season. All men, but one. The old cardinal remained aloft his horse. He did not gawk at the deer like the others. Instead, he gazed warily deep into the forest, to the spot where the sunlight danced on the floor. He squinted his piggy eyes as if searching for something. Searching, perhaps, for the spot in the distance where a small fire had burst forth and extinguished seconds later in a tiny plume of smoke.

1514

HEVER CASTLE, ENGLAND

The first royal hunt ended in a grand fete. White tents nestled in the gardens and dozens of flags of Tudor green and gold fluttered in the obliging breeze. The air carried the scent of apple blossoms, and torches lined the walkways, turning the shadows long. Minstrels strolled the grounds, delighting the guests with their joyful music, the sweet song of recorders and fifes blending in splendid harmony.

A pile of timber was alight at the edge of the wood and a bonfire danced bright into the navy blue of twilight. Servants bustled, clearing away plates of uneaten venison, rabbit, and grouse. Two skinny kitchen lads struggled to carry the heavy carcass of a fat boar back to the larder, an apple still stuffed in its mouth. The servants of Hever Castle would eat well tonight.

The hunt had been magical, and throughout the weeklong event, Anne and the king had become inseparable. Though her mother had insisted she return to the castle each evening, Anne found her way back to the hunt party every morning at dawn. Day after day, she and the king walked ahead of the group, talking and jesting like old friends. Henry wanted Anne's opinions on all matters, amazed by her insights and perspectives.

The men had not seemed to mind. Though Henry had diverted his attention to this beautiful young girl, Anne had kept the others happy with her masterful scouting. Once she had found the rhythm in her role, she had been unstoppable. Anne had been responsible for the capture of five more deer, six rabbits, and a wild boar.

Cardinal Wolsey however, was seething. The king had always been careful to share his attentions among his men on hunting days, giving particular industry to the cardinal. But Henry was so enraptured by Anne, he had lost interest in everything else. He had not even noticed when a great boar fell at George's hands after a bloody battle between man and beast. Instead, the king and Anne wandered merrily in the woods, lost in their own little world.

The queen and her ladies had stayed as guests at the castle, rather than having to suffer the difficulties of the out of doors. Her health was clearly not good, and Anne felt rather sorry for her. Having such a vivacious husband seemed to exhaust her, and she had spent most of her time resting in preparation for his return.

The final evening's meal had been a feast the likes of which Anne had never seen. The gaiety had carried on many hours after the meal had finished. The queen had retired to bed, followed by Anne's parents and Mary, and finally George. Only a few men remained by the fire, their faces red with drink.

The small crowd was boorish for the likes of a young lady, but Anne was at ease. She felt quite at home amongst this oafish crew as they bantered and joked like a group of overgrown boys. Only the cardinal remained sullen. He sat aloft a large log in front of the fire, his paunchy belly hanging low between his legs.

"Mistress Anne, do you think it appropriate you are out this late? What reputation might you acquire in the company of these bawdy men?"

Anne ignored the cardinal and laughed at a joke Henry whispered in her ear.

"Anne can stay as long as she likes." The king dismissed him with a wave.

The cardinal leaned in, speaking low to the king. "But, sire. We have work to do. May I remind you about the matter of great urgency? These matters are not for the fairer sex. Perhaps it is time for Mistress Boleyn to retire for the night."

The king paid him no mind. Instead, Henry leaned in to whisper a new wonderful tidbit into Anne's delicate ear. She burst into a fit of giggles.

The cardinal narrowed his eyes, impatience growing upon his features. With nostrils flaring, he made a direct attack. "Sire, I await your final decision on the betrothal."

Henry stiffened. A muscle flexed along his jawline. "Wolsey, you are like a dog with a bone on this matter. Can it not wait until tomorrow?"

"A decision must be made this night, sire." The cardinal cocked his eye and folded his thick arms across his chest.

Henry stared into the forest, unable to lock gaze with the man before him.

The cardinal pressed now with a sycophantic whine. "Even Anne's father, Sir Thomas Boleyn, has recommended it. It is certain to seal the peace with France. It seems a minor cost if you consider the issue more broadly."

Suddenly the king was on his feet, his muscular form towering above the Cardinal's stout paunch. "My sister, the English princess, is never a minor cost!" he shouted for the first time. "It will not be a marriage she wishes. I shall not sell her heart to a man she does not want, to a man she does not know."

The cardinal continued to press. "But, my king, the princess shall do it dutifully. She will do it for her country. She will do it for you." Wolsey gave Anne a quick sneer.

A hush wound around the group like a spool of black thread as the king grappled with this terrible decision. His shoulders hunched heavily over his frame and he paced a journey in front of the fire. Finally, Henry waved his hands in defeat.

"Make it so. But I warn you, negotiate well. I will not have my sister suffer at his hands. She must have the all riches of the world. She must have ladies at her disposal to give her friendship."

The cardinal grinned, shadows swirling upon his face in the light of the fire. Then with a snap of his fingers, the activity around the camp shifted from idle to hustling. The remaining men readied themselves to mount their horses as the cardinal called orders.

Wolsey slipped a swollen foot into his stirrup, and with a heave of his arse, swung himself into the saddle. "I assure you, sire, the princess will have her every need cared for. I shall select her gowns, her jewels, her ladies-in-wait, everything. She will want for nothing."

The cardinal gave Anne one last hateful look and with a hard pull on his horse's mouth, he rode off with his men into the night.

King Henry sat down beside Anne, rubbing his forehead. The bonfire burned low and the softened glow of the embers danced upon his troubled face. Anne had not understood the exchange between Wolsey and the king, but she knew it plagued Henry. They sat quietly for a time. He stared at a lone log in the fire still glowing red. Anne's instincts told her to wait until Henry was ready, and she allowed him a moment to work through his worries.

After what seemed an eternity, Henry spoke, his voice full of regret. "I am not a kind man, Anne. I hope you do not think too high of me."

Anne put her hand on his shoulder. "What say you, good king? You are a most kind and noble man, loved by all in your country."

The king looked at her, dismayed. "No, not you. Please do not bring me a courtier's tongue. Do not flatter me because I am king. I am sick to death of it." His brow furrowed with lines she had not noticed before. "You are the only one—the only one who will tell me true and not cajole me."

Anne did not know what to say. She dropped her eyes, another long pause welling up between them.

"Anne," Henry whispered. "Be my friend. I have never had a true one before you." He searched her eyes. "And please stop calling me sire and king. My name is Henry. I am but a man when I'm with you. I make mistakes. I make choices for the sake of duty and country I would not make otherwise."

Anne nodded.

"You are so honest and fearless. Just be my friend. Just tell me true. That is all I ask."

She sat for a while in contemplation, the weight of his request upon her. It had been easy between them as they jostled and bumped through the woods today, a world away from the reality of their true stations. But the game had changed, and she was unsure of how to meet the king's new request. How could she show her friendship? How could she ease his woes?

A mischievous thought snuck its way into her mind. She smiled impishly and bit her lip to contain it.

"What?" he asked.

"'Tis nothing." Her voice trailed with hint of a giggle.

Henry leaned in, intrigued. "Come now. You have promised to tell me true."

Anne rolled her eyes in a girlish gesture. "Well, Henry." She emphasized his name and delighted in how it played on her tongue. "If the truth is what you seek..." Her eyes danced with naughty amusement. "The truth is...I am a better rider than you. I caught you in the race this morning, but you would never have captured me thus." She laughed aloud.

Henry sat back in utter surprise, a smile pulling at his lips.

"And, the truth is..." She continued, drawing him into her beguilement. "I am a better hunter than you. You almost rode into the canyon after that rabbit. Had I not stopped you, you might have sailed right off the edge." A new fit of giggles consumed her.

Henry's mouth hung open.

"But the worst truth of all..." She bit her lip to suppress another smile. "Was your dancing tonight by the fire. It really was quite awful."

Henry's eyes widened at the criticism. Anne knew no one else would have dared insult his dancing. "Anne Boleyn, you have gone too far with these truths and I will see you punished." A dazzling smile lit his face.

The king grabbed her by the waist and pushed her forward. They rolled together as the heavy log that held them jarred back. The two screamed with delight as the ground caught their bodies with a soft thud.

Anne felt herself beneath the delicious weight of this man. His muscular body lay atop hers, her arms pinned back by his in a playful wrestle. His face hovered above hers in the darkness, only the low embers lighting its silhouette. His sweet breath warmed her lips. In this impossibly close position, she felt their innocent game shift from one of jest to one of passion. The yearning she saw in his eyes made her breath catch. The closeness of his lips was tantalizing.

"Anne," he whispered. "You are unlike any woman I have ever known."

"It is you who are splendid," she whispered. The roughness of his beard set her young nerves on fire and she yearned to feel his lips upon her mouth. This was a new sensation for her, but it was raw and honest in its need.

"How is it possible?" His voice was tender. "That this happiness cannot last forever."

"I do not know. But if I could, I would will it so."

He rubbed his cheek against hers in gentle agony, breathing in her scent as if to burn the sweet memory of it into his mind. "Do you believe in true love, Anne? Between a man and a woman?"

She caressed his cheek. "I do."

His breath caught as she touched his face. "Do you think under different circumstances you could have loved me?"

She smiled. "I think I may love you now."

He looked into her eyes, deep blue wells of emotion. "And I you."

As he lowered his mouth to hers, she felt a pull, an irresistible need to feel his lips upon hers. As he kissed her there in the wood, the pressure of his tongue upon her own lit her senses on fire. It was soft and intimate but passion skittered beneath. She wanted nothing more than to give over to her instincts—instincts that cried out to pull him closer. He pushed his body harder into hers and her passion ignited. For a moment, she did not care about anything else.

But her chaste upbringing held firm and at last she pushed him away.

"Henry, please. I am but a young maid and you are a married man. The King of England." She winced as she struggled to contain her own desire.

Henry stopped. "You do not want me?"

Anne's lips throbbed for more, but she forced her head back to gain clearance from his delicious mouth. "My Lord. I want you more than night and more than day. But it cannot be, and we both know it."

"Anne, I need you."

"Please, do not ask this of me."

Henry's shadowed features concealed his hurt, but the clenching muscle in his jaw was signal enough of the frustration that surged within. He rolled off her body in a bewildered state of lust.

They lay on the leaf-covered ground, staring up into the starry sky, the crescent moon pulsating above them.

"Anne?" he whispered into the darkness, taking her delicate hand in his.

Anne took a deep, slow breath. "Yes?"

Henry's voice was gritty now, full of fear for her truthful answer. "If I asked you to love me forever, not as a king but as a man, would you promise me your heart?"

"Yes."

He rolled onto his side and lay a muscular arm across her stomach. "Even if we had to keep our love secret?"

"Could you?" she asked.

Henry pulled her face to his to look into her eyes. "I have fallen in love with you, Anne Boleyn. You have bewitched me."

Anne leaned over and kissed his lips so slowly that her torture registered among the heavens. He tasted musky and masculine, the scruff of his beard catching against her delicate skin. A jolt of electricity coursed through her belly and lower still. Pulling away once more, Anne ran a finger along his rugged jaw.

"I must take my leave, Henry, before I lack the strength to go."

PRESENT DAY
QUEEN'S UNIVERSITY, CANADA

I raced down the street, a book-laden knapsack bouncing precariously on my back. Unkempt student houses whirred by as I sprinted toward my destination. A couple of football players sitting on a tattered couch on the front lawn cat-called after me as I flew by. I gave them a serious scowl, flipped them the bird, and continued.

"Shit," I cursed under my breath. Today I was late for my appointment with Lily the librarian.

The light turned red and I screeched to a halt at the corner of University Ave and Union. This was the epicenter of Queen's University. Majestic limestone buildings boasted monastic architecture, grand arched entrances, and impressive towers. Mature sugar maples ran the distance from Ontario Street all the way up University Avenue. I breathed in the earthy scent of fall, the smell of a new school season.

A strange honking noise, rather like a Canada goose, started up a few feet away. It was wheezy and off-key but the notes soon morphed into a melodious tune as the bagpipes found their harmony. The piper, wearing his Queen's tam and quilts, drew a crowd. Everyone knew the school song and they all joined in to sing. Without a moments notice, a crowd of proud Queen's students were standing together, linked arm in arm, howling out the words to Old Queen's Sweater.

I sang along for a bit, caught up in the infectious school pride, until the light turned green and I tore myself away from the singing revellers.

Today I had no time for fun. Today I was headed straight for the bowels of the old university library.

The stacks were the least sexy part of the university. Eight floors of nerdy goodness housed obscure books from floor to ceiling. The Special Collections department on the bottom floor held the university's most ancient historical works. The level was especially unappealing by the special Plexiglas barriers installed to ensure the proper humidity levels for optimal book preservation. It was ugly—plain and simple.

Lily, the librarian, sat at her desk sporting a mousy mushroom hair-do and a ruffled polka-dot blouse. She looked up with her thick glasses and gave me a weak smile.

This was the best one could hope for in a Lily-greeting. Usually she forgot to smile at all. Lily was an unusual character. Her voice was flat, her demeanor deflated, her words came slow. She reminded me of a balloon with a slow leak, all the air gone out of it. But she was one of the brightest minds in this library, and despite her subdued pace, she was passionate. Lily was a superstar. She would keep going when everyone else had given up. Lily was the ultimate nerd and I trusted her.

"Hey, Lil, sorry I'm late," I breathed. "You're doing well?"

She sat slumped in her chair, inert for a longer-than-usual moment. "Uh huh..."

I paused to see if I could read any other signs of life, but on seeing nothing, I pressed on. "Okay, the exam question is a little odd. I'm wrapping my head around it, and I thought we could discuss a few approaches. You ready?"

"Mmmm...hmmm..."

Ignoring her flaccid reaction, I continued. "So far I've done a bunch of research on Anne Boleyn, her family, and her rise to power. It's a remarkable story, how Anne could convince King Henry to divorce his first wife."

She stared back through coke-bottom glasses.

"Really, Lil. She wasn't just a pretty face. Anne Boleyn was instrumental in politics and religion in sixteenth-century England. Heck, she influenced the entire English Reformation." I checked for signs of life once again.

"Interesting," she wheezed.

Victory! Now I knew I had her, her tiny reaction fueling a fire that had begun burning in my belly.

"I'm obviously not going to argue she was a witch. Instead, I plan to argue Anne Boleyn was a modern woman before her time, a thinker, a strategist, a leader." I was feeling rather enthusiastic now. This was the approach my father would have taken, I felt sure of it.

"But I need to find the research to support it. I mean, how did Anne Boleyn, a well-bred English lady in sixteenth-century Britain, become one of the most influential women in history? Back then women were subservient, certainly not leaders in their own right."

Lily sat slumped behind her desk with eyes closed now. If I hadn't known her better, I would have sworn she was sleeping.

"Let's pull together a list of search terms and we'll comb the literature." The tiniest hint of interest entered her voice and I wondered if I was imagining it. "We'll want to understand who Anne Boleyn was and who she was influenced by." She pulled up the query page on her computer screen. "Females in particular. We'll do a scan of modern women in Europe in the early 1500s. Women of influence."

Touch down! Lily was in. I considered giving her a high-five but thought the better of it. Baby steps.

Heading to my study carrel at the end of a row of books, I realized I was a little excited about this crazy exam question. The notes I had taken were a long jumble of scribbled pages of history basics: dates, places, births, and deaths. I had always thought of this part of the research as 'his-story.'

But for me, the real thrill of any historical research was breaking through those basic facts to find the nuggets of insight. I wanted to understand the palpable reality of a person's existence. I'd always thought of this as 'her-story.' And this bizarre research question seemed to be pushing me there. So this was my research game plan. I would begin by researching 'his-story' and with any luck, I would find 'her-story' along the way.

The books swallowed me up for several hours as I attacked the question about women of influence in the sixteenth century with gusto. Strangely, the same name I had given beautiful John at the séance last night surfaced again. A French royal, Marguerite de Navarre was an author in her own right, an important patron of the humanist reform, and a key figure in the French Renaissance. Scholars described her as the first modern woman. That made her a woman of influence. The problem was geography. Marguerite de Navarre lived in France and Anne Boleyn lived in England.

My mind spun with possibilities as I headed back down the book aisle to see how Lily was doing. My hunch about Marguerite de Navarre wasn't much to go on, but it was a start. Lily was sitting in the same spot I left her in this morning, immobilized behind her desk. Only her eyes moved from behind thick lenses.

"You find anything interesting?" I asked.

"Mmmmm...."

I sat beside her to compare notes. We had done this many times before over the years, discussing our findings, looking for connections between them. We could lose an entire Saturday afternoon without even noticing. It happened more often than I cared to admit.

"I'm thinking we need to look into Marguerite de Navarre."

"Mmmm...hmmm..."

We passed the next few hours working together to develop a clear research plan on this woman-or-witch problem. We made good headway in determining the key pieces of information required. Nerdy as it was, we found our natural stride in the research. It wasn't exactly a party, but there was something satisfying about being in the stacks with Lily.

Lily and I had been a research duo ever since the day I started in the PhD program. That first day of school, I had decided to try to overcome my antisocial nature by attending the annual History Department student barbecue. It hadn't gone well. The director's welcome speech was nothing short of terrifying. Every time Dr. Landon Fishburn opened his mouth, I felt sick to my stomach. He was so haughty and sure of himself, he reminded me of an African bullfrog, all puffed up and ready for mating. That afternoon, I had fled to the stacks, determined to get away from the egos and competitive brownnosing.

Lily had been sitting behind her desk, poring over Aristotle, a book that had been one of dad's favorites. He had read it to me many times as a child. At that moment, I knew Lily was a kindred spirit. We spent the day reading the Greek romances. Xenophon's *Ephesian Tale*... Lucian's *The Life of Aesop*... It was like finding a long-lost sister. I had been coming back to the stacks ever since. And though she had guided me through my research career, she hadn't asked for even as much as a thank you.

"You're so smart, Lil," I said after our brainstorming session had run its course. "You could have a prolific publication record if you wanted to. Everyone would want to work with you and you wouldn't be stuck here in the stacks."

"I don't want fame. I've seen too many academics go crazy looking for that kind of glory." She shrugged. "Besides, you know how it works. Only the *big people* publish around here. Librarians are the little people that help them publish. Don't be fooled, Ellie. Students are little people too."

The university system had always been rather cannibalistic. Bigwig professors leaned on students to do the majority of the work, but the students almost never got the recognition. I was about to launch into a rant about the tyranny of the modern-day teaching institution, when I noticed it from the corner of my eye. Lily was fidgeting. There was a slight twitch in her thumbs. My very own inert Lily-the-librarian seemed nervous. I eyed her again to confirm my suspicion.

"I've got a date tonight," Lily volunteered, stone faced.

Her news hit me hard. Outside of work, I knew nothing about this woman I realized. Lily was always in the library. She didn't have a life, did she? If someone had said she had a little bed in the corner of the Special Collections room, I might have believed it. I couldn't imagine her leaving the library even to get a cup of coffee, much less going on a date.

The expression she wore now hinted at terror. Lily was out of her element. That much was obvious. I wondered about how to react to this personal information. Truth be told, we were just two awkward ducks hiding eight floors below ground in the bowels of a library. Our special connection had always been historical research. Discussing anything as intimate as dating was well beyond our collective element.

Nonetheless, I tried to be supportive. "Well....you go girl," I offered, stiff as a starched shirt.

"Mmmm...hmmm..." she replied.

PRESENT DAY
QUEEN'S UNIVERSITY, CANADA

Instead of my ritual morning run, Grapes and I spent time together watching reruns of her favorite soap opera. My great-grandmother often boasted she had taped every single episode since 1984, the year she got her first VCR. Today, the main characters were renewing their wedding vows on the little black and white TV sitting on the kitchen countertop.

Grapes bustled about with her three-step-shuffle, *schlum-bum...bum, schlum-bum...bum*. I sat at the table with my feet propped up on a chair. I made a point of never getting in the way when Grapes was cooking. Over the years, Grapes and I had established the rules of the kitchen. Grapes insisted these three simple rules 'protected our harmonious relationship.'

Rule #1 – Ellie bought the groceries. Grapes cooked the meals.

Rule #2 – Ellie could never operate the stove or the microwave.

Rule #3 – Ellie would—*under no circumstances*—add salt, pepper, or any other spices to the pot, as it disturbed Grapes' artistic composition.

"I looked at Dad's boxes of research yesterday," I broke in between a teary set of I-do's on TV. I wasn't sure I wanted to introduce the topic of my dead parents but it slipped out anyway.

Grapes whipped the scrambled eggs in the frying pan. "Well, good for you, dear."

I drummed my fingers on the table. "I found a strange envelope from Kingston Travel when I was down there."

She stabbed a fork into the eggs. "Oh?

I took a sip of Earl Grey tea and told her about the plane tickets for Mom, Dad, and Grandma I had found in the basement. Something about the tickets didn't add up. They had left for London, England only days before they died on their camping trip here in Canada. I still hadn't been able to figure it out.

Grapes' eyebrows danced as she poured the orange juice. "That must be a mistake, dear. I remember the day they dropped you off at my house." She shook her head. "They were excited about their trip. They bought new backpacks and everything."

Grapes stopped for a moment, overcome by the memory. She and Beth had been best friends. It was hard to believe they were mother and daughter. We sat for a minute, unsure of where to go with the conversation now that it had moved into our off-limits territory.

Her blue eyes glistened. "It's still hard to believe they're gone, isn't it? Even after all these years. Some days I half-expect to see Beth come through the door with a new herbal tea I've got to try."

I didn't agree with Grapes on this at all. Losing my parents and grandmother wasn't part of a childhood memory I gazed through like a pretty gauze curtain. For me, I had stowed all the memories about my childhood into one big imaginary room in the attic of my mind, locked the door, and threw away the key. It was easier that way.

"Do you remember, Ellie? How we loved to cook together?" asked Grapes, her voice thick with her own lingering memories.

Sweet wisps of memory floated from beneath the attic door in my mind.

The women in my family did love to cook. Tomatoes were my mother's specialty. Mom could transform her little red beauties into an arsenal of tomato-ey deliciousness. Grandma Beth's speciality was beer. She used the hops from the garden to brew a craft beer laced with the tiniest hint of chilies. But Grapes' culinary specialties were the most impressive. She had a knack for elevating any food to a new plane of otherworldly yummy-ness. She could divine a simple peanut butter sandwich with such perfection that a choir of tiny angels would dance a waltz on your tongue. Everything she cooked still tasted this way. It was a most unusual gift.

The house had felt surreal on the days they cooked together. They worked with such synchronicity that they hardly spoke at all. Cooking was like a three-part harmony, with not more than a whisper among them. A pinch of something here, a stir of a pot there, and like magic a new dish was conjured.

"Ellie." Grapes smiled as the toast popped up. "I'm glad we're talking about this. We've gone on too long pretending they didn't exist."

I caught the last happy wisps of memory and tucked them back into the attic.

She took my face in her hands, leaving floury handprints on my cheeks, and planted a big kiss on top of my head. Then she arranged the scrambled eggs and toast, making a ketchup smiley face on my plate.

"At least we've still got teach other," she said softly.

* * *

The Sleeping Goat was a favorite hangout for Fine Arts students of Queen's University. Its eclectic motif drew the theater crowd. Red velvet curtains covered the walls and collections of artistic urns occupied each corner of the café. An enormous harp sat beside the checkout counter and a few violins and saxophones hung from the ceiling.

The centerpiece in this strange coffee shop was a Renaissance portrait that adorned the main wall. In a gold gilt frame, an oil canvas portrayed a medieval noble lady wearing a furtive facial expression. She wore a double string of black pearls and a thin leather band secured a gauzy veil over her head. But the most curious thing about the portrait was the large white ferret the woman held in her lap. I stopped to admire her image. She had a mysterious quality that made me want to linger.

"Don't you love her?" asked an enthusiastic voice behind me.

This morning Mindy was sporting a large diamond nose ring. Her dangling earrings were silver pentagrams.

I smile weakly. "Yeah, she is captivating. But why is she holding a ferret?"

Mindy nodded with her usual intensity. "It's a Leonardo da Vinci, circa 1500. No one knows who the woman is. And that's not a ferret. It's an ermine. Look, the inscription below tells you, *Lady with an Ermine*."

We gazed at the haunting young woman in the portrait. Her image burned into the back of my eyes. The ermine did too.

"Mindy, what's an ermine?" I asked after a while.

Mindy shrugged. "I don't know, I guess it's basically a ferret." She glanced at my face and her eyes grew wide. "You know, it's weird how much she looks like you. She has the same chestnut hair and those dark mysterious eyes. Even the shape of her face..." Her voice took on a theatrical tone I had little patience for.

I walked away from the ferret woman. "Come on. Let's grab a table."

We found a spot on cow-fur-covered chairs and made our orders. Mindy was having a soymilk mocha-choca-caramel latte with protein sprinkles and whip cream. I was having tea. The waiter looked annoyed by my lack of creativity.

"So, Mindy. Tell me about Wicca," I asked with a resentful edge.

Mindy's eyes lit up at my fact-finding directness, but I just wanted to get this little learning session over with. Once the drinks arrived, and we settled in, Mindy prepared to give her lecture on the ways of the Wiccan.

"First of all, Wicca is a religion. It's not just silly hocus-pocus, you know. We live by the Wiccan Rede, which teaches about connections in the world and everything in it."

"Mmm...hmmm..." I wheezed, Lily-style.

Mindy took this tiny sentiment for a resounding interest and launched into a rather intelligent overview of the modern-day religion. It was strange. Mindy was articulate and flaky, all at the same time. I took notes on a napkin to make sure I kept up.

"There are lots of crossovers between the modern Wiccan religion and ancient forms of witchcraft. It all goes back to the creative elements. They each have positive and negative aspects. These elements make up everything, and so we celebrate them across the four points of the compass. They are earth, air, fire and water. All witches have a certain proclivity for one element and this proclivity gives the witch a set of powers."

"And what kind of witch are you?" I asked with a smirk.

Mindy shrugged as she fiddled with one of her pentagram earrings. "I'm not sure yet. I like the idea of being of the North—an Earth witch. They do a lot of stuff with spells and potions. They're the healers."

I gave her a long look. I had a ridiculous mental image of Mindy dressed up in a Halloween witch costume, pointy hat, broomstick and all, cooking up potions on her stovetop.

Mindy slumped down in her cow-fur chair. "But I don't think I'm very good. I tried a truth serum on Carl two months ago because I suspected him of cheating. But the only *truth* he told was to my mother when he said she could stand to lose a few pounds. Talk about making a bad first impression."

I snorted, almost choking on my tea.

Mindy laughed too. "Yeah, it was terrible. But it is true. She is a little overweight. So maybe the spell worked." She took a sip of her latte, getting whipped cream on her nose.

In spite of myself, I was warming to Mindy, flaky stories and all. She was big hearted and there was a good brain in her head, when she used it. We chatted for a while longer as she provided the basics on the other three creative elements.

"There are water witches of the east point. They can manipulate water and do stuff with the weather. There are the wind witches of the west point. They use the wind to transport things. Some very talented witches can pass objects through time. Then there are the fire witches of the south point. They control fire."

Her eyes grew big again. "Ellie, if you were a witch, that's the one you would be. I mean, did you see the way those flames pointed at you last night?"

My back stiffened. Panic rose at the memory of the séance, and as usual, my throat started to close. I had suddenly had enough of this conversation. "Thanks for all the info. I really do appreciate it."

"Listen, Ellie, before you go." She put her hand on my arm with renewed determination. "There is one fundamental rule that modern Wiccans follow. It's linked to the ancient Craft, so you need to know about it. Witches must practice magic only for good. No dark magic. Dark magic has a way of coming back to you."

I sank down in my cow-fur chair.

"Dark magic has to do with death. Any spell that changes the natural order of living and dying is part of dark magic. And if you do it, you bear a dark mark—a curse that can haunt you for the rest of your life."

"Okay, so no dark magic. Got it," I said stiffly, hoping that wrapped it up.

But Mindy maintained her vice like grip on my arm. "Listen, Ellie, this is important. Last night the voice said, '*Beware the dark mark on your name; we have felt it for many generations.*' Remember?"

I now wished I hadn't come for a breakfast latte with this girl.

"I think the dark mark on your family might have resulted from some-one, a long lost relative of yours, who did some terrible magic. Something that was horrible enough to put a curse on your whole family."

A voice inside my head told me to leave, to get out while I still could. The invisible hands wrapped themselves around my neck and squeezed.

"I've got to go." I stood and backed away from the table.

Mindy glanced up and shrugged as if she was used to people not taking her seriously. "Okay, but think about it, Ellie." Her tone changed back to perky casual. "If you have any other questions, I'm your Wiccan."

"Thanks, Mindy. Oh and hey, you've got whipped cream on your nose."

Anne dragged a leather-gloved finger across the barn door, a secretive smile playing upon her lips.

The horse stables were bustling with their usual activity. Groomsmen brushed horses, mucked stalls, and clamored about with the requirements of a busy household. Anne floated through the commotion, stepping over a puddle of horse piss and a sack of sweet grains. Light shone through the barn's cobwebbed window, illuminating a thousand tiny flecks of dust in its beams. A chorus of tiny fairy sprites.

Lingering thoughts of the king clung to Anne like wood smoke. A warm sensation pulsed through her every time she thought of him. She remembered the weight of his body on hers, the heat of his breath on her lips, the look of longing in his eyes. Last night had awakened something in Anne, igniting her sex, igniting her heart. And with it, she had the unmistakeable urge to ride, to drive the mare beneath her as she galloped through the fields. She needed to feel alive.

Anne spent most of the morning alone, lost in her thoughts, daydreaming about what might have been if she had let their kisses go further.

"You liked him too, didn't you?" Anne wove her fingers through the horse's mane.

She rode for hours, lost in the delicious memory. The softness of his lips. The longing in his voice. It was a perfect morning ride. The spring meadows welcomed her as she raced through the fields, her hair dancing in the wind. She daydreamed of another reality when she and the king could be together, madly in love and devastatingly happy.

As she circled alongside the castle, returning from her pleasant morning run, she spied a well-dressed woman pacing in the flower gardens near the bronze cherub. Anne knew, even at a distance, it was her mother.

"Good morning, Maman," she bellowed. Anne dismounted with ease and gave her mother a hug.

Elizabeth stiffened, a shadow passing over her features. "Hush, child. Come and sit down. There is much to discuss."

Anne floated to the bench. Her mood was so high that even her mother's scolding could not bring her down. She raised her arms in the air and spun around before she plopped onto the bench. It was a silly gesture, but she couldn't help herself. As children, she and Mary had danced like faeries on this very lawn, and she had never forgotten the pleasure of it.

Elizabeth hesitated. "Anne, you will leave Hever Castle in a fortnight. You are to accompany the English princess, Mary Tudor, to France. You will serve as her maid of honor at the royal wedding."

Anne stared at her mother. Her words made no sense.

"But I do not even know Princess Mary!" It was all Anne could think to say.

Elizabeth took Anne's hands in her own. "It was decided last night. Princess Mary, the king's sister, has been betrothed to King Louis of France. He is an older man and wishes for a young bride. Their marriage will secure the peace between England and France. It is an honor that you should accompany the princess."

Anne's happy world melted around her. How had her lovely days of hunting with the king resulted in her exile? She could not leave Hever. She could not leave her precious woods, her childhood home, her beloved brother and sister.

Elizabeth pressed on, a look of torment upon her face. "The king did not wish to send his sister away to France without lady friends to comfort her. Rose told me this morning the princess has resisted this union for some time. The English princess is not more than twenty and the French king is almost sixty. It will be a most awkward match."

Anne imagined the horror of being forced to marry an old man. She shuddered, thinking of him peeling her clothes off on their wedding night, his graying teeth seeking her youthful lips for a lingering kiss.

"But why me, Maman?" Anne was sympathetic, but she still didn't understand why it had to be her.

Elizabeth stared at her gloves for long moment. "You, my daughter, impressed the king during the hunt. However, you had the opposite effect on Cardinal Wolsey. You did not make a friend of him." Elizabeth's eyes stayed on Anne's, nodding to see if she would catch the implications of her words.

Anne had no difficulty in seeing the truth of it. She had jousted with Cardinal Wolsey all week. She had bested him at riding, she had ignored him when he had called her out, but worst of all, she had stolen the affection of the king. Was that the sin she was being punished for?

"The cardinal," Anne whispered, remembering the exchange between Wolsey and the king by the fire. "Of course it was the cardinal's idea."

"The cardinal is a powerful man, my child," Elizabeth said warily.

Anne shook her head. She did not care. She had not liked the cardinal. He was gluttonous and ugly, a pompous stuffed shirt.

"I hate that man and his piggy face. I will not go," she shouted. "He cannot make me leave Hever."

As Anne's rage boiled over like a pot over flame, a strange new energy filled the air in the garden. The birds perched in the apple trees nearby scattered and a hot wind began to blow.

"Anne, calm yourself. You must learn to control the storm brewing inside you."

The wind continued to surge, flipping over the leaves, exposing their light green underbellies.

"I do not care!"

"Anne, stop!" Elizabeth's voice was sharp.

But Anne would not be cowed. The sky darkened as storm clouds closed in. The branches of the apple trees swayed in the gale that had sprung up from nowhere.

Elizabeth slapped Anne's cheek.

"Stop!"

Anne's rage melted into self-pity as her mother's hand connected with her cheek. The wind died down as quickly as it began. Anne fell forward into a sob, burying her face in her hands.

Elizabeth rubbed Anne's back for a while, urging Anne to see reason. "Don't you understand what is happening here, daughter? You must go. You are a threat to your very self. It is as Aga has foretold. She saw it in her visions."

Anne was unable to take her hands away from her face.

Her mother's voice softened. "I thought if I pretended you were like other girls, this would all go away."

"But I *am* like other girls."

"No, Anne, you are not. I have worried about you since you were born with that extra finger. Every time you got angry and a storm blew in. There are so many signs. Don't you see them?"

Anne looked up at her mother with bewilderment in her gaze. None of this was making any sense. What did her exile have to do with the weather? What did it matter if it rained? And what of her fingers?

Elizabeth looked imploringly into Anne's dark eyes as she readied herself to tell Anne something she clearly never wished to share.

"You come from a line of women who have practiced the Craft for many generations...witchcraft."

Anne moved down the bench from her mother now, needing space to breath.

"What are you saying, Mother? I am a witch?"

Elizabeth held a finger to her lips and glanced around the garden. "Shhh, those words will have you dead."

But things were lining up for Anne, as though her world was in color for the first time. The wind, the trees, the universe—it was all connected, and she was a part of it. All the questions she had been meaning to ask since that winter night surged forward.

"Are you a witch too, Mother?"

Elizabeth squirmed for a moment, twisting her hands in her lap. "Yes, I have the gift. My grandmother taught me about the Craft, about the Goddess."

Anne's eyes were as wide as saucers. "The Goddess?"

Elizabeth searched the gardens again for any passers-by. "Yes. The Goddess. She lives among us in the soil and the trees. Every petal of every flower is bursting with her energy. She is born and reborn with every coming of the moon. She is everywhere."

While none of this made any sense to Anne, she felt the instinctive truth of it. It comforted her like an unacquainted truth she had always known was there.

"You come from a line of women with a special gift. For generations, our name was Bullen. We kept it as a sign of our strength and loyalty to the Goddess. But the name became marked with witchcraft. We lost many

Bullen women to burning and torture. It was safer to hide under a different name from those who sought to persecute us."

"But I am a Boleyn, not a Bullen." Anne's curiosity was piqued.

"My grandmother saw her opportunity when she betrothed me to your father. His surname was Boleyn. Bullen was still not safe, but Boleyn was close enough to Bullen to be the connection to the Craft. To maintain our magical lineage."

Anne was entranced. She wanted to know. She needed to know.

"The Craft is to be studied and respected. One must not take it lightly. I thought if I did not teach you, that you would be safe. But you have never been safe from it. It has been seeking you since you were a child. Don't you understand how dangerous that is?"

Some of Anne's usual defiance was returning and the feeling in her belly was growing hotter. It was true she always had a special connection with animals. They seemed to understand her. The weather too was hers to control. It had come in handy when her sister made her angry. Anne could have Mary caught in a rainstorm, soaked to the bone, at the most inopportune moments. But none of this seemed dangerous. It was a gift—in the same way she was gifted at Latin and calculus.

"Anne, listen." Fear laced her mother's words. "Witches are burned. Witches are drowned. They are cut open. Their eyes are gouged out." She paused, letting her words sink in. "It doesn't take much to convict a woman of witchcraft. She has only to be suspected. Then men like the cardinal will make a point of finding evidence against them—true or false. He could be a real danger to you when you don't know how to control your powers."

"I can control myself," said Anne.

Elizabeth shook her head. "No, Anne. That is not true. Many people witnessed it when you spoke to that deer. They all watched. They all saw it. You did it right in front of the cardinal and the king."

The hairs on the back of Anne's neck stood on end. "How did you know about that?"

Elizabeth took her daughter's hands in her own. "Everyone is talking about it."

Anne felt dampness under her arms. She rubbed her palms, now sticky, on her skirt. She remembered the small fire she had started beneath the feet of the deer, but it had stopped just as soon. The whole occurrence felt so natural, it had been too hard to resist.

Reassurance returned to her mother's voice. "This is the best solution.

You shall go to France and serve the English princess. I cannot teach you while you are here. It would be too dangerous. And refusing the cardinal will raise further suspicion."

For once, Anne could not find any words.

Elizabeth gave her daughter's hand a reassuring squeeze. "You are in need of a teacher and thankfully I have one for you. Her name is Marguerite. She will seek you out."

"But what about Mary and George? I shall be lonely."

"Mary does not have your gifts. She wants nothing to do with the Craft. It is you who must go. Remember, you will have the English princess. She is close in age to you and will be grateful for your companionship. And Rose shall accompany you too. You will find happiness in France. I promise."

"Rose shall accompany me?" said Anne, her voice thick with relief at the knowledge her nursemaid would join her on this journey. Tears welled in her eyes. Her life was melting away like her favorite marzipan sweets left in the rain.

"It won't be forever, Anne. Things will settle down here after a couple of months and then you will be called home. Think of it as a new adventure."

PRESENT DAY

QUEEN'S UNIVERSITY, CANADA

Dez and I trundled up Princess Street, each of us carrying heavy grocery bags. It had always been our ritual to spend Saturday afternoons buying everything on Grapes' complicated shopping list. The job was never an easy one, given the weird and wonderful things she asked us to find. Usually we had to hit several grocery stores, a few health-food shops, and sometimes even a gardening center to complete the errand. It always made Dez a little grumpy, but I knew he enjoyed the challenge.

"Why the heck does your Grapes need dried knotweed?" he scoffed, a little out of breath.

"I don't know. She just needs it. I learned a long time ago never to ask about her secret recipes."

"But honestly, knotweed? Is that even edible?"

I shrugged. "I think she uses it in one of her herbal teas."

Dez groaned under the weight of a cumbersome bag.

"Don't be such a baby. Walking is good for you. You spend too much time in the biology lab."

He ignored the jab about his own nerdy work habits. "Hey, did you read the paper I gave you?"

I shook my head. "Haven't read the paper, no. I'm trying to take a less 'witchy' approach to this comprehensive exam." I scrunched up my nose as a thought occurred to me. "But I did find something weird in my dad's research when I was looking around. Actually Dez, do you mind if we make one more stop. It's right across the road."

Kingston Travel had been on Princess Street for as long as I could remember. It was a sad little shop with not much more than a desk and a few travel brochures. Paint peeled from the walls and the distinct smell of coffee and cigarettes permeated the air. Travel posters covered the cracked plaster with images f destinations from around the world, promising fun, sun, and relaxation.

I glanced at one poster that read, '*Visit the Tower of London—Step Back in Time.*' An image of Anne Boleyn's head, sliced clean off, sailed through my mind. A little shiver passed through me.

A young woman at the front desk looked bored as we entered. The new age of internet travel companies had obviously done some serious damage to their business. The store was empty and the phone was silent. The woman glanced up before returning her attention to a pile of paper-clips. She was making a replica of the Eiffel Tower. It was pretty good—for paperclips.

"Excuse me." My voice sounded hollow in the empty space. "I'm hoping you can help me find some information about a travel receipt from several years ago?"

Dez put his shopping bags down with an exaggerated sigh of relief.

The woman looked up slowly from her paperclip masterpiece. "How many years ago?" Her eyelashes, clumpy with mascara, stuck together in a rather unattractive way.

I gave her my most charming smile. "The receipt is from 2007."

The woman scoffed. "You're kidding. That was, like..." She did the math in her head. "More than ten years ago."

I laughed nervously. "Yeah...but can you help me?"

Dez raised an eyebrow. I hadn't mentioned the travel folder I had found, but he was a quick study and I knew it wouldn't take him long to figure things out.

The woman blinked those sticky eyes and resumed work on her paper-clip creation. She used tweezers to affix three little iron platforms to the top of the Eiffel Tower structure. It was so fascinating, we couldn't look away. She was ignoring us, but we watched her all the same. It was painstakingly slow work but when she finished, the tiny tower was impres-sive. She even remembered to include the elevator that moved up and down inside the columns.

Just as I wondered if she had forgotten us altogether, she screamed into the back office. "Ma!"

"What!" A gravelly voice shot back.

"There's some people here who want to talk about a travel receipt from the turn of the century."

"Okay, Rachel, honey, hold on." The voice croaked over a bone-rattling cough that hinted at years of smoking. From behind the door emerged a small round woman in her late sixties, wearing another no-nonsense scowl that matched her daughter's.

Dez crossed him arms, an amused expression on his face, ready to see what else I had in store.

"Umm... I'm Ellie Bowlan," I stammered.

The woman's puckered lips were rather unnerving. A black hairy mole bobbed on her sagging jowls.

"I'm hoping you might have some information about three plane tickets sold to an Arthur Wright in 2007?"

She narrowed her eyes. "I hope you're not looking for a refund."

I shook my head.

"Look. If you don't have an invoice number I wouldn't be able to find it in our computer. I'm afraid I can't help you."

I bit my lip. My backpack was stuffed with research notes, journal articles, and books, but I thought I remembered sticking the travel folder in there too. Plopping the bag on the ground, I searched through the chaos until my fingers settled on the colorful Kingston Travel package. I waved it in the air with a hopeful expression.

"Actually, I do have the invoice..."

The woman's glower advanced into a snarl, but she nodded all the same. She shooed Rachel out of the seat and sat with a thud in front of the computer. "And why do you need this information?" She peered over her glasses as she typed in the password, the Eiffel tower paperclip miniature sitting proudly beside the keyboard.

Hope swelled inside me like a teabag in hot water. Taking a move from Dez's rulebook, I decided my next step was to play the pity card. "The travel receipts were for my parents and grandmother. They died on that trip." I sniffed and wiped away an invisible tear.

Mrs. No-Nonsense looked up at me. "Oh."

Dez's lip curled imperceptibly as he finally caught on. "She is desperate to find the truth," he added. "That trip made her an orphan."

"Can you confirm they went to London?" My voice cracked, this time with a hint of legitimate emotion.

The woman sized me up, her dark eyes burrowing into mine like fleas on a bloodhound. With a grunt she began typing. "Okay, honey, let's see what I can find. A travel receipt for one Arthur Wright... Hmmm... Yes."

I held my breath. I didn't know what else to do. Dez leaned in closer to see the screen.

Scanning the file for interesting tidbits, she was interrupted by a few hacking coughs. It took a while, but I waited with growing excitement, trying to remember to breathe occasionally. When she finished, she lifted her round face, jowls and all, and gave us a long look.

"I'm just gonna say this. I don't remember many specific clients in my years as an agent. I've had this business for over forty years. There are too many to remember." She shook her head in disbelief. "But this man, Arthur Wright, I do remember."

My palms went sweaty. "You remember booking this trip for my dad?" I squeaked.

"He came in with your mother that summer. They were real nervous about something. Paranoid even. They booked their flights without even asking what it would cost. I love customers like that. They paid up front for the whole thing in cash." The woman's scowl transformed into smile, the hairy mole disappearing inside a dimple.

I tried to remain calm. "Do you have any idea where they stayed?"

"Sure. I got them a reservation for the Royal Horse Guards Hotel in London. Send all my clients there. It's on file here. Look. Two hotel rooms —one for him and the wife, the other one for the mother-in-law."

"Holy shit," Dez whispered. "That's them."

"Yes!" I shouted. My reaction was embarrassing but I didn't care. "That's them! So if I call this Royal Horse Guards Hotel, maybe I can confirm they stayed there?"

She hacked out another long phlegmy cough before she continued. "Sure, but don't get your knickers in a knot just yet. It gets more interesting. As I said, your dad was edgy, maybe even afraid. He asked that I use aliases when I booked the reservation for the hotel. He said he didn't want anyone to be able to find them in London. They needed to be 'incognito' or something. To be honest, I figured they were criminals...or at least running from criminals."

My mind reeled with this new information.

"Oh," I breathed.

The woman's face had returned to its usual scowl, but the tone of her voice was still motherly. She stood up and gave me an awkward hug that smelled like day-old cigarettes and mildew. I must have looked like I needed it, or maybe she just wanted us out of her store.

Mrs. No-Nonsense waddled to the exit, pulling at the hair on her mole. She yanked the door open, the bell above the frame tinkling, and gestured for us to take our leave.

"Listen, honey." She gave my hand a squeeze as she shooed us away. "Good luck in figuring out your mystery. No one likes to be responsible for the making of an orphan."

* * *

The air outside the travel agency was cool and crisp. It felt good on my face and I took a deep breath. My mind swirled with information and I needed time to think it through.

We had always been a hard-core camping family. No European vacations or sunny Caribbean beaches for us. We camped in Algonquin Park every August like clockwork. If my family left on August 20th, they would have been deep in the backwoods, off the grid, nowhere near a road or access to an airport. Camping and London in the same week? No, the two truths were simply incongruent.

"So, are you gonna tell me what's going on?" Dez asked.

Rubbing my temples, I tried to make the pieces of my world fit together. But no matter what I did with this new information, the puzzle seemed irreconcilably broken.

"How is it possible that my parents and grandmother were in London, the same week they went camping here in Canada?" I asked the question aloud, although I wasn't really talking to Dez.

Dez put his bags down on the sidewalk and took me by the shoulders. "Ellie. What the hell are you talking about?"

Dez's face slid into focus. He wore a look of genuine concern, not to mention confusion. We hadn't discussed my parent's deaths in years, so it was no wonder he didn't understand. But something about the travel folder had been itching at the back of my brain.

I put my groceries down too and told Dez the whole story. He listened as I walked him through the confusing events of the last few days, a look of clinical skepticism on his brow. When I finished, he rubbed his purple fingers over his chin.

"So your parents went missing. We know that part is a fact." He kept rubbing and a violet smudge was emerging on his face. "But just because you always believed they were on a camping trip doesn't mean they couldn't have disappeared in Europe. Missing is missing, no matter where they went."

I shook my head. "Yeah but why would they lie? Why would they tell us they were going camping if they were actually going to London?"

The attic door in my mind trembled on its hinges. Childhood memories threatened to spill forth and I did my best to reinforce the seal around the door. Though I didn't voice it, a small memory slipped into my stream of consciousness.

On the night of my eleventh birthday, I awoke at midnight in search of a glass of water. Heading to the kitchen, I found Mom, Dad and Grandma deep in discussion. Something about the intensity of their conversation made me stop. Under any other circumstance, I would have barged in and plopped onto my father's lap. I had always been a daddy's girl, but that night I listened at the door. Dad was doing most of the talking. He was speaking about a change of plans and a need to collect samples. Or had he said specimens? I couldn't be sure.

I didn't understand everything they were talking about, but there was mention of London. "We'll meet by Big Ben. We should have the results by then," he explained as Mom and Grandma nodded. Then he followed with something strange. "We have to keep Ellie safe from this. Just in case."

Dez interrupted my train of thought.

"Ellie, what is happening to you? You zoned out there. Are you feeling okay?"

I shook my head, trying to clear away the memories. "Yeah, sorry. I'm just... I have a lot on my mind.

My phone vibrated in my pocket and I jumped at the tingling sensation running up my leg. Somehow answering it seemed like a better option than answering more of Dez's probing questions.

"Ellie. It's John Chelsea."

"Who?" I sputtered as I attempted to shove the childhood memories back into the attic. Silence swelled though the phone line.

Think Ellie. Think. Who was John Chelsea?

Then it hit me. The person on the other end of the phone was beautiful John from the séance. Handsome, athletic, smooth-guy John. John-the-guy-in-the-wet-towel.

Dez leaned in and whispered too loudly, "Who is it?"

I waved away my pestering best friend. "Oh hi." I tried to recover by sounding super casual.

John gave an embarrassed laugh. "Listen, I wanted to call to say thank you for the advice on my Comp question. You told me to look into Marguerite de Navarre? Remember?"

I said nothing. The events from last night and today were colliding in my head like bumper cars. And to make matters worse, I was overcome with nerves. This was drop-dead-sexy John, after all.

John now sounded uncertain about calling. "Well you were right. Marguerite is the perfect proto-feminist case study. I wanted to say thank you. I thought I should let you know."

A full ten seconds lapsed before I replied. "I'm glad I could help?" It came out like a question. My tongue was thick and uncooperative.

"Hey, are you okay? You sound a bit lost," he asked.

"I'm okay," I replied a little too quickly.

I could almost see the perplexed expression on his face. He must have thought I was a total wacko. "Okay, well hang in there Ellie-from-the-kitchen. You are definitely one of a kind."

I hung up the phone, my face flushed red, and looked into Dez's curious eyes.

"Who was that?"

"It was John Chelsea." I sounded a little stunned, but the day's events had overwhelmed my ability to think clearly.

Dez whistled. "Ooooo, Ellie. I didn't know you and John were at the 'chatting on the phone stage.' I mean, he's been asking a lot of questions about you, but wow. That's terrific. Usually you move a lot slower."

I punched him in the arm. "Shut up, Dez. We're not at the 'chatting on the phone stage.' He called to talk about Comps."

Dez smirked. "Okay, sure. Whatever you say."

I put my hands on my hips and gave him my fiercest scowl. "Listen, mind your own business. You're making me crazy."

Dez opened his mouth to get another jab in, but I stopped him.

"Just pick up your grocery bags. We need to get home. Grapes needs her dried knotweed and the rest of this stuff. Maybe she can make you an herbal tea that will get you to stop asking so many questions."

1514

CHATEAU DE BLOIS, LOIRE VALLEY, FRANCE

R ose pinched Anne's cheeks for a bit of color. "Now don't ya be complainin' girl. Yoo are as white as a chicken egg."

"Ouch," Anne shouted. "Stop it. I don't care if my complexion pleases the King of France."

Rose made another grab for her face. "Anne, yoo are stubborn as a wart, ya are!"

Anne kept a safe distance. "I hardly think the king will care. We have seen none of him, nor the English princess since we arrived. They have kept us alone in these damp rooms like prisoners. If this is how they want to treat us, they shall have to endure my sallow complexion."

It had been nothing but deep fog and rain since they crossed the English Channel into France, and the poor weather had stayed with them as they made their way across the Loire Valley. The clouds hung so low Anne saw little of the rolling French countryside.

Once at Chateau de Blois, the same inclement weather had concealed most of the castle's exterior majesty and the charming city surrounding it. Anne saw only the chateau's red and white stone façade. The grand entrance in gothic style architecture boasted an ostentatious stone statue of the king flourishing a sword on horseback. It had seemed a silly thing to do to build a castle here in this dismal swamp land.

A knock at the door announced it was time for Anne's presentation to the king. Rose gave her a quick hug. "You'll do just fine, luv."

Ann tucked a loose strand of hair from beneath her coif and smoothed her skirts.

She nodded to the servant and stepped into the castle for the first time since her arrival. The chateau was enormous. Sumptuous wood-paneled walls went on forever, boasting ornately carved archways in every corner. A dark navy blue ceiling painted with golden fleur-de-lis luminesced above. Anne glanced into one open door and spied a grand dining room with a fireplace that could fit a dozen men inside.

Courtiers milled the about the castle without a care in the world. In a small room that likely served as a water closet, Anne saw two people copulating like dogs. A heavily painted woman flashed her a black-toothed smile and Anne looked away before she saw more. This was no English countryside. Of that she was certain.

After a distance, the servant stopped at a set of large wooden doors and knocked. From within, a tall mustached man emerged jangling a set of keys. He wore a set of unusual round spectacles on his nose. A blue peacock feather in his cap twitched with nervous energy as he cleared his throat.

"Mistress Boleyn. You have arrived," he said in polished French. "You may enter now, but I warn you, this is not a good day. I suggest you keep a low profile."

Anne's French was as a good as her English and she had no trouble conversing in the language of her new home. She took a breath and stepped into the room, ready to be received by the King of France.

The king sat in a large chair adorned with dozens of gems. Unlike her handsome English king, this man was greasy and pencil thin, with a patchy beard and overgrown ears. He sat slung over the throne, with his feet hiked up over one of the side arms. He was elderly, the gray hair at his temples revealing his age. When he spoke, though, his voice was high, like that of a pubescent teenage boy. A tiny man, no more than three feet tall, was busy washing and oiling the king's feet. He seemed to take great pleasure in massaging the king's toes.

"Frederique," barked the king in his shrill tone. "Look at the nail on my big toe. It has given me an itch of late. Yes...there. Do you see anything growing?" The king leaned forward to see it for himself.

The little man inspected the offending digit. "Aye, sir, I do spy a bit of fungus." Frederique's voice was surprisingly low.

Repulsed by the spectacle, Anne forced her gaze around the room. The king's receiving room was rather empty save for a few cowering servants. It took Anne a moment to spot the English princess sitting at the opposite end of the room. She sat motionless on her velvet chaise, her gray eyes staring into the shadows, more a marble statue than a real flesh and blood woman. Her skin was pale and flawless. Thick waves of strawberry blond hair cascaded loose over her shoulders. Her white gown was trimmed with gold, a heavy jewel-encrusted necklace double strung across her petite bust.

In spite of her interest in Princess Mary, Anne's attention was diverted back to the king. A small dark woman had entered the room and was now pacing in front of his throne. She was olive skinned and raven haired, with a most impressive air of confidence. She placed petite hands on her supple hips and narrowed her eyes.

"Louis, Paris is full of disease this summer. Your people are dying every day. You cannot raise the taxes for the poor. It would kill them all." The woman spoke with an intelligence and authority that would rival any man.

King Louis glanced up, as if noticing a buzzing fly, and then went back to his feet.

"Marguerite," he sneered. "I do not give a fig about the people of Paris and their sickness. I am the king." He poked a long finger into his chest. "And if I want to raise taxes to fund my fight with Milan, it shall be so. Plague or no plague."

The dark woman's face flushed. "Louis, it is the *plague*! For all that is holy, you must recognize this. The people are hungry. Their children are dying. They are desperate. And desperate people can rise against you. If you ignore this, then you are a fool."

The king's head snapped up again. "How dare you, woman! I am the Father of the People. The great King Louis of France. Loved by all. Revered by all." He kicked at Frederique to free his feet and stood to face her.

Marguerite crossed her arms, refusing to be cowed. "Yes. They do call you the Father of the People, and we both know why. I have created this image for you by caring for the commoners, by extending the generosity of the royal hold. So the people will love you. How can you care so little?"

Louis puffed up his chest like a strutting cock. "I care so much for my kingdom, I will take a new bride in only a matter of months." He gestured to the corner of the room toward the inanimate princess. "And this virgin bride will bear me a son. He shall be my gift to France. That is the greatness of my generosity."

Marguerite's lips formed a grim line. "I hardly call that generosity when you already have an heir who will make a magnificent monarch. Why can you not treasure your own daughter? Claude has done all you have asked. She married Francis. My brother was the man of your choosing and she did so without question or complaint. Yet you continue to detest her."

"And who might you be?" the king barked as he noticed Anne standing in the doorway.

The tall man with the moustache stepped forward and issued an edgy bow. "This is Mistress Anne Boleyn. She is the lady-in-wait for the English princess, Mary."

King Louis eyed her with a sneer. "Anne Boleyn...eh." He sucked spittle from between his front teeth. "Mistress Boleyn, tell me this. Do you like hunchbacks?"

Anne's eyes widened but she did not reply.

"Hunchbacks, you daft girl! Do you like hunchbacks?" He stared at Anne, as if her response would settle some great argument.

"Sire, I do not know..."

Marguerite came to Anne's rescue. She stood between Anne and King Louis like a shield. "Louis, you cannot put this upon our newcomer. Your daughter is a beautiful woman, regardless of the pitch in her back. She is intelligent, and she is kind. She carries your grandchild. Perhaps a grandson."

Louis spit on the floor. "Do not call that thing my 'daughter.' She is the spawn of the devil." He waved her off and headed to the door. "I wish to take some air in the gardens. Frederique, get my shoes."

"Fine." Marguerite smiled, smooth as an oyster pearl, as she watched the small man scramble to dress the king's naked feet. "I shall take my leave of you for the summer. But I warn you, you shall not have the benefit of my advice over these next months. I do more than you know." She turned to gather her belongings and added with a casual tone, "I will be taking Claude with me to the country. She requires fresh air at this point in her pregnancy."

"Good. I shall not to have to see the hunchback for a time."

The king turned to the door, his face flushed with irritation. Frederique had rolled up his stockings and was installing his slippers. The bows on his shoes were larger than any Anne had seen before.

Once redressed, the king stormed from the room, his small manservant trailing in his wake.

"Louis, there is one last thing," Marguerite called after him, clearly not finished with their business.

The royal entourage exited in a huff, followed by the litany of cowering servants. Once the room had emptied, Anne looked around, unsure of what to do. The only remaining soul was the English princess.

The young woman sat in the corner, still unmoving. After what Anne had witnessed, she felt a keen sadness for Princess Mary. There had been butterflies aplenty in Anne's belly when she had imagined meeting this royal couple, but they had since disappeared. The English princess was just a girl she realized, much like herself, frightened and alone.

Anne approached her slowly, curtsying low before she introduced herself.

"Princess?"

The woman did not break her stare.

Anne stepped towards her. "Princess?"

Once again, the woman remained motionless.

Anne placed her own hand on top of Princess Mary's. The woman's hands were cool, nails chewed low, cuticles bloodied. "My name is Anne Boleyn."

No response.

Anne wasn't sure what to do next. She took a step backward and gazed again at the woman's petrified form. Perhaps, she thought, her heart is too broken to speak. Anne sat down, arranging herself at the woman's feet, and traced her fingers along the floral pattern of the rug.

"I come from Hever." Anne tried to reach her in a new way. "I have never served a royal before and can only hope to perform my duties to your satisfaction. I do wish to serve you well."

Silence.

"I feel your heartbreak. It echoes my own. I too was sad to leave my family. Perhaps we can be friends?"

Nothing.

"I think you are brave, to do your duty for your country. For your king."

Anne noticed a silent tear streaming down the princess' cheek. She waited a few moments longer, hoping for a response, but got no other sign of interest.

Anne rose to her feet, her head hung low, and turned to go.

Finally, as if inspired by Anne's renunciation, the princess spoke.

"I have no friends." The woman's voice was low.

Anne turned back in surprise. "Oh, I am sorry to have assumed we could be."

The princess shook her head. "No, I am sorry for it, Anne Boleyn. I am sorry you must join me. I did not ask it."

Anne did not know what to say. She did not understand.

The princess returned her gaze to the shadows. "I cannot be your friend. I must endure my fate alone."

Anne stepped towards the young woman, but the princess held up her hand. "No, please... I will not be swayed. I hope you can find happiness while you are in France, but you will not find that happiness with me."

"But princess," Anne pleaded.

In a broken voice the princess whispered, "Please just go."

L ily looked up with those impossibly thick glasses and gave me a tiny smile. Something about my beloved Lily-the-librarian quieted my neurotic tendencies. I wasn't sure why, but I was more at ease in the stacks with her than anywhere else in the world. The dusty shelves and the smell of ancient parchment comforted me. It was safe down here. There was no one to impress, no one to judge us. It was just Lily, the books, and me.

"How was your date, Lil?"

Lily's eyes shifted back to the computer screen. "Okay," she offered. "He was a bit boring. And a little funny looking." She provided no further information but the flush on her cheeks was apparent.

Laughing at her honesty, I waved her off. "Funny looking isn't so bad. It's the charming, *good-looking* ones you have to watch out for. They're nothing but trouble."

"Mmmmm...hmmmm..."

I patted Lily on the arm and padded away from her desk. "I'll be at my favorite study carrel if you need company." The sarcastic remark was lost on her. Lily needed company like she needed a hole in the head.

I thought she would dive into her work right away, but a miniscule twitch triggered in her left eyebrow, causing it to arch a tenth of a millimetre above her frames. It was almost imperceptible, but I recognized the shift in an instant. Lily had found a lead.

"I pulled this text from the Medieval European History section," she wheezed. "Might be of use. It turns out Anne Boleyn lived in France for a while—before she moved to the English court and started all that business with King Henry in England. So maybe she did know that Marguerite de Navarre of yours."

"Oh yeah?" I asked with a hint of enthusiasm, scooping the large book out of her arms. "That's awesome, Lil."

Lily's small smile emerged. It brightened her face and made her look almost pretty.

At the end of the aisle, nestled into my study carrel, I spent the next few hours reviewing the text Lily had given me. It was an enormous volume, and I had to hunch over its pages to make my way through it. The book focused on Anne Boleyn's formative years. It told a part of her story I hadn't known of before. Much of the literature was focused on Anne Boleyn's rise to power through her marriage to Henry Tudor. Her teenage years were usually an invisible period in her life. But this text helped me to understand the young Anne Boleyn and how she may have become her own version of the 'first modern woman.'

The historical evidence suggested Anne spent seven years in France when she was growing up. Most scholars believed she was the maid-of-honor in the wedding of Princess Mary Tudor to King Louis XII of France.

There is strong historical evidence to suggest that Marguerite de Navarre, while at the French court, tutored Anne Boleyn. Marguerite, the sister of the future King Francis I, was a celebrated intellectual and patron of humanists and reformers alike. Several historians have hypothesized Marguerite de Navarre influenced Anne Boleyn's belief system, which later became fundamental in defining her role in the English reformation.

I held my finger under the passage and reread it a few more times. This was the connection I'd been looking for. Anne Boleyn knew Marguerite de Navarre. One piece of the puzzle had fallen into place. I loved when that happened. My father nodded with approval in my mind's eye.

I bounded back to Lily's desk.

"Look at this, Lil. You were right," I shouted down the book aisle. "Marguerite de Navarre tutored Anne Boleyn. This is evidence I needed. You are a genius!"

"Uhhh-huh..." She didn't seem altogether impressed with my find. "Listen, Ellie, I found more. I did a bit of digging on the witchcraft angle."

She refilled her lungs. "Most of the historical record suggests Anne Boleyn had six fingers on her right hand. Many people said it was a witch's mark. In fact, that sixth finger was part of the evidence used against her at her own trial."

I slumped down on the edge of Lily's desk. The thrill of my Marguerite de Navarre discovery vanished into thin air.

Lily eyed me over the frames of her glasses. "Ellie, don't overlook the possibility that Anne Boleyn was a witch. They call it the Comprehensive exam for a reason—because you are expected to be *comprehensive* in your research. You have to explore both sides. Woman *or* witch—remember?"

"I guess." My voice sagged.

I had been looking forward to our usual end-of-day research debrief, incorporating a good discussion about where we could go next with our Anne Boleyn investigations. But Lily's advice stopped me. I needed to change direction and rebalance my research strategy.

Turning back to my study carrel, I growled. Lily was right. I needed to explore the possibility that Anne Boleyn was a witch, if only to refute the idea as unfounded. But this witchcraft thing seemed ridiculous—and creepy. Looking into Anne Boleyn's encounters with the supernatural made me uncomfortable. It hit too close to home. Images of the séance washed over me again. The wine glass, the pointing flames, the voice saying, '*The answers you seek are contained in your father's research.*' A shudder passed through me.

* * *

After several more hours poring over books, I ascended from the bowels of the library. The lights seemed a lot brighter above ground and I squinted my eyes to adjust. I felt like a bookish vampire emerging from her underground lair.

The student body scurried about, eager to start class assignments and get a jump on early term papers. Most people were gathered in the more appealing parts of the library, plugged into their laptops like futuristic robots. This was a new electronic generation of students, a generation that didn't remember when books were printed on paper. In fact, many students didn't seem interested in learning at all. One guy in the corner played Candy Crush on his phone, and a group of girls with low-cut shirts eyed a handsome professor by the photocopier.

A stout, balding man, dressed in his university tweeds, stood near the checkout counter, his big eyes bulging as he fiddled with his necktie. I recognized this puffed-up bullfrog in an instant. It was the director of the History Department, Dr. Landon Fishburn. The arrogant way he peered over his glasses made me want to sneak away, to escape unnoticed. I had never liked this man. But now that I was writing his Comprehensive exam, I wanted nothing to do with him.

I put my head down and headed for the exit. Unfortunately, the squeak of the door hinge drew his attention. He looked up from his book and gestured across the library.

"Ms. Bowlan." He croaked. "How nice to see you at the library. Working on the Comprehensive exam, are we?" Fishburn raised an eyebrow as though he had just spied his next meal.

"Uh...yes?" I replied. Again, my statement sounded like more of a question.

His eyes narrowed conspiratorially. "I've been looking for you."

"Oh?" Oily nerves ran through my guts.

Fishburn tutted at my reaction in a way that made me feel stupid. "I wanted to speak with you about the exam. How are you doing with everything? Don't you love the subject matter?"

"Yeah. It's great," I lied.

He leaned in close with a new hungry intensity. "And how are you doing?"

I took a step back, feeling rather put off by his enthusiasm. Why was he showing interest in me? Throughout my time in the PhD program, I had barely ever interacted with the great Dr. Landon Fishburn. At the student summer barbecue, he had seemed utterly unimpressed, even though I had the highest grade point average in the department.

Today, he eyed me like a hungry frog—and I was the unsuspecting fly. "Fine, thank you." I kept my answer short, hoping he would lose interest and allow me to make my escape.

Fishburn fixed me with an amphibious eye. "Perhaps I could give you a hand with your research?"

Alarm bells rang in my head. I couldn't be sure how to read this man's sudden interest, but something was out of place. Was it a trap? Was he trying to trick me into violating school rules? I didn't know, but my instincts told me to get away from him as fast as I could.

"Dr. Fishburn... Uh... I'm not supposed to talk about the exam with faculty...remember?"

His face dropped imperceptibly, but he managed a warm response. "Of course, Ellie. Listen, I wanted to give you this book. It's a text called the *Malleus Maleficarum*. Have you come across it yet in your research?"

He plopped it into my hands. The text sat limp against my palms like a dirty rag. I shook my head, uncertain of whether I should talk or not.

Fishburn appeared mildly disgusted. "Right, well that's okay. Just review it, would you?"

I tried to smile, but it came off as more of a painful grimace.

He turned to take his leave, chalk wafting from the back of his pants. He glanced back over his shoulder one more time as he pushed open the heavy library door.

"I'm expecting great things from you, Ms. Bowlan. Great things."

Anne lay in bed, enjoying the morning light. It was the first time she had seen the sun since they arrived in France. She had awoken from a dream that felt so real, her heart was still pounding. In it, she was alone in the woods in the arms of her beautiful King Henry. He had begged her to wait for him, to love him forever. And she had agreed, succumbing to his kisses in the forest. She could still feel the warmth of his lips upon her own.

Anne had not stopped thinking of Henry since she promised her heart to him the night they spent by the campfire. Her desire had only heightened with the distance. She had spent the morning writing and rewriting a letter to him. Her latest draft was short but full of yearning.

My dearest king,

> *I hope this letter finds you in good health and good stand. I write to you as the friend I always promised to be. I write to you also as your wanting lover. My heart breaks to know I cannot be with you. Alas, the fates have not deemed it possible. And so, dear Henry, I lie alone in my bed in France, wishing for you, wanting for you. Knowing when the day comes that we can be together, it will be heaven on Earth.*

> *Your forever heart,*
> *Anne*

She was underscoring her name with several gratuitous swirls when a knock at the door set the last line askew. She tucked the king's handkerchief under her pillow and jostled her nursemaid in the sleeping trundle beside her bed.

"Rose. Make haste. Someone is come."

Rose rolled over, groaning as she creaked out of her bed. Her nightcap failed to contain the mess of curls. She scratched a sizeable rump and pried her eyes open. Anne giggled at the sight of her.

"Who comes at this hour to disturb us? I can't thenk what is worse— bein' ignored all day or bein' interrupted from a blissful slumber...eh, Anne. These French are truly savages." Rose shuffled to the door, her flat-footed feet naked against the stones.

The knock came again. "Alright, you don't have to pound to dooor down... I'm a comin'...fast as a fury." Her voice was a groggy growl. Flipping the latch upward, Rose pulled the door open and gasped. "Oh, your ladyship...I...please forgive meh appearance. We weren't expectin' companie."

A familiar voice answered back. "I apologize for coming unannounced. I wanted to make introductions between Anne and the king's daughter. We leave for Amboise tomorrow and there is much to prepare."

Rose swung the door open wide. "Of course, m'lady."

Anne jumped off the bed with the reflexes of a cat and curtsied to the two ladies now standing in her room.

The olive-skinned woman who had argued with the old king yesterday moved towards her in earnest. The expression she wore had changed since their last meeting. Instead of a fierce scowl, she now smiled with warmth.

"Anne, how nice we can replay our first meeting. I do apologize for the display yesterday. I was unable to welcome you properly to France. I am Marguerite de Navarre, a member of the royal house—and I dare say—an advisor to King Louis." Marguerite curtsied, her years of training apparent.

Anne bobbed. "It is an honor to make your acquaintance."

The woman searched Anne's face, fine lines gathering around her eyes as her recognition grew. "I didn't see it yesterday with the other distractions, but I do see the resemblance now. I see your mother in you. Despite your dark coloring, you possess many of her features."

Anne wasn't sure what to say.

Marguerite took Anne's hands in her own. "I knew your mother years ago. She sent a letter to tell me of your arrival. She asked me to watch over you, to tutor you..." The woman searched Anne's face again.

Anne swallowed back a combined surge of excitement and fear. "I... I have always been a willing and eager student."

Marguerite clucked. "You mustn't be afraid, Anne. Your mother asked I tutor you in the Craft. It shall be a most intriguing summer."

Anne's eyes grew wide but she remained silent.

"I have but one other student, Claude. She is the king's daughter. I wanted to make formal introductions between you. She is an excellent scholar in the Craft and in traditional academics too. She is the same age as you. I am looking forward to a summer filled with learning and friendship."

Anne gazed at the somber girl standing in the corner. She was dressed as impeccably as her much older sister-in-law, but her pretty face conveyed none of the same authority. She gave a small curtsy in response. The right side of her body did not stand up quite as high as her left. Anne thought she could see a hump on her back, not deforming, but noticeable. The young woman cradled her petite hands around the base of a large belly.

Anne tried to imagine being so young and pregnant, already preparing to be a mother.

"Ouff," whispered Claude. "Please forgive me. The child kicks." Her voice was more childlike than Anne expected.

Anne lit up with the thought of a babe inside this young girl. She was fascinated by the mechanics of it. "The child kicks? And you can feel her?" she asked, forgetting the formalities of the introduction between them.

"Aye, she kicks hard. Marguerite says that means she is strong and healthy." The girl rubbed her stomach. "I pray it will be."

Anne moved in closer to spy the baby's movement through the folds of cloth in Claude's dress. Together, they watched the moving fabric for a time, tiny twitches tracing across the top of the belly.

Claude giggled. "Do you want to feel her kick?" She took Anne by the hand, placing it atop her dancing stomach.

Anne's lips parted in astonishment. A tiny foot from below the fabric kicked into her palm. She stood in utter fascination.

Claude whispered, "I think she likes you."

The girls smiled at each other, a new friendship born.

Marguerite was the one to interrupt their silent bonding. "Anne," she asked. "Would it please you to accompany us to the country this summer?

We leave tomorrow for the chateau at Clos Lucé. It is a much simpler estate house in Amboise, much more comfortable than this drafty old palace."

"But what of the English princess?" asked Anne. "I am her lady-in-wait."

Marguerite smiled. "Princess Mary has been most generous. She was the one who suggested you join us. For your health."

Anne curtsied again. "We do miss the countryside, madame. It has been lonely for Rose and me since we arrived." She glanced at her beloved nursemaid, a silent request that Rose could come along too.

Marguerite eyed Rose's stout form as she hovered by the bed, draped in a large white night dress. Her cheeks were flushed with anticipation, her eyes full of longing.

"We would never ask you to come away without your nursemaid." Marguerite smiled.

Rose squeezed her hands together and leapt with gratitude, her great breasts swinging loose beneath her nightgown. "Oooooo...we should love luv to go. Thank you, madame."

Marguerite placed her hands on her hips. "Then it is all set. We shall go to the country for the summer." She guided Claude to the door as they made ready to leave. "Anne, the king is having his public supper tonight. It is to be our last before our departure. Would you join us? Claude could do with the companionship."

Anne responded without a moment's hesitation. "I should love to."

* * *

A long table dressed in white cloth and silver plate stood at the center of a large dining room. The king sat at the head, a thin golden crown cresting his greasy pate. He wore a matching blue velvet doublet with enormous puffed sleeves that seemed to be trying to swallow him. Flanking the king, a panel of dinner guests sat talking amongst themselves. The English princess sat stoic and silent at the other end of the table.

Anne was not sure which French custom she found more queer, the two pronged forks set at each plate or the courtiers who stood at the edges of the room watching the king's every move.

"We shall take the battle to Milan this summer. She will be an exquisite prize. There is much culture to pilfer from the Italians," King Louis announced. He looked down the table at the statue-like princess. "Unlike the English, which I doubt have much culture to offer at all."

Princess Mary remained unresponsive, although a flush settled over her cheeks.

Failing to elicit a reaction from his bride-to-be, the king turned his attention to Anne. "You must wonder, Anne Boleyn, about this new Italian fork we have adopted here at my French table. I believe you English still use your fingers and stab at your meat like savages. Do you not?"

Frederique snickered sycophantically.

Anne gaped, unsure of how to respond.

"Louis." Marguerite returned the conversation to the invasion of Milan. "I do hope you consider our discussion yesterday regarding the timing of the battle. This summer, our troops are ever sick with the plague. The chances of our success are low, especially with the war coffers depleted."

Louis gave her a threatening stare. Even Anne understood this ominous warning. It was one thing for Marguerite to castigate the king in his private rooms, but not at a public supper. "I have these matters well under control. Do not press me, woman."

The man in the feather cap cleared his throat. "Sire, I believe Milan will make an excellent target and this time we shall take her for certain." His moustache twitched as he stabbed a piece of pigeon pie with his two-pronged fork. "However, with our priorities around the royal wedding, delaying the Italian invasion until the spring may be pertinent. In the meantime, we shall ensure the royal house continues to collect all things Italian for your pleasure."

Claude's husband, Francis, chimed in carefully. "Sire, it may please you to know that Leonardo da Vinci, the greatest Italian scholar of our day, has agreed to summer here in France. In Amboise, as a matter of fact. They say he is the light of Italy, famous for both his artistic talent and his knowledge of science."

Francis reached across the table and placed his hand atop of his wife's. Upon seeing the king's pinched expression he added, "Perhaps Da Vinci will paint a masterpiece in your honor?"

The king raised an eyebrow but did not respond. The group sat silent for a moment, waiting for his reaction, but he seemed uninterested in this bit of news.

"The royal wedding," Louis redirected. "We should set a date. What say you, my English princess?" He spied down the long table. "Do you prefer a late summer union or perhaps early fall?"

Everyone paused to hear the princess' reply. Anne anticipated a pretty smile or perhaps a warm nod, but the English princess remained inert, her eyes fixed in the shadows. It seemed she might dare refuse to respond.

Louis turned a deep shade of pink. "Well, out with it woman!"

The English princess blinked her pale gray eyes, still holding her gaze in the corner. "Please yourself, sire."

The vein in the king's forehead throbbed.

"Father?" Claude spoke for the first time. She had been cowering at the far end of the dining table. It was obvious she rarely invited the king's attention. "Perhaps the wedding date could be set for October? It is such a lovely time of year. And the leaves of the oak trees will have turned a shade of amber to match the color of Princess Mary's hair."

Louis shifted his gaze towards his daughter, his eyes full of loathing.

"Did I hear a dog barking?" He sniffed the air like one of his bloodhounds.

Claude's face fell. She pulled her uneven shoulders upwards to affect a straight line and tried again. "Father, the babe comes in autumn too. Perhaps we could celebrate both—your happy union and the birth of your first grandchild. Maybe a boy?"

The king stood up with a clatter, his chair tipping backwards behind him. He moved slowly toward Claude with a menacing gate.

She shrank into her chair as he approached. Then without warning, King Louis snatched up Claude's plate and raised it high in the air. Claude cringed as he threw the plate to the ground. Pieces of pigeon pie and soupy cassoulet smeared across the floor.

The room froze. Courtiers no longer laughed obligingly, nor did the dinner guests.

King Louis spoke now, his voice low and dangerous. "Do *not* address me father, you deformed devil spawn." He spat on the table where her plate had been. "Now go and fetch your food like the dog you are."

He heaved Claude from her seat and threw her pregnant form down upon the mess of food. She fell upon her knees, cradling her belly. She dared not look him in the eye but instead did his bidding, shuffling towards the food along the wall.

The king watched her as she collected her wasted supper. One of the King's hounds snatched a piece of bread from her trembling hands and scurried off with its prize. A look of satisfaction crawled across the king's face.

"Come, Frederique." Louis spun on his heel, gesturing to his small man. "Make haste. I feel a shit coming on. And I shall need my Groom of the Stool to wipe my ass."

PRESENT DAY
QUEEN'S UNIVERSITY, CANADA

T he rain was coming down like a monsoon over the South China
Sea. A clap of thunder split the sky as a gust of wind threatened
to blow my car right off the road.

Despite the torrential downpour, Bernice's yellow clapboard house in
the suburbs looked cheerful. Lacy white curtains framed handsome
windowpanes. The sculpted shrubbery and potted petunias emitted an all-
is-well-with-the-world vibe, except for one little garden gnome who had
fallen over face first in the mud. He looked like he had given up on the
world.

I was greeted by the scent of instant coffee and fresh baked cookies. I
had always loved the smell of Bernice's house. No matter the time of day,
it always smelled of baking. Fresh bread. Chocolate cake. Apple crumble.
And to complement the enticing aroma, a variety of needlepoint pictures
adorned the walls. There was even picture of a polar bear wearing a top
hat and pink tutu.

Despite the peaceful setting, the squabbling arguments of the Titanium Trio could be heard from the foyer. This was common after a
daylong poker tournament or any other day they spent together.

"Gerty, you are in a snit. Does it always have to rain on poker days?
Your tantrums are ridiculous." Grapes scolded her best friend.

"I'm not in a snit," Gerty retorted, hot as a hen. She crossed her thin
arms across her chest and leaned back in her Lazy Boy chair. She was tiny

as a bird, but she was easily the feistiest member of the Trio. Her blue hair took on a darker hue when she was angry.

"Hi everyone," I said.

Three old faces looked up and the argument was forgotten. The prodigal granddaughter had arrived. Neither Bernice nor Gerty had any grandchildren of their own, so I had been the center of attention since I was a kid. It was like having three great-grandmothers instead of one.

"Come over here and give me a nice big hug, darlin'," Bernice chirped from the pink velour sofa.

Her sweater vest was stitched with tiny needlepoint hearts. Bernice was an incredible seamstress even though she was legally blind. The woman couldn't see a damn thing, but it didn't seem to stop her. She had stowed her white cane in the hall closet and refused to use it. "Canes are for old ladies," she always said.

After a series of hearty hugs, things settled down enough to get the news on the latest poker tournament scuffle. In spite of her visual impairment, Bernice always seemed to win the money. Naturally, this was a source of great conflict for the Trio. With Gerty's tempestuous nature, it never took long before accusations of cheating started to fly. From there, the arguments would escalate until after a while Bernice's house became a war zone of yelling and fist waving. I often wondered why they played poker together. After one of Bernice's clean sweeps, they usually didn't speak for days.

"How much did you guys play for today?" I asked.

Bernice pointed to the pile of pennies on the TV tray in front of her. "The usual ten dollar maximum...but when you play with pennies, you can play alllll day."

"And where did Vernon get off to?" I asked, hoping to divert the conversation away from another argument.

The Trio took turns explaining the events of the day. Their stories were always long winded and embellished with ridiculous mistruths, but I enjoyed them anyway. After they covered all the painful details of Vernon's intestinal problems, Bernice explained a complex needlepoint design that required half-cross tent stitches. Gerty reported on Zach's attempts to get into the garbage while no one was looking. The dog lay snoring on a needlepoint dog bed in the corner.

Grapes gave my hand a squeeze. "How was your day dear? Did you get lots done?"

"Yep," I replied tightly. I wasn't thrilled about discussing my academic pursuits with the Titanium Trio. I appreciated their support, I did. But I knew these women too well. A conversation about Anne Boleyn would morph into a discussion about the TV series, *The Tudors*. The three of them binge-watched the show on Netflix a few years back and it set them into a girlish frenzy. Bernice and Gerty had a heart-pounding crush on the actor who played King Henry. They talked about how handsome he was for weeks.

Grapes changed the subject before Gerty could start in about the benefits of muscular men in tights. "Ellie, tell the girls about the plane tickets you found in the basement the other day. That's an interesting bit of news."

I gave Grapes a grateful look and slumped down in the pink velour sofa. It was so safe and relaxing at Bernice's house, I relayed the whole story, right up to my most recent discovery at Kingston Travel.

"It looks like Mom, Dad and Grandma were in London that week. It really calls into question whether or not they died here in Canada."

Bernice swatted the air. "I knew it! I knew something wasn't right."

"The travel agent also said Mom and Dad seemed nervous when they booked their trip. They wanted their hotel reservations booked under alias names. They were supposed to be 'incognito.'"

"You don't say." Gerty whistled through her teeth. She poured a swig of gin in her teacup and threw it back, cowboy style.

Bernice closed her eyes as a memory made its way across her wrinkled face. "Lizzie, do you remember the policeman who came to the door to give us news that day? You know, tall fellow, white hair, with the bushy white moustache. I remember thinking there was something funny about him. Something that didn't feel right."

"I remember." Gerty nodded. Her hair was lighter blue now, no longer the color of storm clouds. "You did say it, Bernice. You said something was fishy. But Ellie and Lizzie were so devastated, we thought it best not to push it."

That day, all those years ago, we were together baking cookies in the kitchen when the police officer knocked on the door. Bernice dropped the cookie sheet and we all knew it was bad. Huddling together on the front porch, the moustached officer gave us the news. Grapes held me tight while Bernice and Gerty circled around us. We stayed on the porch for what felt like forever, the four of us sobbing.

"We figure the three of them took a tumble over the edge of the Baron Canyon. It's a long way down. Very treacherous out there in the back woods," the officer had explained with a strained voice. "We found only these spectacles, their rain coats, and Arthur Wright's wallet."

It was the worst day of my life. It was the day I locked away all my childhood memories and threw away the key. I had kept only my father's glasses, and even those were carefully stowed in a shoebox at the back of my closet.

But our lives did continue. I grew up. I survived. Thanks to these three women. Each in their own way, they guided and taught me. This Titanium Trio became my new little family, never replacing my parents, but determined to create bonds just as strong. We had many special times together. Some were crazier than others, but they were always full of love. Bernice taught me to play the piano, and though I was tone deaf, she never lost her patience. Gerty hosted the pajama parties. The four of us often stayed up all night watching horror movies and eating tubs of chocolate ripple ice cream. One year the Trio even convinced me to join their synchronized swim team, frilly bathing caps and all. Grapes, competitive as always, choreographed a water-wheel maneuver that was impressive even by Olympic standards.

"We've been through a lot. Haven't we, girls?" Bernice sighed, nostalgia hanging in the air.

I swallowed back a lump in my throat. "You want to know the other weird thing I found in Dad's research?"

Bernice squeezed my hand. The Titanium Trio leaned in closer.

"I was reading one of Dad's published papers about unusual naming conventions from the sixteenth century. He was interested in a particular convention where the child takes the mother's name..."

"Like you do in your family," said Gerty.

I was about to continue when her comment stopped me. "Hold on— that's true. I never thought of that."

Gerty nodded, as though it were obvious. "You guys are unique. That's for sure. All the women in your family take the name Bowlan. And if you hadn't noticed, they all take a variation of the name Elizabeth too. I remember you mom and dad discussing it when you were born, before they decided they would call you Ellie, for short. The name has been a part of your family for generations."

"So dad was interested in this 'matriarchal naming convention' because it was part of our family tradition?" I asked.

Grapes nodded. "Your mom helped with his research too. She was the one who did all the tedious tracking of the family trees. She preferred it to her nursing job where she had to be away from you for so many hours in the day."

I sat up straight. This was news to me. "Hold on. Mom was a nurse?"

Bernice smiled with pride, looking into nowhere. "Before you were born, dear. She was a mighty fine nurse. Wasn't she, Lizzie?"

Gerty rocked in her Lazy Boy, her stockings slouched down around her ankles. "That's another thing you didn't know about the Bowlan women. They all have a knack for healing. Your Grapes can put together an herbal tea that will sort you out in a sweet jiffy. Your Grandmother Beth practiced the healing touch. And your mom was a nurse."

"Oh," I said, a twinge of self-pity pulling through me. "But if healing runs in the family, why am I terrible with stuff like that?" Blood and guts had always freaked me out. I could barely manage a hot compress and a Band Aid.

Grapes hugged me now. "You take after your father, dear. You have his inquisitive spirit. You were both intelligent, stubborn, and a little bit high-strung. We've known you would be an academic since the day you were born."

Gerty handed me a shot of gin in a teacup. "We wouldn't have you any other way. Neurotic, stubborn, and perfect!"

Bernice patted my leg. "And you're no more stubborn than any of us. Heck, look at Gerty. She would have sulked for weeks about the poker game if you hadn't come to cheer her up."

"Don't start with that again." Grapes put up her hands like a referee in a soccer match.

I suppressed a laugh. "Okay, Bernice, since we are uncovering truths, here's one for you. How can you win at poker every single time? You can't even see." I nuzzled her with my shoulder.

The Titanium Trio burst into giggles. They were like teenage girls at a high school dance as a new set of arguments broke out in a henhouse squabble of bickering.

"I'll tell you how she wins," Gerty shouted above the laughter. "She cheats!"

PRESENT DAY
QUEEN'S UNIVERSITY, CANADA

L andon Fishburn's *Malleus Maleficarum* was a macabre little book. Written by Dominican clergy in the late 1400s, it had been the authoritative manual for the persecution of witches for over three hundred years. It was the European go-to guide on heretic torture throughout the Middle Ages, and by all accounts it was one of the most horrible examples of female degradation and disempowerment I had ever seen.

I had spent the last several hours reviewing its contents. Given my Type A tendencies, I wanted to make sure I was as thorough as possible. But as I dug into its details, I grew more uncomfortable with the turn of every page.

The most offensive sections dealt with the proper steps for the interrogation and torture of the suspected witch. A woman was to be stripped naked and searched for witch's marks, tortured by any means necessary, and then a confession taken. Finally, the book recommended burning the witch so the evil contained within her organic form could not be interred in the sacred Earth for all eternity.

"Nice book, Fishburn. Very edifying," I whispered under my breath.

After several hours of reading, I had completed my review of the text. The manual was informative about medieval perspectives on witchcraft, but I still hadn't figured out its connection to Anne Boleyn. No matter

how many times I reviewed it, I couldn't see the link. Why had the
director of the History Department given this to me?

The little scar on my hand had started to itch and I gave it a fierce
scratching. In the commotion, I dropped the book on the desk, frustration working its way up my neck. I could feel a headache coming on under
the fluorescents. Every time I closed my eyes to block out the flickering
light, Fishburn's bulging amphibious pupils swam into view.

"Get out of my head, frog face," I growled.

The *Malleus Maleficarum* sat at the edge of the study carrel. I tapped
the book with my pencil, maybe a little more roughly than necessary, and
the book fell to the ground with a loud thwap.

"Shit."

I snatched the book up off the floor. As I wiped the dust bunnies from
its back cover, I noticed a little piece of lined paper that had fallen from
between its pages. Lifting the paper between my thumb and forefinger,
the scrap of parchment dangled in the air like a dead mouse caught by the
tail. In small, neat handwriting, seven names were listed.

> X Agnes Sampson, died 1591, Scotland, confession given,
>   burned alive
> X Walpurga Hausmanrich, died 1587, Austria, confession
>   given, tortured to death and burned
> √ Christenze Kruckow, died 1621, Denmark, confession
>   given, beheaded, buried Fryendale Cemetery, Albory
> X Anna Pappenheimer, died 1660, Germany, confession
>   given, burned at the stake
> √ Anne Boleyn, died 1536, England, written confession,
>   beheaded, buried Tower of London, reinterred to crypt
>   at St. Peter's
> X Rachel Stedeln, died 1400, Switzerland, confession given,
>   hanged and burned at the stake
> √ Giovanna Boannaro, died 1789, Italy, hanged and buried,
>   De Zizo Quarter Cemetery, PAlermo

"What is this?"

I reread the paper again. It was obviously a list of women tried for
witchcraft. Anne Boleyn was among them. And based on what I read, the
trials hadn't gone well for any of them. They had all been killed in horrible, terrifying ways.

The list meant something, but what? Why did three names have check marks beside them while the others did not?

I chewed the pencil with irritation, chipping off yellow paint onto my lips until my brain responded. The electrical circuit switch flipped on and a little light bulb glowed in my mind. The remains of the three women marked with checkmarks lay in consecrated ground. They had not met with fiery deaths like the others. But why would anyone need a list like this? Why would Landon Fishburn care who was burned and who was buried? My brain hit a brick wall.

"Ellie?" Lily's hand on my arm startled me. "Are you okay?"

"Yeah, just frustrated." I growled.

Today Lily was wearing a violent pea green jumper with a billowy white blouse. The large built-in shoulder pads created an odd effect. She looked like a cross between a kindergarten teacher and a football linebacker. Lily put an awkward hand on her hip and stared at me for a while.

"Would you feel better if I told you I found something?" She blinked behind those large glasses. "Something...amazing." Lily's voice was as flat as ever, but I'd never heard her describe anything as amazing before.

"What do you mean...amazing?"

A smile pulled at the corners of her mouth. "I mean *amazing*." This time, the whole smile appeared.

Lily spun on her heels and started back down the book aisle. I had to run to catch up.

"I got to thinking about the books in the Special Collections section of the library. I wondered if they might be of use for your Comp exam. We have a lot of old books from around the world. Many of them are diaries and almanacs authored by women over the centuries. They rarely have a title and are often listed as Author Unknown. That makes them difficult to search, you see?" Lily was unusually verbose.

"Okay?"

"Most of the books in the special collection come from private donations from wealthy families. Often they have a connection to historical figures in European history. Over the years, I've gotten to know books and the families that donated them." Lily finally took a long breath, re-inflating those languishing lungs.

"When you mentioned Marguerite de Navarre the other day, it struck a chord, but I couldn't place the name. It hit me this morning as I was restocking the Greek romances. I almost fell right off my stool. De Navarre was a family name I'd seen on one of the reference sheets for the books in the special collection. I wondered if I could find a clue about Marguerite de Navarre."

"Wow, that's brilliant," I said.

Lily kept walking as I trailed behind her. "I searched the files and found a book. The de Navarre family of France donated it after they had a flood at the Chateau d'Amboise in 1862."

We arrived at the door to the Special Collections room and put on blue overcoats, ugly shower caps and latex gloves. Lily pushed her back into the heavy door, releasing a pocket of compressed, humidity-controlled air. She looked at me over the glasses that had slid down her nose.

"You ready?"

"As I'll ever be!" I grinned like an idiot. I just loved this crazy woman.

She ushered me over to a long steel table beneath a bright light fixture. Disappearing for a moment, she returned, holding a black, damaged leather-bound book that looked ancient. She set it on the table with care.

"I found a grimoire," she whispered.

We stared at the black leather specimen. It lay on the table naked and exposed. It seemed to cower under the bright light, as though it would rather be hiding in the almanacs section with the other books.

"Lil, what the heck's a grimoire?"

Lily's face lit up like a Christmas tree. "A grimoire is a book of spells, Ellie. Magic spells. They were handwritten and fiercely guarded by their owners. Owning one was dangerous. Unless you had need of a grimoire, you didn't want to own a grimoire."

She placed her hand over mine for a moment, brushing over the itchy scar, and gave it a pat. "Now, look at this." Lily opened the front cover, the book's spine cracking under the pressure. The pages were yellowed, and the ink faded. A heavy water mark made its way across the lower edge, buckling the pages along the bottom.

I leaned in to get a better view.

Lily continued with newfound enthusiasm. "The first page of a grimoire always contains a blessing to the book itself. The owner recites this blessing each time she uses its spells. It's a way of making a pact with the book of magic, a way of asking for its protection." She rubbed her gloved hands together. "Now this is where it gets interesting." Lily opened the book to reveal a yellowed page, frayed with frequent use.

Greetings of the Grimoire

I call unto mine booke, thine blessings be,
Steere and comfort, magic adorn.
I pledge mine heart, a pact is sworne,
Marguerite Navarre, my power borne.

I ran a latex-covered finger over the words of the last sentence. "Holy shit, this is the spell book of Marguerite de Navarre?"

"Mmm...hmmm..."

My mind revved as the facts connected in my mind.

"If Anne Boleyn's mentor was a witch...maybe Anne Boleyn was a witch too."

"Mmm...hmmm..."

The silence between us sparked with electricity. "Can we look at it?" I asked.

"Yes, but be careful. It's fragile."

I skimmed the leather cover, trying to find a natural break in the book's spine. A well-worn seam opened to a set of pages titled in the same feminine script. The pages in this section listed a variety of spells: *"A Healing Prayer—for Recovery from Sicknesse," "A Tonic for Truth," "Redirecting Love's Fancy," "Instructionne For the Fire Goddess"* Each page described an incantation or spell. The handwriting was flowing and careful, and each instruction was complex. Phases of the moon, ingredients for elixirs, rituals and procedures. Each spell contained a thorough set of direction that left no room for error. It was clear Marguerite de Navarre had been an exacting woman.

The next page was unlike the others. It bore no title, nor any recipes. An image of a naked man had been sketched inside of a circle and a square. Whoever had drawn this image was skilled, likely an artist. The figure looked like the Vitruvian man from medical textbooks. But on this version, small detailed animals had been sketched across parts of the body. A bull with large horns gored the man's heart, a venomous snake bit into his foot, and a ferret sat at the center of his head.

"What the heck is this?" I asked.

The image of the naked man sat silent on the page, unwilling to share its secrets. I focused on the little rodent drawn on the man's forehead. It seemed to be gnawing the man's skull.

A cell phone in Lily's pocket rang into the empty room.

"Hello?" she wheezed. "Mmmm...hmmm." There was a long pause. "Okay, seven o'clock." She hung up with a swift click.

She turned, her pale cheeks flushing. "Ummm... Ellie, we need to wrap this up for today. I've got to get going." Her voice was still flaccid, but I detected a hint of fluster.

"But Lily!" I protested. Just when things were getting interesting Lily called it quits? This wasn't my Lily-the-librarian. I pointed to the image of the naked man with the weird skull-eating ferret thing, hoping she would change her mind.

But she shook her head. "I have another date tonight. I have to go home and get myself looking...presentable." She gestured to her whole body as if she was unsure if it was even possible. Her hands moved subconsciously to the orange barrettes she wore behind her temples. It wasn't much of a style but it kept the hair out of her face.

She packed up the precious grimoire and I followed her from the humidity-controlled Special Collections room.

"Another big date?" I asked with a pout. Lily, the girl who never left the library, was kicking my butt in the man department.

"Mmmm...hmmmm...." she replied but offered nothing more.

Well, at least one of us had a date—funny looking or otherwise.

PRESENT DAY
QUEEN'S UNIVERSITY, CANADA

The smell of Grapes' Sunday roast cooking was heavenly. It greeted me the moment I walked through the door like a dose of aromatic heroin. Grapes took particular pride in her Yorkshire pudding and homemade horseradish. Every time she made the dish, the Yorkshires came out of the oven golden brown, puffed up high atop the muffin tin. Her horseradish was fiery hot with a tang that kept us coming back for more. We heaped it onto each cut of beef until we were rubbing our eyes and blowing our noses. Grapes had named this impeccable combination of Yorkshire and horseradish, "Heaven and Hell on the Dining Room Table." She made Kleenex the centerpiece for these Sunday night suppers.

"Quit looking at me with those big dog eyes of yours. I already gave you three pieces of fat," Grapes scolded the dog in the kitchen. Zach sat in a puddle of drool.

As Grapes thumped around the kitchen with her strange three-step shuffle, *schlumb-bum, bum...schlumb-bum, bum...*, I made myself useful by setting the dinner table. Grapes was a stickler for Sunday night dinners in the dining room. "Sunday suppers should be fancy," she always said. Each week, I pulled out the good china and set up a candlelight dinner for two.

"Oh Ellie," Grapes called from the kitchen. "Could you stir the chicken noodle soup on the stove? I'm right in the middle of the tricky part of the Yorkshire puddings and I don't want it to suffer."

I advanced towards the stove with caution. This was a most unusual request.

"Are you sure Grapes?" I asked with trepidation. She hadn't asked me to stir anything since I set a pan of scrambled eggs on fire a few years back. The house smelled like an outhouse for months and Grapes had never forgotten it.

Grapes gripped her walker as she plopped fat drippings into each dimple of the scalding muffin tin. "Mr. Kontiki hasn't been well since the dance marathon. Terrible case of the sniffles, I'm afraid. I wanted to see if my chicken soup would fix him up. You need to reach the top shelf and add a few drops of the green elixir. Do it fast. The timing has to be just right."

"But Grapes, what if I ruin it?" I protested.

The broth bubbled away on the stove top, hearty chunks of chicken and potato tossed in the flavescent churning brew. The bottle on the top shelf sat menacingly, daring me to touch it.

"Make sure you stir the broth when you add the elixir. It needs a nice swirl when it's going in," she instructed as she worked on the Yorkshire recipe.

Eager to help, I unstopped the bottle and dumped the contents into the burbling broth. Thick green liquid hit the surface and I stirred with a large wooden spoon. For a second, I thought I had been successful, until I noticed the flames. In seconds, the elixir had ignited in a small green fire on the surface of the soup.

"Grapes!" I shouted. But it was too late. The flames petered out as soon as they had begun. The soup was a dull, ugly gray.

Grapes looked up from between the bars of her walker. Her head was practically inside the oven as she tended to her proud puddings. "Oh dear. I worried that might happen. Were there flames?"

"Yep." I pulled my hands away from the boiling goo on the stove, the little scar itching again. The wooden spoon dripped with phlegmy blobs. "Sorry, Grapes."

She shuffled over to the stove, shooing me away from the disaster. "That's okay. Mr. Kontiki will have to take cough syrup. This is why we have rule #3: Ellie may not—*under any circumstances*—add salt, pepper, or any other spices to the pot."

We recited the rule together.

Grapes gestured to the kitchen chair and I assumed my usual position. I propped up my feet and stayed out of her way. It seemed safer that way.

After more apologies, Grapes dumped the unsalvageable mess into the compost bin and we re-established our happy Sunday night rhythm. Grapes updated me on the latest gossip from the seniors center. She had big plans for the Titanium Trio's contribution to the community bake sale. They were working on plans for the fund-raising contest that would make them the reigning Kingston Charity Champions. Apparently Bernice was working on a special costume for Zach too so he didn't feel left out.

I updated Grapes on my recent library endeavors and more news about Mom, Dad, and Grandma.

"I called the Royal Horse Guards Hotel in England this morning. They confirmed three people checked in to the hotel. But get this... They never checked out. They left their luggage behind and vanished."

"Oh?" Grapes stirred the gravy on the stove.

"The hotel promised to send us their stuff. They've had it in storage all these years." I chewed a fingernail. "The more I think about it, the more I'm starting to believe something bad happened to them. I mean, why else would they leave their things behind and just disappear?"

My great-grandmother stared at the Yorkshires getting fat and full under the intense heat.

"Something must have happened to them in London. Something that stopped them from coming back. Don't you think?"

Grapes eyebrows were dancing. "I don't know, dear. I really don't know."

I screwed up my courage to tell her about the séance. I had been avoiding it for the last few days, but raising it now seemed like the right time. I covered the details of Madame Lazarre and her ridiculous theatrics as she called the spirits from beyond. Then with hesitation, I told her about the sliding wine glass and the unbidden visitor Madame Lazarre hadn't expected.

"A voice said it had a message for me, a message from Beth Bowlan."

Grapes blanched. "You mean my Bethy?"

"I don't think so. She didn't talk like Grandma. But she said...'*Beware the dark mark on your name, we have felt it for many generations. Seek your father's research for answers, among the boxes, unheralded work, hidden within.*'"

Grapes mouth formed the shape of an O. "She talked about the dark mark?"

I continued with my confession. "She said, '*Only a Bowlan among the living can end the curse, to do it the circle must be complete, find the beginning to find the end, and save the life of the man who killed your parents.*'"

"Oh God," Grapes sat on a chair with a thump. "They were murdered."
We sat in silence as the realization sunk in.

Grapes wrung her hands. "Ellie, my grandmother used to talk about a dark mark on the Bowlan name. She told of a mark—a curse—that has been following the Bowlan women for generations. Every woman in the family carries the curse, but for each woman the curse is different. That way it can't be anticipated. It can't be avoided for the next woman in the Bowlan line."

"Oh come on. You don't believe that, do you?" I scoffed, but the hairs on the back of my neck were standing on end.

She nodded. "I do believe it. My grandmother lost all but one of her children in a terrible house fire. Mother lost her brother in a steam train accident when he was only five years old. My own Nathan died in the prime of his life in a printing press accident, and Bethy's husband died in a mineshaft in Sudbury. Then your parents and my Bethy.... I'm telling you, it's the family curse. It must be."

I rubbed my temples. A dull headache was now pulsing through my skull.

Grapes put her wrinkled hand on my own. "I've always worried about what you'll have to face in your lifetime. And what your children will have to face too..."

The creepy feeling from the séance washed over me. Suddenly, I didn't want to talk about this anymore.

But Grapes pressed on. "The voice said the curse could be ended, right? This might be the clue we've been waiting for. Wouldn't you want to end the curse? For your own sake and the sake of your children?"

"I guess." My head was spinning.

Grapes jumped up from her chair, her optimism returning. The snowy white caterpillars were dancing above her eyes. "Think about the message, Ellie.... *The answers you seek are in your father's research, among the boxes, unheralded work, hidden within.*"

I whispered the words from the séance back again until the answer hit me. "Grapes, you're a genius. The word *unheralded* could mean unpublished. It could mean I need to check out Dad's unpublished works."

A smile crossed Grapes' lips. "Yes, that's it, dear. I've been thinking about the last few months leading up to their deaths. Your dad, mom and grandmother were excited about something. A new discovery maybe?"

"So whatever Dad was working on might have taken them to London?" The memory that had slipped out from beneath the attic door in my mind poked at me. My parents had been discussing a new discovery in the kitchen that night.

She nodded. "When they left they said they needed to collect something. Samples was it? I'm not sure but it required both Eliza and Bethy. I thought they were going camping. That's why I assumed they were collecting plant specimens. You know, for making herbal teas."

"I wonder if they found what they were looking for before they...died." My voice caught in my throat.

Grapes patted me on the shoulder. "You've got to go back down to the basement to get the answers." She made her way to the oven and pulled out the Yorkshire puddings. As usual, they were a perfect golden brown. "You keep doing your research and we'll sort this out."

She brought the sliced roast beef to the dining room table, balancing it with the pitcher of gravy and horseradish too. It was amazing what this woman could do with a walker. Zach licked his lips as he watched the meat go by, drool dripping shamelessly on the floor.

Grapes placed the mashed potatoes and a bowl of brown-sugar-cinnamon butternut squash at the center and sat down at the table. Dinner was served.

"I give you Heaven and Hell on the Dining Room Table," she said with most of her usual finesse.

"Looks delicious." I smiled.

"Oh shoot, Ellie. We forgot the most important thing." She gestured to the kitchen with urgency. "We forgot the box of Kleenex."

* * *

Grapes and I spent our Sunday night supper reminiscing about my teenage years. We had become our own little special family by then. I suppressed an embarrassed laugh as I remembered the year the Titanium Trio convinced me to join them in a dance competition. Three old ladies and a skinny thirteen-year-old girl were decked out in black tights and body suits. Bernice had sewn red sequins on our shoes and top hats. The dance routine ended when Grapes did a cartwheel across the stage. Needless to say, we won the contest.

Zach and I had set up in the musty basement again. I was getting used to the gloomy jumble of family junk that lay scattered around the cavernous hole beneath our house. Each blue glass medicine bottle, every macramé plant holder, and even the funky smelling ceramic chamber pot in the corner was part of my history, after all. Zach was as relaxed as ever. He lay on the blue and green family quilt, chewing on his hockey puck.

Upstairs, Grapes had jacked up a 1980's music workout video. She always did aerobics after her Sunday night roast beef dinners. She said it helped with digestion. She cranked out a Cindy Lauper tune, *Girls Just Want to Have Fun,* her voice warbling as she screeched along with the music.

The music was deafening. The basement ceiling bounced up and down as dust bunnies fell onto our heads. I looked at Zach and shrugged. "Yeah, we're weird but you love us. Don't you, bud?"

Zach thumped his tail.

Running a knife along the box marked, 'Arthur's Unpublished Works,' I peered inside. I was pleased to see this box wasn't as organized as the others. It was more like the messy dad I remembered. I grabbed the first few papers and notepads and headed back to the quilt with Zach. I scratched his belly as I examined the first few papers under the light bulb dangling from the ceiling.

"Look at this one, bud. This paper is about Queen Elizabeth. That's interesting, isn't it? She was Anne Boleyn's daughter."

Elizabeth Tudor's Bastard: A Theory and a Model of Care

The private life of Queen Elizabeth the First has been a historic fascination amongst scholars for centuries. As one of England's longest ruling queens, her iconic image as the Virgin Queen—married to her job and her people— has created a pretense of piousness and purity that may be inaccurate. Historical evidence suggests Elizabeth had at least one lover, Robert Dudley, and that she may have had a child by him. This paper details evidence to support this hypothesis. We then propose a possible model of childcare for the unclaimed bastard that would have allowed Elizabeth to play a secret role in the child's upbringing.

"Hmmm... This paper says the good old Virgin Queen Elizabeth was less of a virgin than we thought."

Zach looked up, scandalized by the news.

"Okay, buddy. Let's change it up. How about this yellow notepad? There's something scribbled here."

I gave my wooden HB pencil a good chew as I scanned my father's handwritten notes. I zoomed in when I recognized my mother's name.

- *ELIZA AND BETH MAKING EXCELLENT PROGRESS
  TRACKING THE BOWLAN FAMILY TREE —
  GOING BACK 500 YEARS*

- *ELIZA STUCK — CAN'T GO BACK ANY FURTHER*

- *LOOK INTO HENRI CAREY — HE MAY BE THE LINK*

In my excitement, I kissed Zach on the top of the head. The dog chewed his hockey puck, unimpressed by my discovery. Grapes' music switched to Duran Duran. She sang along to the swoony song, howling every lyric with breathless glee.

Ignoring her warbling voice, I scanned the yellow notepad pages for a while. It all seemed like more of the same, until I came across another name I hadn't expected to see.

- *ELIZA'S WORK OVER 500 YEARS IS ONE OF OUR
  LONGEST SPANNING RECORDS YET*

- *WE NEED A NEW METHOD TO CONFIRM
  ACCURACY OF THE FAMILY LINEAGE*

- *MET WITH DR. IVOR CULLEN, HUMAN GENETICS,
  AT THE CANADIAN GENEOLOGY CONFERENCE
  LAST WEEK. HE SUGGESTED A METHOD OF
  ISOLATING DNA*

- *THE DNA METHOD MAY BE AN EXCELLENT TOOL
  FOR GENEOLOGICAL RESEARCH*

- *CULLEN HAS PROPOSED WE WORK TOGETHER ON
  A PILOT PROJECT TO TRACK THE BOWLAN
  LINEAGE*

"Holy shit, Zach. Dad was working with Ivor Cullen—the human genetics guy? He was the one who wrote the paper called, "The DNA of Witchcraft." Dez gave me that paper at the séance. I had forgotten all about it."

The dog groaned.

I held the notepad up to the light to confirm what I was seeing. The name Ivor Cullen was written in my father's handwriting at the end of the page. It was undeniable.

"Ivor Cullen... Ivor Cullen..." I repeated the name over and over in the darkness. "I wonder what he had to do with all of this?"

VOLUME 3

LITHA

Summer swoons, the Sun stands still
Mother Goddess calls the fire
And the witches dance

"Who pray tell is that?" Claude's voice conveyed a hint of girlish amusement as she peered over the manicured lawns below.

Anne and Claude had spent only a few weeks together, but in that time they had become inseparable friends. Perhaps it was something in Claude's soft-spoken manner that reminded Anne of her sister. Perhaps it was Anne's abounding confidence that helped Claude find a little of her own. Regardless of the reason, they had become a perfect pairing, like a mild wine with a sharp, zesty cheese.

For their summer away, Marguerite de Navarre had sent for books on every subject, Latin and Greek literature, arithmetic, geometry, and science. She had challenged her two students to tackle them all by the end of their holidays. For the last couple of days they had been reading one of Marguerite's engineering favorites, *The Mathematical Principles of Petrus Ramus* and Anne had been thoroughly enjoying the challenge.

More importantly, Marguerite had introduced the girls to the Craft. They had learned about herbs for the making of medicines. Birch bark for pain, frankincense for swollen joints, figwort for burns, and bluebells for truth.

Claude called to Anne again, this time with urgency. "You must come and see this. It is Petrus Ramus' engineering theory come to life."

Anne eased herself from the chaise. "Aren't we supposed to be studying?"

"Just come. Hurry."

Down in the gardens of the Clos-Lucé, Anne spied a twiggy, long-legged man wearing a deep purple night jacket trimmed with gold. The white linen of his nightgown peeked out from the flowing fabric. A rough piece of brown twine tied up a long silver beard.

The old man sat atop the frame of a wooden horse, but two large wagon wheels replaced its legs. He pushed along the ground as he held fast to a set of handlebars. Every several minutes, as he got up enough speed to propel himself forward, he stuck out his gangly legs, screamed with delight, and then slammed his feet back to the ground. Anne thought it was the queerest thing she had ever seen.

"Who on Earth is that?"

Claude put her hand to her lips and stifled a giggle. "I don't know but he looks like an old spider."

The man remounted and set about repeating the same sequence of running, lifting, and slamming. It was a ridiculous spectacle indeed.

Marguerite sailed into the room as the girls continued to stare. "I see you girls have discovered Signor Leonardo Da Vinci, our infamous Italian scholar. He is staying with us this summer at the Clos Lucé. I have been meaning to make introductions."

The man eddied around the garden on his peculiar contraption, urging it forward with as much force as he could muster. For a moment, he seemed to achieve success and his contraption glided across the green lawn, the fabric of his purple robe flowing behind him. A satisfied smile lit his face. It was a look of immense pleasure and Anne found it rather endearing. Her brother always got the same look when he galloped through the forest on his favorite mare.

But the man's face dropped as his machine hit a rock sending his delicate balance askew. His legs bolted outright as he pitched and wobbled. He righted himself for a moment, and warbled again, and then he crashed into the stone wall of the garden. A spray of pink rose petals flew into the air.

"Oh my," cried Claude.

The women raced to his aid. Anne, the most athletic, took the marble stairs two at a time. She was careful not to slip on the polished floors as she flew across the entrance hall and through the heavy oak doors of the chateau. The old man lay still in the grass, staring up at the sky. A set of bright blue eyes peered from behind a couple of scruffy gray eyebrows.

"Monsieur, are you alright?" Anne breathed heavily as she knelt at his side.

The man's eyes met hers, confusion swirling in their depths. Soon his beard began to twitch. "It works!"

Anne furrowed her brow.

Leonardo da Vinci attempted to right himself, his arms and legs as thin as a grasshopper's. "I am all right." He flailed. "Would you be a dear and help me up? My ancient body cannot always keep up with my intellectual exuberance."

Anne was grateful to see Claude and Marguerite arriving. They all went about helping the old man to his feet. It was not an easy task, but once he was righted, he uttered a small cry.

"Oooophhh," he exclaimed. "I fear that is the end of the experiment for today. My body has retired in spite of itself."

"Leonardo," Marguerite announced. "I would like to introduce my two students, Princess Claude of France and Lady Anne Boleyn of England. They both have excellent minds and diverse talents."

Leo winced as he bobbed in greeting but soon a smile made its way across his ancient face.

Anne eyed the apparatus lying on the ground. Its fine wooden surfaces had been carefully sanded, its proportions precisely balanced and exacting. "It is a sad thing you cannot continue with your experiment. 'Tis a most impressive machine you have built," she said.

Leonardo glanced at the contraption on the lawn, disappointment devouring his expression. "I have been working on it for months now, and just when I discover how to propel it forward, I find I have damaged my old body."

Anne moved towards the thing laying in the grass. Its spindles and gears fascinated her. She ran her finger along its smooth round wheels and pressed against its pedals. The wooden tires rotated. Anne smiled. It was a spectacular feat of engineering.

Leonardo shouted to her, "Is it damaged?"

"It looks to be in good order," Anne called back. She picked it up the by the handlebars and walked the contraption back and forth, watching as the wheels rotated in correspondence with the foot pedals. A delicious thought popped into her head. "Signor da Vinci?"

"Mmmmmm?" Leonardo replied despondently.

"Could I try to ride it?" she asked.

Marguerite interjected. "I think that is a bad idea, Anne."

But Leonardo was replenished with youthful ebullience. "Do you think you could, Anne? I should love to see it work."

Anne had never been one to back down from an athletic challenge. With all her years of riding horses, she knew she could master it. She swung her right leg over the frame and pulled her skirts up, fiddling with her dress so the fabric would not impede the pedaling mechanism. Once she was ready, she placed her right foot atop of the stirrup-pedal.

Leo rubbed his hands together, his shoulder injury long forgotten. "You must go fast. This machine requires...momentum."

"I love to go fast," she whispered.

"Then go like the wind," Leonardo said with a wink.

Anne pushed her foot down on the pedal and the apparatus was set in motion. It lurched to the right, but Anne's balance was impeccable. She counteracted the pull with a strong push to the left.

"Faster! Faster!" shouted Leo. "You must go faster!"

Anne pushed with her right foot again, and then with her left. Soon a rhythmic motion streamed through her legs, right, left, right, left, right. All the while, she steered the machine with the wooden handlebars in front.

"Faster!"

Anne pedaled harder. The wind blew hair as though she were on the back of her horse. Tulip beds and marble statues whirred by. Even the clouds in the sky couldn't keep up as she gained speed. Her heart fluttered in her chest as her athletic body urged the machine forward, faster, faster, faster.

"Wheeeeeeeeee!" Anne squealed.

"Wheeeeeeee!" Leonardo echoed back.

After several more minutes of sheer ecstasy, Anne dragged her feet on the grass to slow herself down. She stopped right in front of Leonardo and beamed at him. The group gathered around her, applauding as they delighted in her athletic accomplishment.

Leonardo danced Anne around the lawns, his injury now long forgotten. Anne couldn't help but dance along with him, laughing with delight at his graceful movements.

"Leonardo, perhaps you should take care," Marguerite scolded lightly. "There is rather large goose egg forming on your brow."

Leonardo rubbed at his temple. A purple bruise was making its way across his forehead, an inky dark mound above his left eye that matched the violet of his robes. He stumbled a little and Anne caught him in her arms, placing her arm around his waist to stabilize him.

"Monsieur da Vinci. Perhaps you should sit down," she said as she guided him to the wooden bench among the daffodils.

He plopped on the bench and looked up at Anne. "Thank you, dear. You are a most wonderful rider."

Leonardo took her hands with an indebted smile. She wore no gloves and her sleeves were pushed up high from blowing in the wind.

Leonardo's eye's widened as he took her delicate fingers in his own. "You have six fingers on your right hand."

Anne recoiled her hand under her sleeve, an instinctive reaction. No one had ever been impudent enough to point out her deformity before. She felt every bit a child again, humiliated and ashamed.

But Leonardo took no notice. He brought Anne's fingers up to his nose, peering at the delicate sixth digit as though it was sent from heaven. He wiggled the finger, inspected each of its joints, and tapped on the perfectly formed fingernail.

Marguerite smiled. "I told you she was special."

Anne's eyes widened. She could not believe what she was hearing. This humiliation, this deformity, was being discussed like a great gift. Her thoughts returned to the winter night when she and her sister had accompanied their mother to the half-timber cottage in Hever Village.

"It is perfect," Leonardo whispered.

"Yes, it is perfect. *She* is perfect," Marguerite paused, her voice low. "Do you see now, Leo? She bears the mark. She needs someone to teach her. Someone like you."

Leonardo scratched his forehead. For a time he did not reply. He simply sat transfixed in the garden, eyes closed, humming a little tune. His frail body swayed in the light breeze, his foot thumped along with the music that passed soundlessly across his lips. Anne glanced at the others in the group, but their eyes were glued on Leo.

One thing was for sure. Anne's sixth finger had inspired this man, and for the second time that day, her heart fluttered like a hummingbird taking nectar from a flower. Her sixth finger burned with a prickling red heat.

Finally he opened his eyes and a smile lit his face.

"You are right Marguerite. This is an important sign, indeed. We shall teach them both—together. You and I will tutor Anne and Claude this summer." Leonardo da Vinci got to his feet and flourished a low bow. "And it shall be glorious!"

PRESENT DAY
QUEEN'S UNIVERSITY, CANADA

The sun shone through the window with the promise of a new day. Zach lay beside me in bed in an upside-down-dog position. Grapes and I had agreed to dog sit for a few days while his owners were out of town. I had drawn the short straw, so he was sleeping with me. His legs stood straight in the air as he lay on his back, snoring like a diesel engine. I had covered him with the family quilt from the basement to keep him warm. It was a strange sight. It looked like I was in bed with a coffee table.

In spite of Zach's somnolent distractions, Ivor Cullen's research had held me captive all morning. I chewed my pencil as I sorted through my notes. In the late 1990s, Cullen and his team had been the first to develop the method for isolating human DNA. It was work that would transform genetic science forever. His team built the very first Polymerase Chain Reaction Machine at Cambridge University. Although the machine had been a prototype, its revolutionary technology had become the basic sequencing blueprint for the human genome project in 2000. After that, his publications seemed to double in number and prestige. He published on everything in the field of eugenics from the DNA of genius to the DNA of athleticism.

The article entitled "The DNA of Witchcraft" had been particularly fascinating. It had helped put a number of pieces of the puzzle together. I fiddled with the edges of the crumpled journal and reread its contents for a third time. Cullen claimed to have identified the DNA for witch-craft, the particular genetic sequence that gave witches the ability to harness the power of the universe. His test subject had been Nathalia Vantur, a famous Romanian witch with the powers of prediction likened to that of Nostradamus. The article was rigorous from a methodological perspective, not at all flaky like I might have guessed. Strangely though, after the witchcraft paper, Ivor G. Cullen stopped publishing completely.

A low voice called my name from down the hall.

"Up and at 'em, lazy bones," said Dez as he sailed through my room with a steaming mug of tea. "Grapes sent me up here to drag your ass out of bed. And what the hell is she cooking down there anyway? She's got weird herbs and dried flowers all over the counter."

I looked up from the Ivor Cullen paper, temporarily distracted from my mission. Dez had a backpack slung over one shoulder and a fresh set of purple stains on his fingers.

"Not now, Dez. I'm in the middle of something."

He sat on the edge of the bed and the mattress groaned under his weight. "Come on. I'm heading to the lab. I'll walk you to the library."

I took the steaming cup of Earl Grey from him and tossed the Ivor Cullen paper in his direction. "I finally got around to reading the article you gave me."

Dez smirked at the well-worn pages. "Looks like you've read it several times."

I nodded distractedly.

"I've been poring over it all morning. It turns out Ivor Cullen was working with my father. I found dad's notes in the basement. But I don't quite understand the link between them."

Zach stretched beneath the quilt with a long groan and the coffee table tipped over.

I reached for my laptop, heading straight for Google. If Cullen had been such a big name in genomics there might be a webpage that explained the connection. Better than Zach or Dez could explain it, anyway.

A couple of search terms later, I located a promising website. There was a link that read, 'Ivor G. Cullen, Professor of Human Genetics, Cambridge University wins the Singer DNA Research Award.' Clicking on it, the page arranged itself on the screen and Dez leaned in to see it. A large photo sat in the middle of the text. It was a headshot of Dr. Ivor Cullen, his scruffy hair a mess atop his head. An extra bushy white moustache perched menacingly above his lip. His brown eyes were strange.

The image almost stopped my heart. I brought laptop within an inch of my nose as the moustached man stared back at me.

"Holy shit, Dez. This can't be Ivor Cullen."

Zach popped his head out from beneath the blankets. Dez raised an eyebrow. "Why not?"

"This can't be Ivor Cullen, because this is the police officer who delivered the news the day my parents died."

I jumped out of bed, slippers flying. Dez shouted something behind me as I zoomed down the stairs. In the kitchen Grapes was singing old show tunes. She didn't glance up from the onion she was cutting.

"Good morning, sleepy head. I'm making omelettes this morning. Gonna be goooo—oood."

"Grapes, you've got to see this." I ushered her hands away from the pile of chopped onions. "Do you recognize this guy or am I going crazy?"

Dez and Zach arrived in the kitchen as Grapes was wiping the tears from her eyes. We all gazed at the screen. It took a second for Grapes to make the connection but when she did, she took a step back.

"My heavens, that's the policeman." Her voice was hollow.

"I know—right?" I arranged the laptop so we could all see it better. "The white hair and the bushy moustache are the same...but the eyes are the dead giveaway. He has the same strange glare, doesn't he?"

Grapes nodded. She looked as though she had seen a ghost.

"Ellie," Dez asked with exasperation. "What the hell is going on?"

I shook my head, trying to find a way to explain it.

"Look." I stumbled. "This isn't a photo of the police officer who came to the house when I was a kid. This is Dr. Ivor G. Cullen, professor of human genetics from Cambridge University. He was studying the DNA of witchcraft."

A shadow passed behind Grapes' eyes. "Sorry, did you say the DNA of witchcraft?"

I nodded. "Yeah, but here's the weird thing. This researcher was also collaborating with Dad to map out the Bowlan family tree."

A hush fell over our group as we processed the news. I plopped a bowl of kibble on the floor for Zach in the meantime. A puddle of drool had formed around his food dish and if I didn't feed him, the kitchen linoleum would become a slippery mess.

After a while, Grapes shook her head, her coifed white hair helmet frazzled. "I just don't understand."

"Me neither," I said. "I mean, why would this guy masquerade as a policeman? The same policeman who gave us the news about their deaths. Grapes, do you think Ivor Cullen is the murderer?"

She gripped her walker tighter than usual. "Maybe we should go to the police?"

Dez nodded. "Yeah, El. The police need to know about this. It's getting a bit too weird."

I stared at the screen again. The resemblance was uncanny. I was certain it was the same man. But at this point, we had no real evidence. And I wasn't ready to explain the whole bizarre story to the police without a glimmer of proof.

"No police yet. What would we to tell them? That we found a picture on the internet of someone who looked like a police officer that came to our door more than ten years ago? That's not much to go on."

"No." Grapes' snowy white caterpillars danced. "It's not much to go on."

"I don't know, you guys." Dez said with hesitation. "I think the cops could help."

I shook my head. "Let's wait and see if we can find any more information. Right now, it's all too crazy to believe."

We stared at the screen a moment longer. Ivor Cullen stared back. His eyes were cold, perhaps even a little dangerous. Worse than that, his eyes were familiar. A shiver walked its way up my spine.

PRESENT DAY
QUEEN'S UNIVERSITY, CANADA

A s I ran along Lake Ontario, I tried to shake the creepy feeling that had been growing inside me all morning. I had managed to ditch Dez by suggesting he fix the flashing blue light on Grapes' VCR. It had gone wonky a few days ago and I knew Dez loved techy antiques. In the meantime, I had been able to escape for a run.

In spite of my intense pace, my nerves were still frazzled as I rounded the bend on Water Street. It didn't help that I was planning to go out for lunch with beautiful, athletic John this afternoon. He had called last night to ask if we could compare notes for our Comprehensive exams. It had seemed like a good idea at the time, but as I ran along limestone shoreline, I was regretting that I had said yes.

Over the course of my university career, I had only three boyfriends. The first was a football player, and I loved his athletic body. About six months into our relationship, he asked if I would consider a ménage-a-trois. Needless to say, that relationship ended swiftly. My second boyfriend was a body builder, and I adored his huge muscles. But that relationship went the way of the dodo when I realized he was more interested in his illegal steroid drug business than his actual business degree. My third boyfriend was a basketball player. He was only available on Tuesday and Thursday nights. It took me almost a year to realize that on the other days he had to be home with his wife and kids. After that, I decided to give up on men.

The run felt particularly awful and by the time I arrived home, I was a ball of nerves. Dating brought out the worst of my Type A personality. I couldn't help but overthink every detail. What to wear? What to do with my hair? How much mascara to apply?

After a quick shower, I threw on a rumpled red hoodie and a pair of tights. I passed on the makeup entirely. My sweatshirt had a stain on the shoulder and I wiped at it, hoping it would just go away.

"How do I look?" I asked the dog.

Zach brought me his hockey puck. The drool from the little orb left a slimy smear on my pants.

I eyed the black lab and instantly felt a little better. Zach was too chubby for his stout frame. His ears were crooked and his red collar frayed. The "Z" on his name tag had fallen off, and it now read "ACH." But his brown eyes were loving and his pink slobbery tongue gave his lips a certain grin when he held the puck in his mouth.

"Come on, bud," I announced. "We're going on a date."

Zach and I made our way to the student center in the heart of the university campus. A riotous group of first-year frosh filled the lobby, chanting sophomoric school songs for all the world to hear. Beautiful John sat on a bench, wearing an amused expression beneath a large sign reading, "Go Gaels Go! Homecoming Weekend—Coming Soon!"

John gave me a friendly wave and then broke into a serious grin when he saw the Zach. The dog had that effect on people. He sniffed his way through the crowd, his bushy tail wagging as we approached.

John wore a pressed blue button-down and a pair of khakis. He was tall and chiselled like a Greek god. The sun had bleached his sandy hair and his eyes were an awesome amber color—not quite green and not quite brown, but flecked with gold. He was cuter than all three of my previous boyfriends put together.

Zach sniffed John's crotch. A good sign.

"This is Zach. We are dog-sitting," I said stiffly.

John didn't seem to notice the beads of sweat on my lip, nor the stain on my shirt. Instead, he became engrossed in a boyish game of hockey puck tug-of-war.

"Hey bud," said John. "What's that you've got there."

Zach dropped his hockey puck at John's feet, and he threw it through a wall of students in a riotous game of fetch.

"Oooops," said John.

"Uhh..." I said awkwardly as Zach took a girl out at the knees. "Maybe
we should go."

We settled on a restaurant with a dog-friendly outdoor patio. A pretty
blond waitress with lots of cleavage appeared with our menus and gave
John an overzealous smile. She flirted with him for a while, giggling at
every word he uttered. She even folded a paper napkin into a butterfly-
shaped origami and wrote her phone number on it. When she left, my
cheeks were burning.

John looked at me with a smirk.

"What?" I said sharply. My tongue felt fat again and I chewed on it to
try to force it into action. I sat there looking like a piece of pink bubble
gum ready to burst.

He glanced down at the tablecloth and played with his fork. "It's just
that I have a lot of questions for you."

"Like what?" I didn't mean to, but I came off sounding defensive.

John only seemed amused by my reaction and relaxed into his chair. He
put his large arms behind his head and held my gaze for a while. "Like...
where were you when I called last night? It sounded like you were at a keg
party."

I laughed, forgetting my nerves for a second. "Oh no, I was in the
basement doing research. Terrible phone reception down there. My
Grapes was upstairs doing aerobics. She likes to crank out Duran Duran."

His brow creased. "Sorry, did you say grapes?"

"Yeah. Grapes is my ninety-three-year-old great-grandmother. She
swears physical fitness keeps her alive. She works out every day...yoga,
aerobics, Kung Fu..."

John's face was hard to read, but I worried I had divulged too much
information. I had a habit of rambling when I was nervous.

"Your great-grandmother's name is...Grapes?"

I swirled the ice cubes in my water glass. "Yeah, I've called her Grapes
since I was a kid. In my family, it was important to differentiate between
my grandmother and my great-grandmother. When I was little, it came as
out *grape*-grandma. It got shortened to Grapes over time...." I tried to stop
talking but once my tongue had been set in motion, it just kept going.
"Grapes says she likes the nickname. She thinks it makes her sound like a
hipster."

I noticed he was watching me with those incredible amber eyes.

"Pretty dumb, huh?" I shrugged.

He gave me another hard-to-read look. "Actually, my family didn't do nicknames. Mom and Dad didn't believe in them. They thought they were...unnecessary," he said.

My cheeks flushed. I felt like an idiot. I was acting like a big weirdo. A big weirdo with a weirdo family.

"Oh, I didn't mean that as an insult, Ellie. I've always liked that sort of stuff. People with nicknames always come from cool families. My parents are really straight and narrow. You know the type...really boring...and kind of beige."

The waitress reappeared, this time with a bowl of water for Zach. She made gooey eyes at John again and tossed her long blonde hair over her shoulder. Even the way she held her pen was sexy. John ordered three grilled chicken sandwiches, an extra-large salad, and a baked potato. I ordered a slice of pizza.

Now it was my turn to raise an eyebrow. Who ordered three chicken sandwiches in one sitting?

John noticed my expression and blushed for the first time. He folded his massive arms across his chest. "I play a lot of rugby. It really burns up the calories."

I glared at the waitress as her voluptuous rump disappeared behind the door to the kitchen. To my surprise, John paid her no notice. Instead, he balled up his custom-made origami butterfly and tossed it playfully at me.

In spite of my jitters, we settled into a nice conversation. We found a natural rhythm discussing our Comprehensive exams and the fact our topics were acquainted. Before I knew it, I found I was enjoying myself. There was something incredibility sexy about talking to a muscular jock who was brimming with intelligence and not just brimming with testosterone.

"Marguerite de Navarre is the perfect case study for my Comp," John said with gratitude. "She really was the first modern woman. She even wrote a book called *The Heptameron*." He fished a rumpled text from the bottom of his bag. "Marguerite wrote these stories based on the actual events of her life. Apparently, she removed the real names of her characters before publishing."

I peered at the dog-eared book from across the table.

John dragged his chair around and sat beside me. "Here, let me show you my favorite story." As he leaned in, I could smell his aftershave. It was soapy with a hint of musk with a little fresh-mowed grass for good measure.

Redirecting Love's Fancy

It was on this day a comely princess could be found sitting at her armoire, a single tear running down her lovely cheek. The princess was a beautiful woman who was admired by all the court. But her most resplendent attribute was her heart, for she had the heart of angel, so kind that no one could find even its slightest flaw.

The princess had married her prince not but a year ago. They fell in love and she became pregnant with his child. But during her summer away, her husband's heart strayed. This is a tale of broken hearts and a husband's straying fancy. More important, this is a tale of how three women set things right...

"Yeah, it's a love story. I am a sucker for love stories," he admitted. Then, as if recreating a level of machismo, he added, "But they do magic in it too. It's right here. The three witches use a love potion on the prince."

Together the women brewed a love potion so pure and intoxicating it could sway even the darkest of hearts. That night, the three women stole into the prince's rooms and gathered around his bed. The first friend called upon the moon to redirect love's fancy and send the prince's heart back to the princess. The second friend poured the love elixir into the prince's sleeping mouth. And the princess herself kissed the prince upon his cheek and begged him to love her again.

After reading the story together side-by-side the waitress arrived with four meals. She arranged three plates in front of John and then threw a slice of pizza at me.

John launched into his first chicken sandwich with zeal. With one bite, he devoured almost the whole thing. I watched him with fascination as he swallowed it and dove into his second. It was like watching someone in an eating contest. He sucked in food like an overzealous vacuum cleaner. The way he stuffed his face made me laugh. He reminded me of Zach when he got into the garbage. He had this loveable, half-crazed look about him.

"I have my own Marguerite de Navarre secrets to reveal, you know..." I said playfully, finally relaxing a little.

John gave me a look of interest between bites.

I nodded and threw my hair over my shoulder the way the waitress did, sexy-style. "Yesterday, in the library, we found the grimoire of Marguerite de Navarre."

"Whrolly cow, whratz a gremour?" John asked with a bite of sandwich stuffed in his mouth.

"A grimoire is a book of spells." I leaned in with dramatic flair. "So it looks like your favorite proto-feminist was also...a witch."

John's eyebrows shot up between chews.

"I'm going to take a look at it this afternoon at the library if you want to join me?"

John stopped chewing. "I'd love to."

We fell back into more pleasant conversation. John was busy eating so I did most of the talking. We moved from academic topics to the latest news on my parents' murders and finally on to more personal stuff. I told John stories about my childhood I hadn't allowed myself to think about for years. I told him about the time I fell off the stage during a ballet recital when I was six. I told him about the zombie-chicken costume my mother made me for Halloween when I was nine. I told him about the science fair experiment that Dad and I worked on, and the small explosion in the basement that followed.

Through it all, John wolfed back sandwiches and listened with interest. After twenty minutes, he had finished all three chicken sandwiches, the salad, and the baked potato. And I had run out of stories.

"Sounds like you have a terrific family." He slid a piece of crust under the table to Zach.

"*Had* a terrific family," I said. "They died when I was eleven, remember?"

"Yeah." He paused. "But you still have your Grapes, and anyone who does aerobics to Duran Duran is okay in my books. You guys are definitely not beige."

I blushed again. "Sometimes I wish we were more...beige."

John wiped his mouth with a napkin. "No way. You will never be beige. You're more like..." He thought for a second and gave me a sexy half-smile. "You're more like fire engine red—complete with flames."

* * *

"Geez, how many floors below ground are we?" asked John as we descended into the bowels of the library.

I had never brought another person down to the stacks, not even Dez, and I hoped John thought it was as great as I did. As we headed down the stairs, Zach charged ahead, making a beeline to the bottom floor. He knew where he was going and exactly who he was going to visit.

When we arrived, Zach and Lily were already engaged in their own peculiar reunion. It was the same ritual every time. Zach wagged his tail and barked madly, turning in circles in a bizarre doggy dance. Lily spoke to him in a high-pitched Elmo voice.

"Yes you are my friend, Zachy...yes you are my friend, Zachy..."

We watched as Lily put Zach's slobbery hockey puck in her mouth. She growled at the dog and lunged around the room. Zach assumed the puppy pose.

"Hey, Lil," I called out, hoping to put a stop the embarrassing game before it escalated. I didn't need John thinking we were any more weird than he already did.

Lily removed the hockey puck from her mouth and wiped the dog drool from her lip, her face sinking like the Titanic.

"Hello," she said stiffly.

I made introductions, but the exchange was incredibly awkward. Lily was acting as though I had invited a guest to her house for dinner without letting her know. As the names and how-do-you-do's were exchanged, Lily's glare was as hard as a boiled egg.

"Great place you have here," John joked.

Lily didn't reply.

She stood with her arms gripped across her chest as John made attempts at conversation. Zach was the only one who seemed happy. He stuck his head inside the garbage can beside Lily's desk and helped himself to a bit of leftover soup.

In an effort to clear the tension, I opted to get down to business. "I was hoping we could look at the grimoire you found yesterday?"

A pause hung like a hangman's noose as Lily considered my request. It was even worse because of the snorting and licking noises emanating from the garbage can. After a good hard squint, Lily acquiesced.

"Mmmm...hmmmm..."

She grabbed three gowns, latex gloves, and shower caps and headed for the door.

"You have to stay here..." said Lily, Elmo-style, and planted a kiss on Zach's muzzle. "No doggy-woggies in the Special Collections room."

We snapped on the gloves and gowned up. Despite the fact that John wore a blue coat and shower cap, he was still handsome as hell. Lily gave the door a shove and the pressure inside the Special Collections room gave way.

"I had no idea this place existed," whispered John.

I smiled. "Why are you whispering?"

"I don't know," he whispered back with a goofy grin.

Lily returned with the precious grimoire, cradling it in her arms like a newborn child. She laid the book flat on the table and stood back with hesitation.

"Lily's the one who found the grimoire, and it's definitely Marguerite de Navarre's," I said, pointing to the blessing on the first page. "See? *I pledge mine heart, a pact is sworne, Marguerite Navarre my power borne.*"

John turned his amber gaze upon Lily. "This is incredible. Lily, how did you find it?"

She didn't answer his question right away, but it was apparent she appreciated his acknowledgement of her bibliothecarial brilliance. She pulled a third chair up to the steel table.

Now in her element, Lily walked John through the key aspects of the grimoire and relayed the story about how she had come upon it in the unmarked almanacs. It was amazing to watch him work on Lily, the girl who was terrified of men. He asked all the right questions and demonstrated the right amount of interest. He even managed to get her to smile once or twice. To my relief, it wasn't long before the awkwardness of our threesome was forgotten.

Lily, John, and I found our own rhythm while poring over the text. We scanned each section with intensity. Fascinating potions, incantations, and rituals filled the pages of the grimoire.

"Look at this one," said John, his own inner-nerd shining through. "It's a love potion... *Redirecting Love's Fancy*... This is how Marguerite described the love spell in *The Heptameron*. With the three witches and the kiss... Remember Ellie?"

Redirecting Love's Fancy

Construct this amorous potion during the last quarter of the moon, and call the spell when the waning gibbous hangs low in the night sky. Take caution. Effects are immediate and intense.
One part clear water, taken from a spring that runs by the roots of an ancient oak
One part red claret, brewed with Benedictine grapes crushed by snakestones
Four leaves of fresh green basil, two daisy petals, and a sprig of white jasmine
One skinned Althea root and the Balm of Gilead
One drop of virgin's blood, taken from the tip of the finger

I held the spot on the page and tapped it with my pencil. "I guess that makes sense. Marguerite wrote *The Heptameron* based on events from her own life. She probably used this recipe from her grimoire to conjure the love potion."

A boyish grin made its way across John's face. "I wonder who the lucky guy was she used the spell on?"

I smiled back. "I wonder what the *immediate and intense* effects were..."

As we moved on to new parts of the grimoire, John was careful to acknowledge Lily's ideas. After all she was the one who discovered the text. The afternoon melted away with enthusiastic discussions boiling up out of every new incantation. Lily was the one to identify the next big find.

Instructionne for the Fire Goddess.

For the true daughter of Prometheus no incantation is required
No ritual is of need
The true daughter of Prometheus is marked by her hand
And lives by her magic in instinct alone.
The Fire Goddess need only to feel the fire within her belly
And feel the heat upon her skin
And when she wills a thing burn
It will burn for her unquestioningly.

"Do you think Marguerite was referring to Anne Boleyn? She was marked by her hand with her sixth finger, remember?" asked Lily.

Her flaccid voice hinted at the inspiration that was working its way through each of us. We were on to something here, and we all knew it. The little scar on my hand itched like crazy, and I rubbed it on my tights to get rid of the sensation.

A crash in the next room broke the spell, drawing our attention away from the magical grimoire. Following the clatter, a ferocious barking rang through the space, vibrating the Plexiglas barrier with seismic ripples.

"Zach?" I gulped.

The three of us jumped from our seats and shuffled to the exit. John gave the heavy door a push and we spilled from the Special Collections room into the main part of the library.

Zach stood near Lily's desk, his four legs braced for combat. His lips were pulled back along his muzzle, exposing a set of sharp incisors and the pink of his gums beneath. He snarled like a wild animal defending his territory. When the dog noticed us standing there, he began pacing back and forth, hackles raised. He lowered his growl but he kept his eyes trained on the exit.

"What's happening?" asked Lily, looking panicked.

John and I searched the perimeter of the room and down each book aisle. Rows of texts sat undisturbed. The fluorescent lights pulsed with their usual headache-inducing cadence. A few stacks of papers had fallen off a library cart, but otherwise, nothing was out of place.

"Zach just freaked out. I've never seen him do that before," I said.

John smoothed the hair along the dog's spine. "It's almost like he scared off an intruder. But who would want to break into a library?"

Zach was still agitated. His growl had become a nervous whine as we continued our inspection. Lily's desk was untouched. Her orange purse hadn't been disturbed. An old coffee cup sat beside her computer screen filled with miscellaneous pens. The library looked the same as always. Dingy, old, and boring.

The dog settled down a bit as I scratched his hackled scruff.

"Maybe I should take him home," I said.

John rubbed Zach's ears now too. "I can do it, Ellie. I need to get going now anyway."

"But..." I resisted.

John waved off my concern. "I know where you live, remember? I'll drop him off at your house. It's no problem."

I glanced at Lily. She had dumped the pens onto the desk and was inspecting each of them as though they were her beloved children. As much as I wanted to take Zach home, I knew I couldn't abandon Lily down here in the stacks.

"Okay, thanks, John. I'll stay here with Lily...just in case."

Anne wandered along the fresh green lawns of the Close Lucé. The freestone dovecote set against the deep blue sky was the perfect summer home, inviting and quaint. Fields of red poppies surrounding the manse swayed in the obliging wind, filling the air with a gentle peppered fragrance.

Blocking the sun with the back of her hand, Anne gazed up at the chateau. From her position in the gardens below, she could see a bearded man dressed in white robes pacing in a second story window. Leonardo was no doubt working on some new experiment.

A black cat wound its way around Anne's legs, its tail curled along the inside of her bare calves. The women had abandoned their shoes and stockings that summer, many thanks to Leonardo da Vinci. Most days the old man didn't even bother to change into day clothes, preferring the flowing fabric of his nightgown. He had encouraged Claude, now ripe with child, to do the same. This led to a slow but happy degradation of the formality normally surrounding members of the upper class. No rules could contain them that summer. Nothing could dissuade them from two marvelous things, the pursuit of learning and the pursuit of fun.

She and Claude had spent the last few weeks learning the basic tenants of magic and its guiding laws. Marguerite emphasized the laws of magical rites and the principles associated with worship. Leonardo pointed to the feminine presence in everything around them. They payed homage to the divine mother by teaching their young apprentices how to direct the course of action, emotion, energy, and life. And Anne felt more alive than ever.

Anne scooped up the cat and scratched him behind the ears. "Come on, Salai, you little devil. Leonardo will wonder where you have gotten off to."

The house was cool in the quiet of the morning. Not even the servants stirred in the kitchens below. Before she could set her basket of bluebells upon the chaise, a riotous crash from above shook the floorboards. A great waft of dust exhaled from the study on the second floor. Anne heard Claude giggling.

"Leo! It took us days to inventory those books. Why, pray tell, were you standing upon them?" Marguerite clucked.

Anne raced up the grand staircase, two steps at a time, and plopped Salai on the floor.

Leonard sighed. "I could not wait to begin our lesson. I grew so impatient, I attempted the experiment by myself."

Anne looked around at the freshly destroyed study. Dozens of leatherbound books covered the hardwoods. A rainbow of aristocratic reds, erudite yellows, and monastic blacks had exploded from the corner of the room.

"But now that Anne has arrived, we can begin." Leonardo clapped his hands.

He gave Marguerite a knowing glance and encouraged the girls to settle in. Marguerite, too, wore the look of swollen anticipation. Clearly they were both excited about today's lesson. Leo stroked his beard, deep in thought, as if trying to decide where to begin.

Anne plopped herself down on a cushion and crossed her legs with girlish flexibility as Claude eased herself into the chaise and rubbed her stomach.

"It was a hawk that forms my earliest childhood memory." Leo raised a finger. "I was in a crib—a white one. The window was open and on the railing sat the magnificent creature. The bird jumped onto the blankets beside me, his tail feathers brushing my lips. 'Twas a most fascinating sensation." Leonardo laughed. "For years I have seen this hawk in my dreams. For years I have wondered what blessed this animal with flight."

Claude and Anne exchanged glances.

Leo waggled his eyebrows at the girls. "Flight! That is what we shall tackle today." He gestured to the designs on the large drawing table. "I have created a blueprint for a flying machine. Do you see how the upper surface of the wing curves to create a lower pressure beneath? This will give the apparatus the lift it requires to soar through the sky like a bird."

Marguerite joined in. "Yes flight. 'Tis a fascinating thing. But for a witch, it can also be conjured through magic. Engineering and magic. Today we will teach you both. Today you shall learn how to fly."

"Won't it be dangerous for Claude?" asked Anne.

Leonardo pulled the girls from their seats and arranged them along the outer rim of the room. He pointed a long finger at Marguerite. "You shall both be fine. But you must watch the demonstration carefully."

Marguerite made ready at the center of the room. Taking a long breath, she folded her arms across her chest and stared down at the floorboards, deep in concentration. She exhaled, closed her eyes, and within seconds, Marguerite's toes lifted off the ground. She glided upward, no longer constrained by the Earth's natural forces. She floated up, up, up, until she almost touched the ceiling. Once fully airborne, Marguerite looked down upon the others and flourished her hands.

"For a witch, flight is as simple as a wish," she said.

Anne staggered back, her mind refusing to believe what her eyes beheld.

Marguerite instructed her pupils as she hovered above, her form hanging weightless in the air. "It's a basic skill, acquired with patience and practice. One must request the Goddess' release from the Earth and use one's concentration to create a physical space between the ground and the body. Most witches can accomplish it without too much trouble."

Now Leonardo, too, drifted up into the rafters with ease. His toes dangled from beneath his long linen nightgown as he moved to meet Marguerite in the center.

"Marvellous, isn't it?" He laughed.

Marguerite sailed across the room, taking care not to hit her head upon the lower cross beams in the roof. "Alright, you two. I want you to make room between yourselves. And watch out for the books on the floor."

Anne and Claude hurried to make space between themselves. Leonardo did pirouettes in the air, providing a bit of good humor as the girls readied themselves for their first flying effort.

"You must first ask the Goddess for your release from the Earth." Marguerite paused, making sure they both understood. "'Tis a simple prayer, whispered in your mind's eye."

"Keeper of air, divinity's gain

Maker of wind, snow, sun, and rain

Release me, I beg, from thy earthly plane

My Goddess to cherish from back and again."

Anne took a deep breath and tried to channel the Goddess, to swallow her in, like her mother had instructed all those months ago. To her surprise, it was as instinctive as breathing. Soon, a familiar whir of energy washed through her as she whispered the simple prayer. She focused on the floorboards and pushed her body, light as a feather, away from the ground.

It took a few tries, but on the third attempt, she sensed a mild ping, as light as the snap of a thread. And with it, her release was cast. Anne's feet lifted inches from the hardwoods. The sensation changed in the bottoms of her toes. Rather than a perceptible pressure from the floorboards, her feet tingled with that same fluttering energy that surged within her belly.

"There now," Marguerite encouraged. "Anne has got it."

Anne pushed a little more against the ground as she glided upward to the ceiling. She dared not look away from the ground for fear she would fall. But the sensation was so thrilling, so intoxicating it made her squeal. She was free for the first time from the Earth's bonds, and it felt wonderful. She was as weightless as a cloud in the sky, as atmospheric as a ghost on the moors, as buoyant as a boat on the ocean. Her skin tingled with cool lightness and her hair swirled around her head.

"Well done, Anne." Marguerite praised.

Claude's small feet lifted from the ground now too. She giggled as she floated upwards to join her friends, cradling her belly with care.

"Excellent work, Claude." Marguerite applauded.

As Claude rose through the air to meet the group, she took Anne's hands in hers. They hovered above the floorboards, unable to believe what was happening. Another giggle escaped from Claude's lips. Anne laughed too, delighted by the sensation of hovering in the air. But hers was not a giggle. Hers was a hearty laugh and it was contagious. Before Anne knew it, the others had joined in, alive and energized as the magic surged through them. It was a moment of pure euphoria, of complete and utter happiness.

From below, the door to the study flew open with a clatter. The heavy oak banged hard against the back wall. Rose stood in the doorframe, breathless and alarmed. She glared into the rafters, arms folded across her chest. She marched over to the group suspended in the air and frowned.

"Yoo four get down from there!" she shouted, putting her hands on her hips.

The laughter petered out.

"I mean it!" Rose stomped her foot. "It's bad enough yoo've been prac-tising this unnatural sorcery all summer. It is bad enough the lot of yoo've been traipsing round in your undergarments all night and day. But this flying business, I cannot abide by. Yoo've got a pregnant one up there with you! What'll ya do if she falls?"

Leonardo was the first to return from the rafters. He looked every bit the schoolboy caught red-handed, head lowered, shoulders hunched. The others followed. Their game was up.

Rose gathered another storm of scathing upon her tongue. "Now I luv ye, Anne. Yoo know that. And I'll do anything for ye. But yoo four need to take more care. The servants are startin' to talk. I would ne'er be able to explain this away, if you'd been seen."

She glowered at the group, eyes bulging, lips pursed. It made no differ-ence she ranked lowest among them. At this moment, she was a mother hen and they her ill-mannered chicks.

Marguerite cleared her throat, smoothing the folds in her skirt as she attempted to regain her composure. "You are right Rose. We must take more care. Leonardo and I have become complacent at our summer retreat. 'Tis not as safe as we pretend it to be."

Rose cocked her eyebrow. "Bloody right! And we all know that word getting round of yoo bein' witches would be the end of us. Lord knows what they'd do." She dropped her voice in warning. "I heard tell of a woman tried for witchcraft in these parts. They had her sit the Judas Chair for two days before they drew a confession. 'Twas a bloody affair. Split her almost right up the middle. Lord have mercy that."

The truth of Rose's words hung heavy in the room. The group had become careless and cocksure. Anne remembered her mother's words and a little shiver passed through her. *Witches are killed. Witches are burned.*

"You are right Rose," said Anne. "We shall take more care."

Rose placed her hands on her hips again. "I mean it, yoo lot. I don't want to hear any more about your strange behavior. I don't want to see any more potion making or spell casting." She wagged a chubby finger. "And no more flying. That's final!"

PRESENT DAY

QUEEN'S UNIVERSITY, CANADA

A piece of lemon bobbed in my Earl Grey tea like a cheerful yellow fish. I stared at it resentfully before taking another long sip. The lemon was tasty, but it had done nothing to improve my massive headache. My brain banged against the back of my eyeballs like a jack-hammer on a killing spree. I popped a Tylenol and took another lemony gulp, closing my eyes against the pain.

Ever since this Comprehensive exam had begun, my nightmares had gotten worse—as had the headaches. It was bad enough that every night I had to watch the same disturbing images of Mom and Grandma with a loaded revolver at their heads. But the nightmares had become even more terrifying. Now the dreams were interspersed with flashes of a medieval woman with dark eyes and a strange white ferret. She stood in a darkened room amidst a terrible bone-melting, soul-incinerating fire. Most mornings I woke up soaked in sweat.

The dreams were always confusing. I could make no sense of how the fire started nor why my guts boiled at the sight of it. But I knew who the woman was. Her portrait adorned the wall here at the Sleeping Goat Café, and this morning, I had come to face her.

I headed straight for the da Vinci painting, *Lady with an Ermine*. Glancing around the room to check no one was watching, I prepared for a good long stare. The medieval lady gazed into the corner of the canvas with those dark mysterious eyes. Even at this angle, I could see she was the spitting image of the woman in my dreams. And to my dismay, she was the spitting image of me.

Who are you? I asked her silently. She had my long dark hair. Her nose was a little too long and her cheekbones were high, just like mine. But it was her dark eyes that amazed me. They were *my* eyes. I gazed at them every day in the mirror. Why hadn't I recognized myself in this woman the first time?

"Who are you?" I asked her again, this time aloud.

At my question, the medieval woman turned her head and locked eyes with mine. For a split second, I thought I saw her blink.

I gave my head a shake, sweat breaking out under my arms. This was a bad sign. Dez's comments about my impending nervous breakdown rang through my ears. I leaned in closer to verify it had been a trick of the light. The woman shifted her gaze until we were nose-to-nose. I could almost feel her breath upon my lips.

Then, to my horror, she whispered, *"Burn him...Ellie."*

I stumbled back from the painting, attempting to gather my wits about me. I had suffered sleep deprivation before but never had it resulted in hallucinations. I put my hands over my eyes to block out her image, but the woman's voice rang again in my ears.

"Burn him, Ellie," she whispered with urgency.

I spun on my heel, ready to flee. My throat was starting to close and I wanted to get ahead of the panic attack before it got the better of me.

"It's like looking at yourself in a mirror, isn't it?" Mindy's perky voice behind me was unmistakable. "You two could be twins. Now do you see the resemblance?"

I turned to find Mindy and Tattoo-Carl admiring the painting too. This morning they sipped coffee from their oversized goat-horned mugs. Of all the days I would have preferred to be alone, this was one of them, but the two of them stood there like long-lost friends. I could tell Mindy was itching to give me a hug.

"Yeah," I fumbled. "She does look like me—a bit."

"Ah ha! I knew it!" Mindy vibrated with her usual zeal. She snatched a Sleeping Goat pamphlet from the counter. A picture of the *Lady with an Ermine* sat in its center. She looked at the image again. "Maybe you two are, like, related or something. Wouldn't that be cool?" She stuffed the creepy pamphlet into my hand.

Tattoo-Carl crossed his arms over his chest and gave me a long look. "Ellie, are you okay? Your cheeks are all red."

Thankful for the opportunity to get away from the creepy ferret lady, I allowed Carl to usher me back to the table in the corner of the restaurant. Dropping into the cow-fur chair, my legs gave way. I gripped my Earl Grey tea, watching the little piece of lemon just to make sure it did nothing strange.

Mindy and Tattoo-Carl watched me for a while.

"Sorry about that." I stumbled. "I'm not getting much sleep these days. This Comprehensive exam is making me a little...dizzy."

Mindy fiddled with a silver toolbox as Carl leaned a small ladder against the wall. They exchanged uneasy glances as they sat down.

Mindy put her hand over mine. "What's going on, Ellie? You look like you've just seen a ghost."

I laughed with an embarrassed snort. Having a panic attack was one thing, but having someone else crazier than me witness my panic attack, was quite another. I cleared my throat. The last thing I wanted to do was explain to weird-Mindy and her tattooed boyfriend what I just witnessed.

"I'm fine. Really, I am. What are you two up to, anyway?" I asked, hoping to change the subject.

Mindy opened her toolkit and pulled out a measuring tape. "We took today off because it's Carl's big day." She vibrated again. "Carl's having his first big show at the Kingston Art Gallery. His work will be on display until Friday, if you can imagine."

"Wow," I replied with all the exuberance I could muster.

Carl nodded. "Yeah, I do junk art. Lately I've been focusing on hairdryers. They make for a unique medium."

I stared back. I didn't know what to say. These people were way too weird for me.

Mindy mistook my empty gaze for genuine interest and continued. "Carl transformed a bunch of old hairdryers into the most beautiful ballerina you will ever see. It is a true masterpiece. My man is a genius. You should come see the show."

I managed a polite question. "And where do you find your junk, Carl?"

"He gets it from all over the place," Mindy answered. "In fact, we fell in love in the dumpster behind McLaren's Hardware Store. Remember?" She nudged Carl. "We were looking for toilet seats and copper piping that day. He kissed me right there in the middle of the broken shovels and banana peels."

"Well, good luck with your art show, Carl." I stood on shaky legs, getting ready to make my escape. "I should get going."

Carl put a firm hand on my shoulder. "Ellie, before you go..." He pulled me back into the cow-fur chair. "Have you ever had any strange incidents with fire?"

I wasn't sure how we made the switch from banana peels to fire, but my guts responded with a surge of nausea.

"What?"

Tattoo-Carl was now serious, not at all put-off by my reaction. "Mindy and I have been talking about you ever since the séance. And we want to know. Have you ever set something on fire...without using a match?"

"No," I responded with a defensive snap.

Mindy folded her arms across her chest and settled back into her cow-fur chair. Carl seemed equally unconvinced. They sat there watching me, waiting me out.

"Well, only by accident. I set everything on fire when I cook," I finally confessed.

Carl's smiled as if I had just confirmed something he already knew. "Ellie, I want to show you a little trick."

I wasn't sure how it happened, but in a matter of seconds, goofy Tattoo-Carl had transformed into this wise and confident owl. "Mindy, do you have those séance candles in your backpack?" he asked.

Mindy pulled three pillar candles from her bag and placed them on the table.

"You ready?" he asked.

I didn't respond. I wasn't sure I wanted to see what he was planning to show me. He shifted his gaze to one of the candles in the line and exhaled a long slow breath. Then with the blink of his eyes, the wick of the first candle popped into flame. He looked up to assess my reaction but my eyes remained on the candle. Tattoo-Carl had just lit the candlewick—without using a match.

"You see." He blinked again and the second candle flickered to life. He smiled as the third candle lit up too.

My mouth yawed open like a barn door on squeaky hinges. "How did you do that?"

"I will the fire," Carl explained. "I imagine it and then I will it."

To my utter amazement, the flames began dancing together, extinguishing and reigniting in sequence. The effect was both eerie and profound. It was like watching a light show put on by a symphony of ghosts.

"But that's impossible," I whispered.

Carl narrowed his eyes. "Ellie, I'm showing you this because I think you might have the same gift. There are signs you may be a Fire Goddess."

"A what?" I said a little too loudly before shrinking in my cow-fur chair. I looked around to check if anyone had noticed.

Mindy jumped in. "Do you remember how the flames pointed at you the night of the séance? That was a sign, we think."

Suddenly the *Lady with an Ermine* flashed through my mind. *"Burn him... Burn him..."* I felt myself go tense. The invisible hands at my throat squeezed. My guts became slick too. If I didn't get out of there, I was going to puke.

"Guys." I said, my voice cracking. "Sorry but no... I just can't...no."

Carl smiled casually as I backed away. "Listen, if you ever want to test out your natural gift, I'd be happy to guide you."

"I've gotta go."

Mindy shouted as I stumbled toward the door, "We'll be at the Kingston Gallery all week if you change your mind..."

The moon was as round as a ripe summer peach. It hung low on the horizon, casting orange shadows over the chateau's manicured shrubbery. Anne and Marguerite walked to the edge of the woods where the tree branches jutted like graveyard bones in the darkness. They crossed at the footbridge and then deep into the wildwood, stepping over brambles and avoiding branches at eye height. An old oak tree, long since dead, stood like an ancient augur pointing the women to their final destination.

"Where are we going?" whispered Anne.

Marguerite's face was in shadow, her expression hard to read. She had been surprisingly quiet tonight, not her usual talkative self.

"Tonight is the summer solstice, Anne. The Sabbat marked by the fire festival."

"Fire festival?" asked Anne.

"Yes, my child. Others also worship the Goddess in these parts of the valley. And tonight you are to be the guest of honor."

They walked for a few more minutes through the copse, climbing the steep hill to its crescent. Anne was filled with questions but she kept them to herself. Something told her to stay quiet tonight. The air seemed to crackle with raw energy and she could have sworn the trees were whispering her name.

At the top of the bluff, they arrived at a clearing in the forest. Anne thought she could make out a group of people circling around a campfire. Most of the members of the procession wore long white shifts, fabric blowing in the warm summer night's breeze. Two women walked naked in the moonlight, breasts swinging, flesh jiggling, unconcerned with modesty.

Anne gasped. "Why do those women wear no clothing?"

Marguerite smiled. "We all worship the Goddess in our own way. Some choose to know her in their truest form."

Marguerite stepped from their hiding place in the trees and faced the group of revelers. She put her hands in the air and raised her voice officiously to the crowd. "I am come, dear coven. And I bring the maiden of the festival. I bring you Anne Boleyn."

A sea of faces turned to look upon Anne, charcoal-blackened human masks eying her with greedy fascination. The people circled around her, touching her, eager to catch a glimpse. Anne wanted to run. She wanted to hide. But Marguerite stood beside her with a hand at her back in a small gesture of reassurance.

From the treeline, a dark figure approached. She was a young maid with a belly as round as the moon.

"Claude," Anne gasped, her voice flooded with relief.

"We have been waiting for you," Claude replied.

A rhythmic beat found its way into the voices of the congregation and an erratic dance of black hands and inky faces accompanied the chanting. Some raised their palms to the sky as they stomped upon the willowy field grasses. Others spun in circles with childlike delight, heads tipped up towards the magic of the summer moon.

Torches blazed in the nightfall, painting long streaks of light as the revelers waved them through the air. The smell of wood smoke infused with rosemary and sage welcomed the newcomers with aromatic enchantment. One woman raised herself up and howled at the moon.

Baffled by the scene, Anne averted her gaze to the shadows. She noticed a male figure sitting cross-legged at the edge of the gathering. He was as still as a stone, his long silver beard flowing down his white linen nightshirt. A charcoal pentagram decorated the features of his old face.

"Is that Leonardo?" asked Anne.

Claude nodded.

"What is wrong with him?"

Claude laughed. "He is praying to the Goddess. And when he is finished, the ceremony shall begin."

Leonardo mumbled under his breath, his lips moving with mysterious enchantment. Anne watched with fascination as his eyes rolled back in his head. Finally, Leo got to his feet. He held up his hands and quieted the crowd.

"It's starting," whispered Claude.

Leonardo approached Anne and then waited until the crowd grew silent. "Good Litha, my coven. I thank you for gathering. This Sabbat marks an important night in our earthly calendar and we mark it each year with a fire festival. However, this Litha is special because we are joined by someone who has been marked. I have this seen girl in my visions. This child, Anne Boleyn. She is a powerful creature, much loved by the Goddess and marked with six fingers on her right hand."

Leonardo pulled back Anne's long sleeve and raised her six-fingered hand in the air. The coven members gasped.

"Tonight, on this midsummer's eve we celebrate the sun, we celebrate fire. We bring forth a young fire Goddess!"

A wild cheer erupted from the group as their enigmatic dancing began anew. Bodies contorted as the chanting grew loud again, arms and legs flailing in synchronized chaos. One naked woman took Anne by the arm and led her to the fire at the center of the human circle.

Anne stood motionless, unable to look away from the dancing orange fire. The flames were coppery demons, erratic and fierce. Sinewy fingers appearing and disappearing at random. The campfire seemed to call to her, to seduce her with an energy that both tickled and burned.

"Let your instincts guide you, Anne," shouted Leo, "and call this fire to burn!"

In spite of the peculiarity of the situation, Anne's unease slipped away. The flames welcomed her, their flickering tongues seeking her guidance. She had received no training nor guidance on the matter, but she knew what to do. For the first time in her life, Anne was confident of the power surging within her. A hot energy danced through her, snaking into her loins and tickling her sex, flowing like lava into her arms and legs. Her body was alight with an energy she knew and trusted. It had always been a part of her. She had just never understood it before.

She raised her right hand and whispered, "Burn."

The meagre fire popped and sizzled as a great blaze erupted. Sparks flew in wild disarray as the conflagration took hold. Flames licked into the sky higher and higher, throwing off a ferocious heat. Coven members scrambled to avoid the carnage as Anne willed the fire to burn brighter and truer than ever. In a few minutes, the modest campfire had become a veritable inferno.

The congregation contorted with excitement. A few members ripped off their nightdresses and threw them in the flames. As the energy intensified, the dancers began to levitate around the fire, forming a circle in the air around the blaze. Their bodies hung like weightless dolls in the night sky, hovering around the orange and yellows hues that overwhelmed the darkness.

Taking her cue from the others, Anne too drifted upward into the sky, pushing herself away from the Earth and gliding up to meet her coven. Soon Marguerite, Claude, and Leonardo joined her in the ring of bodies, suspended like marionettes on strings around the blaze.

Suddenly, emerging from the smoke, a shadowy form appeared. Anne struggled to make it out at first, but the ethereal shade soon became a fulsome image. She was a full-breasted maiden, naked from the waist up, long red hair covering ripe nipples. Her lidded green eyes and luscious sensual lips created an image of perfection. She was youth. She was vitality. She was the Goddess.

"Anne Boleyn," the Goddess cooed. Her voice was rich and earthy, as ancient as the stars. "You are come to me at last."

Her voluptuous form swirled through the flames. She snaked and twisted around Anne's floating body. "Anne, you are marked by me, you are cherished by me. You are my fire child."

Anne could only watch, paralyzed by the sight of her.

The Goddess moved in closer to inspect Anne more intimately. The apparition smelled of the trees and the wind, of the earth and the ocean. She dragged a fiery finger along Anne's delicate cheek. "What shall I grant you Anne Boleyn? You need only ask...."

Anne felt a pull in her loins, a deep heat rising, but again she held her tongue.

The Goddess spiraled long and slow, the softness of her naked breasts dancing across Anne's face. "What is your heart's desire?"

Still Anne did not speak. Something about the Goddess felt dangerous. Her beauty, her seduction warned Anne to resist. Until now, she hadn't been afraid, but as the Goddess encircled her body, her skin prickled with alarm.

Now a tickling sensation ran through Anne's chest. It was like a set of searching fingers pressing and pulling through her soul. It searched for Anne's truths. It searched for Anne's secrets. In spite of her desire to resist, Anne opened up like Pandora's Box and her deepest desires pushed their way through, speaking with an urgency of their own.

Images of Anne's childhood floated into view. Her sister dancing on the lawn as a little girl, spinning and laughing, laughing and spinning, until they both fell down. Her brother on the back of a horse, teaching her to ride in the green woods of Hever. "Harder, Anne. Harder. Show the mare you are in charge..." She hadn't allowed herself to think of her brother and sister during her time here in France. But now she missed them dearly. Homesickness pressed down in a fleeting moment with despair.

But the thoughts did not last long. Before she knew it, the prodding hands of the Goddess pushed another secret button. Anne felt the desire click at the base of her naval. All in an instant, her siblings were forgotten, their images fading to nothing. Instead, her thoughts turned to King Henry. His strong jaw and dazzling blue eyes. His slim waist and brawny torso. It was enough to take her breath away. She had thought often of Henry during her time in France and her yearning for him was strong. She wanted him, the taste of him, the weight of his body on her own.

The Goddess smiled. *"I can hear them, you know, the whispers in your heart. Even when you resist me, I can hear them..."* She breathed in Anne's ear, close and seductive.

Anne hung in the night sky, unmoving and stiff.

The Goddess glided away, moving back to the fire. The orange flames licked at the apparition's breasts like suckling puppies. *"Anne Boleyn, you are marked by me, cherished by me, and I will do your bidding."* The Goddess smiled beguilingly. *"And when I do...you and I shall be bound."*

The Goddess vanished with a pop.

In seconds, the warm energy in Anne's belly drained away, as though her fingers and toes had split open and liquid heat poured from her body. She became cold. She became empty. The world was spinning in a swirling, sickening array of orange, yellow, and red against the black sky. Her body spiraled through the night in a kaleidoscope of color. Then it all went dark.

I cleared my head on the walk home from the Sleeping Goat, grateful to have escaped from Mindy and Tattoo-Carl and from that terri-fying talking painting. I still couldn't believe any of it had really happened.

I took the long way home through the university campus, past the student ghetto, and finally to Gate Street. It took some doing, but as I walked, I managed to force the candle-lighting fiasco into the attic of my mind. I wanted it locked away with all the other dangerous family memo-ries. It didn't technically belong in there, but having it out of the way, did make me feel better.

Once it was safely secured behind mental lock and key, my headache miraculously disappeared and my nausea subsided. By the time I arrived at our little hobbit house, I was feeling more like myself again.

Grapes was dressed in a pair of blue men's coveralls with 'FROSH DO IT FASTER' stenciled across the back, and a miner's helmet affixed with a large light. This was Grapes' standard issue cleaning outfit. She wore it every Tuesday without fail when she scoured the house from top to bottom. She bought the coveralls at a used clothing store on Princess Street a few years back, no doubt a leftover relic from frosh week of years past. The miner's helmet was Grandpa Riley's. She said she liked to wear it because it was good for finding dust bunnies in dark corners, and it reminded her of him.

I found Grapes hovering on her hands and knees under the love seat, sucking up dust and dog hair with a handheld vacuum.

"Those bunnies don't stand a chance, Grapes," I said, dropping my oversized backpack in the front hall.

Zach was sitting on the couch, watching with curiosity as Grapes zoomed beneath him. She popped her head from under the couch and smiled.

"You'd be proud of me, dear. I got three big spiders from over there in the corner." She stuck her head back under the sofa and continued zooming.

"What can I do to help? Maybe I could do the high-up windows?"

Grapes was relentless about her weekly cleaning schedule. Over the years, I had learned not to resist. It was much easier to simply get on board. When I was younger, she had assigned me all the easy cleaning jobs, but since she had started using the walker, I usually took on a few of the challenging tasks.

"No, no, dear. I did all the tall windows before you got home."

I looked up to see the high-up windows were sparkling clean.

"Grapes! You promised you wouldn't do them anymore. How did you get up there without a ladder, anyway?" I scolded.

Grapes waved me off. "Now dear. You know I like to do the windows. It's therapeutic for me. You wouldn't deny an old woman her life's greatest pleasure, would you? And besides, you have your research to do."

I shook my head in defeat. This woman was as stubborn as a stain. And besides, she had finished all the work. The house was so clean you could eat off the floor. Lemon furniture polish wafted through the air. The surfaces gleamed. The windows sparkled. Even Zach's food dish had been scoured, no longer smeared with left over kibble and dog drool.

But Grapes' comment about my research plans did strike a chord in my mind. I had been feeling guilty for having wasted precious study time at the coffee shop this morning and I wanted to get back to work.

"Actually, I'm planning to head into the basement this afternoon to see what else I can find in Dad's 'unpublished works.' It was dark down there last night and I'm afraid I may have missed something."

My visit to the Sleeping Goat had left me with a terrible desire to sink my teeth back into my research. I yearned for the simplicity of plain old-fashioned fact-finding, rather than that freaky unexplainable fire ceremony I had witnessed earlier. Grapes popped up from under the couch, limber as ever.

"I was hoping you'd say that. I've been meaning to take my vacuum into the basement. So I'll keep you company." She revved the little engine on her handheld. "You study and I'll get those spiders."

* * *

"Are you looking for something specific, dear?" Grapes asked as she continued her cleaning frenzy in the basement.

She had stowed her walker by an old spinning wheel and was holding on to spare pieces of furniture for support. Her face lit with pleasure each time she spied a new spider web in the light of her miner's helmet and sucked it into her whirring machine. We had already emptied the little vacuum twice, full of the unsuspecting creepy-crawlies she managed to snare.

"Grapes." I squinted into a tall box. "Can you bring your head over here? I need to see what's left at the bottom."

She shuffled along an old wooden rocking horse and arrived with her beaming headlight.

"There. Make the light shine in there... What is that?"

Grapes tipped her helmet and the beam shone into the bottom of a deep storage container. To my delight, the light reflected off a smooth black surface. A small logo in the corner read Barney and Cartwright's Air-Lock Humidity-Controlled Archival Quality Boxes.

"I knew there was something still here," I said with satisfaction. My research instincts were still sharp, despite my insomnia and impending nervous breakdown.

"Atta girl, Ellie." Her eyes sparkled under the brim of her miner's helmet. "But what is it?"

The black archival box was locked up tight with a button and a sliding lock mechanism holding its contents within. We moved to the quilt to inspect it, shoving the dog over so we could both sit cross-legged on the blanket. Grapes' flexibility was apparent when she sat on the floor this way. The woman could practically do the splits.

I pushed the silver button with a pop and slid the metal clasp forward. It opened with a whoosh of air as the vacuum seal mechanism disengaged.

"Arghhh. I'll bet it's filled with pirate treasure," said Grapes, affecting a Long John Silver voice.

Smirking, I raised the lid and the three of us peered inside. Zach thumped his tail and Grapes whistled between her teeth. I bit my lip with a tiny surge of excitement.

The storage box contained two ancient leather-bound books. I wasn't certain of their ages but, based on the cracked leather and the heavy construction of the book's spines, I guessed they were at least several centuries old.

Both of the books cast off an unusual energy, each one unique but powerful in its own way. The first book, a smooth brown calfskin with no other markings, had a humble vibe. It was about the size of a paperback novel, not more than an inch thick. Its pages were thin and tattered, the seam frayed and split. It looked like it had been well loved by its owner. The second book was made of luxurious dimpled red leather edged with gilt borders. It was larger than its companion and it radiated wealth and station. It almost seemed offended to have been locked away all these years.

My heart skittered at the sight of them. This was better than pirate treasure, any day of the week. I glanced up at Grapes. Her eyebrows were going a mile a minute.

"Well?" she said impatiently.

A tingling sensation was now radiating from my scar and I gave my fingers a quick shake. My fingers pulsed as they contacted its calfskin cover, a little snap of electricity running up my arms. I pulled open the front jacket, the book's spine groaning with disuse, and scanned the frontispiece. The cover was inscribed with a spidery handwriting that read, *"Property of Beth Bowlan, 1566."*

I sucked in a gulp of musty basement air. "This must have been owned by someone in our family. Dad's notes say the family tree went back five hundred years."

Grapes eyes twinkled. "My heavens. It's the diary of a long lost Bowlan. A Beth Bowlan, at that. My own Bethy used to keep diaries too, bless her heart."

I passed the book between my hands, feeling the bumpy leather skin cover and the smoothness of the handwritten pages. A hum of electricity crackled where my skin made contact with the pages. Without warning, a tiny blue spark snapped through the air and a jolt of pain fired through my fingers. My scar seared with pain.

"Ouch," I whispered under my breath.

Grapes didn't seem to notice the blue arch of light that zipped through the darkness. "Let's check the other one," she urged.

I rubbed my hands on my jeans, trying to rid them of the bizarre tingling that would not go away. Picking up the dimpled red leather book embellished with gold leaf, I wondered if I was going to be zapped with a new blue voltage.

"Here we go," I said, waiting for another shock. But this time, nothing happened. The prickling in my hands vanished. I hesitated for a moment, trying to determine whether I had imagined the blue spark in the first place.

"Open it, Ellie!" Grapes demanded with the eagerness of a five-year-old.

"Okay, hold your horses," I shot back.

The book's leather cover was richer and its pages far thicker than its counterpart. This time the writing was neat and swirling. I read the words aloud in the dim basement light. "*The Heptameron—Stories by Marguerite de Navarre, 1514.*"

I almost choked on my own tongue. "Oh my God. I've been doing research on this book!"

Grapes' caterpillar eyebrows danced.

"What is that?" she asked.

We leaned in to get a better look in the darkness. The inside frontispiece contained a short written note. The ink was faded but under Grapes' miners light, we could make it out.

To: Beth Bowlan, 1566

My dearest Beth,

Your mother came to visit me before I pass from this world. My time on the Earth shall not be long. Upon my passing, I have asked that you receive my Heptameron. It is my original manuscript. I penned the stories here as they happened in my life.

I am an old woman now, but in my youth, I knew your grandmother. She was a friend of mine, finer and truer than any other. She was like a daughter to me. I think of her every day since her passing. As I have no children of my own, I would like this special keepsake to go to you. Somehow, it feels as though it will remain in the family.

I know your arrangements have been difficult and that your childhood has been strange. I know your mother could only love you in secret and could not claim you for her own. That would be difficult for a child to understand. Please know she loves you more than you will ever know.

> *Please take care of my Heptameron,*
> *Marguerite*

Zach sniffed the leather bindings, nudging it with his nose to unearth its aromatic secrets. I looked at Grapes, the light from her helmet shining in my eyes. My voice came out cracked.

"This is the original draft of Marguerite de Navarre's *Heptameron*. This book is probably priceless. We shouldn't be touching it. And we definitely shouldn't have it in our damp smelly basement."

"Well quick, put it back into its Ziploc thingy."

Grapes held the archive box open as I placed the red leather book alongside the brown calfskin. She closed the lid and handed it to me to seal. The mechanism was simple enough and with a push and a click, I heard the mechanism engage. The air forced outward, recreating the vacuum seal.

"Phew!" I breathed.

"Well it wasn't pirate treasure, but it was pretty darn close," Grapes said with satisfaction.

My mind spun with possibilities and I struggled to get my thoughts under control. Grapes, on the other hand, didn't waste time. She had already come to her own conclusions.

"You need to show these books to Lily," she called over her shoulder as she headed back into her cleaning routine. "She'll tell you how to handle them. Your father obviously tucked them away in that special storage container for a reason."

"You're right." I nodded as I slid the black archival box into my backpack.

My first thought had gone to Lily too. She would know what to do with these ancient texts and how to study them without causing further damage to their delicate pages. But my second thought had gone to John. After all, John was the one studying Marguerite de Navarre for his Comp exam. He was the one who found the *Heptameron* stories in the first place. How could I not tell him I found Marguerite de Navarre's original copy?

I grabbed my cell and scrolled through my list of recent numbers, clicking on the one marked J. Chelsea. I did it quickly before I could chicken out.

Grapes was shimmying along the furniture again. She readied herself to attack a nest of baby spiders in an old armoire. The dustbuster kicked into action, its sucking mechanism whirring away.

"John?" I shouted over the noise of the vacuum.

"Ellie?" The phone line crackled with bad reception.

"Yes. It's me Ellie. Sorry. I'm in the basement again."

John laughed. "Of course you are. So what's up?"

"Listen, I have to tell you something crazy. Are you ready?" I asked, sounding a little crazy myself.

"Uh...sure."

I rubbed my hand on the blanket to stifle the itching. "Grapes and I found the original handwritten version of Marguerite de Navarre's *Heptameron*—in our basement!"

"Are you sure?" His voice was serious now.

"Yes. The book was in my dad's old research boxes!"

I could hear John's mouth hanging open.

I hesitated, a surge of insecurity ripping through me, but the thrill of my discovery gave me the courage I needed. "Do you want to meet somewhere? We can review it together."

"Of course," he said with enthusiasm. "Let's look at it tomorrow. I'm coming over to your place for dinner, right?"

I paused for a split second. "You are?"

"Yeah, your Grapes invited me yesterday...when I dropped off Zach at your house. She didn't mention it?"

I looked slowly up at Grapes, who was still vacuuming. I could have sworn she looked a little sheepish.

"No...she did not mention it," I said, giving my great-grandmother the evil eye.

"She promised me her famous chicken pot pie," John said with enthusiasm.

I kept my voice light. "Oh. Okay. Well, I'll see you tomorrow, John."

I hung up the phone with a tight click. I glared at Grapes.

She looked both guilty and pleased with herself as she stood there in her blue coveralls draped in spider webs.

"You invited John over for dinner?" I accused.

She turned off her dustbuster and feigned a look of innocence only those over the age of ninety can properly manage. "Ellie, you know I can't resist feeding a hungry man." Grapes flicked at a rogue spider climbing up her arm. "I made him two egg salad sandwiches yesterday, and he ate an entire jar of my sweet pickles. He was so cute I thought it would be nice if he joined us for dinner."

I shook my head in defeat for the second time today. This woman was both stubborn and sneaky. I considered balking at her dinner plans, especially given the fact she hadn't let me in on them. In the end, I knew it was hopeless. Grapes was just doing what Grapes always did. She made friends everywhere she went. Everybody loved her. The only thing I could do was to lay out clear ground rules.

"Okay—he's coming over for dinner. Fine. But it's just dinner. I don't want any embarrassing matchmaker stuff."

She held up her vacuum as though she was making a pledge. "Alright dear. Just the chicken pot pie."

"Lily!" I shouted as I tore down the library stairs, two at a time. "You've got to see this."

Today Lily was sitting at her desk staring at a large vase full of pink and white lilies, their dark green stems boasting a dozen magnificent blooms. Her face was arranged in its usual deflated balloon position, but Lily was out of sorts. She didn't look up when she heard me arrive. Instead, she gaped at the flowers like something alien had just landed on her desk.

"Whoa, what are those?" I screeched to a halt in front of the bouquet.

Lily continued staring. "They're lilies."

I laughed. "Yeah, they're lilies. And they're beautiful." I waited her out. She would come up with more information. She just needed time.

"Donny bought them for me. He bought lilies because of my name. I didn't get it at first, but then he explained."

"Donny?" I swatted her playfully.

She nodded. "Donny is the man I have been...dating."

I inspected the flowers with interest. Their heady fragrance created a feminine atmosphere in the dusty old library that was foreign yet fascinating. Their thick waxy leaves held firm against my prodding fingers, withstanding a good poke at the stamens.

"I didn't even know you were dating. I mean, I knew about your dates, but I didn't know you were *dating*."

A lost expression crossed Lily's face. "Neither did I."

"Who is this guy, anyway?"

"He's a professor here at Queen's. We met at the staff social a few weeks ago. He said he thought old books were romantic." She shook her head at the memory. "So I couldn't resist when he asked me out."

I couldn't imagine Lily going to a staff social, but she obviously had a few more tricks up her sleeve than I realized.

"And what does he study?"

"History, I think. I don't know about his specific area of research. He says it's top secret," she said vacantly. "But he's very driven. Last night he told me he was close to making the most exciting breakthrough of his career."

"Well, well, well..." My voice danced. "He sounds great. A driven academic on the verge of a major discovery would be the perfect guy for you."

She looked up at me now. "Actually he's pretty intense. Almost a little too intense."

Placing the vase back on Lily's desk, I gave the bouquet one last spin. The rosy blooms swirled with all the finesse of a Barbie fashion parade. I gave them an approving nod.

"Sometimes love catches you by surprise, Lil," I said, making my voice all soft and gooey. "Do you still think he's boring and funny looking?"

A tiny smile was making its way across Lily's face. "Still as boring and funny looking as ever." She glanced up at me. "But he brought me flowers so..."

I raised my hand for a high-five but she just looked at the palm of my hand, her cheeks flushing red. I waited to see if Lily wanted to disclose anything else about her mystery man. Nothing more came.

"Okay Lil," I said conspiratorially. "Do you want to know what I found in a box of my father's unpublished research this morning?"

"Mmmm?" Lily looked up from the flowers, that microscopic eyebrow arch apparent over her frames.

I was so excited, I felt like a balloon ready to pop. My news was going blow those lilies out of her lily pond. I plunked my backpack down on her desk and stood beside it with a hand on its zipper, like a captain christening a new ship.

"I found two sixteenth century books. One of them is the diary of a long lost Bowlan family member. And the other is the original manuscript of *The Heptameron*—written by Marguerite de Navarre herself!"

The thrill of our find in the basement this morning washed over me again like a tidal wave. I knew this was the kind of thing that would make her day. Heck, it would make her entire year.

Lily opened her mouth, her face an expressionless mask. She actually looked a little scary, but it didn't take long for her to process the news. In seconds, my beloved librarian was out of her seat and gowning up. She grabbed two pairs of gloves and hurried to the door of the Special Collections room.

"What are we waiting for?" Her voice trilled with excitement. This was a new Lily-the-librarian.

As we made our way inside the humidity-controlled environment, I explained the circumstances of my discovery and everything there was to tell about my dad's research. I told her the whole story right from the beginning. I didn't care how weird it sounded. I wanted her to know. She was my research partner, after all.

"The last thing I found in Dad's notes was the name Henri Carey."

"Mmmm...hmmm..." Lily wheezed, but I could hear the enthusiasm behind her sinuses.

"I was planning to see if I could figure out who Henri Carey was, but today when we found the diary of Beth Bowlan and the *Heptameron*. I forgot all about him."

I pushed the button of the locking mechanism on the shiny black storage box and with a flourishing hand, I revealed the two antediluvian texts.

She hissed like a cobra when she saw them, transfixed by their ancient glimmer. Without a word, she lifted up the brown calfskin book and placed it on the table with the deft hands of a special collections librarian. Slowly, carefully, she inspected its binding.

"It's in remarkably good condition for a five-hundred-year-old text," she said as she ran her hands over its cover. "Let's have a look at what Beth Bowlan has to say, shall we?" A smile appeared. A big juicy delicious Lily smile.

April 30, 1566

> *My name is Beth Bowlan. I am nine years old today. I have spent a most splendid day in the gardens with my secret mother. She gave me this book as a gift. She says it is time for me to have my very own book—that I may write my secrets upon its pages and confide my greatest worries within its bindings. She says this book may*

hold me fast when she cannot be with me. It is the most beautiful gift I have ever received. It is beautiful, just like my secret mother.

My secret mother comes to visit me once a week, and at times once a fortnight when she cannot break from her other duties. I wonder what other responsibilities she might bear, but Uncle Henri tells me only that my mother's duties are vast. He tells me she cannot break with them, but if she could, she would be my mother for all the world to see.

I will use this gift to chronicle my thoughts and confide my worries, as my secret has mother bid. I shall cherish this book for always.

Lily and I looked at each other.

"Imagine having a secret mother," she said.

"I don't get it. Why would her mother be a secret?"

Lily frowned. She was fidgeting again, like she had when she went on her first date with Donny. But this time, there was a hint of paranoia in her expression.

"Ellie, before we go any further, we need to think about where we are planning to keep these books. They're fragile but they are also priceless."

I waited. I knew Lily already had the answer. She was the expert on protecting ancient texts and I deferred to her without question.

Lily glanced over her shoulder. "I think we should hide them. Just in case"

"Is this really necessary?" I scoffed.

An eyebrow shot up over her glasses, even higher than before. "After Zach went crazy yesterday, I started to get this funny feeling someone was following me. You know...as though I was being watched," she whispered. "So, I hid the grimoire of Marguerite de Navarre."

I laughed and then realized she was quite serious,

Lily nodded in earnest. "And I think we should put these books in the same place. So only you and I will be able to find them. But they'll be safe in this humidity controlled room."

I looked around the sterile space. There was nothing but a steel table, three chairs, and several neat rows of books. It hardly seemed like a crime scene. She took my hand and led me down the third aisle on the left.

"We'll hide them in here."

She pointed to a tiny line around a floor tile that was slightly larger than the others. Lily took a pen from her hair and used its tip to lift the tile, popping it up with ease. She removed the false tile, setting it on the floor, and pointed into the spacious subfloor below. There, in the darkened hole, sat the ancient grimoire of Marguerite de Navarre.

My eyes grew wide. "This is awesome, Lil. I thought you were going to suggest we hide the books on a shelf but this secret subfloor is even better. How did you know about this hiding spot?"

Lily stood up, wiped off the dust from her daisy print skirt, and produced a smug look. "A librarian knows her library."

"I told you, Anne," Claude said lazily. "You were the only one who spoke to the Goddess. She doesn't present herself to just anyone, you know." She ran a hand over her swollen stomach, tracing the movements of the baby inside.

Anne put her hand on Claude's belly too, just below the naval where there was a lot of action from within.

"She was so real," said Anne dreamily.

Claude pulled her legs up to her stomach and found a more comfortable position. "Tell me again. What did she look like? What did she say?"

Anne shut her eyes to conjure the image in her mind again. They had been discussing it for days.

"Well....she had flaming red hair and eyes like emeralds. She was the most beautiful creature I've ever seen."

Claude closed her eyes too as if to imagine the Goddess herself.

"She bid me tell her my heart's desire, but I could not speak. But after a while, without even meaning to, I thought of..." Anne blushed. "I thought of my true love. It was as though she was pulling the thoughts right from my heart."

"And did the Goddess make you promises?" Claude's voice was thick with admiration.

"I think so." Anne lay back and looked up at the velvet tapestry framing the four posters of her bed. "But none of it seems possible."

Both girls lay on Anne's down-stuffed mattress like wilted flowers. It was too hot for studying, the full heat of summer now upon them. Claude's ankles had swollen to twice their normal size and neither of them had enough energy to do much of anything. Both Leonardo and Marguerite were attending other business and the girls had resigned themselves to an easy morning of rest and chatter.

Rose sat in the corner humming a tune. She had pulled the windows open, trying to get a cross breeze through the room. She squinted at the needlework on the baby booties she was making, beads of sweat gathering on her lip.

"I don't know." Claude wiggled her swollen feet. "The Goddess may well grant your wish for love."

Anne shook her head. She knew it was impossible. The memory of her beautiful King Henry still pulled a melancholy ache through her chest.

"But why not? If he is your true love, there must be a way," asked Claude.

Anne pushed her finger into her friend's fleshy skin leaving an imprint on Claude's bloated foot. "Because my love is obliged to another, so I can never have him—not completely, anyway."

Claude stretched out her arms, trailing her fingers along the red velvet curtains. "Well I am pleased my Francis cannot see me right now. I am grateful he loves me in spite of my crooked back. I cannot imagine him setting eyes upon me, now I am swollen up like a great cow."

Anne laughed. "It must be wonderful to have a love that is truly yours."

"Aye, it is," replied Claude, her voice wistful. "In spite of how my father hates me, Francis has always been kind. I love how he places his hands on mine. It is our little sign, our little affection."

Anne thought of Henry and the way he had kissed her in the wood. It had been their little affection. But there would be nothing more. Henry was a married man and the King of England.

A deep rumbling of hooves distracted the girls from their chatter. Rose dropped her needlework and struggled from her chair. She stood at the window, straining to get a view of the carriage that was arriving down the laneway.

"For all that is holy—could et be?" Rose gave her rump a scratch. "Anne, luv, come here right quick. Ef my eyes don't deceive me, I believe I spy your brother George comin' up the lane."

Anne didn't bother to glance out the window. She sprang from the bed and tore down the staircase, taking two steps at a time. Her night shift trailed behind, her bare feet navigating the stones with athletic prowess. Upon reaching the bottom stair, she made a hard left and raced to the door.

Anne gasped. There in the laneway stood a team of horses pulling a carriage adorned with the Boleyn family crest. Her brother had already dismounted and was dispatching orders to the groom's men and the house servants. She barreled over the marbled walkway and ran to him.

"George!" she cried as she flung herself into his unsuspecting embrace.

"Anne!" He laughed and spun his sister around. He eyed her night-clothes but did not remark upon them.

Anne clung to him with childlike delight. In spite of her strange attire, Anne knew she was a vision of loveliness. She was relaxed and happy and her raven hair trailed down her back.

"We received word Mary was to come to France to join you. She is to attend the English princess as a second maid of honor at the royal wedding," George croaked from inside her embrace. "She is embarking from the carriage over there."

Anne could not believe her ears. "Mary is here too?"

"Go and see for yourself." George peeled away from her.

Across the lane, a groomsman was helping a lady down the steps of the Boleyn carriage. A white gloved hand emerged first, then a set of yellow bustling skirts, and finally the lovely face of her dear sister Mary.

Anne clapped her hands together and ran to her. The sisters grabbed greedily for one another. They stood in an embrace for a long moment, not exchanging a single word. Anne breathed in her sister's familiar scent, a lingering of lavender and honey.

The servants continued with the impressive task of unloading Mary's trunks as Rose arrived at the carriage, howling with delight. She sobbed as she grabbed up George and Mary, inspecting her Boleyn kin, as if they were her own litter of pups.

Marguerite interrupted their happy reunion. "What a wonderful surprise." She smiled cautiously. "We had not received word of your landing."

George bowed low and presented Marguerite with a formal letter, bound with the English monarch's seal. "King Henry of England has sent us. He worries for his sister's welfare and wished to send another maid for her comfort."

Marguerite curtsied in response. "We welcome you both to France.

Please come inside and have a cup of ale. I shall have the cook prepare something for you."

She ushered the newcomers into the chateau, out of the heat of the day. The group followed as she led them through the great arched doors and into the main entry hall. Marguerite was a gracious hostess, asking after their every need, and sending the servants to acquire it. The new arrivals wandered though the impressive home, fawning over this tapestry and that. She pointed out the many aspects of French Renaissance architecture as the group moved through the manse.

At the first moment alone, George pulled Anne aside.

"Go get dressed," he whispered, his eyes dancing with merriment. "We shall have to make our excuses to Madame de Navarre. I need you to come away for a few hours."

Anne laughed. "George, you have only just arrived. Where would you have me go?"

He gave her a brotherly shove towards the staircase. "Go make ready. I can't have you in your night clothes. Hurry. It is a surprise."

* * *

They raced side-by-side on horseback, just as they had as children. George drove his horse hard, kicking at its flank. Anne's dark hair danced in the wind as she urged her mare into a gallop, delighted to be riding with her brother again. They sped along the narrow country roads until they came to a more substantial avenue that would take them into Tours.

As they traveled along the River Loire, the countryside gave way to thatch-roofed homes and cottages. The town grew up around them, the rough road turning to more refined cobblestone. Impossibly narrow half-timbered buildings with pitched terra cotta rooftops lined the streets. The teetering Tudor style of the city with its shadowy closes and cobblestone avenues reminded Anne of more familiar English surrounds.

As the crowds grew thicker, Anne and George slowed their pace. George navigated away from the bustling market square to a quieter part of town. At last, he pointed to their final destination.

"La Taverne Jumeaux," he announced.

A bewildered Anne dismounted. Now that they had arrived, she could contain her questions no longer. "George, what are we doing here?"

"Just follow me, sister. You shall know your surprise soon enough."

The darkened tavern housed several long oak tables with benches tucked beneath. A series of tidy shelves behind the counter held brown jugs of liquor. The smell of savory meat pies wafted through the air. The inn was empty, save for one large man seated in a corner. Anne froze at the sight of him. She knew him in an instant.

He stood when he saw her, a great hulking form in the shadows. As he stepped into the light, Anne looked up into the bonny visage of King Henry. He was as handsome and rugged as she remembered. His square jaw and perfect aquiline nose set her heart aflutter. A hopeful smile played upon his lips.

"This, dear sister, is your surprise." George bowed and took his leave.

Anne forgot her manners altogether and ran to the king.

"Henry," she gasped.

King Henry gathered her small frame in his arms and pulled her in close. She fell against him, the heat of his body made her heart stir. As she breathed in his masculine scent, the smell of leather and outdoors, a warm fluttering flowed through her.

"My love," he whispered.

Henry held her for what seemed a blissful eternity. He nuzzled his bearded face through her dark hair, seeking a private spot behind her ear, and kissed it. It sent tingles up her spine. No one had ever kissed her there before.

Anne thought she might faint from the thrill of it. Still wrapped in his embrace, she could not resist running her hand along his chest, a set of firm pectorals flexing under his linen shirt.

"Henry, you are come to me," she said.

"I could stay away no longer," he breathed, his voice full of wanting. Henry looked into her sun-kissed face. He traced her delicate jawline with his finger and cupped her chin in his rough hands. "I have not stopped thinking of you since the day we met. Every night I dream of you. Every day I wake, yearning to hold you in my arms."

Anne swallowed back the tears that wanted to flow. His words were her thoughts. She had not stopped dreaming of Henry since that day in the wood, the day she had promised him her heart.

Henry's voice was a ragged whisper. "When I received your letter, I knew I had to come. I had to hold you, to feel you, to breathe in your beauty—if only for a moment. I arranged to have your sister join you in France. And I enlisted George to set this meeting so I could look upon you with my own eyes."

For a split second, Anne's thoughts ran to her meeting with the Goddess. Was it she who had arranged this? Her brother and sister, and now Henry? It was exactly as she had wished. For the moment, Anne did not care. She was in the arms of her bonny King Henry and it was the happiest place in the world.

"I have missed you, Henry," she said with trepidation. "I worried you had forgotten me. I worried perhaps I was being silly to love you still."

Henry looked into her eyes. "I promised my heart to you and that shall never change. You are my happiness."

"And you are mine." Anne's knees went weak.

The king slid her into a chair and searched for his traveling satchel. "I cannot stay long. Our boat returns across the Channel tonight. But I needed to give you this token of our bond."

He pulled a handcrafted wooden box from his bag and placed the gift in her hands, looking upon her with affection.

Anne accepted the mahogany treasure, an ornately carved trillium flower decorating the lid. She pressed two fingers against the latch and pried the box open like a prize oyster. A gold chain adorned with a forged golden charm with an embossed letter B sat atop the luxurious silk inlay. Three drop pearls were affixed to its underside. The necklace was stunning.

"B for Boleyn," he whispered with a hopeful smile. "Know that I think of you every day, Anne Boleyn."

She ran her finger over the pearls, glossy and white.

He leaned in close now, his mouth grazing her ear. "Anne, I cannot ask you to marry me because I am already wed. But please accept this gift, my heart's cordon. I shall never love another."

She could not find the words but her eyes brimmed with tears.

A smile played at his lips. "These pearls..." He put his large hand over her small one. "They symbolize my deepest wish for us. There are three, you see? You and I, represent our hearts together forever. And if God wills it one day, the pearl at the center represents the child we shall have. I pray we will someday be married in true, and together we could have a son."

The idea struck her and her heart swelled with warmth. She imagined a wedding—*their* wedding—and the tiny child they would love more than anything else in the world.

"I shall wear it always." Her voice trembled. "I will wait for you always."

He pushed the hair away from her face and caressed her cheek. Then ever so softly, he placed his lips upon hers.

"I love you Anne Boleyn."

PRESENT DAY
QUEEN'S UNIVERSITY, CANADA

"Wow, Lil, you look terrific," I lied.

Lily performed a shuffling spin to show off her new dress. The frock was a brown cotton pinafore patterned with tiny pink paisleys. The sleeves were ruffled, the high neckline was severe, and the skirt went all the way down to the ankles. With this getup, she could have stepped right out of *Little House on the Prairie*. Throwing in her sensible shoes and thick glasses, Lily just screamed librarian.

She fiddled with the ruffles on her sleeve and blushed. "Even librarians can wish for love."

I covered my mouth to contain a smile. "It's perfect. Really. It is. Your date tonight is going to be great."

Lily's face sagged, her ego as fragile as a peeled grape. "I'm really not good with men. They make me nervous. I really don't understand why Donny likes me."

"Come on, Lil. You just need to relax a little," I said, hoping to make her smile. "You're a hot sexy librarian. Isn't that every man's secret fantasy?"

"Mmmm...."

I wanted to keep up with the pep talk, to help pump up Lily's seriously under-inflated ego, but there was nothing more to say. Lily had a way of ending a conversation when she was finished with it. She was already re-stacking books, closing herself off from the world.

Instead of my cheerleading, I headed back into more familiar territory. It was easier for us to discuss bookish things and our talk yesterday about those priceless texts had been bothering me. I wasn't sure why, but I had developed a rather paranoid feeling that someone was following me. It was probably just a bout of delusional paranoia caused by my sleepless nights. After all, a woman in a painting had spoken to me yesterday. But that fact that Lily had felt it, too, made me wonder.

"I think your suggestion to hide those old books was a good one. Remember how you said you had a feeling you were being watched?" I began. I had developed a theory and I wanted to run it by her.

Lily stopped stacking.

"Well, I started to get that same feeling. Its the strangest thing. I thought I saw a man tailing me in the grocery store when I went to pick up a carton of eggs for Grapes. And I could have sworn there was a shadowy figure behind my house when I took out the garbage last night." I glanced at her to read her reaction.

She stood frozen on the stacking ladder.

"I've been wracking my brains to figure out who could be watching us. I mean, we hang out in the stacks every day. No one else knows what we're working on. So who could it be? And why?"

Lily took a couple of steps down, gripping the side rails. It was clear I had her attention.

"Last night I got to thinking. If Ivor Cullen and my dad had been research partners, Cullen probably knew he had those priceless texts. Maybe Cullen wanted them so much he killed my parents to get them."

From her perch on the second rung, Lily's gaze was inscrutable.

"And if that's true, Cullen could still be after them. Maybe by digging around in my dad's old research, I have inadvertently alerted him to the fact the books are still around. Maybe it was Cullen who broke into the library the other day. What do you think?"

Lily stepped off the ladder altogether. Her voice was odd. "Those books would be worth a lot of money to the right collector."

I clicked my pen in the quiet of the room. It made an eerie empty tick, tick, tick that sent shivers up my spine.

"Ellie, someone called the library this morning," Lily confessed. "It was a strange call. The man asked if we had any information on DNA isolation techniques. I told him this was the Historical Special Collections section, but he was persistent. He kept asking if I had come across any DNA research. When I asked for his name, he hung up."

I put my pen down. "Cullen's research was about DNA."

"Maybe it was Cullen," said Lily.

We exchanged astonished looks. Lily seemed fearful at first, panic threatening to overwhelm her, but her expression quickly pivoted to one of resolve.

The muscle in her jaw flexed peevishly. "Well no matter what, the books are hidden now. So that bastard Cullen will never find them."

The ferocity in her voice caught me off guard. It was apparent this librarian would defend her books to the death, and her courage made me feel a little giddy. Lily was a true scholastic superstar.

"Are you ready to dig our precious cargo out of hiding?" A hint of enthusiasm crept into my own voice.

In seconds, Lily was heading towards the Special Collections room. She snatched up our shower caps and we headed in for another day of glorious research.

We spent a companionable morning reading Beth Bowlan's diary, reviewing each page with meticulous precision. The entries gave us a good understanding of this young woman and her life living with her Uncle Henri. Most of the entries outlined her day-to-day activities, perfecting new stitches for needlework, study and prayer, and strolling with her uncle through the gardens. But the entries that focused on her secret mother were the most fascinating.

The hours melted away as we read on. When Beth Bowlan had her twelfth birthday, things got interesting.

April 30, 1569.

> *Today I am twelve. My secret mother came to visit for my special day. Mother says I am old enough to learn about my natural talents in the Craft. She has promised to teach me about my Bowlan family namesake. Mother cautioned that I must tell no one of our tutoring sessions. Not even Uncle Henri. I have promised, but alas, I wish I understood why I must keep so many secrets.*

Lily looked up from the passage. "Wait a second. Beth Bowlan and her secret mother studied the Craft?"

Connections were forming in my mind, but I tried to ignore them. I wasn't quite ready to accept what we had just read. We continued onto the next set of entries.

August 31, 1569.

> *Mother has been teaching me about the Craft for several months now. She has taught*
> *me to work with the wind, to manipulate it, to will it, and to have it do my bidding.*
> *I have learned how to blow the clouds across the sky and to rake a gust across the*
> *lawns. I have perfected the art of scattering dried leaves in the wood. I even knocked*
> *the hat off a gentleman who was taking a morning stroll. Mother tells me there is*
> *much more to my gift. I wonder what that means.*

We stopped at this passage. I needed a minute to process the information. There were real witches in the Bowlan family line. In my family line.

"Beth Bowlan was a witch." My words came out almost like a
confession.

All my life, I had been uneasy about supernatural things. Witches and
warlocks were the stuff of fantasy novels, strictly not part of the real
world. And I had always made a point of avoiding anyone who thought
they were. It was the reason I wanted nothing to do with weird Mindy and
her spooky boyfriend. But I had just discovered there were witches in my
own family. You couldn't get much closer than that.

"Witches in the Bowlan family..." I whispered.

To my surprise, as I heard my own words in the quiet of the library, my
stomach didn't lurch. My guts didn't go slick. I didn't feel the usual
panicked squeeze at my neck. For some unknowable reason, the whole
thing seemed okay. In fact, it seemed rather fascinating.

For the next few hours, Lily and I pored over Beth's journal. I rooted
for young Beth Bowlan and her witchy pursuits. They weren't as strange
when I read them in her words. In fact, being a witch seemed rather
exciting through the eyes of Beth Bowlan.

Towards the end of the day, Lily glanced at the time, her shoulders
sagging. The Mickey Mouse hands on her wristwatch faced up and down
—the dreaded six o'clock position. She had a date, and I did too.

"Let's read one more?" Lily suggested, dragging her feet.

November 14, 1569.

> *Today my secret mother bid me bury two green and yellow ribbons beneath our*
> *favorite apple tree in the orchard. She commanded me to whisper them into the wind*
> *and send the ribbons to a new place. She promised the wind would carry them there*
> *in secret.*

*And do you know what? When I arrived in my bedchamber there were the two
ribbons, one green and one yellow, resting upon my pillow.*

*I am beginning to understand the complexities of my gift. Mother tells me that
next time, she will show me how to ask the wind to carry messages through time.
Imagine such a thing...*

I pushed away from the table and stretched my back out, my spine
snap-crackle-popping. Lily gathered up the diary with care and pried open
the hiding spot in the floor.

"Lil, do you think this stuff is true? I mean, do you think Beth Bowlan
could really do those witchy things?" I hated to ask the question, but my
scientific skepticism was returning. "Or did she make it up just to make
her life seem more exciting?"

Lily knelt over the hole in the sub-floor and eased the book into its
hiding spot. She considered the question for a while and then shook her
head. "I don't think she made it up. We've been reading her diary all day
and Beth Bowlan seemed too grounded, too serious to make up stuff like
that. It seems she was a lot like you."

I agreed with Lily on this one. I didn't know why, but I liked that I was
related to this Beth Bowlan—witch or no witch.

"Oh Lil, hang on. I want to take the *Heptameron* home tonight. I
promised to show it to John."

I scooped the red leather book from the hidey-hole in the subfloor and
slid it into my backpack. Lily eyed me warily, her librarian instincts
kicking in. For a moment, I thought she might tell me I couldn't take it
home but instead she checked her watch again. Man-panic was now
sprawled across her face.

"Put the text in your dad's storage box when you take it to your house.
And take gloves too. I don't want you two getting your dirty fingers all
over it," she insisted.

I laughed and saluted in direction. "Aye aye, captain."

"Ellie," she said quietly, clearly not amused. "Keep it safe."

* * *

Grapes bustled about the kitchen with her three-step shuffle. Today she
was wearing a cornflower blue velour pantsuit, her name 'Lizzie' stitched
in needlepoint letters. She'd been out all day with the Titanium Trio
selling Chocolate-Sprinkle-Marshmallow-Bacon-Whopper cupcakes at the

community center fundraiser. I would have thought a day of cupcake sales would exhaust a ninety-three-year-old woman, but Grapes seemed invigorated. Her cheeks glowed pink and her blue eyes sparkled.

"We did it, Ellie!" She waved the gold medal around her neck. "We're the reigning champions once again. The Titanium Trio pulled in four hundred dollars and seventy-two cents for the charity."

"That's terrific." I laughed.

Grapes poured milk into a measuring cup. "Zach was our secret weapon, of course. He was so cute all dressed up in his special costume," she sing-songed. "Oh and I met that Dr. Fishburn of yours. Lovely man. He asked how you've been doing with your Comprehensive exam."

"Ugh. You didn't talk to the nosey old frog did you?"

"Of course I did. Bulgy eyes and all. He was one of our best customers —bought twenty dollars' worth of cupcakes."

She pulled a casserole dish from the oven. The layers of flaky piecrust were golden brown and sizzling. The chicken pot pie smelled mouthwatering.

"So, are you ready for your date tonight?" she asked with a wink.

"Hey, this isn't a date, remember?" I said tightly.

My phone buzzed with a text message and I glanced at the screen. It was Dez.

Good luck with the date tonight. Tell Grapes to send John home with leftovers. Chicken pot pie is my fav.

I shook my head and texted back.

Not a date!

Grapes and Dez were tag-teaming me on this date stuff without even knowing it.

The doorbell rang and I felt my stomach flip-flop. Zach appeared from nowhere, barking himself into fits at the front door. We had a no-knocking policy at our house, so when someone actually rang the doorbell, it freaked him out.

John stood on the front step looking freshly showered and handsome. He wore a pair of canvas pants and a green plaid button-down. The effect was truly delicious. The green in his shirt highlighted his stunning amber eyes. He seemed nervous at first but broke into a grin when he saw the dog. Zach was still sporting his bake sale costume. He wore a frilly pink bonnet shaped like a cupcake, his black ears sticking out from two special holes in the headpiece. 'This Dog LOVES Chocolate-Sprinkle-Marshmallow-Bacon-Whoppers' was stitched across a cape he wore across his back in perfect needlepoint letters.

"What have they done to you, bud?" John laughed.

I unstrapped the ribbons and wrestled the bonnet from Zach's ears. "Zach was Grapes' secret weapon at the Kingston Community Center bake sale," I said stiffly.

"Of course he was." John scratched the dog, smoothing the fur flattened by the bonnet.

There was a little pause as I fumbled to find something say. I tried to calm my nerves but there was something about getting started into a conversation that baffled me. Once again, John came to the rescue.

"Oh, I brought you something, Ellie," he said. He dug around in his bag and pulled out a crumpled bouquet of wildflowers. The delicate blooms had been accidently lodged between two large textbooks. He handed me the sagging broken bunch.

"Here..." His voice trailed.

I lifted the bouquet to my nose, stems broken, petals crushed. "Thank you."

"I hope you like daisies." He eyed them with an amused expression. "Well, dead daisies anyway."

I laughed. "Dead daisies are my favorite."

We headed into the kitchen in search of a vase and found Grapes chopping carrots like a mad woman.

"Oh hi, John," she cooed as though they were old friends.

He gave her a grandsonly kiss on the cheek and they started into an easy conversation about the charity bake sale. Grapes told a long-winded story about the special recipe the Titanium Trio used to secure their victory in the community competition for highest sales. They had beat out Mrs. Kontiki's apple fritters, Gladys Beaumeister's handmade baby booties, and even Mumbling Murray's fortune-telling booth. All the while John listened with interest. She force fed him two left over cupcakes and squealed with delight when he asked for a third. John clearly had my great-grandmother wrapped around his little finger.

"Okay, you two, out of my kitchen. I don't want you in here distracting me with your cuteness," she scolded.

As we made our way into the living room, John took his time looking at the embarrassing photos lining the china cabinet. I hadn't realized it before, but they were all pictures of me. Ellie as a naked baby. Ellie as a toddler in a diaper. Ellie as a pimply teenager. I wished I could stop him from looking, but my tongue felt fat again.

"You want to sit?" I finally managed.

John looked up from a large framed picture of me sitting on my dad's lap. We were both crossing our eyes and sticking out our tongues.

"Sure," he said and put the photo back on the cabinet.

Zach was asleep upside-down in the wingback chair, his pink gummy worm tongue hanging over a decorative needlepoint pillow. With the armchair taken, John and I sat beside each other on the couch, our legs touching. It was a little too close for comfort but I resisted the urge to find another piece of furniture to sit on.

I wasn't sure who should start the conversation, so we sat for a while in silence again. John seemed happy with the quiet between us but for me it was maddening.

"Do you want to see the *Heptameron?*" I blurted.

John smirked. "I'd love to."

I disappeared into the kitchen and returned with my backpack, sitting back down on the couch. I pulled out my dad's shiny black box and pulled back the latch. The vacuum seal gave way with a tiny whoosh. Prying up the lid, I revealed the red leather-bound book inside.

"Holy cow," breathed John as he reached in to touch it.

"Wait!" I shouted. "Here. Put on gloves. Lily made me promise."

John grinned devilishly. "Figures Lily would be a stickler for latex."

Once John had gloved up, he lifted the *Heptameron* from the storage container with an expression of awe. He caressed the dimpled leather cover, running his long fingers along its binding. I could definitely see the nerd in him. It was very sexy.

"Marguerite de Navarre wrote the original *Heptameron* in this book?" He glanced up at me.

I realized I was staring at him and looked away.

"Can we open it?" he whispered.

"Yep," I whispered back.

He opened the book gingerly and inspected the front cover. I pointed to the inscription on the left-hand side and explained the book's connection with the Beth Bowlan diary. "It looks like Marguerite de Navarre gave her original copy of the *Heptameron* to Beth Bowlan on her death bed. We figure it was the witchcraft connection that created the bond between the two families." I pursed my lips together waiting for his reaction. I was sure he would tell me I was going crazy.

"Amazing," he replied. "Have you looked through it?"

Gaping at his question, I realized we hadn't yet actually examined the book's contents. Lily and I had been so absorbed in Beth Bowlan's diary we had overlooked the priceless text of Marguerite de Navarre.

"I thought we could look at it together?"

He smiled and then bumped me with his shoulder. "Sounds good."

John settled into the couch as though he was tucking into a good novel. I joined him, melting into his arm to get a good view of the pages. I liked this position. He smelled of aftershave and his arm was a wall of muscle.

We scanned a few pages of text until John noticed the story he had shown me at restaurant the other day. The tale was titled, 'Redirecting Love's Fancy,' but this time the characters' real names were still present.

It was on this very day that Claude, a comely princess, could be found sitting at her armoire, a single tear running down her cheek. The princess was a beautiful woman who was admired by all the court. But her most resplendent attribute was her heart, for she had the heart of angel, so kind that no one could find its slightest flaw.

We read the story together, tucked together like two bookworms on the couch, until John put a latex covered finger on the page.

"Look at this." he said with awe. "There she is—Anne Boleyn!"

Together the three women brewed a love potion so pure and intoxicating it could sway even the darkest of hearts. That night, they stole into Prince Francis' rooms and gathered around his bed. The first friend, Marguerite de Navarre, called upon the moon to redirect love's fancy and send the prince's heart back to Claude. The second friend, Anne Boleyn, poured the love elixir into the prince's sleeping mouth with quiet stealth. And Princess Claude herself kissed the prince upon his cheek and begged him to love her again.

"Holy shit!" My heart raced.

John reread the passage and then turned to look at me. "And now you have your proof, Ellie. Anne Boleyn was a witch."

"Anne Boleyn was a witch." I repeated the words.

John's hazel eyes danced with adventure, but for me, the discovery was sobering. I couldn't help but think of the dreaded treadmill and the day I had received the Comprehensive exam question: *Anne Boleyn—Woman or Witch?* I had been terrified of letting my father down, terrified of letting myself down. And now I had the answer to the exam question and the evidence to prove it. Anne Boleyn was a witch. I swallowed back a surge of emotion I couldn't quite name.

"I think you solved your Comprehensive exam," John whispered in my ear. "Congratulations, Dr. Bowlan."

I struggled to find words.

Grapes shuffled into the living room with her walker. "Okay, you two. Dinner is served."

* * *

The dining room was set with a crisp white tablecloth, silver cutlery, and the good china. Candlelight filled the room and two glasses of red wine waited for us on the sideboard. The stereo sang out a jazzy Louis Armstrong tune.

John eyed the magnificent feast. There was chicken potpie, a heaping bowl of fresh bread, zesty orange turnips, crispy green beans, a voluptuous garden salad and an enormous chocolate cake. As usual, Grapes had outdone herself.

"Nice spread," said John as we took our seats across from each other. Candlelight danced across his face as Louis Armstrong's soulful voice crooned in the background.

"Sorry for all this. Grapes must really like you," I said tightly.

John didn't notice the apology. Instead, he dug into the dinner with the enthusiasm of a starving man. He loaded up two huge scoops of casserole and then went back in for more crust. Heaping a mound of turnips and green beans onto the side, he topped it off with a gargantuan pile of salad. His plate looked like a volcano ready to erupt. Remembering his manners, he placed the white linen napkin in his lap and started right in.

As he took his first bite, he scrunched up his face in pleasure. "Oh... my...God. This is sooooo good."

Once the words were out he dove into his meal with abandon. It was as though he hadn't eaten in weeks. It was true that Grapes' food was exceptional, but this guy couldn't seem to get enough. He ate with the rapture of child after a long day in the playground. As I watched him chewing and swallowing, chewing and swallowing, I began to wonder about this beautiful man and the boy he once was. I realized I knew nothing about him, other than his academic pursuits.

John finished his first plate and headed in for a second helping. No wonder Grapes loved him. This was the man she could feed...and feed...and feed.

"So John." I started into my own meal in case he actually ate everything on the table. "Tell me about yourself."

He looked up, his eating frenzy interrupted.

"Hmmm...okay..." He wiped his mouth with his napkin and pondered the question. "I guess it all starts with my family. My dad's a physician. My mom's a lawyer. They weren't around much when I was a kid. They were both dedicated to their careers. Actually, I think that was what ended their marriage. They split when I was fifteen."

"Sorry," I said.

"No. Don't be. They're both happier now. But I didn't have much of a childhood. It was a rather formal upbringing, you know? No chicken zombie costumes or home-brew street parties. Nothing like your amazing childhood."

I smiled. I guess I did have a colorful family. It touched my heart that he remembered my stories.

He watched me from across the table, eyes twinkling in the candlelight. His voice was regretful. "When I'm a father, I'm going to do things differently. You know? I want to do it all. Birthday parties with ponies and clowns, baseball games with hotdogs and beer. Well beer for me...a slushy for her..."

"Her?" I asked.

John smirked, his secret exposed. "Yeah, I've always wanted a daughter. But I would be happy with either a girl or a boy. Kids are great."

"Kids are great." I lowered my eyes, no longer sure where to go with the conversation. I wasn't good with this getting-to-know-you stuff. Here was John pouring his heart out about the daughter he hoped to have one day, and I had seized up like a car engine out of motor oil. My faced flushed red.

We finished our dinner in silence. When John had cleaned every last morsel off his plate, he wiped his mouth and leaned back, folding his arms behind his head. He eyed me for a while.

"You know what would be nice?" he said.

I put my fork down and looked up at him. "What?"

John made his way around the table and extended his hand. "A dance." He smiled. "Ellie Bowlan, will you dance with me?"

I blinked at him vacantly.

"Come on, dance with me." He gave me a wink with those amber eyes as a new jazzy tune came on. "This is one of my favorite Billie Holiday songs."

John led me onto the makeshift dance floor space between the living and dining room as Billie sang in her smoky voice. He put his arms around my waist and pulled me in close. I could feel the firmness of his pectoral muscles and the strength of his arms around me. It made me a little weak in the knees.

As we danced slow and mellow, he sang the words under his breath.

We spun around and around, his rough cheek grazing mine. Our bodies leaned in tighter as a surge of electricity passed between us. The smell of his aftershave made my heart flutter. He pulled my chin upward with his index finger and gazed down with a long slow smile.

"You are beautiful," he whispered.

John's lips were so close to mine, I could feel his sweet breath mingling with my own. My body responded and I leaned in closer, willing him to kiss me. I shuddered as he ran his fingers through my hair. He lowered his delicious lips, ready to deliver a slow yearning kiss. I raised my mouth to his and closed my eyes, waiting for the gentle flush of contact.

But it didn't come.

A slam of the front door startled us from our embrace. Bernice whooped with fright as Gerty chastised her for her reaction. The commotion was anything but subtle and the bickering continued as they made their way down the hall and into the kitchen.

"Come on, Lizzie. Where have you hidden them?" Bernice trilled.

Grapes shushed her friends but it was too late. Bernice and Gerty barged into the dining room, eager-faced and breathless. Grapes trailed behind, her expression apologetic.

"John, can I introduce you to Gerty and Bernice?" Grapes said awkwardly.

Gerty and Bernice were wearing matching cornflower blue velour jumpsuits. They looked like three crazy old sisters when they dressed this way.

"Oh you are handsome, aren't you?" Gerty gushed.

"John, it's a real pleasure, darlin'." Bernice chimed in blindly.

"Hi there," said John.

John released me from our embrace but continued to hold my hand as the Titanium Trio peppered him with questions. He responded with his usual charm and these old women swooned. They launched into a series of long-winded stories about their day of cupcake sales and showed off their matching hand-stitched costumes. John listened politely with an amused expression.

After a while, Grapes shooed her friends towards the door. "Gerty and Bernice just came to drop off the Tupperware containers, right girls?" She worked them from behind.

"Actually," John interjected. "I have to be going too." He locked eyes with mine—a silent exchange between us. "Thank you for the dinner, Mrs. Bowlan. I had a great time."

"But you haven't even had your chocolate cake," Grapes protested. Obviously, the idea of her delicious food going to waste was about to twist her knickers in a knot.

She hurried into the kitchen and re-emerged with a Tupperware container full of leftovers. Two extra large slices of cake wrapped in aluminum foil crowned the top of the pile. She pushed the package into his hands.

"There, now dear. I've packed up enough for you and Dez. He loves my chicken pot pie, but that chocolate cake, well, it's magical."

Nothing was the same after Anne's afternoon with Henry. Everything felt wrong. Their time together had been so short, just enough to allow Anne to remember everything she loved about him. His masculine scent. His firm torso. The scratch of his beard when he kissed her. They had spent only a couple of hours together, laughing and whispering like sweethearts. It had been as wonderful as the night when they first kissed. Where Anne's heart ended, Henry's began. It was love. Anne was sure of it.

Since their parting, Anne had worn Henry's gift every day. The gold embossed B hung in the delicate hollow of her throat. She often played with the pearls that hung from the charm and longed for the day they might have a child of their own.

Henry had sailed back to England that night with George. Anne had begged him to stay but they both knew he could not. He was bound by duty to his country, and England was where he belonged.

Anne sulked. Her sister's arrival had changed things for the worse here in France too. Though it was not her fault, Mary had brought an unwelcome formality back into their happy lives. Mary was too prim and proper to connect with Claude and Marguerite. Nor did she have the mental fortitude to spar with Leonardo.

As a result, Anne felt torn between two worlds. With Claude, Marguerite, and Leonardo, Anne was free to query and question and marvel at the vast world around her. But with Mary, Anne had fallen back into the practices of her more formal upbringing. Dresses and hairstyles, dance steps and music. She had even returned to needlepoint in the afternoons to help her sister feel more at ease.

To make matters worse, old King Louis had seen fit to end their summer holiday by calling them all back to the Chateau du Blois. And just like that Anne's summer fun had vanished in a puff of smoke.

For their first formal supper with the French royals, Mary had insisted on meticulous preparation. Servants swirled around her, applying the final additions to her costume and hair. Anne, in contrast, sat slumped in a chair, unwilling to pretty herself no matter how much Rose cajoled. She had not even flinched when her nursemaid threatened to pinch her cheeks to give her a bit of color.

"Do you prefer the pearl drop earrings or the opals?" Mary crooned. She dusted her bust with powder, the rose pink of her fitted bodice creating an impressive young cleavage.

Anne looked out the window. Even the poor weather had returned. "The opals are fine."

Mary gazed into a small looking glass she had brought along from England. "Should I wear my hair up or leave it down, do you think?"

Anne looked at her sister as her handmaid brushed out her long blonde hair. "Down, dear sister. Your hair shines like the sun when you wear it down."

* * *

Anne and Mary curtsied as they entered the grand dining room, an enormous fire crackling in the hearth. Her sister's face lit with pleasure at the elegance of the evening, the crisp white tablecloths, the busy servants, and minstrels making ready for the feast and entertainment. But Anne was in no mood. Despite the steady stream of arriving dinner guests, King Louis and his dwarf were already eating. She couldn't believe his ill manners.

Louis sat hunched over his plate, shoveling blancmange into his mouth with his new elegant Italian fork. His small man, Frederique, slurped wine from a chalice, unconcerned with the rice that was collecting in his beard.

Stiff-necked courtiers mingled with guarded formality. Anne noticed Leonardo da Vinci looking elegant in his doublet and cap, a strange contrast to his long flowing nightgowns from their summer away. He pulled at the ruffled fabric of his constricting neckline and gave Anne a sympathetic nod as he passed by.

Francis, on the other hand, stood near the grand fireplace looking at ease. Although Anne had met him before, she looked upon Claude's husband as if seeing him for the first time. She had thought little of him on their first encounter but Claude had spoken of him with such warmth this summer, it made her curious.

Francis' eyes were too small and his nose rather large but he was handsome enough in his doublet and hose. Anne could see why Claude admired him. He was refined and well dressed and he had mastered the smooth manners of court. He flitted from guest to guest with the grace of a butterfly, never spending too much time with any one patron. He flattered and beguiled, he chuckled and jested, his conversation as light as a summer breeze.

Claude arrived dressed in a bejeweled dress that made her belly look even larger than it was. She made her way through the crowd with a timid step. Anne waved at her best friend, eager for her to join, but Claude wasn't looking her way. A shy smile played across Claude's face as she gazed at Francis. The two had obviously not yet seen one another since their return from Amboise.

"Claude, my darling. How well you look," said Francis, eyeing her full form.

Claude's bust spilled from her dress. She was thick with pregnancy and her neck seemed to swallow up her face. Her fingers were as fat as sausages.

"Our child grows large," Claude apologized.

Francis took her hand and kissed it. "Indeed. Our son will soon be come to this world."

King Louis barked from across the room. "Your hunch back has grown too!"

The king and his dwarf roared with laughter.

Anne winced at the insult. It hung in the air like an awful smell. At the provocation, Francis' pretty manners faltered. He let go Claude's hand and created a distance between himself and his wife. Claude, now flushing red, retreated to the back of the crowd while Francis made a beeline to his sister.

Anne was not impressed with the exchange. Francis seemed more concerned with blending into the conversation than bothering with his wife's humiliation. But perhaps that was the way of French court. Everything was as polished as silver on the surface but there was ugliness beneath.

In spite of the unease working its way through the crowd, Marguerite was keeping the conversation convivial and easy. She was discussing the finer points of castle life with a couple of well-dressed ladies and the man with the twitching peacock feather. The fashion choices for the season. The musical entertainment. The foul weather that was ruining the annual tennis match.

"Francis, I would like to introduce you to Anne Boleyn's sister," Marguerite said as her brother joined the group. "Mary is come from England to serve as a lady-in-wait to the English princess."

Francis' cheeks flushed as his eyes slid over Mary Boleyn. Unlike Claude, Mary was slim and youthful. Her eyes were the color of the summer sky. Her gown was the height of French fashion and it accentuated her already generous bosom.

Anne scowled.

"It is a pleasure to meet you," said Francis as he kissed Mary's fingers.

Mary lowered her eyelids, a shy smile pulling across her lips.

"May I bid you welcome by asking for a dance?" he asked with a bow.

The minstrels picked up their instruments and began to play an exquisite French chanson for the group. Mary blushed as Francis pulled her in close, the crowd crooning with the elegance of their movements. Mary smiled up at Francis with the heady innocent gaze of youth as they performed the elaborate steps together. It was as though they had danced together a hundred times before.

Anne felt a whirl of nausea in her stomach as she watched them. She wondered if Francis was as praiseworthy as Claude suggested.

"Enough revelry!" the king barked with impatience. "We have things to discuss."

The festivities ended abruptly as the guests dispersed from the dance floor and made their way to the dining table. Servants collided with courtiers as they attempted to assemble under the king's command. Large casseroles of blancmange, now gone cold, were ready for serving. Anne was ushered to a spot beside Leonardo and they both hastened to their seats.

"Now then," the King began unceremoniously. "I wish to discuss the royal wedding." He turned his eyes on Leonardo. "Da Vinci, our Italian scholar, what say you of our new Italian forks? Are they not impressive?"

Leonardo glanced at the silver object clutched in the King's fingers. "Your fork is most impressive, sire."

The king slapped his hand on the table, the vibrations rattling the plates all the way down to Anne's place setting. "Spoken like a true Italian gentleman. That is why I have decided you shall be the banquet organizer for my wedding. You shall bring an air of Italian elegance to our festivities. But I warn you, my expectations are high."

Leonardo picked up his own fork and rotated it between his long fingers, his voice now dripping with sarcasm. "And shall you have forks at this great event?"

The king smiled boastfully. "Of course. It is to be the greatest event of the decade." He waved a finger in the air. "And I shall have fireworks."

Leo nodded carefully. Anne noticed a look of measured patience on her friend's face.

"And the fashion must be high—robes the color of amethyst, trimmed in fur," the king pressed on, lost in his own vision.

"Ermine fur?" Leonardo's face was difficult to read now.

"Fine, yes. Ermine fur." Louis waved off the suggestion.

Leonardo bobbed his head. "Is there anything else you require, sire?"

"Yes, of course. I did not bring you here to laze about, da Vinci. You shall paint a work of art in homage to me—the Great King of France. And you shall present it at my wedding."

Anne wondered if Louis would be capable of appreciating fine art the likes of which Leonardo could produce. He probably wouldn't know the difference between a work of art and the simple sketch of a five-year-old child.

Marguerite waded into the discussion now. Anne had seen her manage the king's mercurial spirit before and wondered if she would have the same luck this evening. "What of the ladies of the court? Are we to be bride's maids to the English princess for this wedding?" she asked lightly.

Louis shifted his gaze down the table, his eyes hardening. "Yes, Marguerite, we shall have all but the dog."

Marguerite laughed at what she mistook for a joke. "The dog, sire?"

But the pause in the conversation was a pregnant one, as pregnant as the woman to whom he had just referred. Anne knew exactly what he meant. The king pointed down the table. The guests watched as he swung his finger in Claude's direction.

"That. I shall not have that...*thing*...at my wedding."

An awkward hush filled the room. No one knew what to say.

Anne could understand none of it. The king's mood had become suddenly boorish, a dangerous tone lurking beneath. But nothing she had learned about this family in her time in France could explain this man's inconsolable hatred for his daughter. All her life, Claude had served her father well. She had done everything he had ever asked of her.

At the other end of the table, Claude cleared her throat. The music died away as dinner guests, courtiers, minstrels, and even the servants turned towards this young girl as she readied herself for a response. Anne marveled at her friend's courage. Claude had become such a confident young woman over the summer. Perhaps it was finally time for her to defend herself against her father.

"But I should attend your wedding. I am your daughter, after all," said Claude with a tiny voice.

Louis froze mid-chew. The muscle in his jaw twitched as his peevish temperament turned to simpering rage. It seemed to swallow him like an apoplexy.

"What...did...you...say?" he managed.

Claude's hands trembled but she pressed on. "I am your daughter and I should like to attend your wedding."

Louis' eyes narrowed into slits as he glowered down the table. He sucked the spittle from between his front teeth, his face reddening to the point of explosion. For a long moment, he tapped at the table with his fork, lost in his own fury.

Marguerite looked as though she might come to Claude's aid, but when she opened her mouth, no words came forth. Anne did not know what to do. If Marguerite dared not speak, it was probably best she too remained silent. There was nothing to do but to wait. All eyes were on the king.

Louis pushed back from his chair and strutted to the other end of the table. Claude cowered under his now hulking form as he stood menacingly over her chair.

"Stand up, dog," he spat.

Claude did as her father commanded and got clumsily to her feet, cradling her belly. She produced a small curtsy and stood with obeisance, eyes dropped to the floor. Anne could see her best friend trembling under the king's terrible gaze.

Louis watched her for a while, allowing her to squirm with the unwanted attention. Finally, he spoke in a voice that was low and dangerous. "I told you before, dog. Do not address me *father*."

Claude kept her eyes lowered. Her shoulders were hunched low and the crook in her back was even more apparent than normal.

"Stand up straight, you deformed freakish imp," he spat.

She attempted to right the pitch in her back so her shoulders were even but she struggled under the weight of her child.

The king scoffed at her effort. He snapped his head up now and addressed the group of dinner guests, musicians, and servants alike. Anne was horrified.

"I would like all of you to look upon this mutilated devil spawn. She is no better than a dog. And she must be punished like a dog."

Claude continued to cringe before him, tears filling her eyes.

"Look at me," he commanded Claude.

She kept her gaze low.

"Look at me, dog!" he roared.

Obediently, she raised her eyes to meet his.

They gazed at each other for what seemed an eternity, his eyes locked on hers, devouring her remaining will with his fury.

Suddenly King Louis drew his hand back and slapped his pregnant daughter hard across the face. His hand connecting with her flesh made a sickening clap through the otherwise silent room.

"I told you, dog. Do. Not. Address. Me. Father."

I drummed my fingers on the edge of Lily's desk and waited for her to return from book stacking. I didn't dare sit in her chair. That would have been too presumptuous, even for me. Instead, I perched on an uncomfortable stool and wiggled with anticipation. Excitement trilled through me like an effervescent string of bubbles.

After John left last night, I had spent a few hours thinking through my approach to my Comprehensive exam. Based on the evidence I had amassed, I decided I would argue Anne Boleyn was a witch. This position went against traditional historical opinion but with the new evidence I had amassed, I felt I could make a strong case. Besides, if the great Landon Fishburn was a lover of ancient witchcraft, he would no doubt appreciate the evidence I had unearthed. I was feeling confident I had this Comp exam under control and the relief was nothing short of miraculous.

Lily came around the corner appearing genuinely pleased with the world. Just by looking at her, I knew something was wrong. She seemed to be floating rather than walking and she wore a dreamy smile that made her look almost drunk. This was not my Lily.

"Oh, hi," Lily trilled.

"Oh hi?" I asked. "Lily, what's going on?"

She wrapped her arms around herself, misty-eyed and breathless. "He kissed me," she whispered.

This news was almost as shocking as my Anne Boleyn discovery. But the smile on her face was proof enough.

"It was my first kiss ever," she said, touching her fingers to her lips.

I smiled. Whoever this Donny guy was had won her heart and I was delighted for her. I jumped off my stool and swooped in for a high five, but Lily was so distracted, I decided against it. Instead, I swatted her arm. "So? How was your first kiss—ever?"

She bit her lip at the memory. "Well, it was soft." She breathed. "And kind of squishy."

We burst into laughter. Lily's belly laugh was fulsome and wonderful. It was the first time I'd ever heard it. It was low and throaty, the kind of laughter that shook her whole body.

"And how about you? How was your dinner with John?" she asked.

"It was nice. But no kiss." I winced, remembering the Titanium Trio barging in on our little dance. I plopped my backpack down dramatically on her desk. "But it's okay because you will never believe what John and I found last night."

She was already putting on her blue jacket and shower cap. Lily had switched gears in an instant.

"We found her, Lil!" I hissed as I followed her into the humidity controlled Special Collections room. "We found Anne Boleyn. She was named in the original draft of *The Heptameron*. The love spell they conjured was the same one written in Marguerite de Navarre's grimoire." I was practically vibrating—Mindy style.

Lily lifted the red leather bound *Heptameron* from the vacuum-sealed storage container and examined the text, obviously needing to see the evidence with her own eyes. She scanned the passage, looked up at me wide-eyed, and then read the passage again.

"Anne Boleyn was a witch," Lily said breathlessly.

I looked like the cat that ate the canary. "Yup."

"Ellie, do you realize how amazing this is? You could publish this work and turn the historical literature on its head. There isn't a university on the planet that wouldn't love to have you. This kind of discovery is what scholars spend their entire career searching for."

"You think?"

"Of course." She blinked at me from behind her glasses. "Yes, of course." Then, without warning, Lily screamed at the top of her lungs, "Anne Boleyn was a witch!"

She flapped her arms like a chicken before launching herself at me. She threw her arms around my neck and hugged me hard. Her show of affection was more intense than I expected, but I hugged her back anyway, laughing at her reaction.

Before I knew it, Lily was dancing a jig around the Special Collections room. Her legs flew out in joyful kicks as she clapped her hands to a mysterious beat only she could hear. I had to admit, she was pretty darn good. It didn't take long before her enthusiasm infected me too and I found myself jigging and shrieking alongside her.

"Anne Boleyn was a witch! Anne Boleyn was a witch!" she sang in her strange Lily beat.

"Anne Boleyn was a witch! Anne Boleyn was a witch!" I sang out too.

Eventually we joined hands and danced in a circle. We spun around like two kids in playground, jumping and leaping, and chanting out the Anne Boleyn cheer. This transformed into a kind of square dance maneuver and we spun each other around until we were both dizzy. After a good round of jigging and squealing, we were both out of breath and Lily's cheeks had gone blotchy. Only then did we calm down enough to sit down at the table and stare at the red leather text like it was an Olympic gold medal.

Lily ran her gloved hands along the ancient book's bindings. "It's amazing to think Marguerite de Navarre's *Heptameron* and Beth Bowlan's diary were sitting in your basement all those years. Thank goodness your father understood their value and knew how to store them properly."

In spite of my excitement, the thought of my dad needled me in the gut. Throughout my academic career, I had always longed to have my father by my side. I had always wished he and I could make our discoveries together. The truth was Dad deserved the accolades for this find, but his murderer made sure he never got the chance.

"Lily," I asked. "Where do you think my father found these books? I mean, we found them in his old research boxes, but where did *he* find them?"

She shrugged. She knew no more than I did. And there was no one else to ask. The only ones who had the answers were dead.

"I don't know. But I did figure out who Henri Carey was," Lily said helpfully. "Turns out, Henri Carey was Anne Boleyn's nephew. He was the son of Anne's sister, Mary Boleyn."

"That's weird," I replied.

She frowned. "Yes. Henri Carey fits into the puzzle. We just have to figure out where."

We fell into our comfortable pattern of reading together side by side, poring over Beth Bowlan's diary. As the hours past, we marveled as young Beth became an increasingly proficient witch. We stopped at a passage towards the end of the journal. The date put Beth at sixteen years of age.

March 23, 1574

> *Today I made a special request to my Uncle. In two days, London is making ready to host the city's Lady Day celebrations. And on this day the great queen herself, our Virgin Queen Elizabeth, will ride through town for all too see. I have never been allowed to attend the parade. But I am sixteen years along now and how I wish to go. I rehearsed my words so many times they still play out in my mind.*
>
> *'Uncle Henri, I have been a member of the Carey family since I was a babe. I have never asked much of you, but today I make a single request. I ask that I may see the Queen of England with my own eyes.'*

"Hold on a second," I said. "Beth Bowlan's beloved uncle was Henri Carey?"

"But if her uncle was Henri Carey, and Henri Carey was the son of Mary Boleyn, then who was her secret mother?" asked Lily.

I frowned. The dots were connecting in my mind, but I couldn't quite draw the line.

March 25, 1574

> *Words cannot express, dear Diary, my disbelief at my discovery today at the Lady Day Parade. Uncle Henri allowed me to attend but he warned that it might cause me a fright. I didn't understand his warning until today when I saw the royal carriage with mine own eyes. I stood among the crowd, bumping and jostling to get a good look. That is when I saw the shocking truth. Do you know what I saw, dear diary?*
>
> *I saw my own secret mother. She was the woman in the royal carriage. My own secret mother was the one that everyone came to see. My own secret mother was Queen Elizabeth of England.*

I coughed as I read the words.

"Holy shit, Lil! Beth Bowlan's mother was Queen frickin' Elizabeth. I guess that explains why her mother had to be a secret. Elizabeth was the Virgin Queen. She never married, so it would have been impossible for her to acknowledge her illegitimate daughter."

Lily picked up a pencil and jotted down a rough family tree. She put

Anne Boleyn's name at the top and filled in the parts we knew. "Beth was raised by her Uncle Henri Carey so she could be close enough to know her mother without being recognized." She circled Anne Boleyn's name to mark the starting point of the lineage.

"And if Beth Bowlan was Queen Elizabeth's daughter, and Elizabeth was Anne Boleyn's daughter," I puzzled, stringing the pieces together like lights on a Christmas tree, "then the Bowlan line is an extension of the Boleyn line."

We exchanged disbelieving looks.

"And that means you are related to Anne Boleyn. She's your long lost great-great-great-grandmother." Lily's heavy glasses slid down her nose as she wrote my name at the bottom of the family tree. "Bowlan—Boleyn. The two names share a lot in common, phonetically speaking."

She circled my name on the paper, Ellie Bowlan, to mark the end of the lineage.

My mouth hung open. I had no words.

But Lily was gaining speed. "This could explain your father's work on matriarchal naming conventions. Maybe the family name was preserved through the lineage by recreating it phonetically, but with a different spelling so people didn't recognize the connection." She pushed the glasses back up her nose. "Queen Elizabeth couldn't ask that her daughter be named Elizabeth Boleyn. The connection would be too obvious. But she could have maintained the sound of the name by recreating it as Bowlan."

I was gob-smacked. "Anne Boleyn was my great-great-great-great-grandmother—like a hundred times removed!"

I raised my hand for a high-five. And Lily slapped it hard.

"Anne Boleyn was a witch! Anne Boleyn was a witch." Lily threw the pencil over her shoulder and started with her strange dance again.

"Anne Boleyn was my grandmother! Anne Boleyn was my grandmother!" I sang along too, kicking my legs to match Lily's bizarre jig.

We danced and howled at this new discovery. We whooped and screamed at the top of our lungs, knowing we were down here alone and nobody would notice our bizarre celebration. No one was here to judge us. No one was here to laugh. We looked like a couple of maniacs on a weekend pass from a mental institution, but we didn't care. We cavorted and boogied with joyful abandon, and it was the best feeling in the world.

"I cannot believe his cruelty!" said Anne through gritted teeth.

Leonardo flicked his brush with irritation, spraying yellow paint on the floor. "Anne, I cannot capture the line of your throat if you keep spinning your head. Each time you move, it changes the light on that string of pearls."

Anne had spent the last several hours modeling for Leonardo's painting and her neck was getting sore. She rotated her head back into position and cradled Salai in her arms. The black cat sat purring on her lap and she scratched him behind the ears.

"Fine. I shall remain still," she acquiesced. "But I will use my mouth to speak. We must do something about King Louis. With our talents in the Craft, we could take action. Don't you think, Marguerite?"

Marguerite looked up from her book. She had been composing a short story for her novel but seemed to be having some difficulty concentrating. The king's outburst had been upsetting for all of them.

"Louis' hatred has grown. That slap was a new level of depravity," Marguerite agreed. "He has never hit her before."

Anne scratched at the coiffure holding her hair in place. She was wearing an ill-fitting Spanish style gown with crimson puffed sleeves. The dress was the height of French fashion but the corset pinched her ribs and the gold brocade cutting across her forehead was itchy.

"I wish the king would die," she spat.

"Anne," cried Leonardo. "Hold still."

"Well, do any of you deny it?" Anne resumed her awkward pose, her muscles groaning in complaint. "He is a monster. Look at what he has done to Claude. She has barely uttered a word since the night of the supper."

Claude lay motionless on the chaise in the corner, staring up at the timbered ceiling. She had been there all morning. The blackened bruise along her eye socket had faded to a sickening greenish yellow in the days following the king's supper, but it was clear her heart had broken. And that would take much longer to mend than any physical injury.

Marguerite put her writing book on the table and went to her sister-in-law, kneeling beside her. She raised a glass of watered ale to Claude's lips.

"Please, darling. You must try to drink something. For the baby."

Claude shook her head. She had eaten almost nothing in the last few days. She had hardly even taken water. Her spirit had been shattered and Anne cringed at her suffering.

"You must, Claude. Take a bit of ale." Anne coaxed now too.

Claude acquiesced and tipped the cup to her mouth and Anne breathed a sigh of relief. At least she would return to physical health and her baby would be all right.

Marguerite took the cup when she had finished. "Here, let me apply a bit of salve to your lips."

"He deserves to die," Anne said steadily.

"Hush, Anne. What you say is treason against the king," Marguerite warned.

Anne harrumphed. She didn't care about treason. She didn't care about anything. Her friend had been assaulted and the perpetrator should pay. King or no king.

"Claude, what say you? Do you not think your father should be punished for his actions?" Anne pressed.

After a morning lying immobile on the chaise, Claude pulled her swollen body into an upright position until her belly rested on top of her legs. The last few days at the French court had destroyed most of her newfound spirit. She had reverted to the cowering timid girl Anne had met months ago.

"I worry for the baby," said Claude.

Marguerite dabbed at Claude's lips with a little more salve. "Louis would surely not harm the child."

Claude lowered her eyes. "He does want a grandson. That much is true. Having a boy would protect the baby. But we all know the babe I carry is a girl. What if she is like me?" She gestured to the hump on her back. "Why would he offer her any more kindness than he offers me?"

Leonardo furrowed his bushy eyebrows at the thought. He put down his paintbrush and plucked up Salai from Anne's lap. The cat nuzzled its face along Leo's long silver beard.

"I have not seen it in my visions," he said. "Perhaps the child will be well, with a straight back and healthy cry. She would be safe then. Would she not?"

Anne leapt from her chair, thankful for the temporary release from modeling duty. She stretched out her arms and flexed her back to loosen the tightened muscles.

"Oh come now. We mustn't be naïve," she insisted. "The king is a threat, regardless. Even if he favors the child, he will continue to make Claude's life a living hell. And for what? What possible reason does he have to hate her?"

Silence hung in the room like a hangman's noose. Anne had wondered about this since her arrival, but she had always been afraid to ask.

"He hates me because of my mother," Claude replied simply.

Marguerite and Claude exchanged looks, a lifetime of painful memories passing between them. It was clear these two had lived through great suffering under this man. Marguerite patted Claude on the arm and explained.

"When Louis was fourteen, he was bid by King Charles to marry Claude's mother. Louis was in line for the throne as a second cousin and his claim was tenuous. Neither of them wanted the royal marriage. But as is often the case for nobles, the two were joined in holy matrimony. From that day forward, their marriage was doomed. There could not have been a more ill-suited match in all of France. It is said the only time they were ever together in a marital sense was the night they consummated their marriage. It was from this union that Claude was born."

"So he hated her mother, and now he hates Claude?" asked Anne with disbelief. The whole story seemed preposterous. How could a man not love his own child, unhappy marriage or otherwise?

Marguerite continued. "Louis wished to marry another. Although it was not her fault, he blamed Claude's mother for blocking his happiness. He was unkind to her right from the start. He tormented her at every opportunity because of the crook she had in her back."

Claude hung her head.

"When Claude was born with the same deformity, King Louis could not love her. In fact, he hated her all the more. He threatened to have Claude sent away, but Claude's mother refused. Louis was forced to accept Claude as his child. But he always disliked the idea that he was her father."

Marguerite gazed at Claude. It was easy to see how much of a mother figure she had been to this sad girl.

"When Charles died and Louis became king, he sought an annulment from his marriage. But it was denied. That is when he became cruel. Claude's mother suffered. She died a young woman. Louis found her dead one morning and had her buried the very same day. It was a most suspicious death."

Marguerite looked to the door and lowered her voice. "It is said that Louis pushed her down a flight of steps. We don't know if the rumors are true, but he would let only his personal coroner tend to her body."

"You mean he killed her?" Anne gasped.

Marguerite shushed the outburst and glanced again toward the door. "No one knows for sure. Such is the power of the king. But we have wondered about it for years."

The story seeped through the air like a poisonous cloud. How could the king be this hateful? How could he kill his own wife? Anne realized, more now than ever, it spelled disaster for Claude and her unborn child.

Anne spoke in a hushed tone, now deadly serious about her idea. "Could we not use the Craft? Could we not ask the Goddess to end his life?"

The others bristled at the suggestion. Claude sat upright, shifting her body to find a more comfortable position. Marguerite wrung her hands as she paced the room. Leonardo put Salai down on the chaise and folded his sinewy arms across his chest.

The silence only fueled Anne's conviction. "For Claude's sake. For the sake of her unborn child. We could use dark magic to kill the king."

"No." Leonardo responded. "We shall not speak of such things. The cost would be too great. We would remove one problem but unleash a fury of others. The Goddess' price is high when murder is what you seek."

"I agree with Leonardo," said Marguerite. "A witch who used the Craft to take the king's life would suffer enduring consequence. The cost of dark magic is high and unpredictable. We shall have to find another solution."

Claude's eyes filled with tears and Anne took her hand in support. The whole situation seemed hopeless. They were up against the most powerful man in France. In spite of his infantile tantrums, King Louis was dangerous and they all knew it. He had killed Claude's mother without consequence. If not with dark magic, how would they protect Claude and her baby from this monster?

Claude rubbed the baby, playing with a bump jutting from just below her naval. "Do you know what is worse than a father who does not love you?"

"That is awful enough, I should think," replied Anne.

"Aye, it is. My father does not love me. It has always been that way." Her voice was raw, stripped bare from the hardship of the last few days. "But a husband who does not love me, that breaks my heart. It hurts because he did love me once. And now even that love is gone."

Anne's stomach clenched at her friend's words. Droplets of guilt began to drip down the back of her neck. Surely Claude had been too occupied in the last few days to notice the insignificant romance that had blossomed between Francis and her sister Mary?

Marguerite waved away Claude's suggestion. "Darling, don't be silly. Francis has always loved you. That will never change."

Claude stood for the first time that morning. It was quite an effort to raise her sizeable form from the chaise. As she got to her feet, she her put her hands at the base of her back to balance herself against the baby's formidable bulge.

"It is true. Francis no longer loves me. But then, look at me. What is there to love? I am ugly and fat. I have a crooked back. My Francis has fallen for another. He has fallen in love with Anne's beautiful sister, Mary Boleyn."

Leonardo glanced at Anne with wide eyes. Marguerite glanced at Leonardo. Their three-part exchange was laden with guilt.

Claude continued. "There are whispers all around the castle. My Francis has spent every day and evening with Mary since her arrival."

Anne wanted to tell Claude she was wrong, but she knew her words were true. Ever since the night of the royal supper, Mary had made a string of pretty excuses to be elsewhere. A game of cards. A day of prayer. A fitting for a new gown. Anne had been so relieved to be free of her sister she had turned a blind eye. She hadn't questioned. She hadn't protected. She hadn't done her duty.

Claude continued. "Rose told me that Mary often walks in the gardens with Francis, laughing and talking the way we used to. He is enamored with her and she with him."

Anne went to the window, the truth of it sinking in. Each in their own way, by holding their tongues, the whole group had been complicit in the budding romance between Francis and Mary. How had their lives become complicated in such a short time? What had happened to their summer happiness at the Chateau Clos Lucé?

She gazed out the window, wishing she could be far away from this place. Perhaps back at their summer retreat when their endless summer days were filled with magic and mischief.

The weather had finally shifted and the August summer sun shone bright, the blue sky the color of sapphires. The rolling hills in the window beyond provided a bucolic setting, except for the horrific site creeping into Anne's field of view.

In the gardens below, Francis and Mary strolled arm-in-arm amongst the ornamental parterres. The smiles they wore were unmistakable. Love was in the air.

"Oh no," Anne gasped.

The others rushed to the window, pushing aside the wet canvas. Leonardo's paintbrushes clattered to the floor as they huddled together to watch the scene unfolding in the gardens below.

Francis cupped Mary's hand, trailing his fingers over the back of her glove. He moved his hand slowly around her waist and pulled her to him. They stood in the garden, close and intimate, gazing into each other's eyes. After a while, Francis drew Mary's face up close to his. Then ever so deliciously, he planted the softest kiss upon her lips.

"Francis," cried Claude.

Anne's heart sank. She knew she had not paid Mary enough attention since her arrival in France. Perhaps she had even resented Mary for spoiling their summer fun. And it had resulted in this. Mary was ruining Claude's marriage. It was all her fault.

"Mary knows not what she does. She is young. She is lonely..." Anne stammered.

But her words were no use. Claude was watching as her husband embracing another woman, the betrayal unraveling before her very eyes. Tears ran down her cheeks and she raised her hand to the bruise over her eye. Then in one swift movement, she ran from the room, gentle whimpers echoing down the hallway.

The remaining friends continued to watch the affair in the gardens below. After more playful kisses and flirtatious giggles, they had all seen enough.

"I am sorry, Anne," Marguerite said, her tone firm. "We shall have to send Mary back to England."

"Aye. Mary will have to go," she agreed.

Leonardo watched on with fascination. "Marguerite, I am not sure sending Mary away will solve this problem. Francis will long for her. Sending Mary back to England will not make Francis love Claude any more than he does now."

Marguerite watched the couple as the kisses continued, her own lips twisted in distaste. After a time, she smoothed her skirts, a new wave of determination passing over her features.

"Yes, Leo. What you say is true. But there are some things best left to the women of the Craft. I shall take care of this little matter of the heart. It is a particular specialty of mine."

PRESENT DAY
QUEEN'S UNIVERSITY, CANADA

I tiptoed down the empty hallway trying hard not to let my Birkenstocks squeak against the polished marble flooring. It was late in the day and most of the students who occupied offices in the history department had long since left the building. I made a point of avoiding my own office here. It was uncomfortably close to Dr. Fishburn's and I always felt like I was being watched. But this evening, I needed to retrieve my APA Reference Manual from my desk. It was an absolute necessity.

Since my discovery earlier this afternoon, I was starting to feel ready to start writing up my Comp exam paper, and I never attempted any serious writing without my reference manual. It seemed a silly thing but citing historical research incorrectly could earn you an instant fail. Academics were funny about getting credit for their work. It was university protocol and I was determined to get my reference manual and sneak out as quickly as possible.

"Ms. Bowlan," a froggy voice echoed down the corridor.

I stopped walking.

"Ms. Bowlan, I recognize the squeak of your sandals. Why don't you come in for a little visit?"

My heart sank. I had been caught. For a second I thought about running away but soon realized that would be foolish. Whether I wanted to or not, I would have to face him. Pushing my shoulders back, I plastered on a fake smile and strode as confidently as I could to Dr. Fishburn's office.

"Hello," I said softly.

Dr. Fishburn sat at his desk like a king on his throne. The office was truly impressive, if I had to be honest. The walls were lined from floor to ceiling with a vast collection of books of all shapes and sizes. Stacked papers covered the floor in haphazard piles, with ant trails just large enough for a human body to pass. One trail lead to Dr. Fishburn's big armchair behind his desk. The second led to a small chair in front. This was clearly the place for the visiting student. My shoulders sinking slightly, I stepped along the trail to the student's seat and sat down.

It was a while before he spoke. Instead, he watched me squirming like a worm on a hook. "You don't come into the office all that often. Do you Ms. Bowlan?"

I blinked at him stupidly. I hoped he didn't think my absence meant I wasn't working hard. "Actually, I do most of my research at the library," I stammered. "And sometimes at home. I find I can get more work done. It's less....distracting."

He nodded slowly. "Hard work is important in academia. I hope you realize that."

I nodded, not sure of what else to say.

He gazed at me with his amphibious green eyes for another long minute, before he put his arms behind his head. It looked as though he was readying himself to impart a piece of great wisdom.

"Do you know the secret to getting your PhD, Miss Bowlan. Do you know about the three P's?"

I blinked again.

He looked annoyed by my vacant response. "Persist.... Persist... Persist." Each time he said the word he squeezed it between his teeth, coming down hard on the 'ssst' with a snap. "Do you understand my meaning, Ms. Bowlan?"

"I think so. Hard work is part of research?" I floundered.

He smiled now. "That's right. Hard work and digging. And make no mistake. Digging can sometimes take an entire career. But if you....persist...persist...persist...you can get there in the end."

I nodded, hoping that was a cue for my dismissal.

Unfortunately, he continued, but now his eyes became cold. "However, I have learned persistence is not always enough. Do you know what else is required?"

I waited. He was obviously going to tell me regardless of my response.

His lips curled back into a bit of a snarl, a glint of his eye teeth showing. "Innovation!" he said with a raised voice. "Innovation is critical. Research can be more than just difficult. It can be unfair. That's when you have to take things into your own hands, and think...outside...the...box..." He snapped his tongue again.

"Yes, sir," I said, standing up now, ready to flee. "Thank you for your insights. I will make sure I use persistence and innovation."

His face fell back into a friendly frame and I breathed a sigh of relief.

He stood and gave me a slight bow from behind his desk. I put one foot in front of the next, counting the steps along the trail to leave his office. For some reason, I was holding my breath as I reached the doorjamb. Keeping my eyes downcast, I had almost made my escape when Fishburn started up again.

"Your father was a great man," he said, voice trailing like a lure, pulling me in.

I stopped and turned back. Fishburn had never mentioned my father before. Of course, most people knew my father here at Queen's. He was something of a point of pride with the university. He had received the most prestigious awards and most weighty research funding. Not to mention his excellence as a teacher. I knew that much simply by being a student at Queen's. Everyone knew about Dr. Arthur Wright.

Fishburn blinked, his eyelids wrapping around the large orbits of his eyes. "You could say he was one of my greatest inspirations. Do you know that?"

I shook my head stupidly.

"I was pursing my undergrad in biology when I met your father." He smiled at the memory. "But when I heard him give a lecture on the genealogical record and its influence on our knowledge of the history of mankind, I knew I had to change majors. It was brilliant." His next words were almost a hysterical whisper. "It was glorious!"

"I didn't know that," I managed, now equal parts desperate to know more about my father and desperate to keep my memories of him locked in the attic closet.

"Of course, I didn't even realize you were his daughter until recently. You don't have his last name. That's strange isn't it, for a man who studied the genealogical record?"

I shrugged. I was growing increasingly uncomfortable with this exchange. "Umm... Well, we follow a matriarchal naming convention. It's been that way for...generations." Thoughts of my Anne Boleyn discovery flashed through my mind, but I wasn't ready to share this piece of my research. It still felt personal and I still disliked this man.

"Well, as I said the other day, Ms. Bowlan, I am expecting great things from you. I do hope you don't disappoint me."

I backed out of his office. "I'll try my best."

He narrowed his toad-like eyes and harrumphed.

"I hope you try harder than that. This could mean the difference between a successful career and your expulsion from the university."

"Yes, sir."

He smiled again, his face transforming with sugary encouragement. "But if you are anything like your father, I'm sure you will excel beyond my wildest dreams."

PRESENT DAY
QUEEN'S UNIVERSITY, CANADA

Three portage backpacks sat on the kitchen table casting a melancholy gloom over the room. Grapes didn't look up when I came in, but I gave her a kiss on top of the head anyway. She looked as though she needed it.

"They're here," she said with a thick voice, keeping her eyes focused on the luggage. "The delivery guy just brought them."

I ran my hand over one of the bags, its lumpy contents still contained within. A salty wave of trepidation washed over me. This old luggage represented the last of our family, the last of the ones we lost. This evening Grapes and I would face the deaths of my mother, father and grandmother. We would face their deaths together, like we should have done all those years ago.

I pushed my recent exchange with Fishburn into the recesses of my mind. I wanted to be fully present for this moment. I wanted to think about my father as 'Dad' right now, not as an esteemed professor whose shadow still eclipsed me every day.

"Ready?" I asked quietly.

She took a jagged breath. "Ready."

Grapes fumbled with Grandma Beth's tan pack, unzipping it with tenderness. Tears filled her blue eyes as she ran her hands over Beth's things, the clothes folded neatly despite being jumbled inside for almost two decades. Grapes lifted a familiar red sweater to her face and rubbed the cotton fabric across her cheek.

"Bethy," she whispered.

Grapes sat perfectly still for a moment, breathing in and out. I allowed her time to experience her loss. She needed to pay respect to the old memories as much as I did.

Then for the first time in my life, I watched my great-grandmother cry. Really cry. Tears streamed down her beautiful face as she sobbed. Shoulders lurching and lips trembling, she buried her face into the fabric of the sweater. She breathed in her daughter's scent, a scent that still lingered despite the passage of time. Lily of the valley, my grandmother's favorite perfume. It filled the room with her presence, her laughter, her energy. Ghostly memories swirled as Grapes cried unabashedly into the old sweater, admitting her heartbreak after all this time.

I stood watching my beloved Grapes, unsure of what to do. This strong wonderful woman had protected me my whole life, without showing a hint of her own suffering. She had always sheltered me. She had always focused on my needs. But in this moment, I realized her loss was as profound as mine, her hurt no less devastating. And I wasn't eleven years old anymore. It was my turn to comfort her.

I grabbed her up in my arms and gave her a long hug filled with meaning. I wanted to tell her I was sorry. I wanted to tell her I was thankful. I wanted to tell her I loved her. But I didn't. I let the hug say it all. She held on tight and rocked back and forth as the tears flowed. I gripped her hard, ready to take on some of the burden she had lived with all these years.

She wept on. Long, hard, gut-wrenching cries that left her with little else. I didn't stop her. I just kept on holding. Once the tears had run their course, heaving shoulders giving way to sniffles, she dabbed at wet eyes and gave me a grateful smile.

"At least we still have each other, Ellie." She squeezed my hand and gestured to the other two bags. "It's your turn now."

Hands trembling, I prepared to face my parents' deaths. It was my deepest loss, my greatest source of sadness. The attic door in my mind rattled on its hinges, memories desperate to come through.

I unzipped my mother's pack, gingerly pulling one slider to the left and the other to the right. Peeling back the flap, I lifted mom's things out one at a time, relishing each sweater and each pair of pants as though they were priceless treasures. These were my mother's things and it felt wonderful to touch them again. Each item sparked a memory that set a fluttering sensation swirling in the bottom of my stomach.

"Do you remember when Mom wore this scarf to the mall? Do you remember when Mom spilled coffee on these jeans?" I reminisced.

Grapes walked down memory lane with me. In fact, she often remembered more details than me. "Did you know your mom darned that pair of socks three times? She loved them so much she couldn't throw them out."

The conversation was silly as we recalled the trivial details of our lives before that dreaded day. We allowed ourselves to remember them, Mom, Dad and Grandma, and to cherish their wonderful memories. As we talked on and on, my heart swelled with warmth. Grapes felt it too. I could tell by the way it changed her smile. It filled us with something good, something we had both lost all those years ago, and we found ourselves crying and laughing as we told the stories of my childhood.

The mundane details of our lives together seemed the most precious. Mom, Dad and Grandma each had their own idiosyncrasies, each equally ridiculous. Mom ironed everything, even socks and underwear. Each undergarment had to be steamed and folded before it was filed in a drawer in color-coded fashion. Grandma Beth insisted the toilet paper in the bathroom loop paper-side-up and not dangle down from beneath. It was her biggest pet peeve in the world. If she ever discovered the perpetrator of a poorly installed roll, the criminal would be assigned to one full month of toilet cleaning duty. Dad, on the other hand, was determined to be messy. No one was allowed to tidy his office, not even on cleaning day. Not as much as a single filament of dust could be removed without his permission and no one ever dared try. Mine was a real family, complete with squabbling and laughter. Not the perfect family of fairy tales, but the imperfect honest relationship between real people, living real lives. And we were happy. We were complete.

I opened the attic door in my mind a tiny crack and allowed the memories to come through. After all these years, I was finally thankful for them. These memories were my connection to my family. They were my connection to me.

"Should we open Dad's pack?" I asked when we were through.

"Can't stop now." Grapes lips turned up in a sad smile. She still cradled Beth's red sweater in her arms.

This time I was more confident as I lay the largest backpack on the table and unzipped the flap. A jumble of Dad's clothing and toiletries

spilled from the bag with abandon. We laughed at his chaotic, disorga-
nized stuff. This was my father, always packing extra items, just in case.

"Hold on. What's this?" A brown manila envelope sat amongst the
other vacation items.

"What is it?" asked Grapes.

I slid a butter knife along the seal of the envelope and turned it upside
down. Two separate pieces of mail fell onto the kitchen table.

The first was an official document from the Ministry of Justice—
Department of Constitutional Affairs in England. I opened it and read it
aloud.

British License for the Exhumation of Human Remains

> Family Member Applicants: *Eliza Bowlan, Beth Bowlan.*
> Body for Exhumation: *Anne Boleyn*
> Location of Remains: *Original burial Tower of London, re-*
> *interred at the Crypt of St. Peter's, London*
> Application Date: *September 6, 2006*
> Approval Date: *July 12, 2007*
> Special Requests: Do not share DNA results with anyone
> other than the applicants under any circumstances.

Of all the things I thought we might find in my father's luggage, the
license to exhume the body of Anne Boleyn was not among them. I reread
the paper again to make sure I had it straight. This time I noticed the
applicants for this exhumation were Mom and Grandma.

"Hold on. This makes sense. Lily and I figured it out this morning," I
whispered. An image was forming in my mind like a game of Connect-the-
Dots.

I relayed the details of our earlier discovery at the library. Grapes
followed along, her caterpillar eyebrows dancing.

"...so, you and I are relatives of Anne Boleyn. That is why Dad's
research focused on the Boleyn-Bowlan family bloodline."

Grapes mouth formed a perfect O as she processed the news. "But why
would Arthur want to dig up Anne Boleyn's remains if he had the evidence
to prove the lineage?"

I had this one figured out too. Seeing my father's things made me more
certain of our earlier conclusions. "Dad was concerned with the validity of
the matriarchal naming convention. He said it was hard to prove the

lineage because the family name would disappear and reappear several generations later. That left a hole in the lineage calling its certainty into question. He wanted the DNA to prove the lineage without a doubt."

I tore open the second envelope to confirm my theory. This was my brilliant father's stuff, after all. He'd had all the answers from the start. As expected, this piece of mail contained Anne Boleyn's DNA results. That much was clear from the title and the notes written at the top of the page, but the rest of the paper was rather technical. I couldn't make sense of it. I would need an expert in genetics to help me decode it.

"See?" I said pointing at the strange sequence of letters. "Dad was after the DNA evidence for Anne Boleyn. And if I'm right, Ivor Cullen was too. That's why he killed them."

Grapes squinted at the paper. She wore a furtive expression, perhaps a little sad, perhaps a little torn. But it was clear she was struggling with something.

"Grapes?" I asked with concern.

She eased herself out of the chair.

"It's time," she whispered.

Holding a finger in the air, she disappeared down the hall to her bedroom. After a minute, Grapes re-emerged with a medical file labeled "Baby Bowlan." She placed the file on the table in front of me and sat down, grasping her hands tightly in her lap.

"This is an x-ray from when you were a baby, Ellie."

I gave Grapes a tentative look before I picked up the folder. I was still processing the Anne Boleyn DNA letter and I wasn't sure if I could handle any more news. But more than that, I couldn't imagine what it was. There were no secrets between us. Grapes and I had shared everything ever since I was eleven.

I picked up the file. Once again, I slid the butter knife under the seal and opened the folder. A single black and white x-ray fell onto my lap. Thick and glossy, it warped and wobbled in my hands. I held it up to the light to get a better view. There, on the film, was a skeletal image of a baby's right hand with six perfectly formed fingers. It loomed in an array of eerie, ghostly grays.

"Is this my hand?" I whispered.

"Yes dear. Six fingers and all."

I looked at the spot on my right hand where the extra finger was supposed to be. The tiny scar along the edge of my knuckles itched like crazy.

Grapes pursed her lips, willing herself to explain. "Dear, you have a condition called Polydactyly. Your parents had the extra finger removed when you were a baby. The doctors recommended it. They said if they removed it early, the scarring would be almost invisible. And no one would ever need to know it had been there."

I stared at her, my face blanching.

"They did it for you, dear. So you wouldn't be different. So you wouldn't feel...abnormal."

I looked at my hand in disbelief, rubbing the fine scar that had always been there. The scar I had never understood. I thought about the finger they surgically removed when I was a newborn. Self-loathing crawled up my spine like a centipede with a hundred tiny legs. My parents had to remove of piece of me because I hadn't been born normal. I was not normal. I had never been normal.

Grapes continued, summoning her courage to tell me the rest. "Your sixth finger is important, Ellie. It's the mark of a witch—a fire witch."

I said nothing, but the tears spilled from my eyes. To think my whole family had kept this from me. It felt like such a betrayal.

She put her hand on mine, tracing the fine line of the scar. The itching had transformed into a growing heat.

"When you were younger you were unwilling to accept magical things —things that were supernatural. They made you uncomfortable and you would cry. Only your father could comfort you. And he would have to take you away, to the park, or to the museum, to rescue you from it. It terrified you and gave you nightmares. It seemed cruel to force the knowledge upon you. That's why we decided it was better to leave you out of the Bowlan family coven."

"Bowlan family coven?" I whispered, incredulous.

Grapes stood and looked out the window. I knew it pained her to share these truths, to admit she had kept them from me all these years.

"Your mother, grandmother and I—we were the Bowlan coven. A coven of healers. We assumed you would be too. But when you were born, it was obvious your talent was fire. That's why you're such a hazard in the kitchen."

My stomach turned to acid as I tried to process this news. For generations, the women in my family had practiced witchcraft, the powerful art of healing. But when I had come along, they had chosen not to invite me in? The betrayal ripped through me like a blade, like the surgical scalpel that had cut away my sixth finger. I had never belonged, not even to my own family. I was a failure. They had known it all along.

I covered my face to block out the nauseating sensation of falling, falling, falling through the floor. Was everything I had ever believed about myself a lie?

"We wanted to tell you. But you were unwilling to discuss it," Grapes whispered. "You are a witch, Ellie, and your proclivity is fire."

I put my head between my knees because the world was spinning too fast. A familiar set of invisible strangling hands grabbed at my throat and squeezed. *Fire witch...fire witch...* My mind was awash with nightmarish images. The *Lady with an Ermine* portrait at the Sleeping Goat. "*Burn him... burn him...*," she whispered in my ear. Tattoo-Carl winking at me as he set those candles wicks popping into flame. My father's disappointed face staring into mine as he lectured, "When you stand on the shoulders of giants, Ellie..."

I felt like I was going to be sick. How could I be so stupid, stupid, stupid?

The scar on my hand seared with pain as a ferocious crack from the corner rang through the kitchen. I looked up to see the microwave explode into flames, its buttons flashing maniacally. Its little door flew open as a raging fire mushroomed from its center. The blaze pulsed and grew, its heat melting the counter top into a gooey mess. The smoke rose to the ceiling and puffed through the kitchen, blanketing Grapes and me in a gray electrical smog. The scar on my right hand flared in response. It singed and prickled, burning a line of red into my flesh.

"No Ellie!" cried Grapes.

She pulled the extinguisher from under the sink, teetering on her bad hip. Gripping her walker in one hand, she unhinged the safety latch with the other and sprayed a foamy white mess onto the fire. She stood, feet braced wide, gripping the extinguisher as she caught the last of the flames working their way along the daisy print wallpaper in the kitchen. Within seconds, the blaze had vanished.

Grapes breathed a sigh of relief.

I sat looking at the smoky mess in the ruined kitchen, tears streaming down my face as I faced the wreckage. My head spun. My stomach lurched. I was falling into an abyss I couldn't see. The world was going black as I tried to free myself from the invisible hands around my neck.

Grapes wrapped her arms around me before I passed out. "It's okay Ellie," she soothed, "it's going to be okay."

Anne lay in bed, guilt-ridden, and sleepless. She reached into the darkness and searched for Claude beside her. The girls had taken to sleeping in the same bed since Mary had returned to England.

It had been three weeks since Anne's sister had sent been home to England, extradited from France because of her love affair with Francis d'Angeloume. The days leading up to her departure had been bewildering. Images of Mary's tear-streaked face played through Anne's mind. Mary had begged not to be sent away. She had pleaded with Marguerite. In the end, they had packed Mary into the same carriage that brought her to France and returned her to England like an unwanted gift.

But sending Mary home to England had not solved Claude's marriage woes. Francis moped about the castle, listless and uninterested in the daily activities at court. Even Leonardo could not sway him from his depression. Francis wished to do nothing more than sit alone in his rooms, heartbroken and miserable at the loss of his beloved Mary Boleyn.

A click of the door latch caught Anne's attention.

"Girls," Marguerite whispered. "'Tis time."

Soon the three women were making their way through the darkened halls of the Chateau du Blois. They passed the king's chambers and headed down a set of narrow stairs, silent as the mice that scurried below the subfloors. After crossing through the dining room and past the kitchens, they edged along a corridor towards the end of the east hall.

"Did you bring the elixir?" Marguerite asked under her breath.

"Anne has it," Claude replied in the darkness.

"Remember girls," Marguerite warned. "We must not wake him. It is imperative he sleeps."

The three figures stole into Francis' chambers with a tiny slice of moonlight to guide them. Even in the dim light, Anne could make out the room's gloomy disarray. Francis, in his despair, had allowed no servant to tidy it for days and the room lay scattered with empty wine cups and soiled clothing. Plates of half-eaten food, now gone rotten, littered the floor. Books and scrolls, parchment and linens, inkbottles and quill pens lay strewn about the chamber, as if they had been swept from the desk in a desperate act of frustration.

The ladies threaded their way through the mess and approached the bed. Francis lay unconscious upon the pillows, still gripping an empty goblet, the last of the wine spilling down his nightshirt.

"Girls," Marguerite whispered. "Help me open the window. 'Tis best to have the moon in full view."

The women set about removing the window from its frame, allowing only a minute squeak as the hinges gave way to their mounts. Once the pane was unlatched and set along the floorboards, the women focused their attention on the sleeping groom. Even in his drunken slumber, Francis was ill at ease. He tossed and turned in his grief. He moaned under his breath and gritted his teeth against the pillow.

Claude went to his side, sinking to her knees. A single tear streamed down her cheek.

Marguerite was quick to orchestrate the next steps. "Anne, you must pour the circle of ash. But do it quietly or we may be discovered."

Anne hesitated. She wanted to do as Marguerite bid but wondered how she might get around the room without kicking something over. A fluttering whir in her gut answered her question. It presented itself like a gift. She took a deep breath, recited the prayer she had learned only weeks ago and rose through the air, hovering just high enough above the floorboards to be clear of the debris. She opened the jar and poured the ash onto the floor in a large circle.

As the magic of the protective circle was cast, Marguerite presided over their ritual. She too hovered high enough above the floorboards to move about with ease, drifting towards the window and peering out at the thin sliver of waning gibbous moon. She raised her hands to its graying light, swallowing its strength.

"Magic moon, I summon thee,
Bring us favor, our coven three.
Cupid's arrow from above,
Sway the force, redirect true love."

With each verse, the light of the moon pulsated, as if waking from a deep slumber. The wind picked up as Marguerite's words swirled through the room, the bed curtains swaying like dishrags. A tumbler of ale tipped over but the thriving gale stifled its sound.

"Bride loves her groom, groom has forgotten
His heart was turned, temptation rotten.
Their vows hold true, something pure
The child comes soon, love must endure.
"Set back the course, set back the right
Bring bride and groom back to the light."

The wind circled fierce around the bed now, holding the three women and their slumbering patron within its frenzy.

Claude leaned toward Francis, oblivious to the chaos. The couple had fallen into a strange trance, one that connected them in a cloud of sensual lust. Anne didn't understand it, but she knew it was delicious and carnal. Claude held Francis' hands in her own. His eyes lay open and he stared at her with hungry desire.

"Quick, Anne, pour the elixir into his mouth. Do it while the wind holds strong," Marguerite instructed.

With deft fingers, Anne removed a vile from a small pocket in her nightdress. She pulled its tip and the cork gave way with a tiny pop. Francis' mouth yawed open, anticipating its medicine. Anne leaned in close, careful not to disturb the infatuated couple, and poured the elixir into his gullet. Not a drop was wasted. Francis gulped at the liquid like a man in the desert. When he finished, he sucked in a breath. His lips swelled with longing. He moaned with pleasure as reached for Claude, begging for her, pleading for her.

Claude stared at him, unable to move.

Anne gave her a shove. "Kiss him, Claude. What are you waiting for?"

A cry of relief escaped Claude's lips as she moved towards her husband, her lips finding his in the dim light. The embrace was a formidable release for them both, unleashing a colossal passion. They moaned with pleasure, with insatiable need, as they clung to each other in the darkness.

A strange iridescence swirled above them, enveloping the couple in a carnal cocoon as the magic of the love potion gripped them hard. Their moans of pleasure escalated from their writhing sexual shadow. Francis began undressing Claude as she ripped at his codpiece, desperate to unleash his manhood.

Anne stepped back, suddenly uncomfortable with what she was seeing. She turned away but the sounds of insatiable lovemaking echoed behind her in the darkness.

Marguerite cleared her throat. "Well then, the spell is done."

They glanced back at the couple as they made their hasty exit. Claude's naked body swayed atop her husband's, her pregnant belly full and round as her back arched with pleasure.

"What a vixen. I didn't know she had it in her." Anne giggled as she and Marguerite dashed into the night.

1514

CHATEAU DU BLOIS, LOIRE VALLEY, FRANCE

Anne and Marguerite burst through the doors to Leonardo's rooms in the dead of night. A carnal energy still clung to them like lingering perfume.

"We did it, Leo!" cried Anne.

Leonardo glanced up from a set of blueprints and removed his spectacles. "Well done, ladies," he said with a twinkle in his eye.

The women flung themselves down with girlish abandon and relayed the events of the evening.

"You should have seen her, Leo," said Anne. "Our own sweet Claude. She was so overcome with passion, you might have taken her for a lady of the night."

"The spell was perfect," said Marguerite. "Perhaps a little too perfect if I do say so myself."

They took turns telling the story and the role each of them played in righting Claude's marriage woes. When they had finished, Leonardo waggled his bushy eyebrows.

"Well good for Claude. And I should think a nice romp would cheer Francis up too."

This comment put the friends into fits and they giggled with abandon, the thrill of the magic surging around them. Leonardo gathered up the wine goblets to propose a toast.

"We must celebrate," he announced.

Leonardo poured the first glass of wine and then stopped short. He held an arthritic finger in the air, straining to make out a noise. It started as a quiet moaning from the hallway. A low wailing. A chaotic waffling. A rustling of feet? No one could be sure.

"Call the midwife!" Francis bellowed from somewhere in the castle. "Call the midwife! Claude is in labor!"

The friends exchanged worried glances as they leapt to their feet.

Marguerite looked stricken. "But the house physic was just called away on royal business. And Claude's midwife is not expected to arrive until next week."

Leonardo raced through the chamber, gathering supplies. "Anne, you go to Claude. Marguerite, you must fetch Rose. I will find Francis," he commanded.

* * *

It seemed an eternity before Anne reached her destination on the other side of the castle. A single candle cast eerie shadows around the room. A witchy wind blew through the open window and the bed curtains danced in the cool night air.

Claude sat on the canopied bed looking terrified and alone. She looked up at Anne from the freshly soaked linens. "I think I see blood," she whimpered.

Anne tried not to panic as she placed a hand on her friend's swollen stomach. The heavy blankets had been tossed on the floor. Ripped clothing littered the room. Claude cowered, naked and afraid, under a thin white linen. The mattress glistened with the baby's waters and a trickle of deep red blood.

The hairs on the back of Anne's neck stood on end now she was alone with this laboring girl. She knew nothing of childbirth. They had learned nothing of midwifery this summer, and she had no skills nor instincts to guide her.

Soon Claude's panting became cries of distress. She shrieked with agony as labor pains gripped her, uterine muscles constricting to make the curve of the pregnancy an angry rounded cone. She wailed through the contraction, tears streaming down her cheeks.

"Am I dying, Anne?" She panted once the worst of it had subsided.

Anne swallowed. "The babe comes early, 'tis all."

She blotted her friend's forehead as another violent contraction ripped through Claude, this one holding her in its grip for several minutes. Her back arched in agony as the pain tore through her. She balled her hands into fists, throwing her head back and howling like a wolf at the full moon. When the worst of it was over, she fell back into the pillows once again.

"Is it because of the love spell we cast?" asked Claude, breathless.

"Actually, I think it was the love-making that followed," said Anne, the good humor of the evening now long gone.

The contractions were coming hard and fast with barely a moment between them. Claude shrieked as a fresh wave of pain ripped through her, her internal musculature pulling so tight, Anne thought she might rip right in half.

"Hold on, Claude," said Anne. "Marguerite has gone to fetch Rose. She will know what to do."

Claude shook her head, a clammy sheen shimmering on her skin. "No. I can't wait. I have to push. The child wants to come."

"No, please, no," Anne begged.

But it was too late. Claude had succumbed to her body's natural rhythm. She was no longer in control of her own actions. Even without training, it was clear to Anne that her friend needed to push, to allow nature to take its course.

Anne could only hold Claude's hand and grip it tight. "It's okay, Claude. I am here. I am here."

Claude pushed hard, gritting her teeth between wails. After the spell ended, Claude fell back breathless and exhausted, her brow covered in a sweat.

"Anne, you must look for the head of the baby. I fear something is wrong."

"Claude, no. I can't. Please, no..."

Red blood was staining the sheet, spreading like spilled ink across parchment. Though she didn't want to, Anne knew she had to act. Taking a deep breath, she screwed up her courage and pulled back the linens. What she saw was not the baby's crowing head, but a tiny foot.

"Stop! Please stop! The babe is not crowning. She is turned the wrong way."

Claude gulped back a sob. "I'm going to die, Anne." She panted. "I know I'm going to die."

Anne bit her lip with frustration. She didn't know what to do. She didn't know how to help.

"I want you to save my daughter. See that she lives," Claude begged. She panted for a moment longer and then lost consciousness.

Anne dabbed at her forehead but there was no reviving the laboring girl. As the next wave took hold, Claude's body surged hard, but this time she did not cry out. The babe's leg pushed forward, but nothing else emerged. Nothing but deep red blood.

Heavy footsteps from the hallway shook Anne from her nightmare.

"Don't ye be pushin', luv. I'm comin' and we'll get this babe from yoo good and healthy," bellowed Rose.

Anne's nursemaid materialized, great breasts swinging beneath her shift. She huffed and puffed like an old dragon out of breath from her trek across the castle.

"Anne, go fetch fresh water from the basin," she commanded. "We've got to see what kind of mess we're workin' with."

Anne flew to the washbowl across the room and almost tripped over Marguerite, who had sunk to her knees in worry. Marguerite pointed a feeble finger.

"Oh dear God. There is a leg. Only a leg," she gasped.

Rose wiped the bloodied area with a wet cloth and a look of worry crawled over her face. "The wee child is breech."

Claude's back arched once again but still the babe would make no more progress. It all seemed so hopeless. Anne had never felt more inadequate in her life. Her heart clanged in her chest.

"Please, Rose, do something!" she cried.

"I have to push the leg back inside," shouted Rose. "I have to turn the babe round."

Anne and Marguerite fell silent as they watched Rose get to work. She gripped the baby's leg as gently as she could and then attempted to push it back into the womb. Claude screamed in agony, the pain waking her from her unconscious state. The young girl twisted and contorted away from the nursemaid's pushing hands, but Rose persisted, forcing the baby's leg back inside.

After much more toiling and effort, Rose stepped back, her face covered in sweat.

"I can't do it," she whispered. "The babe cannot be turned. The contractions are comin' too hard." She wiped her hand across her brow, a streak of blood smearing across her face.

Anne glanced at Marguerite, their eyes locking in terror.

Claude stirred. "Anne, please." Her voice was almost inaudible, her face pasty with blood loss. "Call the Goddess. We must use magic. She will come to our aid if you bid."

Anne glanced at her nursemaid, uncertain of the request. Rose had been against Anne's witchy pursuits all summer. She had scolded Anne at the first sign of potion making or spell casting. But tonight was different. Tonight there was little other choice. Death waited at the door for Claude like a hungry spider.

"Anne, you must try." Rose agreed.

Anne's mind raced. She knew the Goddess was dangerous, but there was no other choice. Breathing steadily, she constructed the place of calm she had practiced for months. She invited the energy into her body and swallowed it down. It took her a moment to push the fear and panic from her mind, but as she did, she felt a familiar whir. A warm pulsing flutter comforted her, greeted her, acknowledging her power.

Anne closed her eyes and summoned her. "Goddess, I call to you," she said steadily.

As swiftly as the call went out, an ancient force swelled through Anne's body. A shadowy form emerged from her chest and faced her, close and sensual. Anne felt the Goddess' breath on her lips, the supple surge of the Goddess's breasts against her own. The effect was thrilling. The effect was terrifying.

"What do you ask of me, my fire child? We are bound, you and I."

Anne wanted to hide. She wanted to run. The Goddess felt more dangerous than ever.

"Turn the babe 'round," she whispered. "'Tis all I ask."

The Goddess circled Anne's torso like a ribbon of silk, tempting her, enticing her. She trilled through Anne's heart in search of her greatest desires. But this time, Anne held firm. She wanted only to save the lives of Claude and her baby.

"Turn the babe round," she commanded.

The Goddess pouted, lingering to see if she could coax any more from her muse. But Anne resisted her advances, locking her mind up tight. After a time the Goddess acquiesced.

"Alright my child. If that is all you wish."

In a flash, the Goddess transformed herself into a light wind buffeting along Claude's hardened torso. The room filled with a deep earthy scent, the smell of the forest and the trees. Claude writhed as her stomach twisted in an unnatural rotation, her naval circling in an impossible spiral. Anne watched as the spirited gale completed its mighty task. It took only a minute but when it was done, the women knew it. The babe had righted itself before their very eyes.

The Goddess vanished with a pop.

Anne hugged Marguerite, allowing herself to feel the tiniest bit of hope. They clung together as they watched Rose get back to work. The nursemaid did not waste a second. She inserted her hands into Claude's body and readied herself for action.

"Okay, luv. I want you to push like the devil Lucifer himself."

Claude took advantage of a new contraction building to its peak. Sitting up on her elbows, she pushed with every ounce of remaining strength. She howled with pain but this time the babe was coming through safely. She rested as the contraction waned and then pushed hard as the next one urged the babe from her body.

"Come on, Claude," cried Anne, almost giddy with the thrill of it.

"Ye've got one last push. Make it count, lassie!" Rose bellowed.

Anne held her breath as Claude pushed one last time. All at once, the baby was born as a hot rush of liquid washed over Claude's legs.

Rose held the infant and cut the cord. A tiny mewling cry rang out and Anne gasped with relief. She watched as Rose swaddled the cherub with all the adeptness of a nursemaid, a lifetime of babies moving her practiced hands. Marguerite sank to her knees with relief.

Rose gave the child one last check and held her up in the dim light of the candle.

"Claude, you've got yourself a wee girl." She handed the babe to her mother. "A perfect healthy baby girl."

PRESENT DAY

QUEEN'S UNIVERSITY, CANADA

The great maple tree standing at the center of Kingston Park had been on this spot for over two hundred years. It had borne witness to the making of a country, to soldiers and settlers, and to the families that followed. Now it watched over the annual barrage of students at Queen's that came and went with the changing of the seasons.

I had known this particular maple tree since I was a little girl. It was my dad's favorite place to spend a Saturday afternoon. When I was young, he and I visited almost every weekend. Those were the best days of my childhood. Dad always made me feel so special, so loved. He was the only one in the world who truly understood me.

Dad didn't push me on the swing or chase me through the park like the other fathers did. Instead, ours was an intellectual connection. We read books and talked about their deeper meaning. We explored ancient philosophies and contemplated their truths in the modern day world. He answered my questions and challenged my mind. He pushed me to think for myself and question the things the world put before me. My father didn't care I was a child. Instead, he treated me as his intellectual equal. And I loved him for that. I loved him so very, very much.

I hadn't been back to this tree since I was eleven, the week before my parents left on their trip. The trip that would take them from me forever. My dad and I didn't talk much that day, we just watched the waves as they washed along the rugged limestone shoreline. It was a happy moment, one of the happiest in my life. It was the last day I would ever spend with my father.

"Can I join you?" John approached with a worried smile.

We watched the heavy swells crash against the rocky breakers, our backs propped up against the gnarled trunk of the tree. The seagulls soared through the sky, diving against the lusty air currents for a scrap of food.

John took my hand. He seemed to sense my melancholy.

"I miss my father," I whispered.

"I know," John whispered back.

John put his arm around my shoulders and then he held me as I cried, big heavy sobs of anguish. Grapes had cried yesterday, but today it was my turn. I bawled into his shoulder, heartbroken and lost. Memories of my father flowed through the attic door and knocked me down, pulling me into sadness, into emptiness and despair. I couldn't stop the flood of tears and I didn't even try.

For the first time in my life, I let it all out. I cried for the fact he was gone, that I could never prove myself to him, that he was lost to me forever. I cried for the fact I could never know him as an adult, that we would never share the moment of discovery I had always craved. I cried for the little girl, who was still so much a part of me, who lost her daddy when she was only eleven.

John said nothing. He wrapped his arms around me tight, letting me get it out of my system. He let me cling to him, sobbing into his t-shirt, allowing me to show him my vulnerability. He took on some of the hurt I had kept in my heart for years. It burned my skin, my throat, my bones as I faced my loss. Slowly, the pain ebbed away into a dull ache. Once the tears subsided, we sat for a while in silence.

"How did you find me?" I finally asked.

John brushed a tear from my cheek. "Dez called me. Grapes called him. I think they're worried about you." A small smile played at the corners of his mouth. "What's going on El?"

I shook my head. "You don't want to hear about my problems. I'm a train wreck."

John bumped me with an elbow. "Hey, I happen to like this train wreck."

I looked into his amber eyes and saw the sincerity. He wanted to help, but I couldn't tell him the embarrassing details of my life. It was all too weird to admit. I shook my head, silent once again.

"I had a great time last night," he whispered.

This new attempt to reach me through my sadness almost made me smile. "Me too," I said, blushing. "I'm sorry about my great-grandmother's friends. They really are well intentioned."

John chuckled. "They were terrific. I didn't feel uncomfortable at all."

Now I knew he was just trying to be nice.

"Well...except for when I went in for the kiss. That did get a little dicey." His voice became serious now. "But that's okay. I'm willing to wait." He squeezed my hand. "You're worth waiting for."

My breath caught, his words lifting me up somehow. They cut through my sadness and warmed my heart. I realized I needed to tell him my whole lousy story. I finally wanted him to know.

I told him about my dad, that he was my hero. I told him I lived every day in his shadow, terrified of letting him down. I told him about the six fingers on my hand my parents had removed when I was a baby. I told him about the dark curse and the feeling of being a witchy outcast even within my own family. I told him about the fires I set by accident because of my own special brand of weird irrevocably embedded within my DNA. Then I stopped, my story finished, and waited for his reaction.

He didn't answer right away. Instead he looked over the water at the crashing white caps and the seagulls that weaved through the air currents above the foamy surface.

"Amazing," he said under his breath.

I shook my head, full of self-loathing. "No, I'm not amazing John. I'm a circus freak," I sputtered. "All my life I've wanted to be normal. Just fit-in-with-the-other-kids normal. Instead, I was always bookish and shy. I was always younger than everybody else. I was always on the outside, looking in. But if that wasn't weird enough, I just discovered my own parents had to have me surgically modified because I'm such a monster. You don't have to do this, John. You don't have to hang around with me."

John put up his hand to stop me. He almost looked offended at my words. Instead of replying, he lay back in the grass, pulling me with him.

We lay on the freshly mown lawn for what felt like an eternity, saying nothing, just looking up into the withered arms of the old maple. The boughs of the tree swayed oddly from this angle, the blue sky poking from between the branches like a mosaic of stained glass.

"Ellie, do you see how the leaves on the bottom of this maple tree are still green? But the ones at the top are a fiery red?"

"Yeah," I answered.

"Maybe, you should think about yourself in the same way."

"What do you mean?"

He sat up on one elbow. "This maple has stood here for over two centuries. Long before we were born. Heck, long before your Grapes was born. It's been the same tree for two hundred years. But every year, it undergoes a transformation. It turns a burning crimson red, so vibrant you would almost swear it was on fire. It is undergoing its fiery transition now, like you are—but it's still the same tree—and you're still the same you. Just more fantastic and more beautiful than ever."

We were quiet for a while again.

"I like that," I finally whispered, a tiny smile appearing on my lips.

John reached over and took my hand in the grass, threading his fingers through mine. My own tiny digits were safely wedged within his muscular ones.

We lay on the lawn watching the kids play in the park. A group of boys charged around in a riotous game of tag as their mother called after them. Two girls giggled on the teeter-totter, sailing up and down, up and down, without a care in the world.

"One more thing, El."

"Hmmm?"

He looked me in the eye. "If I'm ever lucky enough to have a little girl of my own, I can tell you this. It won't be the awards she wins, or the grades she gets in school, or even the Nobel peace prize that will make me love her. I will love her for simply being mine. And I'm willing to bet that was how your father felt about you. You make him proud every day, just by being you."

* * *

Once John had patched me up and I was feeling better about the world, we wandered up Princess Street. I didn't know where I was taking him, but he seemed happy enough to be walking along beside me.

Swarms of students were milling about on the streets downtown. The Queen's University student body was gearing up for a big weekend of football. A boastful sign was strung across the main street read, 'Go Gaels Go!' Tomorrow was the first at-home football game of the season and there would be raucous bloodthirsty crowds.

As we walked, my eye caught on an artistic storefront across the street. A three-dimensional sign made from old bicycle parts hung outside the door of a limestone building. The sign read, '*The Kingston Gallery Presents: Carl Vander Guild*'. In that instant, I knew where I wanted to take John.

The art gallery was an impressive two-story space painted stark white, structural beams exposed in the ceiling. A variety of sculptures and portraits adorned the walls, some still on display, others packed away into cardboard boxes and bubble wrap.

We wandered through the half-empty gallery. Small pieces of art still sat on pedestals around the room. A pair of running shoes made from aluminum pop cans. A soaring bird made from forks and spoons, with butter knives for wings. A guard dog composed of tiny gears, bolts and screws. The work was impressive and I wished I had come earlier to see the full exhibit.

A full-size statue dominated the center of the room with quiet magnificence. She was a perfect ballerina posed in an elegant arabesque. The movement in the work was breathtaking. She was made entirely of old hair dryer parts.

"Ellie, is that you? O-M-G, Carl, Ellie is here." Mindy squealed as she emerged from the back room and rushed over to give me a hug.

"Hi." I smiled sheepishly. "We thought we'd stop by and take a look at Carl's work. This is John. He was at the séance, remember?"

Tattoo-Carl came in wearing his usual uniform of ripped jeans and a tank top. We made introductions.

"Carl, your stuff is phenomenal," said John.

"Thanks, man. It's been a good week." Carl gave Mindy a playful smack on the butt. "We're clearing out now to make room for the next show."

"I love the ballerina. She's so lifelike." John inspected the ballet slipper fabricated from electrical plug coils.

"Yeah, that's the thing about junk art," Carl said with a nod. "The materials I use have been discarded by society. But if you look at them through a different lens, you see something altogether beautiful."

After showing us around for a while and explaining the essence of his work, I was starting to see Tattoo-Carl in a new light. He had a goofy surfer way of talking and a rather terrifying set of tattoos, but there was an intelligent, thoughtful person behind all those layers of strange.

Carl arched an eyebrow once we had completed the tour. "Uh, Ellie?" A curious smile pulled at his mouth. "Have you been thinking any more about lighting candles?" He looked across to John, uncertain how much more to say.

"Yes," I confessed. "Actually, I was hoping you could help me with something."

Once again, I explained the events of the last couple of days but this time it didn't seem as bizarre. Maybe it was because I was telling my story to two of the weirdest people I had ever met. I had given thought to the 'transitioning maple tree' concept John mentioned earlier. If I was going to transform into a fire witch, like he said, I should probably learn how to light a fire without burning the place down.

"I was hoping you would come around," said Carl as he headed into the back office. "Let's see what you've got."

"Here we go," John draped a large arm around my shoulders.

John and I followed Tattoo-Carl to the back room of the art gallery. Display cases, boxes, and packaging materials filled the space. Carl asked Mindy to get the fire extinguisher—just in case. We cleared a space on the floor large enough for the four of us, arranging ourselves in a circle. It felt a bit like the séance again, but I tried to push the memory from my mind. Carl pulled three candles from Mindy's bag. He reorganized the remaining boxes and bubble-wrap to make sure they were a good distance away. Mindy returned with a fire extinguisher as Tattoo-Carl arranged the candles.

"Okay, I want you to relax, Ellie, and just will the fire," said Carl, his voice calm.

"You've got this El," John said supportively.

I focused on the candles in front of me as the scar on my hand began to itch. It felt weird with the three of them staring at me, but I tried to concentrate nonetheless. My fists clenched tight as my fingernails dug into my flesh.

"Burn, burn, burn, burn, burn..."

Carl interrupted. "Remember, Ellie, a fire witch doesn't need any incantations. She only needs to see the flames in her mind and then she wills the fire to burn."

"Okay. See the flames...see the flames," I repeated.

"Ellie, stop." He put his hand on mine. "This doesn't come from your brain. It comes from your gut. Why don't you try closing your eyes? When you are ready, open them and will the candle to burn."

I took his advice and closed my eyes, the scar on my hand itching like mad. How was a person supposed to *feel* a fire, anyway? I sat there for a while but my mind drew a blank. My face turned red as I held my breath and tried to conjure thoughts of fire. My cheeks puffed. My lips puckered.

DEBORAH COHEN

I furrowed my brow until my forehead became a devilish V-shaped pitch-fork. I must have looked like a fleshy gargoyle having an allergic reaction.

When I opened my eyes, Mindy and Carl were wearing patient expressions. John, on the other hand, was biting his lip. He was trying not to laugh. In fact, I thought I heard him snort.

I clucked in mock disgust and gave John a swat. To my surprise, he swatted me back. This made me laugh as I swatted at him again. John's snort became laughter as he returned the playful smack. Our giddy exchange led to a small wrestling match between us on the floor. There was tickling and a lot of squealing as we wrestled from our crossed legged positions on the ground.

Carl and Mindy looked at us as though we were the strangest people in the world. It took a minute before Carl could reign us in.

"Guys, come on," scolded Carl. "This is serious."

"Sorry," said John, stifling another snort.

Once we had settled down, I took a deep breath and closed my eyes again. Carl looked mildly annoyed I hadn't been taking my lessons seriously, but after our wrestling match, I felt more relaxed. I cleared my mind and prepared to channel the flames. I thought about the blazing inferno from my dreams. I thought about the *Lady with an Ermine* and her urgent whispers. *'Burn him, Burn him...'*

Slowly, I sensed the heat of the fire on my skin. It surged around me, its hot energy pulsating. As the imaginary flames licked against my flesh, I pulled the fire in with my right hand, my newfound scar tingling with a deep instinctive heat. This time when I opened my eyes, I looked directly at the first candle in the line.

"Burn," I whispered.

Without warning, all three candles exploded in a hot inferno. Flames engulfed the tapers as they melted the wax away with bewildering force. Carl and Mindy leaned back and John ducked for cover. Mindy jumped to get away from the fire, tripping over a box behind her.

In spite of the commotion, I was entranced by the blaze. I watched the flames engulf their prey, hungry for anything else they could consume. The heat in my belly surged as I willed the fire to burn brighter. It was like scratching an itch I had never been able to reach, an itch beginning in the scar on my hand and prickling throughout my whole body. It felt so good, I couldn't stop.

John shouted from somewhere far away, but I couldn't make out what he is saying. I could only watch as the flames inched their way towards a group of cardboard boxes.

"Ellie, stop it! Stop the fire!" I thought I heard him shouting, but I was powerless to control the blaze.

The fire raged on. I couldn't find it within myself to extinguish the energy whirring within me. I wanted it to burn. I wanted it to devour everything in the room. It was feeding my body and mind like never had before.

Carl grabbed the extinguisher and sprayed the foamy liquid onto my flaming masterpiece, its blanketing effect strangling the blaze. As quickly as it began, only a smoke-filled room and three puddles of creamy candle wax remained.

John put his hand on my shoulder. "Are you alright?"

His touch brought me around. I tried to clear the haze that had settled over my brain. "Sorry," I stumbled. "I didn't know how to stop it."

"Well, you're gonna want to work on that," said Carl. "Maybe next time we should practice outside."

Mindy's mouth hung open like a fish on a hook wire. Carl collected up the half-incinerated boxes on the storage room floor.

"Well, we have learned something," Carl announced.

"What's that?" Mindy asked as she peeled the cardboard box off her foot.

Carl cocked an eyebrow. "Ellie Bowlan, you are a fire witch."

"Holy shit. That's for sure," said John with a deep chuckle.

"Holy shit," I agreed.

VOLUME 4

MABON

The Earth gives of her bounty as the daylight wanes
Mother Goddess grows old
And the witches seek revenge

Claude lay on the chaise in Leonardo's rooms, nursing her new baby. She had taken to motherhood instinctively, as though she had always been destined for the role. Her infant suckled at her breast, blissfully unaware of how close she had come to not being born at all. Francis, now righted by last night's magic spell, swooned adoringly. He doted upon Claude for her every need, planting kisses on her cheek. He cooed with delight when their daughter made the tiniest of gurgles.

Leonardo had assigned Anne, once again, to modeling duty in the chair by the window. The wedding was but weeks away and a number of other plans required his attention.

"The fireworks shall set France into a frenzy," Leonardo boasted between brush strokes. "Such is the alchemy I have prepared. I have devised the finale as a great lion—to celebrate the royal prowess of the King of France." He raised a furry eyebrow. "Imagine such a thing. A lion to celebrate a man who is nothing more than a rodent."

Anne moaned in agreement. She wanted Leonardo to finish the portrait and she was tired of being scolded for moving.

Without as much as a whisper, the door to Leonardo's rooms creaked open. The group's conversation halted as all eyes glanced up at the interruption. There in the doorframe stood the English princess, as miserable and morose as any suffering soul. Anne noticed the dark circles beneath the poor woman's eyes. A fresh purple bruise adorned her right cheek. Her face was hollow with weight loss and her hair had lost its beautiful shine.

Marguerite gave a quick curtsy and ushered the young woman inside. She glanced down the hallway before shutting the door. "Come, child. What ails?"

The English princess hovered by the door, hands clasped, knuckles white. Even her dress was torn. The gold brocade across the bust line of her gown was broken and her sleeve hung torn across her shoulder.

Anne rose from her seat and curtsied too. Though they had never become friends, she felt an intuitive pang of sadness for this young woman.

"He hurts you—the king—doesn't he?" she asked.

Princess Mary did not respond.

"You can tell us. We are not ignorant of his cruelty. We have only just felt it in different ways."

The group waited for the princess to collect herself. It took a long time, but when she was ready, her words came in a slow whisper.

"He forces himself upon me nightly. And sometimes during the day." She showed them the fresh scratch on her arm. "Though it is awful, I do my duty. But after he takes me—" She swallowed hard. "After he takes me —he lets his dwarf do the same."

Leonardo dropped his paintbrush and it rolled across the floorboards.

"But he cannot do that," Anne demanded, her hands balled into fists. "We shall write to your brother, King Henry. He will have you rescued!"

Princess Mary shook her head. "I am grateful for your kindness, Anne. You have always been good to me." She looked upon the group of friends. "And you have made a happy home here in France. These wonderful people became your family when I could not."

Anne took the princess' hand and led her into the room. She tried to re-affix the torn sleeve over the woman's shoulder. She tried to smooth the stray strands in her hair. "There is a place for you in our circle. There always has been."

But the princess stepped away, rejecting her show of affection. A life of royal training was obviously still well entrenched. She straightened her back and recreated her regal posture before she continued. "Thank you, Anne. But my own suffering is not the reason for my visit today. I bring news of Francis and Claude's new baby."

Her words brought a darkness over the room. Claude pulled her infant in close and covered her with a blanket. She moved towards Claude and knelt at the edge of her chaise, her voice reigned in tight.

"I overheard them talking—the king and his dwarf. The news of your baby girl has reached the king. But I dare say, Louis is not happy."

Claude swallowed, her eyes wide with fear.

The princess pressed on. This was clearly an account she felt she must deliver. "Louis has ordered his dwarf to steal away with your infant. He told Frederique to dispose of her through whatever means was necessary. He will deny the royal baby has been born."

"What! No!" Francis stepped forward, his face blanching. "He cannot."

"But that is not the worst of it." The princess now spoke to the whole group. "The king plans to kill Claude on the night of the wedding. He has ordered his dwarf to do it when she is alone with her baby, unguarded and unprotected. Frederique's commitment is unfailing. I know in my heart he will carry out Louis' wishes." She shook her head. "When the deed is done, the king will announce she died in childbirth. That is why Claude may not attend the wedding. When she dies, he can explain their deaths away without consequence."

Francis gathered Claude up in his arms as the remaining friends exploded with outrage. Now there were no hushed tones or secretive whispers. Anne raised her fist in the air. Leonardo shouted with indignation. Marguerite paced the room with a fierce growl.

More questions, more discussions, and more disbelief at the ghastly news swirled through the chamber. They argued amongst themselves. They demanded answers and more. The English princess gave them as many details as she could, but she had only overheard snippets and was not fully aware of the king's plans. When she had given them all she could, the conversation fell silent again. They stood together in the room, shaken and horrified.

Princess Mary moved towards the door. "I must get back. The king will be looking for me."

Marguerite embraced her. "Thank you, Mary. Thank you for risking your safety to bring us this news."

"I will do what I can to help. You need only ask," she replied.

Marguerite nodded. "Francis, dear brother. Would you please see the princess back to her rooms? See she is returned in good stead. It would not do to have her discovered by the king or his dwarf at this time."

Francis gaped at his sister's request. It was clear he did not wish to leave his wife's side. But Claude patted her husband on the hand.

"Please, Francis, do see her back. Princess Mary has done us a great service."

Francis proceeded to the exit, bowing low to the English princess. She issued a miserable curtsy and left the room without another word. Francis followed behind her, swinging the heavy oak door shut with a soft clunk.

Bile rose in Anne's throat. She was so furious she could barely see straight. "How is it possible a man could be this evil? A father this wicked?"

It was a bewildering question. The love between parent and child was supposed to be the strongest bond in the world, one that could never be broken. Yet here was a man who sought to end his daughter's life and the life of her newborn child. It was an evil that was difficult to fathom.

"We must do something!" Anne shouted as her rage boiled over.

A wind picked up outside the window, rustling through the shrubs in the gardens below. Darkened storm clouds rolled over the blue sky, casting a gray hue over the hills beyond. Even the birds stopped singing.

As the group pondered the princess' words, raindrops began to spatter the beveled windows in Leonardo's rooms, tapping against the glass like a hundred tiny hammers

Marguerite held up her hands, resignation on her face. "King Louis must die."

Leonardo pulled at this beard. "Aye, he must...as must his dwarf."

Marguerite moved toward the chaise she had occupied earlier that day, searching the plush velvet cushions. She ran her hand into the darkened crevices of the furniture seat, feeling her way along until she pulled her grimoire from within the confines of the chaise.

"We must use the Craft," Marguerite announced, flipping through its pages. "Though the cost shall be high. One death will bring great strife to whomever casts the spell, but two deaths...two deaths will bring strife for generations."

"Surely the Goddess would see our need. Surely she would forgive it," said Anne.

Leonardo shook his head sagely. "That is not the way of things, Anne. Dark magic has a cost. And the price must be paid—in full."

The room fell silent once again. But Anne did not care. It was inevitable, their impossible predicament. The king would kill Claude and her baby, a baby they had fought so hard to bring to this world. She could not stand by with this knowledge and do nothing. She would use the Craft to kill the king, in spite of the terrible cost.

But before Anne could get the words out, Marguerite stepped forward, her fingers still searching the pages of her grimoire. She looked up at the group of friends and made the ultimate declaration.

"I shall cast the magic. I shall kill the king. I shall pay the price."

The nighttime air had turned crisp and cold, carrying with it a pungent smell of rotting leaves. The smell of autumn. The smell of death. They gathered in secret under the bright Mabon moon. The trees had lost their leaves and their branches reached like gnarled fingers into the sky. A great fat owl swooped across the forest canopy out for her nightly hunt.

For days, Anne had helped Leonardo with the preparations. They had locked themselves away, conducting the research required to make the killing curse—a curse that, once set in motion, would ensure the death of the king. Marguerite's grimoire had not contained the adequate incantations for such a feat and so Leonardo had volunteered to find the right spell.

Anne had been Leonardo's assistant in all things. She had spent hours poring over the texts he asked her to review. She had taken notes as he paced the room shouting out theories on ancient rites and dark rituals. Anne had even brought his supper each night to ensure no servant would need enter his rooms.

Now that they had come together in the forest, Anne wondered at what new discovery Leonardo might have made. She had left his side for only a few hours that afternoon to care for Claude's baby. But he had obviously found something new. A low fire marked their gathering spot in the wood. The leafy forest floor provided ample seating.

"I brought the wax candles you requested," whispered Marguerite.

Leonardo nodded at the women. "I have finally discovered it. The solution to our problem. It came to me this afternoon while Anne was tending to the child. I wanted to bring everyone together to hear it. It is a complicated formula, I dare say. And there is no time to waste."

Three sets of blinking eyes stared at Leonardo da Vinci over the fire. No one dared interrupt.

"For the killing curse we must fashion a poppet. A figurine fashioned from the wax of Marguerite's candles. The doll must meet the exact proportions of the king in his most natural form. Once the poppet is cast, we shall summon the king's demise."

"A poppet?" asked Marguerite.

Leonardo searched for a scrap of paper to draw a design. "Marguerite, have you your grimoire? I will draw this out. We must all understand quite clearly."

She obliged and pulled the black spell book from her robes.

"You see," Leonardo began as he turned to a fresh page in her grimoire and drew the perfect proportions of a naked man. He superimposed the image in two positions, inscribing the man within a circle and a square. "This drawing signifies the proportions of a man in his most natural form. We shall craft the poppet in this likeness."

The women nodded.

"We shall gather a lock of the king's hair. And once it is in our possession, we shall adhere it to the back of the poppet's head—in this area here." He drew a brush of hair as a halo around the head of his drawing.

"But how shall we acquire a lock of the king's hair?" asked Claude.

Leonardo glanced up. "Let us save this question for a moment, my dear. I need to explain my choice of talisman first, to help you understand my logic. You see, there are many talismans that can bring harm to a man. The first is the fang of a snake." He sketched the image of a simple snake above the naked man's ankle.

"A snake's fang will kill a man in the same manner of true snake's venom. When pressed into the wax poppet at the foot, the poison will enter the body and spread to the heart. Once there, the heart will pump the toxin to the rest of the body, causing great spasms, pain and eventually death." Leonardo shook his head. "But the snake fang is not our talisman. For a fang leaves a mark on the victim. Evidence of a true snakebite will remain in the flesh of the ankle for the coroner to discover. And that would be most problematic for us."

The women crooned with understanding.

"The second talisman is a piece of horn taken from a Spanish bull." As he explained, Leonardo drew the image of a bull over the man's heart. "The piece of horn must pierce the heart of the poppet. If thrust with sufficient force, the horn will enter the heart, and stop it beating in an instant. However, the horn of a bull is not our weapon of choice either. For a horn that gores a man would tear the flesh wide open, and this bruising would remain on the victim's chest. Damage too easy for a coroner to discover."

"But Leo, is there any talisman that does not leave a mark?" Anne asked, her patience wearing thin. She had worked through this part of the plan with him and she knew it well. But until this afternoon they had been unable to find a talisman that would leave no trace.

"Yes, but it has taken me some time to find it. The funny thing is, the solution has been here with us all along." He laughed despite the somber tone of the evening. "You see, though he is a lowly rodent, an ermine can do great damage. The ermine is not vicious like the snake, nor powerful like the bull, but he quietly gnaws until the damage is done. The docile ermine, my dear coven, is our talisman." Leo drew the image of an ermine into the man's forehead.

"When the tooth of the ermine pierces the head of the poppet it will begin to do its work. The rodent will gnaw at the king's brain until nothing is left. The damage will take place inside the skull, leaving no trace, well hidden from the eyes of the coroner. Therefore, when our King Louis dies, having had his brain gnawed to bits, no one will be the wiser. It will appear a simple death from old age." Leonardo smiled, the light of the fire casting eerie shadows over his withered face.

"Brilliant," whispered Anne.

Claude's voice wobbled. "But what of Frederique? Have we a plan for him? He is the one who will come to kill my baby."

Leo got to his feet and paced over the dried leaves on the forest floor. "Yes. I have considered this. The dwarf is an important factor in the plan and we must take care of him too."

This was a surprise to Anne. She and Leo had been so focused on finding a silent killing curse for the king, she had forgotten the dwarf.

Marguerite spoke up. "But Leo. Why not simply fashion two dolls? I can perform the dark ceremony for them both."

"No, Marguerite. This is not a good course of action. We must consider the cost of taking two lives with dark magic. It would be astronomical."

"But I will do it, Leonardo. I shall pay the price," she insisted. "I will have no children of my own. That much I have seen in my visions. The curse would end with me."

Anne could see the logic of it but she could not help feeling she should be the witch to cast the spell. After all, killing the king had been her idea.

Leonardo continued. "It may be true, Marguerite, that the curse would end with you. But we cannot be sure of it. What if the curse continued but it passed on to Claude and then on to her babe? We would have accomplished nothing. No, Marguerite. I have pondered this extensively. We cannot risk it. We simply cannot take both men's lives with dark magic."

"But then how?" Marguerite stood up, her small frame juxtaposed against Leonardo's tall spidery form. She stood stubborn and determined, just as Anne knew she would.

"Fireworks!" Leo wiggled his bushy eyebrows. "The king has asked for a great firework show and I shall give it to him. I will insist his dwarf be the one to light the final cracker. The launching mechanism is rather tiny, so a man of small stature will be required to fit inside. Once he lights the firecracker, I shall fix the apparatus to prevent the ignition from advancing. And with that amount of chemical energy contained within the box..." Leo looked around the fire, his blue eyes sparkling. "Kaboom!"

The women's eyes were wide, pupils dilated. Their faces ghoulish in the light of the fire.

He wagged a long finger. "The final firework shall never transform into a great lion. Instead, it shall blow Frederique to kingdom come. This way, our dwarf problem will be addressed through a bit of clever chemical engineering and *not* by black magic. His death shall appear a most dreadful accident."

Once the plans were set, the group descended into a comfortable rhythm. They stayed on into the night, sitting by the fire and working through each detail to ensure a seamless success. They would need help from the English princess and Francis to set the plan in motion. Rose would assist too, that much was certain.

They made but one pact between them. When the time came, Marguerite would be the one to plunge the ermine tooth into the king's poppet and cast the killing spell. The price be what it may.

PRESENT DAY
QUEEN'S UNIVERSITY, CANADA

E ver since this bloody Comprehensive exam began, I had been riding a rollercoaster of crazy. I had gone up and down, over and under, from elation to despair and back again. But lighting those candles at the art gallery had changed the way I looked at the world. The surge of energy when I called that fire to burn was the most empowered I ever felt in my life. And it was all because of my bizarre DNA and the freaky sixth finger that was removed when I was a baby. I realized as I sat there watching the fire burn, I was not normal. I never would be normal. But maybe, just maybe, that was okay.

John seemed to be okay with it too. The whole experience put us both at ease and we joked all the way home. There was more wrestling and tickling as we wandered along University Avenue. We looked as nutty as fruitcakes, screaming and howling as we chased each other down the tree-lined streets, past Kingston Park, and through the student ghetto. And the best part was that neither of us cared. It was fun to be silly. For the first time in my life, I didn't give a fig about what anyone thought. For the first time, I was free to completely embrace my weird.

The door slammed behind me as I walked into the house, but even our neglected home repair seemed charming today. Floating into the living room, I plopped onto the wingback chair, and let out a long happy sigh.

To my surprise, Bernice lay on the couch propped up on a pile of needlepoint pillows. Grapes was mopping her forehead with a damp cloth.

"Bernice had a spell," Grapes said tightly.

Bernice's eyelids were fluttering.

"What's happened?" I leapt from the chair and knelt beside her.

She stared up at the ceiling. "I'm fine, dear."

Grapes eyed her best friend, worry sprawled across her features. Normally, Grapes was not a pacer. She was not the nervous sort. But today she looked like the anxiety-ridden polar bear at the Toronto zoo, yawing back and forth along a well-worn pattern on the rug.

"Ellie, dear. We have something to tell you," Grapes confessed. "It's important, but we need you to be calm. We can't have another kitchen fire."

I crossed my arms in defiance. I was not interested in revisiting the kitchen fiasco. That was yesterday, and this was today. "Actually, I am doing much better with my fire inclinations. I even went to see my Wiccan friends and got them to show me how to light candles with my mind."

Grapes and Bernice exchanged glances.

"Ellie, we need to be sure you can handle it," Bernice said wearily.

"Of course I can handle it," I insisted, my voice registering a layer of hurt. "If it's important, I need to know. You guys have to stop protecting me from all this stuff. I'm not a child, you know."

Grapes was pacing again. It was not a good sign. I decided to wait her out. After all, it had taken her twenty-six years to tell me I was a fire witch with six fingers on my hand. Today I needed to make sure I didn't scare her off. I sat down in the wingback and tried to project an air of calm. I cocked my head to the side and leaned it lazily into my palm, dangling my Birkenstock from my big toe.

"Remember how I told you about the Bowlan family coven?" Grapes began.

"Mmmm...hmmmm..." I replied, Lily-style.

"Well, Bernice and Gerty were part of it too. Bernice and I are Northern witches—we are healers. Gerty is of the Eastern orientation—she is a water witch. If Gerty wants to, she can call up a rain storm the likes of which you've never seen."

Bernice raised her hand with a hint of annoyance. "That's why it always rains on poker days. She loses and it rains. It never fails. She has flooded my basement three times in as many years."

Grapes shushed her friend. "But none of that is important, Ellie. It's just for you to know that we all have the gift. You aren't alone and we'll never let you struggle by yourself."

I sat as still as possible, still dangling my sandal, trying not to register the surprise on my face.

"Just tell her, Lizzie," said Bernice.

Grapes gripped her walker. "Some witches have an additional talent. Bernice has it. It is the gift of sight. She has a way of seeing the future." Her voice dropped. "And earlier today Bernie saw yours...your future."

Intrigued now, I leaned forward in the wingback chair. My sandal fell to the floor but I continued to will my face into a tranquil expression.

Bernice sat up on the couch, resting on her elbows. "Ellie, dear... I saw... I saw your daughter." She stopped, clearly having difficulty getting the words out.

"My daughter?"

Bernice smiled weakly. "Yes, darling. You will have a beautiful daughter and you will call her Liza—after your mom. She will have chestnut hair like yours, a sweetheart face and the most stunning amber eyes. She will be the center of your universe. Your pride and joy."

My hands flew to my heart as I jumped from my seat. I forgot altogether about being calm and allowed the emotion wash over me. I couldn't believe what I was hearing. To know I would have a child. A daughter. It was incredible.

I closed my eyes and imagined her. My Liza. The delicate skin of her baby cheek against mine. The fine hairs on the top of her head as I nuzzled her with kisses. A little girl in a white tutu leaping across a stage as I applauded with pride. My belly warmed at the thought of her, with an instinct that pulled at my heart and my soul. A daughter—*my* daughter. She would be my little Liza.

Bernice pulled at my arm, distracting me from my daydream. "Ellie, listen." She swallowed hard, tears spilling down her cheeks. "Liza will die. Your little Liza will die when she is nine. I saw it in my visions."

Grapes' eyes filled with tears too and put her hand on my arm. "Your little Liza will die, honey. It is our family curse."

To discover I would have a child and then be told she would be ripped away from me? It was too much to bear. It was too much to process all at once. I turned away from her touch, rejecting her as I rejected her news.

"But it can't be possible," I cried, the pain in my voice palpable.

Bernice sagged. "It's terrible, but it's true. There will be an accident. It will be unavoidable."

"No! We will just be careful. We'll make sure the accident doesn't happen."

Grapes wrapped me up in her arms, her strength calming me, bringing me back from the brink of panic. My guts had turned to an oily ooze, motor oil slipping through my intestines. She rocked me as this new truth settled over me like an unwanted blanket.

"Ellie, it's the dark mark on our family. There will be nothing you can do to stop it—unless we can end the curse."

I looked up from her shoulder. "How can we end the curse?"

"We think there might be a way." Grapes caterpillar eyebrows had started their dance. "Remember at the séance, the voice said, '*Only a Bowlan among the living can end the family curse, to do it you must save the life of the man who killed your parents*.'?"

I nodded frantically.

"We believe this is what we need to do."

I stalked through the living room, thinking it through aloud. "We need to find Cullen. That is what we need to do. We need to find Cullen and then I have to... I have rescue him somehow."

Bernice continued. "Yes, we believe finding Cullen is the place to start. Gerty has been working on trying to find him. She called before you arrived. She's got news."

We waited for what felt like an eternity. Only the ticking from the Grandfather clock in the hall tracked the passage of time. No one had anything more to say. Bernice lay back on her pillows and Grapes paced the living room in an endless circle. I stared out the window at the blue-bells in the garden. There was nothing to do but wait.

Finally, the front door slammed and Gerty appeared in the doorframe. Her hair was dark blue and her stockings sagged at her ankles. Just by looking at her, I knew her news wasn't good. She might as well have had a rain cloud directly over her head. It seemed forever before she made her announcement.

"Cullen is dead," she said in a low voice.

"What!" I cried. "But how do you know? He's our way out of this mess."

Gerty nodded, glacial speed. "He's dead. He died one year after your parents did, Ellie. It was suicide. I found the newspaper article that confirms it was him." She dug through her purse and pulled out a yellowed copy of *The Cambridge Times*. There, in the center, was a picture of Dr. Ivor G. Cullen with his bushy moustache and strange eyes.

I shrank back into my chair, horror swelling through me. I wanted to run and hide. I wanted to stop and fight. But I could do neither. I was frozen.

"What are we going to do now?" My voice was weak.

Without Cullen, my little girl would die. It seemed hopeless but that was the raw truth of it. We sat together as the news of this man's death hit us hard. It felt like it did all those years ago when we found out my parents and grandma were dead. The house held us in the same eerie stillness. The minutes trudged by like prisoners on a chain gang.

Grapes shuffled back and forth in her walker, her polar bear pacing now the only movement in the room.

"There has got to be another way," she mumbled under her breath. "There has got to be another way..."

The grand fete was underway and thousands gathered in the streets to partake in the festivities. Thanks to Leonardo da Vinci, the royal wedding was a spectacle the likes of which France had never seen. A parade of white horses, their manes affixed with bright blue peacock feathers, trotted in unison. Percussionists beat atop leather drums as they marched ceremoniously out in front. Appreciative mobs cheered as court jesters and fire-eaters performed acts of bawdy silliness and death-defying feats.

Marguerite, as expected, had worked behind the scenes to bring gifts to every citizen in the city. She had distributed food and blankets to the poor. The attending crowds had received exotic spices and hundreds of small silver forks had become souvenirs to celebrate this grand royal wedding.

Marguerite had toiled tirelessly to uphold Louis' good reputation. Such was the perceived kindness of the king, the crowds cheered for him. The air outside the castle swelled with chanting, "The Father of the People... The Father of the People..."

Inside the chateau, the merrymaking was even more spectacular. Dozens of tables covered in fine white linen and gold plate accommodated the throngs of wedding guests. A dinner of roast pheasant dripping with ginger and honey, plates of smoked herring, and a boiled swan, cooked and redressed with its magnificent plumage. Every last morsel had been greedily consumed.

King Louis sat looking self-satisfied at the front of the great hall with his new bride. The royal couple wore matching golden wedding attire. Their amethyst robes flowed lavishly over their shoulders boasting the most luxurious ermine fur Europe had to offer. Even the new queen managed a weak smile.

"Do you hear that, Frederique?" The king sniveled as he sucked the spittle from his front teeth. "I am the Father of the People. They do love me so."

"Indeed, sire." His dwarf bowed low.

A group of jugglers and band of tiny dogs provided a distraction for the guests as the formal ceremonies and protocols for the royal union took place. Anne and Marguerite stood behind the new queen, performing their bridesmaids' duties with impeccable poise.

The day had been a long one and Anne had felt the tension through every part of it. She had smiled at the parade, applauded at the ceremony, and feasted with the crowds through the dinner celebration. But she could not help anticipating the precise moment when they would set their plan into action. As soon as she saw Leonardo approaching with a large covered canvas, she was flooded with a renewed energy. She nudged Marguerite with a careful elbow and slid her eyes over the scene. It was time.

"Da Vinci," the king called as he watched Leonardo struggling to bring the painting up the steps to the platform.

Leonardo bowed ceremoniously to the new royal couple and cleared his throat. "To mark this wedding day, it brings me great pleasure to present this portrait. It was a work of some technical significance. I wanted to capture something beautiful and mysterious, to create a painting that honors you, your lordship."

"Yes, yes. Stop talking." The king picked at his cuticles. "Just show me the piece."

Leonardo raised a coiffed eyebrow but showed no other sign of distaste. Instead, he pulled back the cloth with flourish.

"I give you...*Lady with an Ermine*."

A sizable crowd had gathered to witness the great painting's unveiling. As the linen came away from the canvas, the gasp from the onlookers was audible. Wedding guests jostled and bumped to get a look at Leonardo da Vinci's masterpiece

A fair young maiden with a thoughtful expression adorned the canvas. A gauzy veiled coiffure smoothed her raven hair within its confines and a double strand of black pearls sat at her neck. Oddly enough, in her arms, she cradled a large white ermine. Its dark eyes were menacing.

"Leonardo, it is simply perfection," Marguerite crooned.

The king, however, did not seem altogether impressed. He scrunched up his oversized nose as though he had noticed a foul smell. Slowly, he raised his finger.

"Is that Anne Boleyn?"

Leonardo shook his head and readied himself for the lie they had prepared. "No, sire. It is not Mistress Boleyn. You see, a beautiful apparition came to me in a dream. She was an angel. She spoke of your regal heart and bade promises of your long reign over France. When I saw her, I knew she would be the subject for this painting."

The king continued to scowl. "But why does the angel sit with a white rat on her lap?"

Leonardo produced a condescending smile and bobbed at the knee. "That is worthy of an explanation, your highness. You see, the angel sits with an ermine—a symbol of royalty. The ermine adorns the royal robes you and your queen wear today." Leonardo sounded like he was talking to a small child.

"Hmm," the king grunted.

Marguerite stepped forward, recognizing her signal. "Sire," she said, careful not to bring about his bad temper. "Such a masterpiece should be stored somewhere safe, so it cannot be damaged. Don't you agree?"

The new queen now spoke for the first time that evening. "Louis, perhaps the painting should be brought to our sleeping quarters? It would be safest there behind locked doors."

"Fine. Fine. Make it so." The king waved her away, no longer interested in his new gift.

Without hesitation, Marguerite raised her hand into the crowd and called to one of her trusted servants. She spoke to him, her voice hushed, giving him the special instructions. She pressed a gold coin into his hand and returned to her duties with the new queen.

Anne glanced at Leo, who nodded imperceptibly, and they slipped into the crowd like snakes into tall grass.

"That went well," Leonardo whispered to Anne as they met moments later in the corridor.

"Yes." She smiled. "But when did you paint in the ermine? I have only ever seen the portrait with Salai."

Leonardo rubbed his long nose, eyes twinkling. "It seemed fitting. Ermine robes, an ermine portrait, and an ermine death. A balancing of the universe." He scurried off into the crowd.

Anne readied herself to carry out the next part of the plan. As agreed, Rose waited along the back wall with the other servants, watching for her cue. She sat with her hands folded in her lap, her doughy features arranged in a pleasant expression. With Anne's signal received, Rose made her way through the crowd.

Anne pulled her in close. "'Tis time, Rose. Tell Claude to make haste. The king's chamber door shall soon be unlocked."

"I shall do." Rose bobbed her head and disappeared into the castle.

* * *

At Leonardo's command, a new commotion began on the dance floor. Throngs of musicians prepared for a night of reveling and gaiety. Horns honked and strings screeched in an orchestral cacophony of delight as hundreds of guests trilled with anticipation of the ball.

"We shall have dancing," the king shouted. "Dancing in my honor!"

Couples found one another as they made their way to the dance floor, stepping forward and back as they formed a great circle. The music picked up its tempo and the dancers rotated clockwise and counter-clockwise in a glittering ring of elegance. Each woman danced with a new man until the music signaled a change in partners in the pretty French carola.

Anne began at the far side of the room and danced the circle with a courtier's grace. Step after step, she weaved through her partners until she found herself face-to-face with the man she had been waiting for. She looked up at Francis with a questioning eye. He nodded as she extended her hand with gentle grace. In response, he discretely deposited a smooth white tooth into her palm.

"It took a bit of doing to acquire that incisor," Francis whispered from behind a false smile.

Anne bowed low.

"Take care of Claude." His smile faltered.

"I shall," she breathed. "But remember, you must ensure the dwarf is the one to launch the final firework. That is your most important task."

The tempo changed again and Anne moved to her next dance partner in the circle. The Burgundian dance seemed to go on forever now that the tiny ivory package had changed hands. But Anne surged with excitement, knowing she finally had the ermine tooth. Another critical step in their plan had fallen into place.

Alight at the entrance of the king's chambers sliced through the darkness. Marguerite and Anne crept past the antechamber to the outer door with only the eerie glow to guide them. Full of jitters, Anne bumped a table hidden in the shadows and a couple of goblets skittered to the floor. The women cringed at the noise but the festivities in the garden muffled the sound.

Anne scooped up one of the cups. "Marguerite, I cannot see where the other goblet has gotten to."

Marguerite cradled the wax poppet in her arms, its lumpy flesh still and lifeless.

"Worry not, Anne. We have more important things to attend to."

Slipping inside the king's sleeping chambers, Anne saw Claude moving in the shadows. She was inspecting the dressing table laid with the king's many grooming tools. When she found the silver comb, she snatched it up and removed the greasy hairs entangled in its tines.

"You made it," Claude breathed when she noticed her friends.

She ushered them to a spot on the floor she had cleared away, having already completed much of the preparation for their dark ritual.

Claude had drawn and blessed the circle of ash. She had removed the pane of glass from the window so they could do their work in the companionship of the moon. Finally, she had erected a small makeshift altar upon which they would perform the killing curse.

Marguerite looked at Claude's handiwork and nodded with approval. As always, Claude had followed her instructions with exacting precision. She had even remembered to set the king's new painting, *Lady with an Ermine*, inside their circle of ash to preside over their magic.

"Now then, do we have everything?" Marguerite whispered. "I have got the poppet."

"I have got the hair," Claude added.

"And I have got the ermine tooth." Anne held out her hand to show the others. In the candlelight, the small white incisor glimmered menacingly. The ladies murmured with admiration as she returned the tiny piece of ivory to the secret pocket she had installed in her dress. The tooth already felt hungry.

As the three women gathered, the night's energy seemed to shift. The air filled with a deep intensity, something thick and magical swirling within it. In the dim light, Anne glanced at her own image in Leonardo's portrait, shadows dancing across her painted face. Through the canvas, as though through a looking glass, the lady watched over the room. Her ermine watched too.

"Remember, Leo instructed us to wait for the first fireworks. Our timing must be perfect," Marguerite whispered. "Anne, would you go to the window and see if you can determine Leonardo's progress? It shouldn't be long now."

Eager to follow instructions, Anne padded to the window overlooking the gardens below. Her stomach lurched at the height of the tower, easily six stories up. By the light of the torches, she could see a crowd on the garden lawns. More guests funneled from the castle, buzzing with anticipation of the spectacle that would soon begin.

A gurgle from across the room drew her attention. It was tiny and sweet, and utterly unexpected.

"Hush," Claude cooed as she moved toward the noise. "You must hush my darling and sleep."

"Claude, you brought the baby?" asked Anne, incredulous. "But Rose was supposed to watch her."

Claude gave her a sheepish look as she scooped up the child. "I could not let her out of my sight."

Anne could not believe Claude had brought the baby along. This had not been part of the plan.

"Oh, please understand," Claude begged. "My child is to be stolen from me tonight. How could I have left her behind?" She placed the child in the corner upon the king's bed.

The first great firework of the evening squealed through the night air, exploding into a shower of blue and white light, crackling in the blackened sky. The guests in the gardens crowed with delight, as raucous and rowdy as ever. From the city beyond the castle walls, a riotous cheering erupted too. The crowds resumed their faithful chanting, "The Father of the People... The Father of the People..."

Marguerite glanced at the window. "It is time. We must call the Dark Mother."

As the babe settled back into her slumber, the women readied themselves for the dark ritual. They placed a single taper at the center of their protected circle and assumed their positions around the circle of ash. The moon cast an eerie glow as they gazed skyward, wallowing in its magical energy. Marguerite led the incantation, her voice firm and smooth.

"Goddess of Dark, Goddess of Light
We call unto thee, hear our great plight
We summon our courage, we summon the right
Do us our bidding, on this darkest of nights."

Anne felt a familiar sensation build through her body, a warm surge of energy running up her legs and into her sex. It swelled like a ripe red plum through her chest. Now a more seasoned witch, she was comfortable with this feeling of power as it sizzled and popped within her, searing at her toes and fingertips.

The wind swirled around the circle of ash. It tossed at their hair and tickled playfully at their feet.

"The Goddess is close," Marguerite called over the wind. "We must cast the poppet."

Anne felt the Goddess' presence in a visceral way. Her energy lived within the naughty gust trailing up Anne's skirts, caressing her, stroking her. She pushed through Anne's mind, searching for her secrets, searching for her soul. The effect was both terrifying and grand.

Marguerite placed the wax doll upon the altar.

"We offer this wax, its likeness is formed
And affix it with hair of the man who is scorned
Do us our bidding, we summon alarm
Do us our bidding, and bring this man harm."

Claude handed the tangled clump of hair to Marguerite as she ran the poppet's head through the flame, softening the wax to receive its namesake. Marguerite closed her eyes and with dulcet words uttered like prayer, she pressed the greasy strands into the waxy flesh.

"Louis, King of France. This is your likeness. This is your scorn," Marguerite commanded.

As the call left her lips, the wax figure began to move, its tiny body exuding an energy of its own. It twitched in Marguerite's hand.

"I think it's breathing," she gasped.

The wind blew stronger as the women stared down at the doll, an ugly mane flowing from the back of its head. The light of the candle danced over its pale skin creating ghoulish shadows with the rise and fall of its chest. The poppet was suddenly very much alive—alive and evil—just like the man it represented.

Anne fought back a surge of revulsion.

"Let me see." Claude gestured for the poppet in the dim light.

Marguerite passed the living doll to Claude, careful not to let it slip from her fingers.

"Oh, it wriggles!" cried Claude.

Marguerite nodded. "This is good. We were successful in our first step. We have given life to the poppet. And now we must...kill it."

The doll twisted its hairy head towards Marguerite. Alert now, its face rotated backwards on its body in a most unnatural position.

"Someone take it from me, please!" Claude winced as the tiny figure struggled to free itself from her grip. "I don't want to hold it. I don't like it."

A sense of foreboding fell over Anne, weighing on her like a lead blanket, dragging her down, pulling her in. The whispers of the Goddess were louder now, her ancient voice growing haggard and raw in the wind. The sweet smell of rotting flesh filled the air. A smell of dirt. A smell of death.

Something clunked in the room beyond the king's chambers. It began as a subtle knocking against a faraway wall, but it grew into random thuds and crashes. The women listened as the fireworks continued to explode outside.

"Do you hear a woman crying?" asked Anne, straining to hear over the wind.

In the other room, a metal goblet skittered across the floor with a sharp sliding clink, kicked astray by an unknowing foot.

"We are come!" a woman's voice cried into the darkness.

The heavy oak door to the king's room blasted open with an almighty crash. There in the doorframe stood King Louis himself. He was ruffled and bloodied, his teeth clenched with fury. It was apparent someone had tried to stop him from coming to his inner chambers, but he had clearly won the fight. And the loser, based on the pounding from the closet, had been locked away. Anne could see that the brawl had only served to rile him up, to heighten his anger. And when he came upon these women in their witch's circle, King Louis of France was livid.

The women stood immobilized, caught in the act. The wind circled as the Goddess' demonic laughter echoed through the room. Anne glanced at Claude who still held the thrashing wax poppet. It seemed to be scratching a hole through the fabric of her gown with its savage little fingers.

"Witches!" the king screamed.

Louis lunged at the women. He narrowed his eyes on Claude as he leapt through the air, fists clenched. Anne shrieked with terror, horrified by the rage spewing from this man. It belched from him like a disease as he levied his attack. But no matter how many times he tried to get to Claude, the protective magic circle held firm, impervious to his advances.

"No, father...please," Claude begged from within their sanctuary.

"You think I can't get to you?" Louis' rage became frenzy. "You think I cannot end your life? I will kill you, you fiendish goblin, just as I killed your mother!"

The fireworks were coming to their climax. Great booms set the sky ablaze in a symphony of light. He threw himself again against the protective barrier, but still, it held firm. Anne's chest swelled, if only for a second, a sense of hope now coursing through her veins. The magic of the witches circle was as impenetrable as a fortress.

Then, from the shadows of the king's bed, a thin cry found its way into the chaos. It was fragile but it echoed in the dark night. It turned Anne's blood to ice.

A cold-blooded smile spread like a disease across the king's face. "You foolish bitch. You brought your baby?"

Louis wasted no time as he ran towards the noise, in search of the innocent child he hated as much as the woman who had produced it. Claude anticipated her father's actions and lunged forward to stop him. It took only as second for Claude's foot to cross the boundary of the circle. It took only a second for the protective magic to shatter into a thousand tiny pieces. Anne felt it cut through the air like the slice of a blade. The circle's safeguard was broken and they were all exposed.

Marguerite ran for the iron poker by the hearth. Raising it high in the air, she threw her body forward, hurling the weapon at the king. But Louis anticipated her attack. As she dove for him, the king spun round and kicked out her legs. Marguerite tripped, losing her grip on the poker as it fell to the ground. The king saw his chance and seized his hairy hands around its handle. Then with one swift motion, he brought the heavy rod down on Marguerite's head.

Marguerite fell to the ground with a thud.

Anne gasped. Her friend lay lifeless of the ground. There was no magic circle to protect them now. She could do nothing but watch in horror as the night's events spiraled out of control.

And the king was far from finished. Again, he lunged for the child Claude now held her in her arms. Claude fought her father like a wild animal. She howled with fury, desperate to protect her baby. They wrestled and shoved as the child wailed helplessly. Claude thrashed and kicked at the king's legs. She clawed at his face. She bit his flesh. Anything to keep her baby safe.

But it was no use. In one final blow, the king ripped the infant from Claude's arms.

Anne and Claude shrieked in unison, but only for a second.

Claude's precious daughter hung by her feet in Louis' hairy fists. The baby cried for the all world to hear.

The girls stood frozen, too terrified to take another step, too afraid to advance any action that might cause the baby harm. Only the child, hanging upside down like a fish, struggling to be free, bawled madly.

"No," Claude pleaded as the king edged towards the open window. He thrust the baby into the night air, swinging the child from six stories up.

Anne's stomach lurched with the horror of it. Did King Louis mean to throw the infant from the tower? She looked into his terrible face and saw her answer plain and clear. His eyes told her everything.

"Father, please no. She has no deformity..." Claude begged.

The baby hung from the window, wailing and weak. Her cheeks turned deep red as the tiny thing struggled to breathe. Louis glowered at the baby lolling in his grip, swaying in the wind like a piece of meat cut fresh from the butcher.

"Deformed or otherwise, she comes from you and so she is not worthy," he seethed.

A great crack from the gardens below signaled the final firework of the evening. It screamed into existence from a tiny ball of light and then burst forth as a magnificent lion. In a stupefying array of amber and gold, the regal beast with its mighty mane and great teeth lit up the night sky. Louis gazed skyward with a euphoric sneer.

"My regal lion is finally come," he bellowed.

Taking her chance in that razor sharp second, Claude grabbed the squirming poppet from her robes and threw it to Anne. Then she lunged for the king with all of her strength. She pushed his heavy body and kicked him in hard in the knee. As he howled with pain, she pulled her baby into the safety of her own arms. Mother and child fell to the floor. Claude wrapped her body around her baby and bellowed with relief.

"How dare you!" Louis screamed.

Now with the protection of the circle gone, the king's fists connected with Claude's flesh. He levied punch after punch upon his daughter in a tirade of punishing blows. Claude curled into a tight ball, her babe tucked beneath her.

As Anne bore witness to the horrifying assault, time seemed to slow. This man, King Louis of France, did not deserve to live. Anne became aware of a darkness in her heart she had never felt before. It spread like poison through her veins until she could deny it no longer. She hated the king. She loathed him. And she wanted him to die.

She grabbed the doll and squeezed its lumpy body between her fingers. Her other hand went instinctively to the pocket inside her dress where the tiny tooth waited, pulsing with a malevolent energy of its own. With the ermine tooth in one hand and the poppet in the other, the wax creature fought like the devil himself. It twisted and thrashed, biting her fingers and scratching her flesh. But she held it firm.

"*Do it, my fire child,*" the wind whispered in Anne's ear. "*Kill the poppet and take the king's life.*"

Anne faltered as the earthy breath of the Goddess' tickling her cheek. Her voice was as old as the hills. Her touch was powerful and terrifying.

The king issued another blow to Claude's head and she cried with pain. "*Do it!*" shrieked the Goddess,

Anne glanced down at Marguerite who lay in a pool of blood, still as the dead. It was no use thinking of their original plan. She saw the truth of it. It had to be her. It had to be Anne to cast the dark magic.

She pinched the writhing poppet by the head and without further hesitation, plunged the ermine tooth deep into the doll's waxy flesh. It gave almost no resistance as it pierced the pliable surface, right between the eyes, and it sank in deep. Soon the tiny incisor was buried in the poppet's skull. When it was done, she called the words that were supposed to be Marguerite's.

"Take him ermine.

Eat flesh of brain.

Take his life.

End our pain."

With the malevolent magic cast, the king began to scream. His placed his hands over his head and fell to his knees. The pain inside his skull seemed to consume him. Anne watched with satisfaction as it seared in his brain, a gnawing ache, an eating of flesh.

Anne gripped the poppet as it fought for its life. But it did not take long. She felt the doll's life force ebbing away as the ermine did its work, gnashing at Louis' brain until there was nothing left to consume. Anne felt the life leave the king's body like an extinguished flame, snuffed out by the Goddess with a tiny puff of smoke.

As the poppet ceased to fight, so too did the king. Louis fell to the ground dead.

Suddenly Anne's legs felt heavy. Her head throbbed. Her body ached. She threw the lumpy wax figure to the ground, eager to free herself from its slippery flesh. Then she fell to her knees, exhausted.

She crawled to mother and child and wrapped her arms around them. The babe continued to cry but there were no apparent signs of harm. Claude ran her fingers over her infant's delicate head, feeling her legs and arms for any damage. She shushed and cooed, holding her baby close.

Slowly but surely, a quiet settled upon them. Anne held them both tight, unwilling to let them go until her own heart stopped racing. They clung to each other as the baby's crying stilled and Claude's moaning relinquished.

The minutes dripped by like honey from a bottle, slow and sticky, sweet and restorative. It reassured them. It bolstered them. It wrapped around them like a warm family quilt. They were finally safe. It was over.

Anne took in the room's mighty disarray. Chairs were overturned and tables upended. The bed curtains were torn and the foot cushions disemboweled, candlesticks and chalices strewn in every corner. Red claret spilled across the floor and mixed with left over excrement from the capsized chamber pot beneath the king's bed.

And there, in the middle of the broken circle of ash, King Louis lay dead. His skull was unblemished, with no telltale sign of what killed him.

Leonardo's *Lady with an Ermine* looked down with a tiny smile. Her ermine had done its work.

Marguerite, too, lay motionless on the hearth near the fireplace. Her skin was as white as snow against the red blood trickling down her cheek, but her eyelids fluttered with the tiniest movement.

"Marguerite, wake up. Please wake up," Anne whispered as she rallied beside her body. She wiped the blood from Marguerite's forehead, trying to coax their friend back to consciousness. But it was no use. Though she was still warm and drawing breath, Marguerite was not yet ready to come around.

As the minutes ticked by, the weight of the night's events took hold, pulling her deeper and deeper into exhaustion. She sat quiet and stupefied for a time, drawing rasping breaths.

The night sky had become a dull black, bereft of its beautiful lights and raucous explosions. The room filled with a strange silence.

"Claude, something is wrong," Anne whispered in the darkness.

The night had been gruesome and cruel, but it was finally over. The king was dead, and they were safe. What could be amiss? It was Anne who stumbled on the answer first. It was an awful, petrifying realization, and when it came to her, it cracked through her skull like a hammer.

"The final firework! It was never supposed to go off. Frederique lives!"

* * *

Frederique crashed through the door like a wild bear ready for a fight. Tables toppled and goblets smashed as he tore through the room in a vortex of anger.

The dwarf's robes were full of soot and his skin was blackened. His blue eyes glowed in their sockets with fiendish madness. He howled when he saw the king's lifeless body on the floor.

"You bitches!"

He flew at the women in a bestial frenzy, lunging and snarling, ready for blood.

Anne marveled at his power in spite of herself. Despite his small stature, the man moved with incredible speed, growling and snapping as he advanced on them. She tried to scramble to protect the baby, but she was clumsy and slow with fatigue.

The dwarf drew his knife and launched himself in the air, coming down with a force and plunged it deep into Claude's arm. She howled with pain, recoiling from his assault, but still she held fast to her infant. The dwarf withdrew his blade and made ready for another attack.

In the new chaos of the night, Anne's mind cleared. She understood what the dwarf intended. With the next blow, the small man would drive the knife right through the child. And when he had killed the poor little creature, he would murder Claude too. Just as King Louis had commanded.

Anne stumbled to her feet. It took a few tries, but once righted, a renewed vitality bubbled through her. But this energy was different. It fueled her with a dark and formidable force. It was instinctive and ingrained. It was a power she had always held within and it begged for release.

The witchy wind renewed its dance, hot gusts blowing her hair. The Goddess came to her, face to face. Her once beautiful visage was now old and wasted. The mask of time and aging. It was the face of death.

"You have taken the life of one man. Why not take another?" The Goddess spiraled around her like a snake.

Anne was both repulsed and renewed by her presence. The Goddess' idea was appealing, instinctive. It was impossible to resist. The thought pulled at her. It danced within her seductively, drawing on her inner strength and the magical power she readily contained.

"Do it, my child," the Goddess urged. *"What is one more life?"*

Anne closed her eyes and allowed the anger to fill her. It swelled through her, growing large enough it left no place for anything else. Anne could not hold the darkness within her body any longer. As she swallowed it down, she narrowed her eyes upon the tiny brute who rallied attack after attack on her best friend.

"Burn," she whispered.

In an instant, the savage little man was alight with flames. He screamed in agony as his flesh burned. Such was the intensity of her power the dwarf had no time to react. The fire scorched around him, flames licking at his skin. His clothes were alight with hot red tongues, lapping at the fabric that still clung to him. His beard sizzled against the black of his skin, his blue eyes darting about in the smoke.

But Anne's fire curse was far darker than she knew. Her inferno burned at the dwarf's core too, melting his organs from the inside out. His guts became a liquid mess of heat and flame, his lungs turning to lava as he gasped for air.

The dwarf had no time to fight. He had no time for anything. His body succumbed as death consumed him. It wrapped him in its web like a hungry spider issuing its fatal bite. It was so swift, his cremation was but a flash in the darkened room. In less than a second, the dwarf's body was gone. There was nothing left but a pile of ash.

"You've done it, Anne Boleyn!" The Goddess shrieked with laughter.

Anne fell to the ground, bone weary and trembling. The lusty wind danced around her. It circled over the dwarf's ashes, his burned flesh turned to nothing.

With a gurgling howl, a ragged gale blew Frederique's remains right out the window. Snowy white ash flew into the cool night air, wafting like a cloud and disappearing into the dark night.

Anne was frazzled and limp. She closed her eyes, useless with exhaustion. She was too weak to find Claude and the baby. She was too feeble to fight. She could do nothing but lie in a crumpled heap, body drenched with sweat, exposed and vulnerable to the Goddess who loomed above her.

"Two lives you have taken tonight and now you are mine," the Goddess bellowed.

Shrill laughter echoed in the wind as it caressed Anne's ear, winding around her and through her, binding her hands and feet with invisible ties. Anne lay still, powerless to fight her. Powerless to resist.

"Bound you are to me with these rites of dark magic. Bound too is your kin, now and forever more."

Anne became aware of a new sensation at the base of her neck. An invisible set of hands wrapped themselves around her nape, squeezing tightly. A translucent collared shackle was installed with a sharp click. A shackle that would never let her go.

"You shall pay...Anne Boleyn... You shall pay..."

The Goddess vanished with a tiny pop.

PRESENT DAY
QUEEN'S UNIVERSITY, CANADA

My cell phone rang with a new age jangle, waking me from the first pleasant dream I'd had in weeks. I shut my eyes tight against the intrusion, wanting to cling to my blissful slumber. My little girl, the downy skin of her cheek, the trill of her laughter, the weight of her body as I pushed her on a swing. My Liza. My little Liza. She would be the center of my universe, the apple of my eye.

"Up and at 'em, girl," Dez's drill sergeant voice called into my ear. "You need to come to the lab. Your DNA results are ready."

In lightning time, I bolted out of bed, brushed my teeth, splashed water on my face, and threw my hair into a messy ponytail I built a hard run into my commute and made it to the lab in record time. The sterile white doors swung open and a woman wearing protective eye goggles emerged with a cart loaded with test tubes. The glass tubes bumped and jiggled over the partition in the doorjamb and the woman continued down the hallway. She glanced back at me with a raised eyebrow but soon disappeared down the corridor.

A daunting, scientific-looking DNA machine sat in the corner of the lab, clicking and pulsing with impressive efficiency. I grabbed a lab coat from rack by the door and searched the enormous space for my best friend.

Dez sat, as always, at his workbench, poring over a series of complicated notes. John stood beside him, a white lab coat stretched across his muscular arms.

"Hi there," I said, breathing hard, my eyes darting between the two of them. "I got here as quick as I could." I wiped at a rogue bit of toothpaste I could still taste on my lip.

John gave me a boyish grin.

"Took you long enough." Dez winked.

Yesterday, after Bernice's spell, I had called him with the news about my daughter, Liza. Grapes and the Trio had been discussing supernatural options for dealing with the family curse and my pounding headache had returned. After a while, I realized I was out of my element. I needed to return to a place of science where basic facts and hard coded evidence were still king. I had spent my whole life choosing science over the supernatural, and that was when it occurred to me the two might be connected. My witchy power would likely be evidenced in my DNA. And if it was true, so would Anne Boleyn's. After all, that was what Ivor Cullen had been searching for when he worked with my father.

Dez snapped off a pair of latex gloves and popped them in the trash. "You ready for this, El?"

I took a deep breath. "Let me have it."

Dez laid a series of papers on the lab bench, lining them up meticulously like the nerd I knew and loved. He ran a purple finger over his freckled nose and began. "According to these results, you are a 99.999% match with Anne Boleyn. It's incredible."

"Really? That's crazy." I gaped.

"Yes indeed. It's all here in black and white."

John and I squinted at the paper riddled with the confusing cryptogram of letters, our eyes swimming. I bit my lip and John raised his eyebrows. Other than that, we said nothing.

Dez rolled his eyes. "Oh, good Lord. Don't you guys remember anything from high school biology? This is pretty basic stuff."

We stared back at him with vacant expressions.

Dez looked glowered. His eyes darted between the two of us, searching for any small sign of understanding. Seeing nothing, his expression softened.

"Okay, I'm gonna give you the thirty second run down on the human genome. If you don't catch it all—I'm really sorry. But I believe there is an undergrad class down the hall if you need remedial help."

John sided me in the ribs when Dez wasn't looking.

Dez used his tired-of-teaching-students voice as he prepared himself for the lecture. "These letters represent your sequence of nucleotides. All the nucleotides within the DNA form long structures called chromosomes. These letters signify the sequence of the four building blocks: A for adenine, G for guanine, T for thymine, and C for cytosine. We compared your DNA sequence to the DNA report from Anne Boleyn and your alleles are a match. That's the first bit of news."

I nodded, trying to affect a sage expression.

"But it's the eleventh chromosome where things get interesting. The gene for insulin is located right here." He pointed to a highlighted string of letters. "The code right next to it is where you and Anne Boleyn come in. According to your DNA results, you both have a special genetic sequence that is extremely rare. Which is very cool, because until today, no one had confirmed what this particular piece of genetic code was for. You have a genetic mutation—and Anne Boleyn had it too," said Dez, his enthusiasm restored. His bored teacher tone had vanished.

"And that's important because..." My voice trailed with a hint of impatience. This explanation was feeling too technical and I needed Dez to get to the point.

Dez took me by the shoulders. "Because, Ellie, this is also the genetic mutation that Ivor Cullen identified for witchcraft. This gene not only makes you related to Anne Boleyn, it's also the gene mutation that makes you a witch."

The scar on my hand seared with heat as this new information mingled with my brain waves.

"So this is where Ellie's fire talent comes from?" asked John.

"That's right," replied Dez, his words coming faster now. "And this is a really big deal. Like—as in—a huge deal. You see, Cullen took criticism from the scientific community because he couldn't establish this mutation was the gene for witchcraft. It was early work that needed more substantiation. But now, with Anne Boleyn's DNA and your own, El, it's enough to demonstrate the specific function of this sequence of nucleotides. There is a ton of publication potential here. Frankly, it's enough to catapult any scientist into stardom."

My heart clattered in my chest. This was the connection between science and supernatural that I had been looking for. John gave me a playful bump with his shoulder and I jostled him back with my elbow.

Dez watched the exchange between us with a look of mild disgust.

After a while, Dez gave John a pat on the back. "There you go, John. We now have undeniable evidence your girlfriend is a witch."

As always, Dez had said just the right thing. It made me uncomfortable and giddy at the same time.

John smirked. "Yep, she's a fire witch. And a very hot one at that."

Dez crossed his arms across his chest. "One word of advice, buddy," he said, as a new wave of snark readied itself to burst forth. "If you guys ever go camping, just remember not to piss her off while you're roasting marshmallows. Or she might set you on fire."

John and I emerged from the biology building, still enthusiastic about our discovery. Dez's lab results had given me the scientific connection I needed to set my logical mind at ease. The results had helped me formulate my own objective truth, one I had struggled to understand my whole life. I was a witch—yes. I was a nerd—yes. Both were a part of me and I was okay with that.

"What's next, Ellie?" asked John. "Got any more weird and wonderful family secrets up your sleeve?"

"I do indeed," I said mysteriously.

Today, I was hoping John could join Lily and me in reviewing the final chapters of Beth Bowlan's diary. I was certain there would be something to help me put together the final pieces of my family puzzle.

Students wandered up Union Street, already inebriated from their football pregame warm-up parties. Even at this morning hour, students and professors alike had consumed enough alcohol to drown a giant. It was homecoming weekend and the Queen's Golden Gaels were expected to play a bone-crushing game of football.

One drunken frosh bumped into John and continued up the street, swept up with the crowd. John laughed and pointed us toward the stacks.

Strangely enough, when we arrived, Lily was nowhere to be seen. The library was full of dusty old books and several large stacks of paper teetered on the edge of a book tray. A blackened computer screen sat atop Lily's desk, her orange purse tossed beside it.

"Lily?" John called. "Where is she? I thought she was always down here."

"She is—usually." I smiled. "But she's been dating this guy. She's probably out with him. I'm sure she'll be back any minute."

I grabbed two pairs of latex gloves and we headed into the Special Collections room. John found himself a spot at the steel table as I plopped my oversized backpack on the floor. A familiar vase of lilies sat in the room. They brightened up the place with a cheery optimism.

"Lily's lilies," I said. "You should have seen how surprised she was when Donny gave them to her."

"That's great. Lily needs someone in her life. I'll bet she gets lonely down here," said John.

I grabbed the diary from the hiding place in the subfloor and joined John at the table. His research intensity rivaled my own and we passed hours that afternoon, enraptured by the young Beth Bowlan.

June 12, 1574

> *My secret mother came to see me today. She said I was old enough now to know the truth about my family story. I was thankful she trusted me enough to share it.*
>
> *In her youth, my mother, Elizabeth, fell in love with her childhood companion, Robert Dudley. It was the innocence of their bond that gave them hope they might one day marry. Sadly, he did not bear high enough rank and circumstance to be a rightful fit for the likes of a queen. Mother told me I was conceived one night in a love so true she could never see fit to marry any other man. She so has lived out her days alone, without a man to comfort her, without a child to call her own.*
>
> *Mother begged me to learn from her mistakes. She bid me marry for love and not for duty. And I shall. I shall marry a wonderful man and we shall have many wonderful children. And the Bowlan family line shall continue for many years to come.*

"So it was Robert Dudley, after all," I said, thinking of my dad's unpublished paper in the basement. "There have been rumors of their secret love affair, but no one's ever been able to prove it."

This passage pulled us deeper into the threads of Beth Bowlan's life. The hours melted away as we uncovered more details about this fascinating young girl. Before we knew it, we had arrived at the final entry. A twinge of sadness tripped through me at the realization we had reached the end.

"Lily, we're reading the last of Beth Bowlan's diary," I called into the empty room, still harboring some guilt for having completed the remaining pages without her.

"Lily?" I tried one last time, but the room responded with silence.

October 26, 1576

> *Terrible plots against my secret mother abound. Conspiracies lurk in every corner. I am afraid we might be discovered for the witches we are. Mother says precautions must be taken. We must do away with any evidence that might incriminate us. Therefore, it is with great sadness that I must do away with you, my little diary. You hold all my secrets and the secrets of my secret mother.*
>
> *But I cannot destroy you. That would destroy my heart. I have decided I shall whisper you into the wind. I shall whisper you to another time and place when our story can no longer do us harm. I shall whisper you to another Elizabeth Bowlan— who will come to understand the truth about our family and our connection to the Craft.*
>
> *Goodbye my beloved diary. And to the dear Beth Bowlan I shall never know, please love this book well.*

My stomach dropped at the last few sentences of the passage. It finally made sense. The original Beth Bowlan had sent her diary to my grand-mother, Beth Bowlan. That was how this journal had come to be in the possession of my family, hidden away all those years in my father's boxes of unpublished research. My father didn't find the diary. My grandmother did.

I thought about the long journey this book had taken and the connec-tions it made for the women in my line. We had all lived a life of Elizabeth Bowlan, each one different, each journey unique, but tied together by a strange magical name and a strange magical heritage.

"What a family story," said John with awe.

I smiled wistfully. "I only wish Lily had been here to finish it with us."

We looked at the vase of lilies, the fuzzy skin of the white petals looking cheerful in the dull surroundings. It had been nice to have Lily's lilies here, even if she couldn't be. I gave the vase a little spin. As the leaves rustled, a small white note affixed to the flowers fell onto the table.

"Hey, who did you say Lily was dating?" asked John, picking up the small card.

"I don't know. Some guy named Donny."

John passed me the greeting card. "Ellie, these flowers are from Landon Fishburn. Lan-don Fishburn is the 'Donny' Lily has been dating?"

"What?" I croaked.

A repressed memory from the attic in my mind flitted through the open door. It was clearer when I didn't fight it. I was a little girl again, listening at the kitchen door at midnight. My parents and grandmother spoke in hushed tones about their need to change their travel plans. But it wasn't Dad's voice I heard. This time, it was Mom's. She was concerned, resistant even, to something my father had proposed.

"I don't like Ivor Cullen. His research ethics are questionable," she said, pushing the pamphlet for the Tower of London back across the table. "But it's his student that worries me. That Don Fishburn is crazy. I don't trust him. I don't trust him at all."

My legs went weak at the memory. Donny Fishburn was Cullen's student? Was it possible that same man was now Landon Fishburn, the director of the History Department here at Queen's?

Fishburn had claimed to know my father. He told me himself. He had been a student of biology and switched to history because of one of my dad's lectures.

"My father..." I gaped. "Donny Fishburn knew my father."

The words suffocated me even as I said them. My stomach lurched.

The phone rang with mystical bamboo wind chimes, vibrating across the table. It took us both a second before we found it under John's heavy backpack.

"Hello?" I whispered into the dead air.

There was a pause as the line crackled with poor reception. A male voice spoke with deadly calm. "I have your friend Lily."

"What do you mean? Where is she?" The words tumbled out.

"Stop talking, Ellie," the voice warned. "I want you to listen carefully."

I breathed, waiting for more information.

"You will bring your research to the top of Grant Hall Tower in ten minutes—eight o'clock sharp. Bring the ancient texts. Bring the Boleyn DNA results. I want it all. Make sure you come alone. Do not be late and don't call the cops. If you do, I will kill your friend."

"Please no. Please don't hurt her," I begged.

"One more thing, Ellie." The voice crackled over the line. "After I am done with Lily, I'm going to pay your great-grandmother a visit."

The phone line went dead.

* * *

I screamed with fury, burying my face in my hands. Self-loathing climbed up my spine, one vertebrae at a time. For days I had known someone was after those priceless books, but I was too self-interested to take precautions. I hadn't gone to the police because I didn't want to confess the embarrassing details of my life. Instead, I had left it to Lily to deal with my mess.

John smoothed my hair as I railed into his shirt.

"We can handle this, El. It will be okay," he soothed.

"But how?" I looked up. "How are we going to fix this? Fishburn just threatened to kill Lily, and once he's finished, he's going to go after Grapes. I can't lose them, John. I just can't."

"I'll go to the tower with you," he soothed, a muscle flexing in his jaw. "We'll stop him before he gets to Grapes. He'll never get near your grandmother. I won't let him."

"No, no, no, it's too risky," I stammered. "What if we can't stop him? He will go straight to Grapes and he'll kill her. She's an old woman. She won't be able to defend herself."

Tears filled my eyes at the thought of it. I couldn't lose my last surviving family. It was too awful to imagine. A familiar set of strangling hands squeezed at my neck as I hyperventilated. I was losing control. Terror flowed like ice water through my veins.

But something slowed my breathing.

Somewhere within my panic, the image of my father sitting under the old red maple tree presented itself like a gift. I wasn't sure why the vision came at this precise moment, but I was grateful for it. My father, I thought. What would he have done? He had been a calm and unflappable man. There hadn't been a time in his life when he had failed to apply a reasoned systematic logic to any problem he encountered. Dad would have developed a plan. And it would have been a smart plan, not one based on fear.

I forced myself to breathe, to think. And as I did, an idea formed in my mind. Fishburn had been inspired by my father. He had changed majors because of him. I felt sure I could talk him out of his plans to hurt Lily if I could just show him what I had found. So much of the research had been my dad's. Perhaps it would help Fishburn see how amazing it all was. And besides, I was Arthur Wright's daughter. If anyone could shame him into letting Lily go, it would be me.

"John, we have to split up. Fishburn said to come alone. So I will go to the tower and convince him not to hurt Lily." I spoke with growing sense of calm. "And you go to Grapes. You can get her as far away from the house as you can."

"Ellie, I'm not going to leave you alone with that crazy man," John scoffed.

But the plan in my mind was becoming clearer. It was the only way.

"It'll work. I promise. I'll be okay," I insisted. "But I need you to protect Grapes. I need to know she'll be safe. I couldn't live with myself if something happened to her. She's the only family I've got."

* * *

With only Lily on my mind, I raced to Grant Hall. My backpack, loaded with every piece of research I had, weighed on my shoulders. I had stowed the priceless books in the black storage container. I had stuffed my father's papers in there too, along with all of my notes and the Anne Boleyn DNA results. I would show Landon Fishburn everything I had found and then he would let us go.

The university campus was oddly empty tonight as everyone was at the football game at Robertson Stadium on the other side of town. I glanced up to the see the sky filled with a blanket of clouds, perhaps an ominous warning for the confrontation ahead of me. I gritted my teeth and pushed the worry back. I needed to pick up my pace. I was running out of time.

Arriving breathless at Grant Hall, I pulled open the heavy doors. The building was dark and my footsteps echoed around the cavernous space. A whimpering at the top of the staircase drew my attention. I raced up the stairwell towards it, taking the steps two at a time. At the top of the stairs, I made a hard right, sprinted through a storage room and into the tower's belfry.

Behind the great brass bell, a woman lay on the floor, her arms and legs bound with duct tape. Dark blue bruises encircled her eyes. One eyelid was swollen shut and a trickle of dried blood encrusted her nostril.

"Lily, honey, it's me. I'm going to get you out of here," I said breathlessly.

Her left shoulder hung at an unnatural angle and I fought off a surge of nausea at the sight of it. I knelt down and worked the tape to get her hands free. She gritted her teeth, enduring what she could of the pain.

"I would stop doing that if I were you," a male voice echoed from beyond the brass bell.

Lily blanched as her eyes darted to the man in the shadows.

"Run, Ellie. Run," she whispered.

But I did not. Instead, I hovered over her, standing my ground as I called into the darkness. "I know it's you Dr. Fishburn. I know you are the one who has been dating Lily."

The voice laughed, cold and simpering, from the other side of the bell.

"My father wouldn't approve of what you are doing," I said as fiercely as I could. "This is not the way to do good research and we both know it."

His laughter stopped. I thought I could hear his anger behind a snorting scoff.

"You really are like him, aren't you? So high and mighty," Fishburn spat. "So focused on doing things the *right* way.'"

I tried to think quickly, desperate for him to see sense. Surely I would be able to talk him out of this. He was a harmless professor, after all.

"But ethical behavior is all we have as academics. Without it, we become mad scientists. You don't want to become a mad scientist, do you?"

"Don't be naïve, Ms. Bowlan," he simpered. "Mad scientists are the most persistent. The most innovative. Mad scientists are the only ones who know how to achieve true glory."

A lusty wind pulled through the open arches in the belfry. I ignored his threatening tone and knelt down again, working on Lily's bonds. If I could free her from this duct tape, maybe she could run. Maybe Lily could escape.

I heard the click of a revolver behind my head, the pressure of its muzzle hard against the base of my skull.

"Get up."

I stood, raising my hands in the air until I was face-to-face with my aggressor. A stout, balding man with bulging eyes lurked in the shadows. He stood before me with his tweed jacket and chalk-covered pants, every bit the image of a passive professor, but the malicious look in his eyes said something different.

"Did you bring the DNA results?" He pointed the revolver at my head.

I backed away from the barrel of the gun until my backpack bumped against the limestone wall. I kept track of my breathing, refusing to panic.

"Yes," I said with false confidence as a raucous crack of thunder peeled through the sky. "I'll show you what I've found. We can work on it together from here on in. I promise."

"Hah!" he screamed in my face. "You are a dirty little liar. Just like your daddy."

Fishburn tossed two sets of handcuffs at me and gestured for me to secure them around my wrists and ankles. For a second, I thought we might negotiate, but then thought the better of it. This man was not acting like the Dr. Fishburn I knew from the student barbecue, haughty and arrogant. This man was calm and calculating. This man was a murderer.

"Okay," I stammered as I clicked the cuffs into place. First the ones around my ankles. Then the ones that bound my hands. When I was finished, I was completely vulnerable. There was no way I could fight back now.

"I've done what you asked. Now let Lily go free."

He emitted a deep chuckle. "Turn around, you fool."

I fumbled towards the wall. My face pressed up against the damp stone as he took out a hunting knife. He cut the straps of my backpack from my shoulders and dragged the bag into the dying light of the evening. I shuffled around to watch him claw through my things. After a few moments of digging, he held up the manila envelope containing Anne Boleyn's DNA results. A slow smile snaked across his face.

"Good girl. I like a student who can follow direction." Fishburn's dark eyes flashed.

I remained in control. I would not allow the panic to take over. Fishburn glared at me for a time. He seemed to be waiting. Hoping perhaps that I might burst into tears. But I did not cry. I did not flinch. Instead, I still clung to the glimmer of hope that I could appeal to his sense of right and wrong.

"I know you were Ivor Cullen's student. He didn't teach you well. He wasn't an ethical man. But you also knew my dad. Didn't you learn anything from him?" I asked.

The comment seemed to enrage Fishburn, his frog eyes bulging. He tucked his gun into the back of his pants and pulled the knife from its leather sheath. He held it to my neck with a new frothing fury.

"That's right! I was Cullen's student. And let it be a lesson to you, Ellie. Students get screwed!" he screamed.

The sharp edge of the steel pressed into the flesh of my neck, but I would not budge from my post in front of Lily.

Fishburn's face was inches from mine, so close I could feel his breath on my cheek. "I was instrumental in Cullen's infamous paper—"The DNA of Witchcraft." Oh yes, Ivor Cullen was the almighty DNA expert. But he needed me, his lowly student, to do his dirty work. He needed me to find him a witch. And I did! But that pretentious bastard still wouldn't put my name on the paper."

Fishburn seethed at the memory. "It took me a full year to find her—Nathalia Vantur—and what a witch she was. Do you know how hard it is to find a witch who does not wish to be found?"

I tried to affect a look of disinterest. But this was the story I wanted to know more than anything else in the world. This was the last chance I would ever have to understand what happened to my parents.

"Is that when you and Cullen started working with my father?" I asked, no longer able to hold in the question.

Fishburn spat. "No. Your perfect father had nothing to do with our work. He would never have condoned our methods for *encouraging* subjects to participate. It wasn't until after Nathalia spoke up at the ethics review board. Cullen was given a warning, and I was informed I would have to leave the biology program. But that didn't seem fair, did it? Not after everything I had done. Not after everything I was owed!"

A shock of lightning glinted off the hunting knife pressed at my neck. A boom of thunder followed up behind. I decided not to ask any more questions. I realized Fishburn would tell his story in due course.

A slow smile inched across his face. "That is when I came up with an idea so spectacular Cullen had no choice but to keep me on. It occurred to me that using living witches for our research was an inefficient use of resources. Why not use dead ones instead? The DNA of dead witches was as good as the DNA of live ones, and the historical records would point us to the right bodies and the right graves. In fact, they came complete with documented witch trials, confessions, and everything else we needed." His amphibian eyes darted.

"It was Cullen who wanted Anne Boleyn. He said her DNA would catapult us into stardom. He found your father at a genealogy conference and asked him to join us."

Understanding washed through me as the pieces of his story fell into place. It lined up with my dad's notes from the basement.

"But your perfect father turned out to be a real pain in the ass. He insisted on going through the appropriate channels to access Anne

Boleyn's body. He took almost a year to get the official permissions from the British government to exhume her body, based on a ridiculous family connection. By then, Cullen and I had grown impatient."

Pride filled my heart at my father's insistence on doing things right.

"We met your father in London on the night of the exhumation. But your perfect father, Arthur Wright, balked at our research methods. Can you imagine? After all that waiting, he simply refused to share the Boleyn DNA results. That brilliant, yet pretentious, glory-hound father of yours."

Fishburn watched me, clearly enjoying recounting his tale. Soon his face took on a look of sickening satisfaction.

"Your father, mother and grandmother stood there on the Thames that night like a righteous judge and jury. Unwilling to negotiate. That's when I realized I had to be innovative. To take matters into my own hands. I had to eliminate this obstacle." His eyes grew wide with excitement that spoke of madness.

I bit my lip. Flashes of my recurring nightmare echoed through my mind. Three shots in the night.

"I gave your father a choice then. Give us the DNA records or die." Fishburn smiled. "Your father refused, of course. So I did what I had to. I shot your father in the head. I shot them all. Bang, Bang........ Bang."

A swell of anger ripped through me as he made his mad confession. It had not been Cullen after all. This man, Landon Fishburn, was the man who killed my parents. He had taken them away from me when I was a little girl.

"Your father was a brilliant man, Ellie. But he left behind enough research to catapult an academic into true glory. I switched majors, changed my name, and have been working ever since to find it. To find what he left behind. What was rightfully mine!"

I stared into the face of my parents' murderer. A tear had formed in the corner of my eye, but I did not blink for fear it might roll down my cheek.

"Got nothing to say now, eh, Ellie?" His voice was menacing. "Well, let me finish. Cullen was the one who remembered Arthur Wright had a daughter. He went to your house to announce the deaths of your parents, to pose as a police officer and convince you it was all an accident. To make the trail go cold."

His tone now became almost wistful.

"But after London, Ivor Cullen became useless. He wouldn't tell me where you lived. He wouldn't help me find those DNA results. He just

bloody well stopped. So I went to his house, and I shot him too. Bang!"
Fishburn held the revolver to his own head with a savage grin. "I made it
look like suicide. A brilliant move on my part."

Another crack of lightning echoed through the sky. Fishburn walked
over to Lily on the floor and gave her sensible shoes a kick. The wind blew
at the fabric of her brown paisley dress.

"It's all about the three P's isn't it?" he whispered. "Persist. Persist.
Persist." He put his hand on Lily's leg, caressing it with a finger. "And
between you and the librarian here, you did a mighty fine job."

Lily whimpered.

"Don't you touch her!" I shouted, my voice raw.

Fishburn smiled. "Oh yes, I got lots of information from Lily, though
she was a tough nut to crack. She told me everything except for the hiding
place for those precious books. She wouldn't tell me no matter how nice I
was—or how many times I hit her. Eh, Lily? You are a stubborn little
bitch, aren't you?"

"I'm sorry, Ellie. I didn't know," Lily whispered.

"That's right, our little Lily didn't know. Our stupid pathetic Lily." He
glanced at her with a fatherly expression. "Lily thought I might actually be
interested in her. But how could anyone want someone so repulsive?"

"Stop!" I screamed as Lily's face crumbled with humiliation.

"How could any man ever want *this?*"

"I thought you liked me, Donny," she whimpered.

"Then you were a fool."

The wind blew hard around us now, picking up the files Fishburn had
set loose when he had gone through my backpack. Papers scattered like
autumn leaves in a windstorm. The pamphlet from the Sleeping Goat,
emblazoned with the image of Leonardo da Vinci's *Lady with an Ermine*,
sailed through the air and lodged itself under my foot as another crack of
lightning split the sky.

Fishburn knelt by Lily's side. "Perhaps I should hurt you now, like I
promised." He lowered the blade to her face and pressed it into her flesh.
"Wouldn't want me to gouge out your eye, would you darling?"

Lily's whimpering became screams as the blade pierced her flesh. A
trickle of blood ran down her face. Her arms and legs still bound with duct
tape, she thrashed away from the sharp knife. She wriggled hard enough
Fishburn had to use both hands to hold her down.

With this distraction, I took my split-second chance and lunged at this
vile man. Muscles taught and anger coursing through my veins, I cata-

pulted my body forward with as much force as I could muster. But the handcuffs on my ankles clanked together, hobbling my attack. My body sailed clumsily through the air.

As I faltered, feet constrained and knees capsizing, Fishburn lifted his arm up to deflect my trajectory. His knife twisted upright with the wicked precision of a hunter. A sick smile crossed his face as the weapon contacted my flesh. Just before my head cracked into the cement, the frog-eyed man sank the twelve-inch steel blade deep into my thigh.

* * *

Volleys of cold rain ushered me back to a semiconscious state as the storm drilled in sideways through the tower. My right leg throbbed with pain. I tried to swing my leg forward but it was sliced right through to the bone. Realizing I would bleed out fast, I pressed my cuffed hands to the wound to try to slow the flow of blood.

Lightning erupted from the darkened sky and in the bright flash I saw Fishburn's beastly form hovering above Lily. She was no longer screaming. She was no longer fighting. She was frozen with fear.

"Let her go," I called weakly through the driving rain.

"No need for heroics, Ellie. You'll get your turn," he shouted over the wind. "I certainly don't plan to share the research results with you. They are all mine. Mine for the taking. Mine for the glory!"

Fishburn lifted his knife to Lily's face again, just below her eye, and lowered it down. It was clear, even in the darkness, he intended to finish what he had started.

Most of the papers from my backpack had blown away, but the Sleeping Goat pamphlet still cartwheeled in the gale at the top of the tower. It was covered in blood and soaked with water, but as I watched it the thing launched itself underneath my bleeding thigh. The *Lady with an Ermine* looked up from the glossy page, her eyes dark with urgency. In the haziness of my blood loss, she whispered to me.

"*Burn him...*"

It was suddenly so simple. The lady's words had unlocked the solution in my mind. I had worked hard all my life to deny my fire talent. But in that moment, it felt natural. It felt right. Visions of fire infiltrated my mind. The warmth of the flames swelled around me like an old friend. I only had to invite it in. The image of my unborn daughter, Liza, came to me in my fog. I had to make a choice and I had seconds to do it. If I killed this man, the family curse would live on and my Liza would die. If I did nothing, I would pass out from blood loss and this man would murder Lily and me. And it would all be for nothing.

Images of hungry flames gripped my brain. I felt their searing heat on my flesh, the scar on my hand burning into a red welt. I smelled the smoke in my nose. I felt the prickle up my spine. A dark warmth spread across my skin in spite of the cold pelting rain until I had no choice but to set it free.

"Burn," I whispered.

A swell of flames engulfed Fishburn's body in an instant. Shocked and confused, he stepped away from Lily to rid himself of the fire. The driving rain prevented the blaze from taking hold but it dogged him, unwilling to give up the fight. Heat ever rising, smoke billowing around him, he thrashed and kicked in an attempt to throw the fire from his body.

Fishburn raced through the bell tower in terror as the conflagration surged with intensity. He screamed as the flames consumed the sleeves of his shirt and readied themselves to devour his precious flesh. The rain drove down hard, slowing the fire's progress, but still it consumed him, slow and steady, with unrelenting torment.

Lily stirred on the floor, squirming into a corner to stay clear of the heat. She reached back with her bound hands in search of mine. I grabbed one of her fingers and held it tight. We were a force united.

Fishburn ran to the backpack in the center of the room. Even in his final moments, this man was desperate to have his precious research. He picked it up and in no time, the flames found the bag and began their devouring trek across the nylon material.

"No!" shouted Lily as she watched her precious books consumed by the flames.

I could do nothing but watch him burn, to watch the bag burn. I was powerless to stop it. The darkness surged through me like never before.

Fishburn howled as he watched the bag's contents incinerate into nothing. I smiled thickly through my ever-waning mental energy as I witnessed this evil man lose the only thing he ever wanted.

Running to the storage room, Fishburn must have been looking for a fire extinguisher, but the smoke choked at his lungs. His body faltered. His crashed through old broomsticks and mops as cleaning supplies and scrub brushes fell from the shelves above. But it was the cans of paint thinner that ignited the inferno. In seconds, the storage room was alight in a magnificent blaze of red and orange.

The explosion was fierce, so complete that the exits leading to safety were now blocked. The realization came to me swiftly. There would be no escape for any of us. We would die here tonight, Fishburn, Lily, and me. Lost to the fiery inferno at the top of the bell tower.

I lay in a pool of my own blood with nothing left to keep me conscious. I squeezed Lily's hand one last time before the darkness took me.

"I'm sorry, Lil," I whispered.

* * *

Someone pressed against the gaping hole in my leg, a jolt of pain bringing me back to consciousness.

Lily and I were outside the burning building now, the rain still driving down. The smoke from the tower bellowed into the night as a siren in the distance drilled its way into my awareness. In heavy coats and miner's helmets, Dez and John were stumbling from Grant Hall Tower. Blackened and sooty, John laid a shadowy man on the wet grass and Grapes knelt over him with a bag of supplies. Amidst the chaos and the torrential downpour, she administered her salves and ointments. She muttered her incantations and prayers. Finally she delivered mouth-to-mouth resuscitation, pushing on Fishburn's chest.

With her work done, the burned man took his first gasp of air, gulping in the life-giving breath. Then he collapsed back into her arms, begging for water...water...water.

Grapes held a bottle to his lips.

"Thank you...thank you," muttered Landon Fishburn as he drank it down.

The voice of Beth Bowlan flitted through my mind, as ghostly and ethereal as it had been on the night of the séance. *"Only a Bowlan among the living can end the curse. To do it the circle must be complete. Find the beginning to find the end and save the life of the man who killed your parents."*

In my hazy state, I realized the truth it. It dawned on me in the driving rain as the blood drained from my body, the great fire bellowing in the night. I finally understood how the Bowlan curse would end. It would end with Grapes as she pulled my parents' murderer back from the brink of death. Grapes, my beloved great-grandmother. Grapes, my forever protector. Grapes, my enduring hero.

EPILOGUE

1514

CHATEAU DU BLOIS, LOIRE VALLEY, FRANCE

Autumn had arrived and the forests surrounding the chateau were painted deep russet and gold. The summer blooms had died away and the oak leaves skittered across the lawns, dancing forward and back in the capricious breeze. A waning sun lit the grounds with a golden glow and wood smoke lingered on the horizon.

Anne looked over the gardens as she breathed in the fresh, crisp air. There was a finality on the wind today, an ending of a season, the closing of a door.

With King Louis dead, Anne and the English princess had been called back to England. Their time at French royal court was finished. They had served their duties and fulfilled their roles. Now that it was over, England beckoned them home.

"But why must you return so soon?" asked Claude as she cradled her baby girl in her arms. "Won't you stay on with us here?"

Anne ran a melancholy finger across the baby's cheek. "You know the answer, Claude. I am the English princess' lady-in-wait. I always have been. She is returning to England, and I must accompany her. It's what has always been expected of me."

The formalities of royal life were still strange to Anne, even after all this time at court. Though she had been sent to attend the English princess, she had never done thus. Instead, Anne had been allowed to make her life here, to find her own friends. She had been free to learn and grow without burden.

In spite of her many months in France, Anne knew little of the woman she served. She and the English princess had rarely spoken. But in these last few weeks, Anne had become convinced of one thing. The princess had a courageous heart.

Her bravery had been critical on the fateful night of the wedding. Princess Mary had asked no questions as the women freed her from the closet. Marguerite had nursed a welt on her head and Claude's arm coursed with blood. But the princess made no comment. Instead, she followed Marguerite's further instructions with exacting precision.

She had worked alongside the women for the rest of the night, righting the horrendous mess in the king's chambers. They washed away the blood on the floor and mopped up the wine. They mended the king's wedding attire and stitched up the foot pillows. They righted the tables and cleaned the ashes away. And once the room was returned to its former state, the princess undressed the king, put him in his nightshirt, and carried him to bed, his dead body hanging limp in her arms.

"It must be you, princess, to announce Louis' death," Marguerite had explained. "But wait until morning to call the servants, so that they will assume he died in his sleep."

The princess had stayed with the king's dead body, lying stoically beside it through the wee hours of the night. She waited until the sun made its way over the horizon, until she could hear the servants bustling in the kitchens below. Then in the morning light, she had screamed with horror, tears streaming down her cheeks.

"The king is dead!" the English princess had cried, loud enough to wake the castle. "My beloved king is dead!"

Just as Leonardo planned, the coroner had pronounced that King Louis died of natural causes. A happy man on his wedding night. No suspicion was raised, many thanks to the ermine tooth which left no trace of foul play. And many thanks to Rose, a rumor had been circulated amongst the servants that the King's dwarf had run away, devastated by the death of his master.

In the days following the wedding, the group of friends spoke endlessly of the Goddess. Anne's curse had been set in motion with the killing of two men, but she could not bring herself to regret her actions. She had taken the lives of two men. Yes. But they were evil men, and the world was a better place without them.

"If only Frederique had not found the glitch in the firework's launching apparatus," said Leonardo. "A smart little fellow, he was. He repaired the mechanism faster than I could have imagined."

Anne knew in her heart that she had done the right thing. "I will live out my life to the fullest—curse or no curse," she insisted. "And when the Goddess comes for her price, I shall pay it. I shall pay with my life if I must."

Leonardo pulled his long beard in thought. "There may still be hope, Anne," he said with a smile. "I bewitched her, you know—the *Lady with an Ermine.*"

"What do you mean?" asked Anne.

Leo took Anne by the shoulders, his face awash with fatherly emotion. "You see, a painting is immortal in its own way. The *Lady with an Ermine* shall outlive us all. So who better to watch over you and your children and the generations to come? When the time is right, the *Lady with an Ermine* will help set things straight."

"Thank you, Leonardo," Anne whispered.

"It is my gift to you, Anne. My legacy for your legacy." Leonardo gave Anne a low bow and kissed her on the cheek.

PRESENT DAY
QUEEN'S UNIVERSITY, CANADA

My leg throbbed with pain. My lungs felt like a smokehouse. And the skin on my left arm was tight and stinging. So this was me without morphine, I thought, happy to have control of my brain back. It had been days of drug induced stupor in the hospital. Through it all, I had barely registered the friends and family who had come to pay me a visit.

This morning I noticed a hot furry lump at the end of my bed. Zach was curled up in the crook of my legs, and with him, three old faces were waiting patiently.

"Ellie dear, we have been waiting for you to come around. Dez was in earlier while you were still sleeping. That awful morphine made you really woozy." Grapes shuffled over and planted a kiss on my forehead.

Zach nudged me with a wet nose and dropped his hockey puck on my hip.

I gave the dog's muzzle a scratch.

Zach's favorite blue and green quilt lay over me, cozy yet cool to the touch. Though my body was weak and the wound in my leg still pinched, the blanket made me feel homey and safe. I was grateful to have it with me. I was grateful to have them all with me.

Gerty glanced at the door conspiratorially. "We snuck Zach in. So keep an eye out. The nurses can be ornery about having dogs in the hospital."

I watched these three old ladies snicker like a group of schoolgirls. I couldn't believe they were in their nineties when they giggled like that. A warm glow spread through my limbs and into my heart. This was my family, three old ladies and a big black lab. I would love them forever.

A painful thought tripped through my mind. "Lily!"

Grapes ushered my head back to the pillow. "She's fine, dear."

"Oh thank God." I sank back down. "How is her eye?"

She patted my good arm. "It's in terrific shape. I tended to her before the paramedics came. The doctors said the scar will be almost invisible in a few months. She's planning to visit tomorrow so you can see for yourself."

Bernice waved her hands blindly. "Ellie, your Grapes did much more than tend to Lily's eye. She's just being modest. Lizzie here did the impossible. She saved that wretched man, Landon Fishburn. She pulled him right back from death's door."

I flinched at the mention of Fishburn. He was such a horrible man, but the implications of saving his life went far beyond his own personal evil.

Bernice flapped her arms. "The Bowlan curse is no longer. It's over! My visions have changed. Little Liza will be fine. In fact, I saw her this morning while I was baking apple fritters. She was all grown up and graduating from university—Queen's University, I do believe."

Relief flooded through me to know my little girl would be okay. She would grow up to be strong and healthy. I gave the image of my daughter a mental hug. In my mind's eye, she looked up at me with her big amber eyes and my heart melted. I nuzzled my face into her soft chestnut hair.

"I can't take all the credit," Grapes said with modesty. "You have the whole Titanium Trio to thank. And John and Dez too. We all helped. It was quite an operation. Bernice had the vision of the fire. She saw you two in the bell tower in Grant Hall."

"That's right," Bernice chimed in. "I saw it in my visions. You and Lily were lying on a stone floor with that horrible man hovering over you. Right away, I knew he was the man who killed your parents. It hadn't been Cullen after all. It all became clear."

Grapes smiled at Bernice's enthusiasm. "When John and Dez showed up at the house, we knew what to do. We figured you would use your fire talent to protect Lily in the end."

Gerty lit up with a sneaky smile. Her stockings were pulled all the way up today. "To slow you down, I called the rainstorm. I figured we would need a big one to keep that fire power of yours at bay. It was one of my finest storms yet, if I do say so myself."

Bernice jumped in again. "That is where Dez and John came in. They went into the burning building to rescue you and Lily. And then they went back in again to get Fishburn. They could have died with all the smoke they inhaled, but they were unstoppable. They kept going and going until they pulled every last person from the fire."

"And do you know the best part, Ellie?" added Bernice.

I raised an eyebrow.

"Fishburn confessed to everything. He spilled the beans when he came around, confessed to the murders, the kidnapping, the whole nine yards," Bernice announced.

"What? How?" I gaped.

"It's all because of the water we gave him." Gerty laughed. "He begged for it. He even said thank you. Little did he know it was laced with Bernice's most potent truth tonic."

"Bluebells for truth!" Bernice grinned.

I looked into the wrinkled faces of the Titanium Trio. I couldn't imagine a better crew to come to my aid. A lump formed in my throat. What might have happened if these three warrior women had not been on my side?

"Thank you," I said in a small voice.

Grapes gave me a hug. "There is no need for thanks, dear. We will protect you until the end of our days." She raised her white caterpillar eyebrows. "And maybe even longer than that."

Gerty waved a feisty wrinkled fist in the air. "No one messes with the Titanium Trio."

* * *

Today my head was clear, my leg was sore but manageable, and my spirits had returned. I sat up in bed and was pleased to find that my brain stayed put without slamming against the back of my skull.

Lily stood in the doorframe, a bag slung over her shoulder. Her face was set in its usual deflated balloon position, a line of perfect stitches under her eye. Just by the way she looked at me, I could tell something had changed. She rushed over and gave me a long hug. No words, just a plain simple embrace that brought tears to my eyes.

"You okay?" I asked.

She nodded. "You?"

"I'm better now."

So much had happened between us, it was hard to find the words. We sat in silence, holding hands, still a force united.

After a moment, I just had to say it. It had been on my mind since that dreaded night. "Lily, Fishburn was a bastard. None of the stuff he said about you was true."

She put her hand on my arm. "I know," she replied, her large glasses sliding down her nose. "But I'm kind of glad it all happened."

I looked up at her with a perplexed frown.

Lily shrugged. "It's funny, you know. I have spent my whole life hiding in that library, down there in the stacks where nobody could find me. But the last few weeks changed me. The excitement of our research and going on dates. For the first time in my life, I started to feel...alive."

A smile pulled at her mouth and lit up her whole face, a real Lily smile. "And I was dating a psychopath. Imagine how much better it could be if I dated someone nice."

I couldn't help but laugh. Her logic was as solid as ever. "That's awesome, Lil. No more hiding for you."

She pushed those big glasses back up her nose and dug into her shopping bag. "No way. We've got too much work to do."

Lily sat on the edge of the bed and gave my hand a pat. "Your dad was a true genius, you know."

"What do you mean?"

She reached in and pulled the charred storage container into her lap. "Ellie, do you have any idea, how well made your father's vacuum sealed archival box was?" The box was covered in soot. Its edges were buckled and its sides dented, but it remained stubbornly intact. She pushed the silver button, slid the latch, and the box whooshed with a big gulp of air.

"The books survived the fire," Lily announced with pride. Her face no longer sagged. Her lungs were no longer deflated. She was triumphant as she showed off the contents of the blackened box. Three leather-bound texts sat inside, ancient and water damaged, but otherwise no worse for wear.

I touched the calfskin diary. This time, Lily didn't scold me. She simply watched as I caressed its cover.

"Lily, we have work to do," I said, a spark of academic enthusiasm flashing within me.

"Mmmmm...hmmmm..."

She made a beeline for the corner and picked up a new red backpack, placing it on the end of the bed, careful not to disturb my bad leg.

"This is your new backpack. I bought it a couple of days ago when you were still drooling on yourself. It has your laptop in it. The history department is giving you an extension on your Comp exam, but I figured you would want to start working right away."

I laughed. "You know me too well, Lil. Thank you. I will admit, I have the first paragraph mapped out in my head."

She took the computer and placed it on my lap. "So? What are you going to argue? Was Anne Boleyn a woman or a witch?"

My voice came out smooth and confident. "Actually, neither. I'm planning to argue the question is flawed. It's not a matter of either-or. The answer is both. Anne Boleyn was an exceptional woman, and she was an exceptional witch. That is my answer."

"Mmmm...hmmmm... You've got guts, Bowlan." Lily crossed her arms over his chest.

I shrugged my shoulders, more sure of myself than ever. "I have a responsibility to set the story straight. After all, it's my story too."

* * *

John stood in the doorframe looking as handsome as ever, a tall muscular frame with sun-kissed hair and amber eyes. He hovered for a while, holding a fresh, uncrumpled bouquet of wildflowers.

"Hi," I said shyly.

He approached the bed gingerly, eyeing the bandages on my bad leg. The closeness of him sent tingles up my body. I was a bit self-conscious about the bird's nest in the back of my hair but I knew my appearance didn't matter. His eyes were full of adoration.

"I can't believe I almost lost you," he whispered.

I blushed. "But you didn't. You saved me from that burning building. How I can ever thank you?"

He took my hand and brought it to his heart. "No thanks necessary. You don't owe me a thing."

He brought a chair over to the bed but I patted the mattress beside me instead. He sat carefully at my side, arranging the blankets so he could be sure not to hurt me.

"Actually, there might be one thing I owe you," I said once he had made himself comfortable.

He smiled. "Oh yeah?"

I touched his handsome jaw line. "I believe I owe you a kiss."

He looked surprised. "Yes, Ellie Bowlan, I believe you do."

John ran his hand up the tender skin of my throat and pulled my face to his. I closed my eyes as he placed his lips on mine, kissing me tenderly. Our mouths lingered as we let go of our shyness. It was sweet and honest. It was exhilarating and warm. It was heavenly.

His tongue explored mine in this newfound wonder. Goose bumps covered my body as I gave myself over to him. His lips were soft and full of yearning, the roughness of his face scratching against mine.

Our passion ignited and his lips pressed harder on my mine. I returned his kisses with my own hungry ones, a warmth pulsing through my body. Our embrace became more urgent as we explored this wonderful new sensation.

"Excuse me..." A nurse stood in the doorway, her eyes narrowed in a disapproving scowl.

"Foiled again," he whispered, leaning his forehead into mine.

"Visiting hours are over." She jerked her thumb towards the door.

A giggle escaped from the back of my throat. "They're throwing you out, you savage."

John smiled. "I guess they are. But they might as well know, I'll be back for more...tomorrow and the next day and the next day..."

He tucked a loose hair behind my ear and cupped my face in his hands, holding it there as he gazed into my eyes. Then he leaned for one last gentle, lingering kiss. It was full of longing and promises of things to come.

THE END

Thank you for reading! Did you enjoy?

Please Add Your Review! And don't miss more of The Boleyn Bloodline from Deborah Cohen coming soon!

Until then, turn the page for a sneak peek of BOHERMORE by City Owl Author, Jennifer Rose McMahon.

SNEAK PEEK OF BOHERMORE

BY JENNIFER ROSE MCMAHON

Clawing up the steep hill, slipping on loose gravel, I cursed the new rip in my favorite jeans as I vanished into the town cemetery. Every inch of the place was familiar, from the oldest tombstone to the freshest newcomer. It used to be a playground to me for as long as I could remember; hide and seek grew into manhunt, sniffing fresh-laid flowers in the sun turned into stargazing in the black night sky. But it was different now.

My feet dragged through the old section of the graveyard, passing the centuries-old stones of early Massachusetts settlers. The thin slate hand-carved headstones, some cracked or fallen, leaned toward me, straining to be noticed.

I slipped past the World War II monument, avoiding eye contact with the weathered bust-sculpture of some famous general. His eyes supposedly possessed your soul if you looked directly into them. It always gave me that unsettling feeling like I was being watched, so I moved with purpose, flinching at every little sound. I kept focus, past the cannons and into the new section of thick granite stones, shiny on the front, rough on the back, all the same.

The straight rows were packed tight with cold efficiency, draining the warmth of the old section from my core and replacing it with the chill of mass-produced memorials. I shimmied through to the far edge, avoiding stepping directly on any plots, especially ones with fresh-cut sod because, well, the possessed thing again. You're just not supposed to.

Grateful to be somewhat on the outskirts of the grid, I found my mother's grassy patch by the young maple that shaded it.

"Hi, Mom," I whispered as I dropped to my knees in front of her, looking around to be sure I was alone—wondering if every time I looked up, whatever it was that was out there hid, with stealth timing. "I'm gonna hang out with you for a little while. I think I need your help." I paused and tried not to feel dumb.

I plucked the dead leaves from the pot of pansies my grandparents had left and gently pulled a tuft of grass away from the base of her stone to be sure my senior picture was still buried there.

"It's like something's wrong with me," I mumbled. The comment seeped out of my mouth like the sick bile that was churning in my stomach. "Like something's following me...or someone. I don't know."

I flashed back to the smell of wind and rain, the echo of words spoken just out of my hearing. I'd been having the feeling more and more lately—not quite the disturbing visions I had before Mom's death six years ago, but subtle reminders of them.

"Mom, it's my awake dream. The scary wind, the screams, everything. It's coming back. I can feel it. And now that you're gone, I think I'm next."

My heart palpitated in my chest. Hearing my harrowing words made it all the more real. My grandparents and the doctors—they'd all claimed Mom's death was caused by a "heart condition." But I knew better. I knew the truth. It was behind their hushed whispers, behind their tears, behind the hands brushing me away from grown-up talk. My awake dream killed my mother. She was always in the visions, being pulled away from me into the mist. And now...now, it was my turn.

"Am I going crazy?" My exhale expelled resignation and even submission as my hands pulled across my face and into my hair. "I just need to know everything's okay. Like there's not really anything wrong. Can't you just give me a sign?"

A falling leaf, a swooping bird, a rainbow? Anything.

My anxiety twitched in my eye. It lurked in my sweaty palms and my racing heart. I really hated that out-of-control feeling, and it was poisoning every day for me now.

All I needed was reassurance. For my mother to say yes, this was all just my imagination, a ghost story. Maybe my mind had taken my stress and my longing for her and spun it into a remembered nightmare, bad movie-type: *Deadly Wind With a Vengeance*. But now, facing my high school graduation, it was time for me to get a grip.

I sat in the grass tracing the engraved letters and shamrocks in her headstone, waiting for answers that never seemed to come. Finally, I curled up, leaned in against her stone, and rested.

The clink of metal on granite disturbed me—or did it wake me?—and I sat up on my knees, frowning. If I wasn't alone anymore, I'd be out of there so fast.

I peeked over Mom's headstone. The wind had whipped up without warning, flinging mist and twigs at me like shrapnel, making me squint and shield my face. My hair twisted wildly and my jacket flapped against my body, raising alarm in every nerve. I gripped the top of Mom's stone, straining to see past the wind, trying to figure out who was out there.

A thick smell of iron coated my throat and I retched. Blood was in the air, mixed with rage in the violent gusts, and fear burst into my heart. I could swear I heard my name swirling in the blasts, the sounds of an unknown or dead language, and pressed my hands over my ears to stop it. I fell back, wiping the assault from my face and searched Mom's stone, eyes wide with panic.

Desperate for a response, I stared into her monument as if looking into her safe, nurturing face. I blinked for better clarity, leaning in to it, when somewhere deep in my mind, her voice exploded as she commanded me—

"Run!"

My legs sprinted before I was even standing. I had never run faster in my entire life. Every obstacle was against me—rigid headstones, flying petals, loose sod.

I flew out of the cemetery without looking back, my hair trailing behind me, arms pounding me forward. My lungs burned, not only from the effort of sucking extra oxygen, but actually my chest was burning, on my skin, like fire. Something had hurt me. Something unseen.

My pace slowed only when I was within a safe distance from home. Evil self-consciousness washed over me as I considered how crazy I must have looked—early morning May, running for my life, out of a cemetery. Aw, jeez. What an idiot. I prayed the neighbors weren't looking.

What was I running from anyway? Guilt again? Probably. The truth behind my mother's death? I always wondered if I had something to do with it, if I was responsible somehow...I mean, of course I was. Maybe I just wasn't strong enough to help or, more likely, too afraid.

Closing myself off from the rest of the world had always been my best defense from facing it. Worked like a charm, I thought. No one to question me, nobody to need me, no chance of letting anyone else down. I preferred it that way.

But if these crazy visions were coming back, forget it. I couldn't face them. Not again. Especially alone. Without Mom.

No way.

Not a chance.

***

"Maeve Grace...." My grandmother's sing-songy voice called to me from the porch. "Time fer dinner. Fetch some extra tomatoes on yer way up, dear."

Lost in her backyard in my own roaming thoughts again, feeling safer since my earlier "episode" at the cemetery, her voice snapped me back to my present job: filling the wooden salad bowl for dinner. My drawn-out sigh was louder than necessary.

The house would be full of Irish visitors in no time, gathering with my grandfather to watch Ireland play Italy in the World Cup. Michael O'Brien might come with his uncle, Paddy. Blush burned my cheeks just thinking about him and I threw myself back into the vegetable patch.

Searching for more tomatoes seemed way better than a loud soccer match laced with Irish swearing, and definitely better than making an idiot of myself in front of my life-long crush, which was what I managed to do any time Michael was near. I poked around behind the St. Brendan statue, moving the dense greenery in search of anything worthy.

"Are yeh comin', loov?" Gram's voice sounded like a distant echo from the porch high above.

In a knee-jerk response to her call, I tripped on some zucchini vines and landed at the base of the St. Brendan statue in the middle of the garden, my face nearly hitting it.

"Jesus!" The accusation rang clear in my voice. I blamed him for a lot more than nearly breaking my face on one of his anointed ones.

A handmade shelter enclosed the three-foot whitewashed statue of Brendan on three sides. From the back, I couldn't see the religious icon but knew its every feature by heart: peaceful, bearded face, robe-like clothing, cross in one hand, gesturing to the open expanses with the other. Always mocking me.

He was Brendan the Navigator. A courageous mariner, in search of paradise or the Garden of Eden. My grandmother's bedtime stories retold

St. Brendan's Voyage, his epic travel to the promised land, a million times, engraving his fearless curiosity onto my soul.

White paint peeled down in delicate rolls from the outer back wall of Brendan's enclosure, moving my eyes toward its stony base. And there, in the statue's foundation, was a hidden metal door the size of the long side of a shoebox, with countless coats of paint, rusty hinges, and a small, aged padlock.

My eyes widened. How could a little door be here all this time and I never noticed? I cupped my palm around the lock to inspect its tiny designs: Irish artwork, Celtic-type swirls and knots pulled me in, whispering their secrets too quietly for me to hear.

I closed in for a better look, pressing the overgrowth out of my way, drawn to the mystery that only a secret door in an Irish garden could create. A faint burning returned to the skin on my chest, reminding me of my strange injury from the cemetery, heightening my senses.

The pressure of a comforting hand rested on my shoulder, nudging me closer. I turned to ask Gram what it could be and gasped for air when I saw no one there. My eyes darted back and forth, finding only green around me. I snapped back to the secret door without blinking, ignoring the sting of my drying eyes. Strange sounds filled my mind, lonely, haunting sounds of tin whistles lost on the wind, maybe coming from inside the statue.

I reached for the lock again and rubbed the Celtic carvings with my thumb. The metal door was sealed by the paint of countless years. I pushed my fingernails into the top line of the seal, moving along the length, trying to break through—

"*There yeh are!*" My grandmother's voice pierced through my soul.

I flew back from the statue and landed in the zucchinis. "Jeez, Gram!"

"Didn't mean ta startle yeh, dear. Go on, now. What's keepin' ya?"

Gram positioned herself between the statue and me, blocking my view of the secret door. I pushed left and then right, trying to get another glimpse of it, desperate to confirm it wasn't my imagination. But somehow, Gram was able to block it no matter how I squirmed.

"Gram, behind you, in the St. Brendan statue...." I started, dying to show it to her. "What *is* that?" I tilted my head for a better look, reaching around with my curious fingers.

"Oh, nothing." Gram swatted with her dishtowel, stopping my hand from further exploration. I pulled back, feeling like a small child caught with her hand in the cookie jar. "Another one of yer grandfather's projects, 'tis all, his handiwork, sure. Prob'ly keeps some old tools in there or whatnot."

My chin pulled in as I scowled at her. Did she think I was dumb? Her efforts at distracting me from the secret door were useless. I was going to find out what was in there. My eyes were drawn back to it. What *could* be in there?

"Come on now. Stop yer dilly-dallying and daydreamin'. Time to come in. Scooch." She swatted at me again with her dishtowel. God. That was really annoying.

Could she actually be *hiding* something from me?

Walking up the rolling lawn toward the porch stairs, I looked back at the statue. Its head was tipped a little—maybe it always had been—but now it was more obvious. It knew something. I had discovered its secret and now its gentle face was encouraging me to do something about it. Daring me even. The hairs on the back of my neck stood up as we held eye contact.

"Come along now, loov," Gram said.

Climbing the high stairs, I was paralyzed with the need for answers. Real answers. Not just the ones you're given as a child, hollow and flat, that let the adults avoid or move on, but real, concrete answers...about Mom, about my grandparents, about Ireland. Lots more about Ireland. Why was it always shrouded with mystery and secrets in my family? No one ever wanted to talk about it, but it was who we were. It didn't make sense, all the silence.

***

"Are you ever going to *really* tell me why you and Joey left Ireland?" I'd asked a million times before but was never satisfied with the simple or unfinished answer, like I was always "too young" to be told.

Gram's pace slowed on the stairs and she turned to look at me. Her eyes were usually soft and bright, but today, hidden behind her veil of gray strands, they looked steely and guarded.

"Nothin' ta tell, Maeve. You're always lookin' for some grand story."

Did she think I was still ten? I waited for more, not budging.

"There was nothing left fer me at home. Twelve siblings, tiny cottage, no jobs. I had ta go and, sure, I met yer grandfather around that time and he was in a great hurry t' get to America."

Same story as every time. I was sick of all the pleasantries. *Just be honest for once and tell me what really happened. Say what you mean.*

She played with her necklace, the one she loyally wore everyday no matter the outfit, and rolled the heavy, vintage charm around in her fingers. The Celtic swirls and mythical beasts danced on it.

"Ah, there's nothin' left there fer me now," she said, clearing her throat to dispel the tightness in her voice.

"What about Joey?" His name rolled off my lips the way 'Grampy' or 'Pop Pop' would for any other grandchild.

"Never." The word came out of her like a shot, smacking me upside the head, and she was quick to soften her reply. "I mean, yer grandfather won't go back now either, dear. Been hiding for too long. He's too old. 'Tis a shame, really."

"Hiding?" My head cocked to one side.

"Hmm?" Gram reached for her necklace and looked away.

"You said, 'He's been hiding'. From what?" My tight gaze bored into her back.

"I'm just sayin' he's lost touch with home, is all." She stuck her head in the fridge, looking for nothing.

My grandfather used terms like "fled" and "escaped" when he talked about his journey to America at eighteen. He would tell stories, after a bit of whiskey, of struggles for land and wealth, for country and clan. I had faded memories of his fairy tales and legends—battles among clashing chieftains, castles, and ships.

Visitors began to arrive for the soccer match and a symphony of brogues livened up the living room. "Uncle" Paddy, one of Joey's closest friends, filled the space with welcomes, his booming voice bringing a smile to my face. Then I heard Michael. My heart stopped. He was greeting Joey, talking stats about the match and cheering some sports chant, making my grandfather laugh.

I pictured his fitted Irish soccer jacket, the lucky one he wore for every game, and his friendly smile. I'd had a crush on him since kindergarten. Butterflies tickled my stomach, but I snapped back to Gram, looking for a distracting kitchen job so I wouldn't have to go out there.

Gram readied her cast-iron skillet for the steaks. The smell of boiling spuds and the hot, garlic-laced pan filled every inch of the kitchen. As I leaned in against the fridge, my shoulder flinched off its surface as if I'd been tazed.

"Wait. When did you tape my acceptance letter to the fridge?"

I specifically remembered burying it at the bottom of the papers on my desk. But now, the Boston College letterhead was staring out at me, waiting for a reply. Or, worse, a commitment.

Thoughts of my looming college plans made me feel like I was going to puke. My grandmother had been so brave in her journey to America, and here I was, squeamish at the thought of going away to the college down the road.

"I haven't made a final decision, you know." My insecurities flooded to the surface. It was obvious to everyone I would be attending BC. Both my parents were alums.

"Nonsense, dear! Yeh're headed off to university, for pity's sake, not the war. Ya just have the nervous jitters." She looked at me sideways. "Sure, when I was yer age, I was on a ship to the States, eighteen years old, with only a dream in me pocket."

Uncle Paddy wandered into the kitchen and Gram was quick to move her attention to him.

"How're me girls?" he asked as he hugged us, planting a kiss on Gram's head. I looked past him to see if Michael was on his heels, but no sign of him. My breath steadied itself.

"Ach, lassie." He looked at me. "You've grown. Not a kid anymore; sure, those big green eyes of yours would hold any lad hostage. Git out there and say hello to Michael. You'll bewitch 'im completely." His smile was wide and his eyes twinkled. "It's that Norwegian beauty. Ya got that from yer da'."

Noting the look of disappointment in my curled lip and crunched nose, Paddy turned to Gram, looking for more Jameson whiskey.

"Though you're Irish in every way, young lass." He patted my shoulder with his heavy hand, trying to take back his earlier suggestion that I could be Norwegian in any way.

Too late. I'd already heard the message—I wasn't Irish enough.

"Sure, ya should send her off to the Ol' Country, Kate. It'd be good fer her. Stop with the shelterin'. You've kept her hidden long enough," he said over his shoulder as he moved back toward the match with his whiskey and more glasses. He gave a final shout: "Time she found out who she really is. Where she came from. No?"

Gram eyeballed him with a look that could kill. Her eyes spelled each letter of *shut your mouth, you drunken fool.*

Paddy turned to me like a reprimanded puppy and said, "Forgive me, lass, for me big mouth. Yer special though. Destined for greatness. They just don't want ya to know it yet," followed by a wink. He turned back toward the living room and shouted, "Hey Michael, Maeve's in the kitchen waitin' ya."

Gram went after him with her dish rag, like chasing a fox out of a hen house. He ran for the hills.

My knees turned to liquid as I prayed Michael wouldn't listen to him. I froze, wondering.

Paddy's words made me burst with a million more questions for Gram and I turned to her, wide-eyed, ready for information. But she was closed off tight with her back to me, humming an Irish ballad, a little too loud. The kind that always made me cry.

Paddy's comment played over in my mind—how I didn't look Irish. I already knew that but it hit me like a bus anyway. My family looked Irish: strong hands, broad shoulders, twinkling eyes. But I looked more like my dad, and what's ironic about that is he left us when I was a baby. I didn't even know him.

What I did know was that I didn't fit in here. Surrounded by the Irish all my life and still I was different and awkward.

It was weird because when Mom died I didn't fit in at school anymore either. I had just turned thirteen when it happened, so I guess you could say it stole part of my childhood, like I grew up that day. My friends and the other kids around me noticed too. They were still worried about how many likes they got on social media, who they were going to semi with, and if they had the latest phone app. It was all white noise to me. I didn't fit from that point on. I didn't even want to.

And now, I wasn't even fitting in with my own kind. Always hiding in the garden, the kitchen, the cemetery. I was more comfortable alone.

"Hey, Maeve."

I turned like I'd been electrocuted. Michael's smile melted me into muteness.

"Heard you were headed to BC. Go Eagles." The artificial lack of enthusiasm in his tone made me chuckle. He leaned against the door jamb, looking at me with a familiar fondness.

"Um, yeah, well, I don't know yet." I looked at Gram, annoyed about the acceptance letter and now about her telling people. "I guess." I looked down at my phone on the table and pressed the button, hoping some message would appear and whisk me away.

Silence.

"Had you pegged more for a UMass Amherst girl, no? The Zoo?" He laughed, knowing that was the furthest thing from the truth. He didn't seem to care though.

Stuck, as usual, I was blank without any form of witty comeback. The more I tried to come up with one, the more I froze.

"Yeah, BC. That's the one for me." I did not just make a rhyme! Is it possible to die by choking yourself? I envisioned reaching for my own neck.

Michael grinned, probably to be polite. "Well, keep in touch. I'll be workin' with Paddy as his apprentice. Stoneworking, you know. You'll have to keep me up on the college stuff."

"Yeah, okay." I smiled and reached for my phone again. What was wrong with me? He went back to the living room. I blew it. Again!

I dropped my face into my hands trying to erase the previous moment. I snuck a peek through my fingers at Gram and then pulled my face up.

"I should go. To Ireland."

It was like an epiphany. Paddy was right. And he had said something about me finding out where I came from and who I was, like he knew part of the story that was always kept from me. And Gram seemed fixed to keep it that way.

Gram's lined face awakened as she considered my interest in going to Ireland. Then her eyes squinted, closing the topic, and she paused for a second. Her spatula hovered over the pan and she opened her mouth as if she was going to say something. But then she stopped.

Gram was scared.

***

Once the house settled after the match, I found myself in the kitchen again with Gram as I reluctantly helped with the cleanup. I preferred the torture of cleaning my own room. At least I could sweep everything under the bed in there.

"Gram, seriously. What would you think of me going to Ireland?" I pressed her to re-engage as I sat down with my cup of tea, drying the "special occasion" silverware.

Then a sudden sense of urgency flowed through my veins, a chill that hit my marrow. I dropped the serving spoon from my hand onto the table with a loud clang.

Gram blurred out into streaks of color blending into the kitchen. I froze with my eyes bulging and my heart racing.

The wind was coming.

Terror filled me in an instant, reminding me of its occupation of my soul.

I grabbed the wooden legs of my kitchen chair and held on for dear life. Wind, screams, fear—it was coming but I wasn't prepared. I wasn't strong enough. My mother wasn't here this time to help me and—

The wind surrounded me before I had time to draw in a full breath of air. I squeezed my eyes shut and pressed my lips together to block the violent assault. The gusts burst into my ears and up my nose, filling every space in my skull, whirling around in my head, searching for the source of my being.

The urge to look for my mother held more power than my good judgment. I snuck one eye open, hoping for a glimpse of her beautiful face. Maybe she was still trapped there, in the wind, but all around me a vast emptiness swirled with mist and angry gusts.

Wetness clung to my skin as I stumbled forward into the void, shivering through the darkness and confusion. Alarm rose, widening my eyes as thoughts of death swirled around me. My heart pounded with such force I thought it would burst out of my chest. Gram's words of Mom's "heart condition" echoed in my thoughts. My shoulders rounded in as pain surged out of each spastic beat.

I raised my head to gasp for air as a rolling grassy slope appeared. It was like an Irish countryside, so familiar that a wave of relief blanketed my erratic heart. But only for a split second.

A massive rock flew up in front of me then, like a wall, nearly smashing me. I slapped my hands on it, annoyed as it blocked my view and my movement, and maybe a chance to see my mother.

Cold mist and salty spray pelted my face again in harsh slaps as I pushed through the blasts and the thick scent of marine life.

A bone-chilling sensation shuddered up my spine, warning me I wasn't alone and definitely not welcome. My eyes darted around, trapped in my rigid body, searching for my age-old stalker.

I fought the primal urge to run, risking my safety for a possible second of contact with my mother, when from deep within my subconscious a sound began to rise unlike anything I had ever heard or had even known existed in this world. It was a heavy, guttural moan, one of loss and sorrow, and my hair stood on end.

As I squinted into the fog, following the direction of the sound, a form began taking shape and a face came together in the gray haze. It snarled and came at me out of the mist.

My instincts took over. I turned in an instant and ran for my life blindly through the fog. I tore across the green expanse and stumbled on the uneven ground. I didn't have a chance.

Too terrified to look back, I flew through the mist and rain, leaving swirling trails off my elbows and back. The horrifying sound rang louder in my ears as I lost ground. The figure, though I didn't know what or who it was, thundered just steps behind me.

A frozen chill ran through my heart—whatever that thing was had caught up to me. With a newfound burst of energy driven by pure terror, I hit high gear only to be brought to an abrupt halt.

On a shore, I had hit water's edge. Splashing through the shallows, my pace was slowed to molasses, just like a freakish nightmare when you can't run and your voice is lost. With no other option, I turned, hands raised, to face my attacker. A glint of bright light blinded me for a split second and—

SMASH!

My body dropped back down into my chair as my muscles released their death grip on my bones. I drew in a life-saving breath to fill my starving lungs and clutched at my chest to relieve the intense burning on my skin.

I recognized my surroundings: Gram's kitchen. No one chasing me, no massive rock, no wind pounding me. I was safely sitting in my chair at the kitchen table, my cup of tea still steaming in front of me.

Gram stood by the sink, frozen, eyes wide with panic. Fragments of the broken plate she must have just dropped were strewn around the floor.

"I'm okay, Gram," I lied, trying to convince myself as much as her. "I'm okay. It was just a dream."

Yeah, a dream that was stalking me, luring me, maybe even trying to kill me. The nagging burn on my chest raised my inner alarm toward hysterical.

Gram blinked and then shifted her eyes to look directly into mine. Her expression loosened as she glided toward me, reaching for me with outstretched arms, as if she'd almost lost me. She smothered me in her hold.

"T'anks be t' God you're all right."

"I'm so sorry, Gram. I'm okay now." I tried to hide my panic and confusion from her. "This is just a weird thing that used to happen to me sometimes...when I was little."

My awake dream had truly come back to haunt me, and right in front of Gram. Those were the two worst things that could ever have happened. Losing my mind was one thing, but for Gram to have any notion of it was quite another. She would only isolate me from life more now. She already controlled me too much as it was.

I blinked and squished my eyes to release the imposing images. I sniffled to clear the salty mist from my nostrils, surprised by the smell of the sea and damp earth still left there.

"It just hasn't happened in a while, since before Mom...." I paused, smoothing my hair that was still strewn across my face. My dream's connection to Mom and her death was undeniable now, at least in my mind. "But I'm okay. Really."

Her mouth still hung open and her eyes were brimming with tears, proving she needed a better explanation.

"Mom used to help me when this happened, when I was little. She would hold me and talk to me until I came back. We used to call it my 'awake dream.'" I hoped to normalize it as she listened without breathing.

With an uneasy sense of foreboding, I added, "I think it's coming back."

I peeked up from under my lashes, watching for her response.

Gram's face dropped as her eyes searched mine for a different explanation. Judging by her lost stare and the anguish on her face, you'd think I had told her I was dying.

* * *

Don't stop now. Keep reading with your copy of BOHERMORE by City Owl Author, Jennifer Rose McMahon available now.

Don't miss more of The Boleyn Bloodline from Deborah Cohen coming soon! Until then, try BOHERMORE by City Owl Author, Jennifer Rose McMahon.

* * *

When your dreams become reality, being cursed can be a real nightmare.

Like a punch in the face, eighteen-year-old Maeve O'Malley's visions knock her off her path. The Pirate Queen stalking Maeve in her dreams killed her mother years ago, and now, the villain is coming for her. Maeve's decision to ditch Boston College takes everyone by surprise as she packs her bags, leaves America, and heads to the west coast of Ireland to chase her dreams--and end them.

Maeve uncovers an ancient family curse that refuses to remain silent until she accepts her predestined role in what many thought was only a legend. Her Irish history professor--a man she shouldn't be falling for--is the only person who understands the origins of her torment.

Maeve's journey becomes a medieval treasure hunt through Ireland's castles and ruins as she tracks the wrathful Pirate Queen who has her marked for vengeance.

* * *

Please sign up for the City Owl Press newsletter for chances to win special subscriber-only contests and giveaways as well as receiving information on upcoming releases and special excerpts.

All reviews are **welcome** and **appreciated**. Please consider leaving one on your favorite social media and book buying sites.

For books in the world of romance and speculative fiction that embody Innovation, Creativity, and Affordability, check out City Owl Press at www.cityowlpress.com.

ACKNOWLEDGMENTS

I would like to thank a number of people who helped in the making of this book. First and foremost, I would like to thank my family, Michael, Zach and Beth for supporting me in my writing and for giving me room to follow my inspiration. I would like to thank my mom and sister, Diane and Cheryl, and my other friends and family who encouraged me as I was writing this novel. I would like to thank my beta readers Michele Marquis, Laura Guilbeault, Cheryl Evans, and Tegan Whalen for their honest feedback, suggestions to character development and plot revisions as the book was shaped and reshaped in its early drafts. Finally, I would like to thank Yelena Casale at City Owl Press for giving this story a chance. A book is only as good as its editor and Yelena and the team at City Owl Press have helped take this novel across the finish line.

ABOUT THE AUTHOR

DEBORAH COHEN is an author of historical fantasy and mystery. She is an adjunct Professor with the University of Ottawa and an epidemiologist for a National Health Research Institute in Canada. She lives in Ottawa with her hubby, son and daughter, and two large crazy dogs – a Bulldog and a Great Dane – that love to be spoiled rotten.

www.deborahcohen1.wixsite.com

ABOUT THE PUBLISHER

City Owl Press is a cutting edge indie publishing company, bringing the world of romance and speculative fiction to discerning readers.

www.cityowlpress.com

Printed in Great Britain
by Amazon

57453542R00201